FARMINGTON COMMUNITY LIBRARY
FARMINGTON BRANCH
23500 LIBERTY STREET
FARMINGTON, MI 48335-3570
(248) 553-0300

DISCARDED

...l Ernst's depiction of work at a living museum lends authenticity and a sense of place to the involving plot."

—*St. Paul Pioneer Press*

"Greed, passion, skill, and luck all figure in this surprise-filled outing."

—*Publishers Weekly*

"Interesting, well-drawn characters and a complicated plot make this a very satisfying read."

—*The Mystery Reader*

"Entertainment and edification." —*Mystery Scene*

"A wonderfully woven tale that winds in and out of modern and historical Wisconsin with plenty of mysteries. Enchanting!"

—Sandi Ault, author of the WILD mystery series and recipient of the Mary Higgins Clark Award

"Clever plot twists and credible characters make this a far-from-humdrum cozy."

—*Publishers Weekly*

"Propulsive and superbly written, this first entry in a dynamite new series from accomplished author Kathleen Ernst seamlessly melds the 1980s and the 19th century. Character-driven, with mystery aplenty, *Old World Murder* is a sensational read. Think Sue Grafton meets Earlene Fowler, with a dash of Elizabeth Peters."

—Julia Spencer-Fleming, Anthony and Agatha Award-winning author of *I Shall Not Want* and *One Was A Soldier*

W9-ARE-939

"*Old World Murder* is strongest in its charming local color and genuine love for Wisconsin's rolling hills, pastures, and woodlands ... a delightful distraction for an evening or two."

—NYJournalOfBooks.com

"This series debut by an author of children's mysteries rolls out nicely for readers who like a cozy with a dab of antique lore. Jeanne M. Dams fans will like the ethnic background."

—*Library Journal*

"Information on how to conduct historical research, background on Norwegian culture, and details about running an outdoor museum frame the engaging story of a woman devastated by a failed romantic relationship whose sleuthing helps her heal."

—*Booklist*

"[A] museum masterpiece."   —RosebudBookReviews.com

"A real find ... 5 stars."   —OnceUponARomance.net

"Engaging characters, a fascinating (real-life) setting, a gripping and believable plot—this is the traditional mystery at its best."

—Jeanne M. Dams, Agatha Award-winning author of the Dorothy Martin and Hilda Johansson mysteries

ALSO BY KATHLEEN ERNST

Nonfiction

Too Afraid to Cry: Maryland Civilians in the Antietam Campaign,
Stackpole Books, 1999

Fiction

Old World Murder

The Heirloom Murders

The Light Keeper's Legacy

3 0036 01164 8621

A CHLOE ELLEFSON MYSTERY

Heritage of Darkness

KATHLEEN ERNST

MIDNIGHT INK
WOODBURY, MINNESOTA

Heritage of Darkness: A Chloe Ellefson Mystery © 2013 by Kathleen Ernst. All rights reserved. No part of this book may be used or reproduced in any manner whatsoever, including Internet usage, without written permission from Midnight Ink, except in the case of brief quotations embodied in critical articles and reviews.

First Edition
First Printing, 2013

Book design and format by Donna Burch
Cover design by Kevin R. Brown
Cover illustration by Charlie Griak
Cover image: Holly designs: iStockphoto.com/Andrea Hill
Editing by Connie Hill

Midnight Ink, an imprint of Llewellyn Worldwide Ltd.

This is a work of fiction. Names, characters, places, and incidents are either the product of the author's imagination or are used fictitiously, and any resemblance to actual persons, living or dead, business establishments, events, or locales is entirely coincidental.

Library of Congress Cataloging-in-Publication Data
Ernst, Kathleen, 1959–
   Heritage of darkness : a Chloe Ellefson Mystery / Kathleen Ernst. —First Edition.
       pages   cm. — (A Chloe Ellefson Mystery ; #4)
   ISBN 978-0-7387-3698-3
1. Women museum curators—Fiction. 2. Vesterheim Norwegian-American Museum—Fiction. 3. Murder—Investigation—Fiction. 4. Iowa—Fiction. I. Title.
   PS3605.R77H47   2013
   813'.6—dc23   2013021118

Midnight Ink
Llewellyn Worldwide Ltd.
2143 Wooddale Drive
Woodbury, MN 55125-2989
www.midnightinkbooks.com

Printed in the United States of America

DEDICATION

For Andrea Cascardi—
with thanks for twelve momentous years;

and for the Vesterheim/Decorah community—
with thanks for making Scott and me part of the family.

In 2010, while doing research for *Old World Murder* (the first Chloe Ellefson mystery), I traveled to Vesterheim Norwegian-American Museum in Northeast Iowa to photograph antique ale bowls. Since then I've returned again and again to study the collection, take folk-art classes in painting and fiber arts, and enjoy special events.

Vesterheim is the most comprehensive museum in the United States dedicated to a single immigrant group, with a collection that includes more than 24,000 artifacts and more than a dozen historic structures. It is also a cultural center dedicated to documenting and perpetuating folk art and traditions through classes, programs, and tours. Finally, Vesterheim's presentation of the Norwegian experience provides visitors like me, who are not of Scandinavian descent, a chance to reflect upon our own ethnic and family history.

I've done my best to present a snapshot of Vesterheim as it was in Chloe's time, and glimpses of other milestone years as well. Because this is a work of fiction, I did take small liberties to avoid confusion or support the plot. For example, the museum lobby looked quite different in 1982, and the collections storage facility described had not yet been built. Also, since my favorite Vesterheim experiences have been rosemaling classes in July and the Norwegian Christmas Weekend in December, I melded the two into one week.

Most of the places mentioned in the Decorah area are real, including the historic neighborhood near the museum, the Fifth Street bridge over the Upper Iowa River (although it looked quite different in 1982), the Oneota Co-op, Mabe's Pizza, and the Whippy Dip Ice Cream Parlor. My descriptions of private homes are loosely based on real places, but I kept directions vague to respect the property owners' privacy.

You can learn more, and plan your own trip, by visiting these websites:

Vesterheim Norwegian-American Museum:
http://vesterheim.org/index.php
Decorah:
http://www.visitdecorah.com

You can find photos, a tour guide, and maps of relevant places on my website, www.kathleenernst.com

You can also find photographs of some of the artifacts mentioned in the story on pages 340 to 343.

CAST OF CHARACTERS

Chloe Ellefson—curator of collections, Old World Wisconsin

Roelke McKenna—officer, Village of Eagle Police Department

Marit Kallerud—Chloe's mother, member of the Sixty-Seven Club of rosemalers

Frank Ellefson—Chloe's father

Chief Moyer—head of Decorah Police Department

Investigator Buzzelli—liaison for all agencies involved in the murder investigation

Ethan Hendricks—Chloe's college friend

Nika Austin—intern, Old World Wisconsin

Ralph Petty—director, Old World Wisconsin

Sigrid Sorensen—Marit's best friend, member of the Sixty-Seven Club

Violet Sorensen—Sigrid's daughter

Bill Sorensen—(deceased) Sigrid's husband

Emil Bergsbakken—chip carving instructor

Oscar Bergsbakken—(deceased) Emil's brother

Lavinia Carmichael—chip carving student

Gwen—rosemaling student

Petra Lekstrom—member of the Sixty-Seven Club

Adelle Rimestad—member of the Sixty-Seven Club, expert wood carver

Tom Rimestad—Adelle's husband

Howard Hoff—director, Vesterheim Norwegian-American Museum

Phyllis Hoff—(deceased) member of the Sixty-Seven Club

Edwina Ree—retired archivist, expert in Norwegian Christmas traditions

Bestemor Sabo—cookie baker extraordinaire

Peggy Nelson—member of the Sixty-Seven Club

Linda Skatrud—member of the Sixty-Seven Club

Sigmund Aarseth—a beloved rosemaling instructor; the only real person depicted in the novel

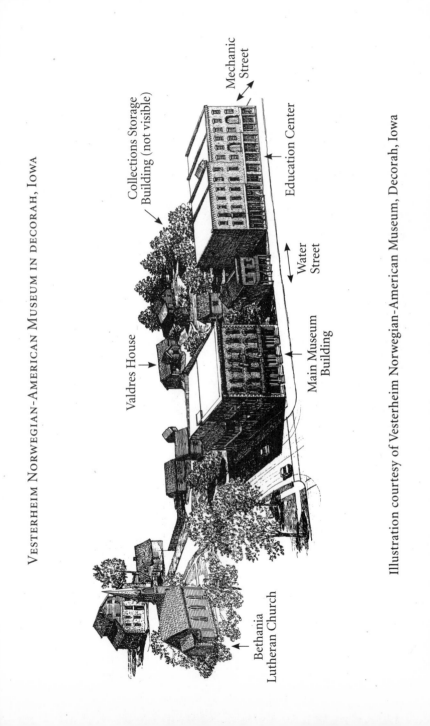

Collections Storage Building (not visible)

Valdres House

Bethania Lutheran Church

Main Museum Building

Water Street

Education Center

Mechanic Street

Illustration courtesy of Vesterheim Norwegian-American Museum, Decorah, Iowa

ONE

ALTHOUGH SHE TRIED TO hide it from Mom and Roelke, Chloe Ellefson's emotional distress inflated with each passing mile. Distress ballooned into panic by the time they left Wisconsin. She exercised driver's prerogative and pulled into the first Iowa gas station she saw. "Pit stop," she announced.

"I need to powder my nose," Mom said. "Roelke, would you fill the tank?"

He already had the car door open. "I'd be glad to."

Chloe got out and leaned against the Buick, hunching turtle-like into her coat. The December wind whipping off the Mississippi River was wicked.

Roelke set the pump and began washing the windshield. "You OK?"

"I'm having second thoughts," Chloe admitted. "This little adventure in family bonding was ill-conceived."

"This little adventure was your idea," he reminded her.

"Do you think it's too late to bail? Maybe Mom could take a cab the rest of the way to Decorah."

"Since we're driving your mother's car, that doesn't seem quite fair." Roelke returned the squeegee to its tank. "Stop stressing. Everything will be fine."

"Easy for you to say." Chloe had officially been dating Roelke McKenna for three months, but he had yet to spend any real time with her mother. "You have no idea what you've gotten into."

"It's going to be a fun week."

Even at her most optimistic, the notion of "fun" had not crossed Chloe's mind.

Roelke put his hands on her shoulders. His cheeks were red from the cold, which was a good look for him. He was younger than she was, and had that cop-persona going for him too: dark hair clipped short, broad shoulders, intense gaze.

That gaze was now focused on Chloe. "Hey. You said you wanted to spend time with your mom on *her* terms. Get to know her better."

"I do, truly." Chloe sighed. She and her mother had drifted along in a superficial *Everything's fine* mode for years. Then, after a solitary visit to a largely deserted island back in September, Chloe had vowed to strengthen her family ties.

While visiting her parents, she'd spotted a flyer from Vesterheim Norwegian-American Museum, announcing simultaneous Beginning Telemark and Advanced Hallingdal Rosemaling classes. "Hey, Mom," Chloe had said. "How about we sign up for these? Beginning for me, Advanced for you." Chloe fully expected the beginners' workshop to end with public humiliation … but for one brief shining moment, it had seemed like a good idea.

She had also fully expected enthusiasm from Mom. Instead, Mom's eyebrows had arched high. "You want to take a *rosemaling* class? You've never wanted anything to do with my little hobby."

Chloe already regretted her impulse. "Well, I thought it would be nice to try it now."

"I suppose we can do that," Mom had conceded skeptically. "If you're sure."

Now Chloe said, "It's the Vesterheim part that's going to bite me in the butt." She watched an old pickup truck rattle by. "There's no way I can live up to the expectations of Marit 'All-Things-Norske' Kallerud this week."

Roelke cocked his head. "Why do you say that?"

"My mother has a Gold Medal in rosemaling," Chloe reminded him. "She wanted me to paint when I was in high school. I didn't, and she's never forgiven me for it."

"That was a long time ago. I wish..." His voice trailed away, and he shrugged.

Roelke's parents were dead, so Chloe could easily imagine what he wished. She felt guilty for complaining. A little.

Mom strolled back across the lot. "Roelke, would you drive the rest of the way to Decorah?"

"Glad to," he said again. Chloe crawled into the back seat. Once they were entombed in the car again, Roelke headed west.

"I can hardly believe it," Mom said. "But here we are, heading off to Decorah!"

"Yes!" Chloe said brightly.

"I've always wanted to share the Vesterheim experience with Chloe," Mom told Roelke, "but she's never shown any interest."

3

"Actually, I have been to Vesterheim before," Chloe reminded her mother. "Several times."

Mom leaned closer to Roelke and confided, "The last time Chloe came was when I earned my Gold Medal. Nineteen seventy-two. A *decade* ago."

Chloe looked out the window. "I spent a decade away from the Midwest, remember? Including five years in Europe? That made it a tad challenging to pop over to Iowa."

Mom ignored her. "Roelke, I'm delighted you wanted to join us. December is a perfect time to visit the museum."

Am I speaking Swiss? Chloe wondered. Perhaps she'd lapsed, and everyone was too polite to mention it.

"After our week of classes," Mom continued, "we'll enjoy the Norwegian Christmas Weekend." She sighed happily. "It's a lovely special event."

"I love Christmas," Roelke assured her.

Chloe was pretty sure that Roelke, who might euphemistically be described as "tightly-wound," hadn't used the words "love" and "Christmas" in the same sentence since he was seven.

"I'm looking forward to my carving class." He sounded genuinely pleased. "I like to whittle, but I'm pretty much self-taught."

"This week will be an epiphany for you," Mom promised. "The Norwegians have *such* a strong woodworking tradition. My favorite pieces are the wooden mangles once used to press linens. Traditionally, a man carved a special mangle for the woman he hoped to marry, and left the mangle on her doorstep. If she took it inside, it meant she accepted his proposal. Once a woman had declined a proposal gift, it couldn't be offered to anyone else. Mothers used to tell their daughters to 'Beware the man with many mangles.'" She laughed. "My husband used to tease that he had hedged his bets by carving several at once, but I know the one he made to propose to me was his one and only."

Chloe winced. She tried sending Mom a mental message: *Please nix the talk of betrothal gifts.*

"A man might carve a love spoon," Mom continued, "for his special girl."

Chloe used one foot to nudge the seat in front of her. She and Roelke had been getting along pretty well, but they hadn't yet been... intimate. She tried harder on the mental message thing: *Please, **please** quit the matrimony talk.*

"And if the couple married, the groom carved *two* spoons linked by a chain." Mom clasped her hands together joyfully.

Chloe clenched her teeth. Perhaps she should just say *Mom, Roelke and I haven't even had sex yet, so give it up!*

"Will I be able to see any of those wedding spoons in the museum?" Roelke asked.

"Vesterheim's collection is incredible," Mom promised him. "I'm sure you'll be inspired."

"*Mom!*"

"I'm sure I will, Ms. Kallerud," Roelke said earnestly.

"Please, Roelke dear. Call me Marit."

Chloe unclicked her seatbelt and curled up on the back seat. If Mom starts prattling about baby cradles, she thought, I will leap out the window.

TWO:

DECEMBER, 1947

MARIT KALLERUD'S FEET SLOWED as she approached the train station, a beautiful old structure with swooping rooflines now graced with evergreen garlands. It was always hard to leave Decorah. She'd attended Luther College here, and she'd started volunteering at the Norwegian-American Museum as a freshman. Some of her dearest friends still lived in town. She felt at home here in a way that was hard to define.

Not that Stoughton isn't a good place, she reminded herself. Her hometown had its own Norwegian identity. She'd been raised hearing elders—people who'd never left Wisconsin—speaking English with a distinct Norwegian accent. Her family's table grace was spoken in that language. She helped at the Lutheran Church's annual *lutefisk* supper and baked sweets for the Women's Society to sell during Syttende Mai—Norway's Constitution Day celebration.

Still, she'd known since the first time she'd stepped from a train, right here, that Decorah would become her second home. My *vesterheim*, she thought. The early immigrants had referred to America's Midwest that way: my western home.

Well, she'd had a lovely visit, but it was time to go. Marit walked resolutely into the station.

She waited in line at the ticket counter behind a young couple snuggled arm-in-arm. "My parents are going to love you as much as I do," the young man murmured. His sweetheart giggled.

Marit studied her shoes. One by one, almost all of her college friends had paired up, gotten married, settled down. Marit had always just assumed that someone would come along for her, too. But it hadn't happened yet.

I have had offers, she reminded herself. She *could* have been married, if that was her only goal. But she didn't want to settle. When the right man came along, she'd know.

Ticket in hand, she picked up her suitcase and headed outside. Well-bundled Luther students crowded the platform. The air rang with shouts: "Merry Christmas!" "Happy holidays!" "Joyful new year!"

The only one who hasn't found the holiday spirit, Marit thought wistfully, is me.

She edged through the crowd, hoping to be among the first to board so she could choose her seat. When a shrill whistle split the air she leaned forward, looking toward the train as it chugged into view. The eager travelers behind her swayed in anticipation, and the sunlight sparkling on nearby snow banks was dazzling. Marit felt a moment of vertigo as someone jostled past—

Then she knew a moment of raw terror as she fell toward the train tracks.

Someone grabbed her arm with a steel grip and jerked her back to safety. "Whoa, there," a man said.

"*Thank* you," Marit gasped. She pressed one hand over her chest, trying to slow her pounding heart. Then she looked up, and her heart began to pound all over again. Her white knight looked a little like Cary Grant and a little like a fresh-faced farm boy who'd just stepped from his tractor.

"Are you all right?" he asked.

"Yes," she said breathlessly. "Thanks to you."

The train slowed to a stop at the platform, and the crowd surged again. The man kept his hand on her arm. "I'm glad I managed to catch you," he said. "I'm Frank Ellefson."

"Marit Kallerud."

She allowed him to take her suitcase. On the train, it seemed the most natural thing in the world to settle into a pair of adjoining seats. "What's your final destination?" Marit asked.

"Stoughton, Wisconsin," Frank said. "My hometown."

Marit stared at him with surprise. "Mine too! How is it we haven't met?"

"My parents have a farm outside of town, and I suspect I was in and out of high school before you. Then I was in the service for a while. I'm back at my folks' place now, although I don't think I want to farm. I've been visiting a friend in Decorah. How about you?"

They chatted about this and that as the train rattled through the frozen Iowa countryside. Frost glazed the window with lace, but Marit scarcely noticed. She *knew*. Somehow, she just knew that Frank Ellefson was the one for her.

And I found him in Decorah, she thought. That made everything perfect.

THREE

Darkness was falling by the time Roelke drove into Decorah. Snow too, and Eastern Iowa's rolling hills were already blanketed with a good six inches. Chloe watched the big flakes caught in the headlights. It's a winter wonderland, she thought, and allowed herself a sliver of hope. Maybe it really would be a good week.

Mom consulted her watch. "The reception for teachers and students has already started. Let's go straight to the museum." She directed Roelke to Water Street in downtown Decorah. "See the old train station? That's where I met Chloe's father. And there's the old Winneshiek Hotel. Perhaps you two can have dinner there one night."

Dinner for two would be nice, Chloe thought. If Roelke hadn't been scared speechless by Mom's romance blitz.

He found a parking spot near Vesterheim's main building. Mom jumped out and hurried away.

Roelke contemplated the old three-story brick structure. "So, this is the place."

"This is the place." Chloe took a deep breath. "Come on. Party time."

They followed Mom into the lobby, which was lavishly decorated with woven paper hearts and evergreens. Christmas carols drifted from stereo speakers. A long table along the back wall held an impressive smorgasbord. Two dozen or so guests were already nibbling cookies, sipping wine, laughing, and chatting. The crowd collectively sported a world-class collection of Norwegian sweaters, although a few people wore colorful *bunads* instead.

"I think I'm under-dressed," Roelke said. He'd worn his best jeans for the occasion, and a green chamois shirt.

"We're fine," Chloe assured him. "We're just the entourage, anyway."

A red-haired woman spotted the new arrivals with delight. "Marit!" she exclaimed, and swept Mom into a hug.

"That's Sigrid Sorensen, one of my mom's best friends," Chloe murmured. "She's a sweetie."

"You and your mom are staying at her house this week, right?"

"Right. And Sigrid is teaching my Beginning Telemark Rosemaling class."

"Ah," Roelke said, which she assumed meant that he didn't know any more about the mysteries of Beginning Telemark Rosemaling than she did.

Several more people joined the reunion. "Marit? Marit! *Marit!*" The decibel level rose with every embrace and happy squeal.

"Wow. Your mom knows a lot of people." Roelke looked impressed. "Want me to hang up your coat?"

"Thanks." Chloe shrugged out of her parka and handed it over. "I'll meet you by the food."

Chloe poured herself a goblet of Riesling. When Roelke caught up he filled a paper plate with carrot sticks, raw broccoli, little chunks of cheese, three meatballs, and two sweet *krumkakke*. "Don't you want anything to eat?"

"I'm not hungry."

"Chloe? Roelke?" Mom called. "Come say hello to Sigrid."

Sigrid squeezed Chloe into a hug of her own. "Oh, *Chloe*. It's been too long."

"It's wonderful to see you." Chloe smiled. Her mother's friend was impeccably dressed in gray wool trousers and a navy-and-cream snowflake cardigan. Her hair was still piled into a sixties-style tower, although the color likely came from a bottle now.

"And this is Roelke McKenna," Mom announced. "Chloe's young man."

Chloe gave Mom points for not introducing Roelke as the future father of her grandchildren. Truth was, Chloe didn't know what to call Roelke either.

"Rell-kee?" Sigrid repeated. "Is that a family name?"

"Yes ma'am. Roelke was my mother's birth name."

Once, months earlier, Chloe had made it clear to Roelke that she preferred "birth name" to "maiden name." Now here he was, completely out of his element but doing his best to fit in. Suddenly, she no longer felt overwhelmed. Maybe having Roelke McKenna along—he of good German and Irish stock—would provide the ballast she needed to get through the week on an even keel.

"How long have you two known each other?" Roelke asked, looking from Marit to Sigrid.

"Over thirty years," Mom said. "I started volunteering at Vesterheim in the forties."

"And Marit and I are members of the Sixty-Seven Club," Sigrid told Roelke. "The very first time Vesterheim brought in a rosemaling teacher, in 1967, we both took the class."

"That was the start of something special!" Mom's face glowed with nostalgia. "We'd been painting, but all we knew how to do was copy old designs."

"At least a couple of Sixty-Sevens will be around all week," Sigrid told Mom. "Lavinia's here, and Petra Lekstrom." Sigrid looked around, then shrugged. "Well, I saw Petra this afternoon. She'll show up sooner or later."

Mom sniffed. "Like a bad penny."

Chloe blinked at that bit of snarkiness. What was that all about? Petra Lekstrom was teaching Mom's class.

"Marit!" A gray-haired man made his way through the crowd. Marit introduced Howard Hoff, the museum's director.

Howard looked at Chloe with a knowing smile. "Do we have a second-generation rosemaler here?"

Mom spread her hands in a rueful gesture. "Actually, Chloe's never picked up a brush."

Here we go, Chloe thought.

Howard blinked. "Surely with an expert like *Marit*—"

"I'm here to learn now," Chloe said in her best cheery voice. She filched a *krumkakke* from Roelke's plate.

"This is the first time we've tried week-long classes in the midst of the Christmas season," Howard said. "But we're in the hole after our recent renovation, and event sponsorship is down. The students' tuition fees are a big boost."

Chloe eyed the director judiciously. Howard Hoff looked exhausted. Dark crescents puffed beneath his eyes. His suit hung on him, as if he'd recently lost weight. His hands moved constantly—smoothing his hair, straightening his tie, exploring his pockets.

"How is the new curator working out?" Mom asked.

Howard rubbed his palms against his pants. "The new curator got pregnant and resigned. She lasted less than four months! Long enough to start projects, not long enough to finish anything. We got funding for a folklore project with a *tight* timeline, and—"

"You've got real challenges, Howard," Sigrid interrupted smoothly, "but it looks like the reception is going perfectly."

"The reception. Yes." Howard made a visible and valiant attempt to refocus. "I need to welcome our guests." He hurried away.

"Poor Howard," Sigrid said. "He's got a tiny staff to begin with."

"It's hard to lose a curator," Chloe said sympathetically. Funding was eternally tight at historic sites and museums. Any vacancy created enormous stress.

"His wife died … what, ten months ago?" Mom looked at Sigrid for confirmation. "Phyllis was a Sixty-Seven too," she explained to Roelke and Chloe. "She died of cancer, poor dear. Howard grew up in Decorah, so we've known him for a long time."

An electronic squeal emanated from a podium, where Howard was fiddling with a microphone. After a couple of false starts, he introduced himself. "We have three wonderful workshops scheduled this week. Emil Bergsbakken is teaching Beginning Chip Carving." He gestured toward a sixty-ish man standing against the wall with hands in pockets.

Emil looked abashed at the attention. He was short and slight, with just a fringe of beard running along his chin. The combination made Chloe think of *nisser*, the barn elves of Norwegian folklore.

"I'm bunking at his place, right?" Roelke whispered in her ear.

"Right. The local hotels are booked solid, and he and Mom go way back." Since the carving class had prompted Roelke to write a check and join this expedition, Chloe hoped that Emil was a good teacher.

Hoff continued, "Sigrid Sorensen is teaching Beginning Telemark Rosemaling." Sigrid smiled and waved. Chloe hoped that Sigrid was a good teacher, too. And patient. Very, *very* patient.

"And our newest Gold Medalist in Rosemaling has just returned from Norway, where she's been studying and teaching, to facilitate a workshop for advanced painters. Petra Lekstrom will teach Advanced Hallingdal Rosemaling." Hoff scanned the room. "Is Petra here?"

Everyone looked around expectantly. A woman behind Chloe muttered, "She's probably off making trouble for somebody."

My, my, Chloe thought. Roelke shot her a *What the heck?* look.

"I'm sure Petra is looking forward to meeting her students." Howard blotted his forehead. "I'm grateful to these accomplished artists for sharing their talents. Vesterheim is more than a museum. It's also a cultural center, dedicated to preserving living traditions that reflect Norwegian heritage..."

"Any regrets yet?" Chloe murmured to Roelke.

He shook his head, clearly determined to flow with the Scandinavian tide.

"The week of classes will end with our Christmas celebration," Hoff was saying. "We will also announce the winner of Vesterheim's Christmas Card design contest. Gold Medalists were invited to submit original designs. Museum staff have pared entries down to six finalists."

Chloe smiled encouragingly at her mother, whose design had made the short list. Mom nodded primly.

"The top designs are on display in the gift shop," Howard added. "Be sure to vote for your favorite. You can also enjoy the exhibit galleries for another hour. Thank you for coming."

The murmur of conversation rose again. Chloe heard another screech of pleasure: "Marit!" Mom was engulfed by more friends.

"Let's wander," Chloe murmured to Roelke. She finished her wine, popped the last bite of *krumkakke* into her mouth, and wiped her hands on her jeans. No food or drinks in the exhibits.

As they left the lobby, Chloe tucked her hand through Roelke's arm. "Sorry I got cranky earlier. I am determined to stay positive."

"Your mother will be busy in her own workshop all week. You'll hardly see her." Roelke stopped in front of a glass case that ran the length of an entire wall, floor to ceiling. The display presented several regions of Norway with artifacts, and life-sized manikins dressed in festive attire. "Colorful!"

"Yeah." Chloe surveyed the exhibit. "*Bunads* have evolved into the national costume for Norwegians, with different styles from different regions. My people go all-out for holidays."

A youngish couple wearing matching sweaters wandered past. The woman's face was pinched with disapproval. "… couldn't be bothered to show up long enough to be introduced to her students!"

Her husband patted her arm. "Petra's ego reached galactic proportions when she earned her Gold Medal last summer."

"Violet deserved to win a Medal, not Petra," the woman huffed. "Everyone thought so."

Chloe gazed after the couple. Violet? Violet Sorensen, Sigrid's daughter? That would explain Mom's burst of pique.

The last thing Chloe wanted to do was eavesdrop on a conversation about the complexities of competition judging, a topic of endless angst for Mom and her friends. "Come see the Norwegian House," she said, and towed Roelke away. "The architecture is Telemark."

His brow crinkled. "I thought Telemark had to do with painting."

"Telemark is a region in Norway," she explained. "My rosemaling class is in the style that emerged from Telemark, and this exhibit replicates a log home from there. It's really cool."

As Chloe led the way inside, she sighed with professional pleasure. The main room was furnished to suggest a well-to-do family living, working, socializing. The painted and carved artifacts on display were stunning.

"This stuff looks really old," Roelke observed.

Chloe pointed to a long table that displayed a variety of kitchen tools and utensils. "Remember the ale bowl that went missing from Old World last summer? Look at that one."

"Very cool," Roelke agreed.

A mangle, displayed with a roller and piece of linen, reminded Chloe of Mom's enthusiastic foray into the nuances of Norwegian courtship customs. Yeah, very romantic, Chloe thought, contemplating the early ironing tools. *Please marry me—so I don't have to do my own laundry.*

Turning her back, she approached a large trunk painted with cherubs and large flourishes in blue and red—faded, but still impressive.

"Can't you imagine a family packing this as they got ready to emigrate? It must have been *so* hard to decide what to take and what to leave behind." Chloe slid her hand beneath the hem of her sweater and reached for the trunk lid's clasp.

Roelke frowned. "I don't think you're supposed to touch anything."

"I just can't use my bare hand. I'm a curator, remember?" She eased up the lid. "I just want to see if the inside is—Oh, *God*!"

The lid crashed down again. Chloe stumbled backward, one hand pressed against her mouth. Her eyes squinched shut, but what she'd glimpsed was etched onto her lids in immutable detail: a brown-haired woman wearing a *bunad* of embroidered red skirt, white blouse and apron, green vest, red cap. She was curled awkwardly in the trunk, unmoving.

Roelke jerked the trunk open again and pressed his fingers against the woman's neck, just beneath the jaw bone. "She's alive. Chloe, go tell someone to call an ambulance. Then stand at the front door. Don't let anyone in or out until the first responders arrive. Got it?"

"Yes." Chloe gulped, turned, and ran.

Back in the lobby, she spotted Howard Hoff and elbowed her way across the room, ignoring the wake of protests and complaints. "Howard!" she gasped. "Call an ambulance. There's a woman in—in the Norwegian House. She's badly hurt."

He stared at her with wide, bloodshot eyes.

"*Go!*"

He hurried away. Chloe made her way to the front door and planted herself as a human barricade.

18

Mom and Sigrid approached, wearing identical frowns. "Chloe?" Mom asked. "What on earth is the matter?"

Chloe fought a wave of dizziness by leaning over, hands on her knees. "I think I just found Petra Lekstrom."

FOUR

WHEN HOWARD HOFF BURST into the Norwegian House, Roelke rose from his crouch to full command presence. "Get out."

The museum director took two more steps and froze, staring white-faced into the trunk. "That's Petra! What *happened*?"

"Sir, you *must* wait in the hall." Roelke stared at Hoff until the older man reluctantly backtracked. It was critical to minimize contamination of evidence. Roelke was pretty sure that Ms. Lekstrom had not reacted to the first signs of heart attack or stroke by climbing into an antique trunk. Someone had attacked and then dumped her in there.

Less than eight minutes later two cops arrived. "You've got a crime scene," Roelke advised. He pulled his badge from his wallet and flashed it their way: *I speak your language.* "Want me on door duty?" It needed to be done, it was something the locals might entrust to a visiting cop, and he wanted to make sure Chloe was OK.

"That'd be great," one of the cops said.

The EMTs arrived as Roelke slid through the crowded lobby. He found Chloe with one arm braced across the door, speaking politely but firmly to an elderly couple. "…afraid not," she was saying. Her face was pale, but she was composed.

"But *why*?" the gentleman demanded. "If someone's hurt, we're only in the way."

Roelke blocked the exit. "Sir, the police have asked all of us to stay."

When the couple had backed off, Sigrid clutched his arm. "Roelke, what happened to Petra?" she exclaimed. "Howard said—"

"I can't speculate," Roelke said. "*None* of us may speculate." He saw Chloe bite her lip, nod. She got it.

Everyone fell silent as the EMTs emerged from the exhibit area with Petra on a gurney. Roelke held the door open and watched them transfer their patient out to the ambulance. More cops arrived—several in uniform, a couple of men in plain clothes.

One of them conferred with the others before clapping his hands loudly. "Attention, please. I'm Chief Moyer, Decorah PD. My officers need to speak with each of you. Your cooperation is both vital and appreciated."

Roelke sized up Moyer. He wore a plaid sports jacket, yellow shirt, dark trousers, and loafers with tassels. His hair—sandy curls—was worn longer than most cops would tolerate, and was accompanied by a Magnum, P.I. mustache. All that would have given Roelke pause if Moyer hadn't accessorized the trendy attire with an unmistakable air of authority.

Chloe leaned close to Roelke. "Was Petra still alive when the EMTs got here?" she whispered.

"Yeah." He was not optimistic, though. Since Lekstrom apparently had been unconscious for some time, he suspected blunt trauma had been involved, probably to the head. "You OK?"

"I've been better," she admitted. "But I'm OK."

Roelke blew out a slow breath. "That's good," he said, "because it's going to be a long night."

His prediction was spot-on. It took time for the local cops to wrangle the reception guests, escorting them in small groups to the nearby police station to give statements; more time for DPD's Investigator Buzzelli, a stocky gray-haired man with flinty eyes and the demeanor of an ex-marine, to interview the two of them about discovering the victim.

Through it all, Roelke kept an eye on Chloe. She's tougher than she looks, he reminded himself. She was thin and fair, but her delicate features hid an inner strength. Although clearly strained, Chloe was holding it together.

Howard Hoff was not. Roelke heard growing agitation in the director's voice as he talked with the authorities. After a few minutes Investigator Buzzelli stepped into view and beckoned. "Miss Ellefson?"

She shot Roelke a perplexed look before obeying the summons. He followed her into the corridor outside the Norwegian House.

The director's shoulders sagged with apparent relief as they approached. "Chloe, I was trying to explain to Investigator Buzzelli that while of *course* we will cooperate in every possible way, it is also vitally important that officers respect the exhibit, the artifacts—most of them were gifts from the Norwegian government—irreplaceable—I—"

"Um … I'm not sure what you want me to do."

Buzzelli sighed. "Director Hoff suggested that we consult with you about any aspect of the crime scene investigation that affects the antiques."

Chloe took a step backward, landing on Roelke's toes in the process. He wasn't sure if that was accidental or if she was looking for literal support. "Why me?" she asked. "I don't work here. I just *got* here."

"But you're a professional," Hoff said. "Since our curator resigned recently …"

"All we've done so far is take photographs," Buzzelli said. "But IDCI agents from the field office in Cedar Falls are due any time now."

Roelke parsed that through: Iowa Division of Criminal Investigation. Made sense. Most towns the size of Decorah did not have the resources to take full responsibility for what likely would become a murder investigation.

"And an evidence team is en route from Des Moines," Buzzelli continued. He looked at Chloe. "They will need to examine the antiques in this exhibit. Director Hoff has asked that you be present."

Hoff nodded earnestly. "I want to assure our Board, and our donors, that Vesterheim did everything possible to preserve and protect the objects entrusted to our care."

It seemed to Roelke that Hoff was just as interested in preserving and protecting his own butt, but he didn't blame the man for that. Sometimes CYA was a sound policy.

Chloe hesitated only briefly. "Sure, Howard. I'll stick around."

Eleven o'clock found Roelke waiting by the cheerfully dressed manikins. Floorboards creaked above his head—cops, no doubt, crawling through every inch of the museum. It would be foolish to assume that evidence was confined to the Norwegian House. Hoff was nearby, slumped in a folding chair.

Chloe stood beside Roelke, arms crossed tightly against her chest. He wanted to get her out of there, but the evidence team was still at work inside the Norwegian House. Through a handy window Roelke caught glimpses of forensics guys doing their thing.

Chief Moyer emerged from the Norwegian House, a pair of protective booties spoiling his otherwise natty appearance. Hoff jumped to his feet, but the chief waved him back into his chair. "Give us a moment, Director Hoff." He extended his hand to Roelke and Chloe in turn. "Officer McKenna? And Miss Ellefson? Thanks for sticking around. I know you've already given statements, but since you two found the victim, I'd like to hear the story from you as well."

Roelke obliged the request. "So," he concluded, "I made sure the scene was secure until the first responders arrived."

"Several people identified the victim as Miss Petra Lekstrom. Neither of you knew her?"

"No," Chloe said. "Her name came up several times this evening, though."

Roelke had made some notes, and now he pulled an index card from his pocket. "People looked for Ms. Lekstrom at the reception. I heard a woman in the crowd say 'She's probably off making trouble for somebody.' About fifteen minutes later, Chloe and I left the lobby and stopped here to look at this display." He gestured. "A couple walking by was complaining about Ms. Lekstrom. Something about winning a Medal?" He looked at Chloe.

Chloe nodded. "Evidently Petra won her Gold Medal at the National Exhibition last July."

"I moved to Decorah in August," Chief Moyer said. "Can you fill me in on that?"

"Decorah celebrates Nordic Fest every July," Chloe said. "You know, a big festival."

Moyer nodded.

"Vesterheim organizes a rosemaling competition and Exhibition at the same time. Ribbon winners get points. Painters who earn enough points over the years earn a Gold Medal. It's a really, *really* big deal."

"I see."

"The couple who walked past me and Roelke earlier seemed miffed that Petra hadn't shown up to meet her students at the reception." Chloe rubbed her arms briskly. "The man said Petra had a big ego, and the lady seemed to think that Petra hadn't deserved to win a Gold Medal in the first place."

"Hmm." The chief's eyes narrowed. I don't think he misses much, Roelke thought.

Two men carried the trunk from the Norwegian House. Chloe looked horrified. "Don't carry that by the handles!"

The techs exchanged a wary glance. "And…how exactly are we supposed to carry it?" one asked.

"Please, support it from the bottom," Chloe begged. "And—oh geez, did you use tape?" She pointed at an identification tag on the trunk.

Howard shot to his feet and hurried over.

"The trunk is going into evidence," Moyer said. "It has to be marked in a manner which permits identification in court, and we have to be able to prove that continuity of possession has been maintained. Right now, it's heading to the Ames lab for analysis. Mr. Hoff, I have a receipt here for you to sign." The chief busied Hoff with paperwork.

"Will the lab people use chemicals or anything when they examine the trunk?" Chloe asked.

"That might be necessary," Moyer conceded. "But in the long run, their work might not be any more damaging than leaving blood or other body fluids on the antique would be."

Chloe swallowed visibly. Another tech emerged from the Norwegian House. He held what appeared to be one whopping rolling pin with carved ridges, sealed into a plastic bag. "Is that …? Did whoever …?"

"It was in the trunk with the victim," Chief Moyer said. "Hidden beneath her long skirt."

"Hunh." Roelke eyed the pin. Swung by one hand, or crashed down with two hands, it would have packed one hell of a wallop. "That's the biggest rolling pin I've ever seen."

"It's a *lefse* pin," Chloe said.

Roelke looked at her. Moyer did too.

"You know." Her voice was getting higher, tighter. "For making *lefse*."

Whatever *lefse* was. Roelke decided to ask questions later. Right now, he really wanted to get Chloe out of here. Turning to the chief he said, "If that's all you need …?"

"Just one more thing. Ms. Ellefson, could you excuse us?"

The chief drew Roelke away. Roelke found himself in front of a mural that depicted a group of immigrants walking to a dock, about to embark on the voyage to America. Petra Lekstrom's ancestors had made that journey. Roelke remembered what Chloe had said about how hard it must have been for immigrants to pack everything needed for the new world in a wooden trunk. It seemed particularly offensive that Petra Lekstrom, dressed in Norwegian finery, had been dumped into such a trunk.

"Officer McKenna?"

OK, concentrate. "What can I do for you?"

"I understand that tonight's reception was held to welcome teachers and students to the museum. And that you and Miss Ellefson are scheduled to participate in classes this week."

Roelke glanced back at Chloe. God, she was beautiful. With her long blonde hair coiled behind her head, and her chicory-blue eyes, she could easily have stepped from the mural.

The chief cleared his throat.

"Right," Roelke confirmed.

"Mr. Hoff told me he's determined to keep the classes going."

Roelke chewed that over. "Makes sense. Hoff exhibited signs of anxiety earlier, evidently due at least in part to the museum's financial stability."

Moyer spoke with a hint of suppressed anger. "Someone put Miss Lekstrom into that trunk."

"Yeah." Roelke drummed one thumb against his thigh.

"This crime does not feel random. DCI will take the lead in this investigation, but my department will conduct a parallel and joint investigation. Although Investigator Buzzelli is the official liaison with the DCI team, I will remain involved."

Roelke nodded. Chief Moyer was new—to the job, to Decorah. If this crime went unsolved, his career would end up chipped on toast.

"I don't know the local people," the chief said. "And I'm not Norwegian. Nor is Investigator Buzzelli."

"Neither am I."

"But you're a police officer. And you'll be in the center of activity this week. Keep your eyes and ears open, and please stay in touch." Moyer pulled out his wallet, extracted a business card, and handed it over.

As Roelke tucked it into his billfold, he glanced over his shoulder again. Chloe was sitting on the floor now, knees pulled up. Dammit all, he thought. He'd come on this trip with the vague but glorious intent of helping Chloe and Marit improve their relationship. Now Chloe was upset. Marit was upset. And he'd just been asked to help out with what seemed destined to become a murder investigation.

The home Sigrid shared with her daughter was a beautiful Queen Anne structure just blocks from Vesterheim. Chloe let Roelke carry her suitcase inside, and she couldn't focus on the impressive architecture or the antiques furnishing the parlor.

Yikes, she thought. I *am* upset.

Roelke took Mom's and Chloe's luggage upstairs, and Sigrid ushered Mom into the kitchen. After Roelke returned Chloe followed him to the front door. "Thanks for everything."

"Are you really OK?" He smoothed a strand of hair away from her face.

"Not entirely," she admitted. She reached for his hand, twining her fingers through his. It still felt strange, sometimes, this business of being with Roelke McKenna. They had almost nothing in common. His cop demeanor had sorta freaked her out when they first met. During today's car trip, when he charmed her mother, she'd seen a completely new personality—which made her wonder just what else she did not know about him. But tonight . . . well, she was very glad he'd been present when she opened that trunk.

"I need to go." He put his free hand behind her head and kissed her. "Emil's waiting out front."

Emil. Right. Emil Bergsbakken, Roelke's host. "Of course," Chloe said. "I'll see you in the morning." She stayed by the front window until Roelke had gotten into Emil's old pickup and driven away. Something about those disappearing taillights made her feel lonely.

She turned away. Get a grip, she ordered herself. She might be dating a cop, but she was not willing to pin her entire sense of security on his presence. Next time she'd carry her own suitcase, too.

Before following the low murmur of conversation into the kitchen she paused in the dim foyer, taking a moment to consider the house, opening herself. Sigrid's home was, she guessed, about a century old. Chloe was sometimes receptive to lingering emotions in historic structures, great joys or piercing sorrows too strong to contain in a human soul. Most often, she perceived only a faint jumble that she was able to tune out. That was the case here in Sigrid's home.

Which was good, since she'd be staying here all week. If some dark emotion had sent her running, she would have had a hard time explaining it to Sigrid and Mom. Or Roelke. Roelke was many things, but "fanciful" didn't make the list. She had no idea how to tell Roelke about her little gift of heightened perception.

Well, Chloe thought, that will have to wait for another day. Preferably one that doesn't include finding an injured woman stuffed into a trunk.

She joined the others. Unlike the immaculate living room, the kitchen was clearly a busy, lived-in place. Cookbooks lined a shelf, with extras poked sideways on top. Dishes were drying in the drainer. A fruit bowl contained one lonely tangerine.

Mom, Sigrid, and Sigrid's daughter, Violet, were sitting at the table drinking tea. During Chloe's high school years, the Sorensens had sometimes visited her family in Wisconsin. Violet was closer in age to Chloe's sister Kari, but they'd all gotten along fine. Chloe hadn't seen Violet in years. She was still slim, but her long honey-toned hair was now styled in feathered layers.

"Chloe!" Violet got to her feet. "It's been a long time."

"Too long," Chloe agreed, returning the other woman's hug before dropping into the empty chair.

"Tea?" Violet asked. "It's chamomile."

"Have some, sweetie," Sigrid urged. "We all need to settle our nerves." Violet pulled a mug from the cupboard.

"I just don't *believe* it," Mom murmured. "I saw Petra on that stretcher, but ..."

Good thing you didn't see her before she made it to the stretcher, Chloe thought, suppressing a shudder.

"I know." Sigrid's eyes brimmed with tears. "Someone attacked Petra. In the *museum*."

Chloe felt a fierce stab of anger toward whatever SOB was responsible. Committing such a crime inside the museum that symbolized something precious to so many people added an extra degree of offense.

Violet murmured, "I can't take it in."

"Just who is Petra Lekstrom, anyway?" Chloe asked. "I mean, I know she's an instructor, but it seems as if she wasn't on real good terms with people—"

"Chloe!" Mom snapped. "This is hardly the time to speak of such things."

An awkward silence settled over the room. Chloe opened her mouth to defend herself, then closed it again.

Violet filled the mug and pushed it across the table toward Chloe. Then she approached Mom and put an arm around her shoulders. "Everyone's upset, Aunt Marit," she said with soothing sympathy. Mom patted Violet's hand.

So much for mother-daughter bonding. Chloe felt too weary to decide if she was grateful or annoyed by Violet's intervention. Maybe Mom felt guilty about calling Petra "a bad penny."

"Petra may recover," Violet reminded them. "We really have no idea how badly she was injured."

Mom stared into her mug. Sigrid stared at the wall. Chloe studied her tea. The refrigerator hummed, and a clock above the sink ticked.

"I can't say I was close to Petra," Mom said finally. "But I would never wish her harm."

Chloe figured that was as close to an apology as she was going to get for Mom's rebuke. "Of course not," she said.

"Petra is a member of the Sixty-Seven Club," Mom added quietly. "And our numbers are dwindling."

Sigrid leaned toward Chloe. "Marit was the baby in the class," she said in an undertone.

"It hasn't been that long since Phyllis Hoff died," Mom said. She looked at Sigrid. "How is Adelle Rimestad doing?"

Sigrid shook her head. "Not well. Be sure to visit her while you're here."

"Adelle has lung problems," Violet whispered to Chloe.

Somewhere in the dusty crannies of Chloe's brain, a light bulb flickered on. No wonder Mom was ever eager to visit Decorah and see her friends. They were all older than she was. It must be hard for Mom to hear the latest litany of sad news ... and ghastly to have the evening ruined by the discovery that one of the diminishing band had been attacked and left to die inside an immigrant trunk.

They all jumped when the phone rang. Violet waved her mother off and answered it. "Hello? Oh, hey, Howard. Is there any news of ... no, we haven't heard any more either." She listened. "Of course I'll tell them ... What?" Her shoulders slumped. "Sure, I can do that." She replaced the receiver.

"Well?" Sigrid asked. "Any news on Petra?"

"No. Howard's decided to have a breakfast for teachers and students at eight-thirty tomorrow morning. He'll share whatever news he has then." Violet gave a little shrug. "I agreed to bake muffins."

Chloe glanced at the clock. It was very late. "I can help, if you want."

Violet shook her head. "Thanks, but I'll do it. Howard's like family." She retrieved a large mixing bowl from a cupboard. "I'm supposed to be at work by eight, but fortunately I have a five-minute commute." Violet, Chloe knew, worked as a secretary in the music department at Luther College.

Mom pushed to her feet. "I need to go to bed."

"Me too." Sigrid rose as well, and carried their mugs to the sink. "I won't be able to teach a duck to swim tomorrow if I don't get some sleep."

And the unteachable duck will likely be me, Chloe thought, as the older women left the room.

"Maybe Petra will be all right," Violet said. She opened the refrigerator and pulled out a carton of eggs. "If not, I'm afraid the police are going to end up with a pretty long list of suspects."

"Petra is . . ." Chloe hesitated, "disliked?"

Violet cracked an egg into the mixing bowl. "It's no secret." She gave Chloe a *What can I say?* shrug.

"Hmm," Chloe said. It seemed wise to leave things at that.

Violet sighed. "I can't think of anything more horrible to spoil the beginning of Vesterheim's big week of classes and Christmas festivities."

I can, Chloe thought morosely. If Petra Lekstrom didn't survive her attack, the mood at Vesterheim would only get worse.

FIVE

Chloe, Sigrid, and Mom arrived at Vesterheim's Education Center, down the block from the museum, just after eight the next morning. All of them were loaded down with totes and tubs stuffed with the copious amount of stuff rosemaling evidently required. Chloe, who'd vaguely imagined needing to purchase a brush and a few tubes of paint, had been shocked by a "Needed Supplies" list that included Q-tips, tracing paper, masking tape, a stylus, multiple sable and foam brushes, a palette knife, and an expensive pad of something called Painter's Palette.

"We have new classrooms," Sigrid said, as she led the way inside. "Beautifully lit, away from public view … we even have our own lounge and kitchen."

"Remember how cramped we were back in sixty-seven?" Mom said. "And none of us cared."

Mom's words were right, but her tone was subdued. Chloe felt true remorse for resenting her mother's enthusiasms. That Marit Kallerud was subdued here, at Vesterheim, was just plain wrong.

Chloe managed to make it to the third floor without dropping either her supplies or Violet's pumpkin spice muffins. In the lounge, several women were setting out trays of coffeecake and bowls of fruit. Chloe spotted Roelke leaning against the wall in a far corner. Something tight beneath her ribs eased a bit.

"Sigrid! Marit!" Howard Hoff hurried across the room, looking an inch away from total meltdown. "We need to talk." The museum director hustled the older women away.

Chloe surrendered the muffins and joined Roelke. He gave her a quick kiss and an appraising look. "I'm all right," she told him firmly. "Is there any news?"

"Yeah," he said. "Petra Lekstrom died last night."

Dammit. Chloe hung her head for a moment. Petra … Vesterheim … Mom … this was bad, bad, bad. "Do the cops have any suspects?"

"I don't know."

Chloe asked the question she'd avoided last night. "What did the police chief want to talk to you about before we left?"

"Since I'm going to be on the inside this week, he asked me to keep my eyes open, and—"

"What?" Chloe eyed him with dismay. It hadn't occurred to her that Roelke might get sucked into this tragedy. "'On the inside?' I thought cops hated working with cops from other places."

"I give the chief credit for being open to all sources of information. He's new here. He doesn't know the community, or the museum, or anything about Norwegian stuff. I guess Investigator Buzzelli doesn't know much about Norwegian stuff either."

Chloe didn't want to believe that "Norwegian stuff" had anything to do with Petra's murder. She also didn't want Roelke to spend the week in cop mode—tense, terse, focused like a laser.

He was already at it, in fact—not-so-casually scrutinizing the students straggling into the lounge. "What did you hear about Petra Lekstrom after I left last night?" he asked. "Did your mom and Sigrid talk about her?"

"They didn't want to."

Roelke was still eyeing the growing group as if Jack the Ripper might appear in a painter's smock. "Your mom might tell you stuff about Lekstrom that she wouldn't share with the police..." He frowned when Chloe began massaging her forehead. "What?"

"I asked about Petra last night," she told him. "Mom just about bit my head off."

"Can you try again? This is important."

"I *know* it's important, but—"

"May I have your attention?" Howard had emerged from his huddle with Sigrid and Mom. Twenty or so students were now nibbling muffins and sipping juice from paper cups.

"I am sorry to begin with more bad news," Howard said. "Petra Lekstrom passed away at the hospital last night."

That announcement brought a dismayed buzz. Chloe shifted her weight slightly, so her shoulder rested against Roelke's.

"This is tragic," Howard continued. "But the Vesterheim community is a family, and at times like these, families pull together."

Nods, a few murmurs.

"Petra's death obviously impacts our workshop schedule. Some of you traveled across the country to attend her class. Rest assured, your workshop is still a go."

More murmurs, some questioning looks.

"Sigrid Sorensen, one of our most popular instructors, is stepping in to teach the advanced class," Howard said.

"Sigrid is moving up to teach the advanced class?" Chloe said blankly. "Then who …"

"Fortunately," Howard said, "one of the students enrolled in the advanced class is also an experienced teacher. I am *very* happy to announce that Marit Kallerud has agreed to teach the Beginning Telemark class."

⚬⚬⚬

This is not good, Roelke thought. Chloe's expression suggested that she'd been smacked in the face with a pickled herring. "Remember," he whispered, "the whole idea of this trip was for you to spend time with …"

Chloe pinned him to the wall with a look that had gone from stunned to mutinous. He stopped talking.

"We have every reason to believe that what happened last night was an isolated incident, and Chief Moyer has assured me that his officers will keep a special eye on the museum," Hoff was saying. "I hope that you all can move past the terrible shock and throw yourselves into your creative endeavors."

Roelke glanced at Chloe. She had a *Yeah, right,* expression on her face.

"The painting classes will start a little late today, to give our instructors a chance to get organized," Howard concluded, "but I suggest that you students go ahead and settle into your classrooms."

People drained their cups and started gathering their things.

"This is not going to work," Chloe said bleakly. "My mother will be on my case every minute."

"No, she won't."

"Maybe I could switch to the carving class."

Roelke shook his head. "If you drop out of your mom's class, all you'll do is embarrass her, and—" Over Chloe's shoulder he saw Marit approaching, and he raised his voice. "Hello, Marit."

"Good morning, Roelke." Chloe's mother looked composed, but Roelke saw the tight pinch to her mouth. Evidently Marit also had some reservations.

Marit turned to her daughter. "I'm sure you're disappointed about the new arrangements."

"Not at all," Chloe said. "I'll be learning from the best." Roelke gave her credit for a game attempt.

Marit smoothed her hair, which did not need smoothing. "Sigrid has more experience teaching Hallingdal than I do."

"It's *fine*, Mom."

"So you'll just have to muddle along with me." Marit glanced at the wall clock. "I need to speak with you about another matter, Chloe. Do you recall Howard saying last night that Vesterheim's curator recently resigned?"

Roelke felt Chloe stiffen. "Ye-es," she said slowly.

"She wrote a grant application for a folklore project. The museum received funds to conduct oral history interviews about Norwegian-American Christmas traditions. There are several interviews left to do, and the project must be completed by the end of the calendar year or the money will disappear. As you can imagine, Howard's worried."

"Ye-e-es," Chloe said, even more slowly. Roelke marveled at the degree of wariness she managed to convey in that single word.

"So I told Howard that you'd conduct the final interviews."

Chloe blinked. "You *what*? Mom, I'm a curator, not a folklorist!"

"For heaven's sake, Chloe," Marit said. "You work for the Historical Society of Wisconsin. You've got a master's degree in museum studies. You've been involved in folklore your entire life."

"But I'm supposed to be painting, remember?" Something in Chloe's eyes changed. "Or ... do you not want the daughter who's 'never picked up a brush' in your class? Is *that* it?"

Roelke groaned silently.

"You can do both!" Marit waved an airy hand. "Just schedule the interviews for evenings. Since you've never shown a *jot* of interest in painting before, I don't imagine you'll be spending all of your time—"

"Next time, please ask before volunteering me to—"

"Vesterheim needs help," Marit said crisply. "And after everything's Howard's had to handle ... well, I can't imagine that you'd even consider refusing."

Across the room, a student snatched a banana. Howard poured himself a cup of coffee. One of the food ladies started filling the sink with hot water. Everyone was evidently oblivious to the hushed exchange taking place in the corner ... but Roelke felt something crackle in the air like electricity before a storm.

And at that moment, he realized that he was a complete and utter moron. Why had he thought he could help ease tension between Chloe, who he was only beginning to understand, and Marit, who he barely knew? What the hell had possessed him?

At last Chloe said, "Fine, Mom. Whatever you want."

"Thank you, dear." Marit gave her daughter an *All is well* nod. "Stop by Howard's office sometime and pick up the files. Now, I must get to the classroom. Don't be late!" She smiled brightly and hurried away.

Chloe turned to Roelke. "What was she thinking?"

Roelke had no idea what Marit was thinking.

Chloe folded her arms. "I just agreed to spend my evenings interviewing octogenarians about paper hearts and *smultringer*."

Now Roelke had no idea what Chloe was thinking. Just be supportive, he told himself. "Maybe the interviews won't be so bad."

"No, no," she said impatiently. "The assignment doesn't bother me. I love meeting elderly people and hearing their stories. But I suggested this trip in an effort to improve relations with my mother, who has been known to observe that I don't spend time with her or share any of her interests."

"And yet?" Roelke asked, since she seemed to be waiting for a response.

"And *yet,* she just gave away my spare time. Silly me, but I'd expected to spend time with her this week. And with you. Now I'll be spending my evenings talking about goats and—"

"Goats?" He really was struggling to keep up.

"*Julebukkers.* Don't ask. I hate them."

Roelke tried to remember if he'd ever heard Chloe use the word "hate" before. He came up empty.

"The real issue is that my mother, evidently, does not want to spend time with *me.*"

Roelke started to say something along the lines of *At least you'll be sharing class time.* Fortunately, common sense kicked in. Stymied by the notion of a verbal response, he switched into action mode and picked up her tub of supplies. "Come on."

He helped Chloe haul her stuff to her classroom. Marit was busy at the front. Seven women and two men were already seated at tables, laying out tubes of paint and jars of rice and a bewildering variety of other clutter. They reminded Roelke of his grandmother and friends playing bingo in the church basement long ago. Some of the ladies set out their game cards with equal precision, and surrounded them with troll dolls and oversized dice and whatever else they considered lucky.

Chloe picked a spot in the back row, far corner. "Thanks, Roelke. Can we meet in the lounge at lunchtime?"

"It's a date," he promised.

⌘

Roelke's classroom was a big industrial-looking room on the ground floor. Three tables had been placed in a U in front of a blackboard. Emil Bergsbakken was arranging decoratively carved objects on another table. Roelke slid into the lone empty chair.

The woman on his left had warm gray eyes and a long mane of silver hair held in place with butterfly barrettes. "Lavinia Carmichael," she said in response to Roelke's introduction, and offered a firm handshake.

"Good morning," Emil called. The carving instructor looked tired. Well, Roelke thought, it was a short night. The evening before, when they'd arrived at his farmhouse just north of Decorah, Emil had politely showed Roelke to the guest bedroom and immediately retired. Emil had likely known Petra, and was shaken by her death. Hell of a way to start the week, Roelke thought.

"Norway has a rich tradition in woodcarving." Emil held up an ornately carved mantel clock. "This is an example of acanthus work. Note the flowing leaves and vines."

"Stunning fluid energy in that piece," Lavinia murmured.

Roelke, who knew nothing about fluid energy, nodded.

Emil continued, "Now, this platter shows chip carving, which is the style we'll be working with this week." His voice gained strength. "V-shaped gouges carved into the wood create intricate but balanced patterns, because life is made up of darkness and light. This carving tradition stretches back over 1,500 years. The most common motifs are geometric."

Lavinia shook her head in admiration. "Look at the symmetry in those rosettes."

Roelke, who knew nothing about rosettes symmetrical or otherwise, nodded again. Since his objective had been to accompany Chloe and Marit, he really hadn't given this chip carving class much thought. He could whittle a simple bird or turtle, but that was about it. Now he wondered if he was in over his head.

"I'm going to pass around some handouts," Emil said. "Then we'll begin."

Lavinia took two knives stored in plastic tubes from a well-worn canvas bag. "Thank heavens," she murmured. "I've been looking forward to this class for months, and when I heard about Petra last night, I was afraid Howard would cancel everything. Trust Petra to go out with a bang."

That seemed cold. "I beg your pardon?"

Lavinia flapped a hand. "I shouldn't have said that. Never mind."

"Sure," Roelke said. "I take it you knew Ms. Lekstrom, though?"

"Oh, I knew her." Lavinia flipped through an over-stuffed three-ring binder and opened it to a blank page. "If it weren't for her, I never would have discovered chip carving, which I love."

"Wasn't Petra a painter? Did she carve, too?"

"No, Petra stuck to painting. That's the point." Lavinia accepted a packet of papers and passed the stack to Roelke. "But I shouldn't speak ill of the dead."

Emil said, "I want to analyze some designs so you understand the foundations of chip carving. The first important element is focal point." He held up the platter. "As you can see here ..."

Roelke tried to follow along, but his mind was turning over Lavinia's cryptic comments. At the reception, Sigrid had mentioned that Lavinia was a member of the Sixty-Seven Club, but evidently Petra had said or done something that caused Lavinia to give up painting altogether.

He turned that over in his brain. Simply passing that tidbit on to Chief Moyer would lead to official questioning. That might be inevitable, but it would be much more pleasant for Lavinia—who, after all, had no idea she'd just been chatting with a cop—if he could discover the story unofficially.

He drummed one thumb against the table. Someone—maybe him, maybe Chloe—needed to talk to Marit.

SIX

Chloe watched the clock's minute hand creep toward noon with tensed muscles, ready to bolt. *Yes—*

"Remember," Mom called, "I want everyone to finish mixing their paints before lunch."

Chloe dropped back into her chair. Shit. The long morning wasn't over yet.

The first thing Chloe had learned about rosemaling was that she evidently had the eye-hand coordination of a goldfish. Mom had begun by teaching some basic brush strokes. As she'd wandered the aisles, she'd found nothing to compliment in her daughter's attempts. *There are no flat lines in a C-stroke, Chloe. ... Hold the brush straight up and down, Chloe ... You must **turn** the brush in an S-stroke, Chloe.* Chloe had been enormously relieved when Mom announced that they were moving on to the preparation of their paints.

Now, Chloe dubiously regarded the blobs on her palette. She had imagined squeezing dollops of paint from their tubes, grabbing a brush, and going to town. Instead, the class had just spent over an hour mixing their own shades from complex equations. The second thing Chloe had learned about rosemaling was that she had no eye for color. Mom had yet to approve any of her daughter's efforts. *Try adding a pea-sized dollop of yellow ochre. ... Fold in the light hue instead of squashing it, your color's getting muddy ... Don't use so much Prussian blue, it's too strong.*

I am not staying here through lunch, Chloe thought. In desperation she leaned toward the woman sitting to her right. Gwen was a ringer—clearly an experienced painter. Chloe had spent the morning both feeling intimidated by her tablemate and trying to copy everything she did.

Time to copy. "Gwen?" Chloe asked politely. "Do you think my dark green is OK?"

Gwen, a round-faced brunette woman perhaps a decade older than Chloe, leaned over. "Looks good to me."

"*Thank* you." Chloe silently declared victory and diapered her palette in plastic wrap to keep the paint from drying. Then she went to find Roelke.

He was waiting for her in the lounge. "Hey," she said. "How was your morning?"

"Great!"

"Really?" She tipped her head. Roelke McKenna was not a man to enthuse lightly. But he did look honestly and truly pleased.

"I learned how to sharpen my knife. How about your morning?"

"About what I expected. I did not succeed in satisfying my mother."

"Sorry." Roelke kissed her forehead. "What do you want to do about lunch? I was hoping we'd have time to visit the museum's carving exhibit."

"I packed lunch for us," Chloe told him. "That'll be quick, and then we can go."

They ate cheese and tomato sandwiches, chatting with the other students, before excusing themselves and heading for the formal museum. "This is quite the building," Roelke remarked.

Chloe looked up at the brick building trimmed with ornate window arches and carved balconies, recently and lovingly restored in an effort that had strained Vesterheim's budget. "It began as a luxury hotel. And the Education Center once housed a foundry shop where plows and wagon parts were made. It's great that Vesterheim repurposed historic structures. And you haven't even seen the Open Air Division yet."

Inside the museum, volunteers were adding more holiday decorations to the lobby. Life goes on, Chloe thought. Wrapping the entire museum in real or metaphorical black crepe wouldn't accomplish anything.

Roelke eyed a plywood figure. "What's with all the gnomes?"

"*Nisser.* They're mischievous barn elves," Chloe explained. "They always make an appearance at Christmastime."

She carefully avoided the Norwegian House exhibit by taking a back stairwell. When they reached the permanent exhibit titled *Wood And Its Decoration,* Roelke's jaw actually dropped.

Chloe smiled. The collection of folk art never failed to astonish her, either. The artifacts ranged from tiny bowls to massive furniture. She trailed behind as Roelke admired the antiques.

He pointed to a shelf carved with flowing lines. "Acanthus style. Vines and stuff. And—Holy *toboggans*." He'd spotted the case of artifacts decorated with chip carving. "Look at that workmanship."

The display included several mangles—those betrothal gifts Mom had described with such glee. Chloe touched his arm. "It's gorgeous. We need to keep an eye on the time, though."

As they retraced their steps, he paused in front of a flat piece of wood—roughly thirty-five inches by four inches, and carved with a variety of symbols. "What is that?"

"It's a *primstav*—a calendar stick." Chloe regarded the piece with professional appreciation and personal distaste. "Centuries ago, people used them to keep track of time."

"So... those tiny notches are for days?"

"Right. Each stick has a winter side and a summer side." She indicated a carved mitten. "This marked the beginning of winter. The symbols represent seasonal activities. Some of the traditions came from pagan times, like..." Her voice trailed away. The first story that popped to mind had to do with women who wished to marry running around a cuckoo tree three times. Good God, she thought. Shades of my mother's encyclopedic knowledge of marriage folklore.

Roelke squinted at the stick. "Do you know what all these symbols stand for?"

"Not off the top of my head. I think there's a flail for threshing grain in there somewhere. And... see that bonfire? That probably stands for the winter solstice. Right next to it is a drinking horn. Merry Christmas, have some beer."

"Well, hunh," Roelke said.

"But lots of those symbols represent saints' days. There was a time when the church punished people if they didn't honor the saints. These *primstavs* helped peasants keep track." Chloe frowned at the calendar stick. "When I was about eight, I sat through a slide show at my dad's Sons of Norway lodge where the speaker described all the martyrs' deaths in great, gory detail. I was traumatized."

Roelke put an arm around her shoulders. "No fun."

Chloe let her head rest against him for a moment. Maybe they could play hooky that afternoon …

"Chloe?" Roelke asked. "I need you to do me a favor."

That didn't sound good. Her sense of refuge disappeared. "What is it?" she asked, way too savvy to agree up front.

He told her about the conversation he'd had with Lavinia that morning. "So there's some kind of old conflict between her and Petra, and …"

"And you want me to find out what happened."

"Right. I mean, *I* could question your mom—"

Chloe had seen Roelke in formal cop form. It was not fun to be on the receiving end. Right now Mom really liked Roelke, and Chloe didn't want anything to jeopardize that. She sighed, deeply and dramatically. "No, I'll talk to her."

"Thanks."

The reference to Mom reminded her of something else. "You go on ahead. I should stop by Howard's office and pick up the folklore project notes."

Roelke made a big show of glancing at his watch.

"It won't hurt if I'm a *little* late for the afternoon session," Chloe said. "Besides, since my mother volunteered me for this little gig, she can hardly complain." She hoped.

Roelke started to frown. Then his expression changed in a way Chloe couldn't quite identify. "It's just a file or two, right?" he said. "I'll get them for you."

Chloe's eyes narrowed. She couldn't tell if he was intervening for personal or professional reasons. Did the cop want a moment alone with Howard Hoff, or did her companion want to facilitate peace between her and Mom?

She decided that the question was not worth deep analysis. "Be my guest," she said. "I'll meet you after the afternoon session."

It didn't take long for Roelke to find Hoff's office. The door stood half-open, and the director's voice drifted into the hall. "... No, I don't think you should come." Pause. "It's a sweet offer, Judy, but I'm really fine."

The man was obviously in the middle of a personal call. Roelke stepped away and leaned against the wall.

Hoff raised his voice. "No, I insist. Judy, I—no, honey, just listen for a moment. You're the best daughter in the world, but you've got a fiancé in California. There's no good reason for you to spend money on an airplane ticket."

Now, that was a surprise. Roelke would have figured that Hoff would leap at the offer of moral support from his daughter.

"I'm sure the police will find whoever did this terrible thing to Petra," Hoff was saying. "...Yes, I promise. I'll call you soon."

Roelke gave the director a moment before stepping to the door. Hoff stood holding a photograph in a silver frame. Roelke raised his hand to knock, but something about the director's profile made him pause. Howard stared at the photograph with an expression of grief and loneliness...and something else too.

This errand was already proving interesting.

Roelke stepped backward and coughed discreetly before presenting himself. Hoff swiveled, blinking in surprise. "Excuse me," Roelke said. "I told Chloe I'd pick up some files. Something about that folklore project?"

"Oh! Yes, of course." Hoff glanced down and seemed surprised that he was still holding the photograph. He put it back on a credenza, positioning it just so. Roelke could now see a black-and-white image of a woman, head and shoulders held in an awkward studio pose. She had a heart-shaped face, an elaborate upswept hairdo, and a genuine smile. The only other thing on the gleaming expanse of polished wood was a rosemaled bowl, which she'd probably painted.

Hoff's desk was covered with files, binders, sloppy stacks of phone message slips. The director rummaged through a teetering stack of folders. When he reached the bottom without success he began excavating in a drawer. "Oh," he murmured, looking perplexed, "*there's* the accreditation file." He put it on top of the manila Matterhorn and dug farther. Finally he extricated several fat files.

"Here you go." He held them out to Roelke. "And..." After another few minutes' search Hoff unearthed a small recorder and some blank tapes. "She'll need these, too. I'm so glad Chloe was willing to pick up the final interviews."

"She's delighted with the opportunity," Roelke assured him. Then he left the director to his work and his memories.

I need to learn more about Director Howard Hoff, Roelke thought as he hurried away. He'd studied a lot of faces, gotten pretty good at reading people. And he was pretty sure that the emotion clouding Hoff's grief was guilt.

"Be sure to clean your brushes thoroughly before leaving," Mom reminded her students.

Chloe took that as permission to quit for the day. Thank the good Lord, she thought fervently.

The afternoon had been even more stressful than the morning. A clerk in Vesterheim's folk art supplies shop had helped the beginning students trade the platters Petra had listed on her supply sheet for oval trays that fit one of Mom's designs. Chloe had sanded her tray and slapped on a base coat of dark acrylic. She also managed to transfer Mom's pattern to the tray without calamity.

But all too soon, Mom had moved on to actual rosemaling. "Since Telemark motifs are asymmetrical," she explained, "this style is ideal for beginners." She walked her students through the first few steps, calling them forward so she could demonstrate each bit of the pattern before sending them back to try it themselves. Chloe never finished one assigned motif before Mom moved on to the next, and she was ending the day behind.

Now Chloe shot a surreptitious glance at Gwen's work. Her tablemate's work was even further along than Chloe had expected. That means I'm even more behind than I realized, Chloe thought.

Gwen sealed her palette into a spiffy plastic container that looked much more professional than Chloe's plastic-wrapped sandwich. "Want some help cleaning up?" she asked Chloe.

"Thanks, I'd love some help," Chloe replied gratefully. "I'm the slowest person in the room."

Gwen reached for one of Chloe's brushes and began pulling the bristles through a scrap of newsprint to remove pigment. "You'll get the hang of it."

"I sure hope so." Chloe went to work on another brush. "Gwen, please tell me that you're not really a beginner."

Gwen laughed. "No, I've been painting for years."

"Then . . . why this class?"

"I've taken beginner classes many times. I—"

The lights went off. In the classroom's sudden silence came the sound of adolescent laughter and pounding footsteps.

"I think some *nisser* are playing pranks," Mom said. She made her way to the wall and flicked the switches again. "Some of the volunteers preparing the museum for Christmas obviously brought their children and grandchildren along."

"My sister and I used to do the same thing," Chloe admitted to Gwen. "It seemed so hilarious when I was eight."

Gwen chuckled. "Perhaps I should think twice about leaving my paints here overnight. I don't want some disgruntled elf to mix my colors." She reached for a baby food jar of muddy-looking turpentine. "As I was saying, I keep taking classes because I always learn something new. And there aren't any other painters where I live."

Chloe had grown up in Stoughton, Wisconsin, where it was impossible to walk down the street without seeing rosemaled embellishments on shutters, business signs, park benches. "Well, your work is beautiful," she said, nodding toward Gwen's tray. "Do you compete in the annual Exhibition?"

"No *way*." Gwen lowered her voice. "I give people like your mom a whole lot of credit. I do this for fun, and that whole competition aspect…" She shook her head. "I think the point of entering is to inspire other artists, and to celebrate one's accomplishment. That's probably the case for most people, I guess, but I've heard some pretty nasty remarks over the years." She set the first brush aside and reached for another. "Sour grapes from people who didn't win a ribbon, most likely."

Chloe remembered the complaint she and Roelke had overheard the evening before about last summer's Exhibition. "I suppose judging is somewhat subjective, too."

"To a point," Gwen conceded. "The process has to be transparent. The judges provide critiques, and the good ones are clear and constructive. But every once in a while…"

Chloe swished her brush in some paint thinner, wiped it on her palm, and frowned at the traces of red paint left behind. "Like last year, maybe? I heard someone complaining about—about the Gold Medal." At the last moment she backed away from saying Petra's name aloud.

"There were a *lot* of complaints," Gwen murmured. "Two painters had accumulated enough points that if they earned a blue ribbon, they'd each earn a Gold Medal. Petra Lekstrom did just that. But a lot of people thought that Petra was scored too high, and that Violet Sorensen's work—which got a red ribbon—scored too low."

"So Violet ended up one point short of Medal status, right?" Chloe tested her brush again. Dammit! Still threads of pigment.

"Right. Violet painted a butter churn, and it was stunning." Gwen gave Chloe a *What can you do?* look. "There were a lot of mutters about Petra somehow influencing one of the judges. But there are three judges, so it wouldn't be easy to do."

"I know that winning a Gold Medal is huge," Chloe mused.

"Beyond the honor, it leads to all kinds of opportunities. Well— you know that, of course, since your mother is a Medalist."

Yes, Chloe thought, I do know a bit about that. "What did Petra enter in the competition?"

"An antique trunk."

Petra had painted an immigrant trunk? Chloe winced.

"I know," Gwen muttered, as if reading Chloe's thoughts. She handed over several clean brushes. "Here you go."

"Thanks." Chloe carefully settled the brushes, wooden ends down, into her jar of rice. She tried not to linger on the fact that Gwen had cleaned three brushes in less time than it was taking her to do one. "I really appreciate it."

"No problem." Gwen pushed her chair back. "See you tomor- row."

Chloe got back to work. She didn't notice Mom passing by until she spoke: "Gently, Chloe. We must protect our brushes."

Yeah, yeah, Chloe thought. For once, she didn't take the criti- cism to heart. Her mind was too focused on the painful image of Petra selecting a trunk, spending hundreds of hours planning and preparing and painting, with no way of knowing that six months later ...

Chloe wiped her brush one last time, decided to ignore the remaining wisp of red, and set it aside. Everyone seemed to agree that Petra Lekstrom had not been well-liked. But had someone hated her enough to plan such a brutally ironic attack?

SEVEN

TIME TO AM-SCRAY, CHLOE thought. Brushes clean and paint protected, she jogged down the stairs to meet Roelke. He met her with a smile and a kiss, and the combination smoothed out the afternoon's rough edges.

"Here's the stuff from Hoff." Roelke held out some files and a microcassette recorder.

She slipped them into her totebag. "Thanks."

"Did you plan to eat dinner at Sigrid's house?"

"No." Chloe shrugged into her parka. "I've already had eight hours of my mother's company today, and very little of yours. Is Emil expecting you?"

"No," Roelke echoed. "I was hoping I'd have a date tonight. I hear there's a good pizza place nearby."

"Mabe's," Chloe confirmed. "Let's go."

When settled into a booth at the restaurant, with BBQ pizza for Roelke and veggie pizza for her on the way, Chloe felt her tense muscles begin to relax. "How was your afternoon?"

"Great!" Roelke said again, with the same surprised-but-pleased smile he'd displayed at lunchtime. "Emil's a good instructor."

"Did you start on a project?"

He shook his head. "We're working on practice boards."

"I wish we could have practiced more," Chloe said wistfully. "Mom made us start on a wooden tray."

"Well, here's something to take your mind off painting. I overheard Hoff telling his daughter, who evidently wanted to fly out from California after she heard about Petra's murder, to stay home."

"Really? I would have thought he'd be thrilled to have his daughter come visit."

"Me too."

"I heard something interesting about Petra this afternoon..." She frowned as Roelke pulled out a stack of index cards so he could make notes. "Do you have to do that? It makes it all so—so official."

"Since a woman was killed yesterday, yeah, I do. You were saying?"

Chloe told Roelke that Petra had won her Medal for painting an antique immigrant trunk. "Isn't that creepy?"

"It is," he admitted. "I'll—oh, thanks." Before continuing he made room for the pizza a young waiter delivered. "I'll make sure the chief knows that."

Chloe leaned forward on her elbows so she could whisper. "Do you think somebody might have...you know, actually *planned* to attack Petra and stuff her body into an immigrant trunk? Was someone trying to make a statement?"

"A statement about what?"

"About the Gold Medal she earned last summer." Chloe took her first bite of pizza and was momentarily distracted. "Oh my God, this is good. They must use Wisconsin cheese."

"I imagine that a few people in Iowa make good cheese, too."

"It's possible, I suppose," she mumbled around another bite. She wiped her mouth before getting back to the point. "Petra Lekstrom and Violet Sorensen were both close to winning a Medal. Evidently a lot of people were unhappy when Petra earned one, but not Violet."

"That hardly seems like motive for murder. Are you suggesting that Violet Sorensen—"

"No!" The word burst out loud enough to turn heads. Chloe tried again. "No, of course not. I've known Violet for years. I'm just saying that in broad terms…some people might take the whole competition thing a bit too seriously."

Roelke sipped his water. "My grandmother and her friends took the Jefferson County Fair pie competition too seriously, but no one ever came to blows about it. Even though nobody ever beat my grandma's strawberry-rhubarb pie." He sounded a bit smug about that.

Chloe made a mental note to trot out her own strawberry-rhubarb-*maple* pie recipe come spring. "No disrespect to your grandma and the Jefferson County Fair, but this is a national competition. Gold Medalists are put up on a pedestal. Collectors and museums buy their work. They write books and teach classes. Petra had just taught a class in Norway, for crying out loud."

"OK, OK." Roelke made a few more notes on a new index card. "Anything's possible, and jealousy can simmer for a long time before erupting. I've seen people fly into a rage for less."

Chloe eyed her last sliver of pizza with regret, too full to join the clean plate club. "Let's talk about something else. If I can line up an interview for this evening, do you want to come along?"

"Sorry, but I can't. This afternoon I got a note to call Chief Moyer. He asked if I could come by the station tonight at seven."

Chloe used her straw to swirl the ice cubes in her glass. Just as she'd anticipated: cop stuff trumped gentleman-caller stuff. "That's OK," she said. "It was just an idea."

$$\infty$$

Roelke arrived at the police station at 6:55 P.M. Buzzelli was running something through a photocopy machine. Chief Moyer stepped from his office as Roelke stamped snow from his boots. "Thanks for coming by," Moyer said.

"No problem."

Moyer gestured both men into his office, which looked a lot like every other chief's office Roelke had ever seen: tidy desk (sloppiness did not send a good message to the visiting public), a few framed citations on the wall (certifications attesting to professional prowess, and plaques of appreciation from the Kiwanis, Rotary, and Lions Club attesting to community involvement), and pictures of young children (because a family man understood problems on a personal level). Roelke and Buzzelli dropped into the chairs facing the desk.

"Twenty-four hours have passed since Ms. Lekstrom was found," Moyer said. "Officer McKenna, I have explained to the investigator here, and also to the DCI agent in charge, that I've asked you to participate informally in this investigation."

Roelke nodded. Buzzelli did not. Definite friction here, Roelke thought, but thankfully not my problem.

"I have spoken with Chief Naborski in Eagle," Moyer continued. "He assured me that you can hold your own counsel."

That made Roelke feel good.

"It would of course be inappropriate to share any confidential information we learn during the investigation," Moyer added.

"Of course," Roelke agreed.

"But discussing basic details might be helpful as you get to know people this week. Investigator?"

Buzzelli opened a file folder, extracted a color photograph, and slapped it down on Moyer's desk. "Petra Lekstrom, age fifty-four, of Preston, Minnesota."

Roelke picked up the head-and-shoulders shot. Petra looked to be wearing the same getup she'd died in—red wool cap, white blouse, green vest. She was what his grandmother would have called "a handsome woman"—hair a soft brown, face largely clear of wrinkles, dark eyes, full mouth curved in a smile that contained a hint of seduction.

"The victim was five-foot-three and slight of build," Buzzelli continued. "That big rolling pin found in the trunk was the probable weapon—"

Roelke cleared his throat. "It's a *lefse* pin."

Buzzelli looked at him.

"For making *lefse*." Roelke added helpfully. He liked being helpful. He really did need to find out what *lefse* was, though.

"Let's move on," Moyer said. "Family, Buzz?"

"Lekstrom never married, had no known children," Buzzelli continued. "She attended Luther College here in Decorah. Next of kin, a sister in Seattle, has been notified. The sister hadn't seen the victim in eighteen months."

"How did Ms. Lekstrom support herself?" Roelke asked.

"Largely through an inheritance from her maternal grandfather."

Roelke considered. "Was it enough to kill for?

"We're not talking millions here." Buzzelli waggled one hand. "But Lekstrom's house in Preston is paid for, and she doesn't have any known debt. She got interest payments every six months. Otherwise she had a business doing genealogy for people. Sometimes she taught art classes, and she sold some of her painted stuff."

Roelke made some notes.

"One of the DCI agents is talking to acquaintances in Preston," Buzzelli added, "but he's not getting a whole lot. Lekstrom's neighbors are elderly. Very polite, but not very talkative."

Moyer leaned forward, forearms on his desk. "Yesterday the museum was closed from four o'clock until five-thirty, when the reception began. If Miss Lekstrom was assaulted before the museum closed, the assailant was likely either an employee or someone who purchased a ticket."

"Or," Roelke countered, "she might have been attacked by a volunteer who helped with the reception, or one of the students or instructors who attended."

Moyer picked up several stapled pieces of paper and handed them to Roelke. "This is a list of everyone known to be inside the museum yesterday between noon and the time the victim was found. It is incomplete. Obviously any museum visitor who paid for their ticket with cash, and did not sign the guest book, left no identification behind."

Roelke scanned the sheet, typed on a machine that produced a solid circle for every O. Each name was followed by a designation: visitor, volunteer, museum staff, class instructor, student. It was a long list.

"I wanted you to have a copy," Moyer added, "because you may hear something about one of the people on this list."

The older man shifted in his chair again. "I don't think—" he began, then closed his mouth. Either Buzzelli had second thoughts about what he'd been going to say, or he truly did not think.

Roelke filled the silence before it could become awkward. "Petra Lekstrom won a Medal in that big-time rosemaling Exhibition last summer. You probably know this already, but the object Ms. Lekstrom painted for the competition was an immigrant trunk."

More silence suggested that the other men had not known that. Moyer's eyes narrowed thoughtfully. Buzzelli grudgingly pulled a small notebook from his pocket and scribbled a note. Nobody thought to ask, Roelke thought. But hell, he hadn't either. That tidbit might have sailed by if Chloe hadn't picked up on it.

After a moment Moyer asked, "Anything else?"

Roelke tapped his thigh with his thumb. "A woman in my carving class knew Ms. Lekstrom for many years, and clearly disliked her."

"Who?" Buzz asked.

"Lavinia Carmichael." Roelke kept his tone mild. "If you can give me another day, I might be able to learn what caused the discord. She might respond better to casual conversation than formal questioning."

"Investigator?" Moyer asked.

Buzzelli looked bored. "Sure."

"Anything else, Officer McKenna?"

"No."

Buzzelli stood. "I have work to do." Moyer nodded, and the investigator left the office.

A moment later Roelke heard the front door open and close. He looked at the chief.

"I serve as Decorah's police chief at the pleasure of the mayor," Moyer said. "In the four months since I arrived, I have come to suspect that the good investigator had hoped to serve Decorah in that particular capacity."

Roelke nodded. That would do it. Buzzelli was old-school, a tough cop who'd likely seen plenty of hard action and worked himself up the ladder rung by rung. Chief Moyer represented a new generation: college-educated, overdressed, perhaps—in the eyes of a veteran cop—more worried about a suspect's legal rights than getting some asshole off the street.

"Let's connect again tomorrow evening." Moyer picked up a stack of papers and tapped the already tidy edges on the desk: *We're done here.*

"Sure," Roelke said, and left.

After Roelke headed for the police station, Chloe lingered over her soda and reviewed the folklore project files. She was relieved to find a well-organized plan and clear notes. The come-and-gone curator had listed potential informants with a brief note about topics that had emerged during preliminary contact. Most of them had already been interviewed. Chloe considered the remaining names and decided to start with a widow famous for her holiday baking. The woman was known locally as "Bestemor Sabo"—Grandmother Sabo. Can't go wrong there, Chloe thought hopefully. She found a phone booth near the front door, called the given number, and received a warm welcome to visit that evening.

After hanging up, Chloe fished a fistful of change from her wallet and dialed a familiar number. "Ethan?"

"Chloe? That you?"

Chloe smiled. Her best friend Ethan, who worked for the U.S. Forest Service, lived in Idaho. Just hearing his voice made her feel good. "It's me. I'm in Decorah with my mom and Roelke."

"How's it going?"

"My mom ended up teaching my rosemaling class. It's a long story—" one she did not want to go into at long-distance rates— "but basically I can do no right in her eyes."

Ethan's voice was low, sympathetic. "Sorry it's such a challenge. You did good to suggest the trip, though. Family's worth holding onto."

Chloe bit her lip. Ethan's parents had not handled well his coming out as a gay man. Chloe knew how much the estrangement hurt him. I should remember that, she thought. At least Mom still considers me part of the family.

"I'll keep trying," she told Ethan with dogged resolve. "I promise."

"How are things going with Roelke? First family adventure and all?"

Chloe considered. "Well, *he's* bonding with Mom."

"That's good, right?"

"I guess so. Mom keeps wafting into tales of Norwegian courtship and marriage, which makes me want to bury myself in the nearest snow drift, but Roelke seems to be taking it in stride." A noisy group of teens burst through the door to Mabe's. Chloe pressed the receiver harder against her ear, plugged her other ear with a finger, and turned her back. "And he seems to be doing OK with his carving class. I wish I'd signed up for that one." She sighed. "Remember back in forestry school when we used to quiz each other on tree identification with those blocks of wood? I do love all the visual variety."

Ethan laughed. "Me too."

"Softwood trees, hardwood trees, I love 'em all. Remember that time when we got presented with a piece of diseased wood at the mid-term?"

"Yeah," Ethan said. "It was so beautiful that as soon as the exam was over I begged the prof to let me take it home. I made a cookbook shelf for my mom with it. She loved it. Of course that was before…" His voice trailed away.

Shit, Chloe thought. She was not doing well by her friend today. That's what came of being self-absorbed with her own problems. "Well, you can make me a cookbook shelf for Christmas," she said. "Out of any kind of wood. I'd treasure it."

"Only if you bake something for me from one of those cookbooks. Chris is a pretty good cook, but neither one of us does well in the baking department."

"Will do," she promised. And speaking of baking, she thought, I need to go see what Bestemor Sabo wants to share.

EIGHT

AFTER LEAVING THE POLICE station Roelke got his bearings, hunched his shoulders, and struck out briskly for Emil's place. The sidewalks were mostly clear of snow and ice. The worst bit was crossing over the Upper Iowa River. The single-lane bridge had an impressive double arrangement of angular iron trusses, but no sidewalk and nothing to shield him from the wind.

Emil lived less than a mile beyond the river on an old farm tucked beneath a bluff on Skyline Road. The frame house was small, and the barn where Emil kept chickens and milked a couple of cows was small, too. There were also a couple of other outbuildings, a little pasture, and a narrow field where he probably raised hay.

Roelke let himself into the house, pulled off his boots, and left them on the mat. He liked things tidy. Besides, Emil's place was immaculate.

"You're back!" Emil called from the living room, where he was settled with a knife and practice board. "Want a beer?"

"I'd rather something hot," Roelke admitted. "If you've got it."

"There's tea in a canister by the stove."

"Thanks." Roelke watched Emil make a short, quick stroke. "After teaching us all-thumbs students today, aren't you ready for a break?"

"I'm trying a new design. If I like it, I'll show you all tomorrow." Emil paused, shrugged, and made another cut. "Carving makes me feel good."

Then you must feel good all the time, Roelke thought as he headed into the kitchen. The furniture in Emil's house was decades old—not antique, just outdated—but that didn't matter because the man's carvings took the spotlight. Wooden spoons, plates, bowls, boxes, shelves, clocks, tables, chairs, and a variety of items Roelke didn't even recognize were *everywhere*. Many patterns included rosettes—he now knew that rosettes were circular designs —while others featured straight lines and hundreds of tiny triangles, carved in patterns that always, *always*, seemed perfectly suited to the object itself.

Roelke filled the kettle and turned on the burner. He studied the kitchen idly while waiting. The toaster looked twenty years old, the stove thirty, the fridge maybe forty. The room was purely functional—no curtains at the window, no cookie jar on the counter, no well-thumbed cookbooks on a shelf.

Then Roelke noticed a big crock on the floor. It held a few stray kitchen tools that, to his unprofessional eye, must have passed from old to antique a ways back. One was a big, grooved rolling pin.

"Hey Emil, is this a *lefse* pin you've got here?" he called, hefting the pin. It was heavy—four pounds, maybe five. He carried the pin into the living room.

"*Ja.*" Emil's face clouded with sorrow. "That was my *mor's.* My mother's. She died when I was just a boy. Why are you wondering?"

"Just curious," Roelke said mildly, reminding himself that the pin found beneath Petra's body was not common knowledge. "What is *lefse,* anyway?"

"Flatbread. Made with potatoes."

Roelke contemplated the pin. "What are the grooves for?"

"I don't know. You better ask one of the women at Vesterheim. Any good Norwegian woman knows how to make *lefse.*" Emil's voice was husky. "My *mor,* she spread warm *lefse* with butter and a little brown sugar. Now, that was good eating."

Roelke was sorry that he'd triggered sad memories. His own mother was dead too, and he knew how bittersweet reminiscing could be. "I think I hear the kettle," he said, and retreated back to the kitchen.

The tea was hard-core, so Roelke made do by only dipping the bag a few times. Then he carried the steaming mug into the living room and settled down where he could watch his host work. He waited until Emil paused, wiping his design with a cloth to remove any stray bits of wood, before asking, "Did you learn to carve as a boy?"

"Oh, *ja.*" Emil pronounced the affirmation as *yawh.* "My father was a good carver. All the men were, back in the old days. In Norway, you know, everything was made of wood—tools, kitchen utensils, furniture, houses." Emil pointed to an oval lidded box. "My grandfather made that, back in the old country."

I have to get Chloe out here, Roelke thought. This place is a museum itself. "Have you always concentrated on chip carving?"

"Pretty much. Some of them carvers, they need a big work bench and big tools. Lots of equipment, lots of fuss. You get that complicated, and all of a sudden you got to worry about ventilation and noise and not cutting your hand off with a power saw. All I need is a couple of knives, a ruler and compass, and a pencil. I like things simple."

Roelke nodded.

Emil pointed again. "That bowl there? My brother Oscar did that one. Oscar, he was one good carver."

"Oscar has passed away?"

"Last spring." Emil returned to his work. "A heart attack, they said it was."

"I'm sorry," Roelke said.

"Maybe he'll be back soon," Emil said. "The old Norwegians believe that the souls of family members who died come back at Christmastime, you know."

"I didn't know, actually." Roelke waited to see if the older man was speaking in jest, but Emil went back to his work.

Roelke glanced around the room. No television. Just a few books and a basket holding old issues of *National Geographic*. It was a good thing Emil was so involved at Vesterheim, because otherwise he'd live a very lonely life.

Well, he didn't want to dwell on that. "I really enjoyed class today."

Emil smiled. "You did good."

Roelke leaned back in his chair and sipped the tea, feeling ridiculously pleased. Dad used to say that, he thought suddenly. Didn't he? Roelke tried to remember. Back when he was little, before his father's boozing got out of control. Once or twice at peewee baseball games, when Roelke had made a good catch or hit a long drive. "You did good," his dad would say. Then he'd pull Roelke's cap off and smack him on the butt with it, laughing. Roelke had never understood the butt-smacking part, but the rest had made him stand tall for the rest of the day. If only…

He suddenly realized that his left knee was jiggling up and down. He shoved all the "if onlies" back into a box in his brain. "Emil, you must have known Petra Lekstrom, right?"

"Sure." Emil moved his shoulders up and down. "She lived over the border, but she came down to Decorah all the time."

Roelke understood that "over the border" meant southern Minnesota. "What was she like?"

Emil finished another triangle before responding. "She was a real piece of work."

"Yeah?" Roelke sipped his tea. Its heat slid down through his chest, dispelling the last chill. "How so?"

It took Emil a few moments to answer. Roelke couldn't tell if he was trying to choose his words carefully, or waiting until he reached a good stopping point in his work. "There was this one time," the carver said finally, "maybe … five, six years ago, when she was taking some class upstairs and I was teaching one downstairs. All of a sudden she just marches right into the shop and starts tossing pieces of wood around."

"What for?"

Emil waved a hand. "That's what I wanted to know. She said she needed some wood to make a drying stand. Something like that, anyway. So everybody gets up and helps her look. Finally she takes some stuff and sashays right back out. Then just when I got everybody all settled again, she's back. This time she grabs this pretty piece I'd been saving for a box."

"Did you say something?"

"I said, 'Hey, I want that. I'll find you something else.' And she said, 'It's just a board. Don't be such a *chisler*.' She thought she was very clever, that Petra Lekstrom."

Roelke rolled his eyes. He wasn't big on puns.

"She took that board," Emil said. "But that night, I told Oscar what happened. He just settled down with some wood like most every evening. He was still at it when I went to bed. In the morning, I see he's carved a woman holding a paint brush. It looks half like Petra and half like a witch. I laughed when I saw it. Oscar says to me, 'You tell Petra Lekstrom that rosemalers sniff turpentine.'"

"And … did you tell her that?"

"No," Emil conceded, eyes twinkling. "But Oscar and me took that carving to the rosemalers' classroom real early, before anyone else was around, and put it up on a shelf. That Petra, she laughed when she took the wood. But we got the last laugh." He held his board toward Roelke. "You see this curved design in between these two straight-edge borders? I'll show you how to do that tomorrow."

The lacey design looked difficult. "Then I better get to bed," Roelke said. "Thank you, Emil. Good night."

After washing the mug, Roelke headed up the steep stairs to the guest room tucked beneath the eaves. His mind raced with thoughts … of Petra Lekstrom, of his father.

Finally, after tossing and turning beneath the blankets for way too long, he made a deliberate mental switch and thought of Chloe instead. Usually thinking of Chloe—of the miracle of her actually dating him—was enough. Tonight, it wasn't. They weren't together and that was wrong, just plain wrong.

Roelke had no intention of pushing things with Chloe. He'd wanted to date her for three months before she finally agreed to give things a try. Now three more months had passed, and he still sometimes felt as if he was trying to hold milkweed fluff in his hands. Chloe was fragile and strong. He didn't really understand her work, or the things that made her happy, or the way her mind processed information. But none of that shook his faith that they'd do well together.

He did not want to rush her. But tonight, with a killer wandering Decorah and a December wind rattling the windows, he really, *really* wished he could fall asleep with Chloe in his arms.

Chloe spent a high-calorie evening with Bestemor Sabo, who was as plump and endearing as Mrs. Claus. Bestemor Sabo began with a heartfelt apology: "I'm sorry I only have nineteen kinds of cookies made, Miss Ellefson. If you can come back in a few days, I'll be up to my usual two dozen."

Chloe needed two cassettes to record Bestemor's family stories about holiday baking. She was less successful with the taste-test the elderly woman had prepared, begging off after half a dozen cookies.

"Well, I'll just pack up the rest for you," Bestemor Sabo said cheerfully.

"Your children and grandchildren are lucky," Chloe observed, watching as Bestemor made a nest of waxed paper in a cookie tin that looked old enough to accession into Vesterheim's collection. "And everyone else on your list."

"I like to make people smile." Bestemor Sabo paused, a delicate almond cookie in hand. "And this year ... after what happened to Petra Lekstrom ... well, we all must try extra-hard to bring holiday cheer back to Decorah."

"Did you know Petra?"

The older woman got back to work. "Of course."

Of course, Chloe thought. It was that kind of community. "It's awful. I know a lot of people didn't really like Petra, but still ..."

"True enough," Bestemor agreed. "Except for the ones who liked her a bit too well, if you know what I mean."

Chloe thought she did. "You mean men, right?"

Bestemor Sabo ripped off another piece of waxed paper with one sharp jerk against the strip of tiny metal teeth. "Some say she had an affair with one of the competition judges last summer. As for what people say about her and Howard ... well."

Petra and *Howard*? Howard Hoff? Chloe tried to look receptive to, but not eager for, gossip.

"I don't like to speak of such things." Bestemor Sabo placed the last cookie in the tin and pressed the lid into place. "You take this along with you."

Darn, Chloe thought. She thanked her hostess and headed out.

Despite layers of thick wool, Chloe's toes and fingertips were soon numb. Decorah felt like a different place than the town they'd reached ... was it just the evening before? Yesterday's sparkling Christmas charm was gone. The night was dark and cloudy. The air held a damp cold that leached straight to the marrow. Christmas lights seemed more garish than festive. Chloe walked quickly, alert for any furtive movements. Petra Lekstrom's murder was giving her the heebie-jeebies.

At Sigrid's house, a welcome glow and hum of voices pulled her to the kitchen. The counter was dusted with flour, dirty bowls filled the sink, and the room smelled of ginger and cloves. Sigrid was nowhere in sight. Mom sat with forearms resting on the table, staring at a mug of tea. Violet sat beside her, visible in profile. "...know I shouldn't let it get to me," Mom was saying.

Violet put a hand on Mom's arm. "Don't be so hard on yourself, Aunt Marit," she murmured. "How could it not?"

"Hey," Chloe said. Too loudly.

Mom straightened. "Why...good evening, Chloe. We were starting to wonder about you."

"I was doing my first interview for Vesterheim," Chloe said. "Remember? That project you volunteered me for?"

Violet didn't allow an uncomfortable silence to take root. "How did it go?"

"It went fine." Chloe walked to the stove and turned on the burner beneath the kettle.

"Well, I'm going to call it a night," Mom said. "Good-night, girls."

"Good-night," Chloe echoed. She stared at her mother's back until it disappeared, and then listened to her footsteps fading as she climbed the stairs.

Violet picked up her own mug, sipped.

Let it go, Chloe counseled herself silently. Letitgo. Let. It. Go.

Violet sipped again.

"So Violet," Chloe said, as conversationally as humanly possible, "did I interrupt something?"

"No. Your mom's just … you know. Rattled about everything that's happened. My mother is too. She went to bed an hour ago."

Like I'm not rattled? Chloe thought. Like I'm incapable of providing a word of solace? She closed her eyes and rubbed her forehead. Shit. *Was* she incapable of providing a word of solace? Had the past few years, filled with what might euphemistically be called "challenges," desensitized her to other people's feelings? Chloe had no idea. What she did know was that Mom was upset, and needed to talk about it … and she seemed to prefer doing that with anyone other than her own daughter.

The kettle began to steam. Chloe made a cup of tea and retreated to the table.

"Want a cookie with that? I made *pepparkakor*."

Death, family dysfunction, and Christmas cookies. *God Jul*, everyone. "No, thanks," Chloe said. "I visited Bestemor Sabo this evening, and—"

"Say no more." Violet laughed. "Speaking of food, I'd love to have Roelke and Emil to dinner tomorrow night. Can you pass that along?"

"Sure." Chloe made a mental note before returning to her topic of … well, if not her choice, Roelke's. "Violet? Can I ask you about something else?"

"Of course."

"Bestemor made a couple of references to some … um, connection between Petra and Howard …?" Chloe leaned back in her chair, stretching her legs, pretending that digging up dirt didn't make her feel sleazy.

"Oh, Lordy." Violet got up and began putting the gingersnaps into a cookie jar. "Well, it's a pretty open secret. Aunt Marit knows all about it, I'm sure."

Chloe rolled her eyes. That did not, of course, mean that Mom would ever tell *her* about it.

Violet must have figured that out too. "Rumor says Howard and Petra had an affair."

Chloe tried to find a tidy slot in her brain for that little factoid. "Seriously?"

"Seriously. The rumors are serious, anyway."

"Howard seems an unlikely lothario."

"I agree," Violet said dryly. "My guess is that Petra acted as lotharia, if that's a word. I bet she went after Howard just because she could."

"But everyone says Howard adored his wife."

Violet sighed. "He did. I didn't believe the whispers until my mom spotted Petra and Howard in a ... shall we say ... passionate embrace late one night in the parking lot."

Chloe wrinkled her nose. Ew.

"It's really tragic," Violet added. "Maybe nothing more happened, and at worst the relationship evidently didn't last long. But a couple of months later Howard's wife was diagnosed with cancer."

"Did Phyllis know about her husband's maybe-affair?"

"I have no idea," Violet said.

Chloe really, *really* wanted to go to bed. But Roelke's request—that she try to find out how Petra had driven Lavinia from painting in days of yore—was still unfulfilled. *Geez*, he owes me, Chloe thought. Big time. "Violet? Do you know Lavinia Carmichael?"

"Sure."

"She's in Roelke's carving class, but she's also a Sixty-Seven. Do you know why she stopped painting?"

Violet began running hot water into the sink, and squirted in some dish soap. "That happened a long time ago. I've heard your mom and my mom allude to it, but you know how they are. I was in college at St. Olaf at the time, living on campus in Northfield, so I never heard the scoop."

"I was just wondering," Chloe said. "I keep hearing about those early painting days." She tried to think of something that would make her seem like less of a sordid rumor-monger. "That first class sure had an impact on my mother."

"My mom kept scrapbooks." Violet plunged a cookie tin into the sink. "They're in the tower room off the parlor. I'm sure she wouldn't mind if you poke around."

"Thanks. I'll do that." Chloe used the invitation to take her leave.

The small circular room was a charming space. Whimsical wooden animals paraded toward a Noah's Ark tucked beneath a small Christmas tree. Chloe moved a child-sized wicker rocking chair so she could sit on the floor by a row of scrapbooks. When she pulled the first album free and saw the date lettered on the front, her eyebrows rose. Nineteen forty-nine? Yikes. That was eighteen years before Vesterheim's first rosemaling class. But Chloe had not gone into the history field for nothing. Curiosity piqued, she opened the album.

NINE:
JUNE, 1949

By the time the parade wound its way through Decorah, Sigrid was exhausted. From her perch on the Norwegian-American Museum's float, she forced herself to keep smiling and waving as they inched past the last of the crowds lining the sidewalk.

"Oh, what fun!" Marit exclaimed. "All our work was worth it. The Norwegian community was well-represented in Decorah's Centennial Celebration."

"It was indeed," Frank Ellefson agreed, smiling fondly at his wife.

Sigrid felt her heart constrict with envy. She knew Frank wouldn't have taken the time to travel to Decorah and spend two days decorating the museum float on his own. But it was important to Marit, and therefore it was important to him.

Sigrid realized she was twirling her wedding band on her finger, and forced her hands to stillness. Preparing the float *had* been fun. Many of the museum's stalwart volunteers had gotten involved. The girls made hundreds of crepe paper flowers. Howard Hoff and the Bergsbakken brothers had taken care of the actual construction. Howard, who hoped to win a job at Vesterheim one day, was in his element. Emil was sweet and efficient. Oscar had a wicked sense of humor that diffused minor bickering. One pithy comment from him got everyone laughing.

Well, everyone but Petra.

Now, Sigrid glanced over her shoulder to the highest seat on the float. Petra had enthroned herself with queenly glory in the elaborate *bunad* she'd sewn for the occasion. That woman, Sigrid thought, thrives on conflict.

Although both of them volunteered at the museum, this float was the first big project they'd worked on together. Sigrid and Marit had privately agreed that Petra actually seemed uncomfortable with harmony. She'd usually been the one to introduce tension: "Your flowers are too big ... You're putting too many red ones on this side ... No, that's where *I'm* going to sit."

"I don't think she even cares what the float looks like," Marit whispered. "Petra seems to enjoy tossing monkey wrenches into the process and then standing back to see what happens."

"You weren't here for the early planning sessions." Sigrid had rolled her eyes. "Lavinia Carmichael and I had brainstormed a few ideas to bring to our first meeting. Petra had some plans of her own, but she went to the museum director *first* and got his tacit seal of approval."

None of that matters, Sigrid thought now, fanning herself. The sunshine, the crowds, the noise, the warmth of her own wool *bunad*—it was all making her feel a bit queasy. Thank God the parade was almost over.

Emil, who was driving the tractor pulling the float, navigated the final corner and parked. Everyone cheered.

"Frank," Petra called, "could you give me a hand?" She aimed an all-eyes-for-you smile at Frank, pretending herself incapable of stepping down from her throne. Marit and Sigrid, who'd been riding on the edge of the float with legs dangling, exchanged a look of mutual disgust. That, Petra, is a losing battle, Sigrid thought. Anyone with a pair of eyes could see that Frank was crazy about his wife.

Which was, of course, why Petra was angling to lever herself between them.

Frank, looking splendid in his own ceremonial attire, politely helped Petra step down. Then he turned his back and tucked Marit's hand through the crook of his arm. Although she wasn't showing yet, Marit was three months pregnant.

Marit smiled at him, then caught Sigrid's gaze. "I think the gang's going for ice cream cones at the Whippy Dip. Are you coming?"

Sigrid shook her head. "I got a bit overheated. I'm heading home."

Marit looked concerned. "Do you want to meet for one of the concerts at the fairgrounds later? Or maybe join us for dinner at the Winneshiek?"

Sigrid liked Frank, but she missed the old days when Marit stayed at her house while visiting Decorah, instead of the Winneshiek Hotel. "Maybe," she hedged. "I'll see how I feel later." She waved good-bye to her friends.

Minutes later, she reached the old Queen Anne she'd inherited from her parents. The house felt warm and stuffy, but at least it was quiet. Sigrid settled on the window seat in the tower room off the main parlor. She loved this space—small, peaceful. She often retreated here because she hated rattling around this big house by herself.

Of course she wouldn't *be* alone if Bill had made different choices.

Sergeant Bill Sorensen, U.S. Army, had served his country during the war. She'd lived with the agony shared by millions of newlywed women until he came home safe and whole after VE Day. Except ... he hadn't been whole. The man who survived combat wasn't the man she'd married. The new Bill was moody, restless, remote. Six months later he'd decided to return to military service without discussing it with her. Hurt, shocked, angry, she'd argued bitterly with him about their future—especially their living arrangements. "You can come to the base," he'd said, clearly astonished that she would consider anything else.

"I live in Decorah," she'd said. And she meant it.

So Bill left, and Sigrid stayed. She'd seen him last about two months earlier when he'd come home on leave. His visit had been rocky, and he'd spent the first several evenings away from home. "I need to be with other vets," he'd said, avoiding her eye.

In fairness, by the second week, he'd tried to be a good husband. He took her to see *The Heiress* because Sigrid liked Olivia de Havilland, and they strolled through Dunnings Spring Park, and ... well. The point was, she felt sad and happy whenever he came home, and sad and happy whenever he left.

Sigrid sighed and picked up her current needlework project, a baby bib she was embroidering with a sweet little *nisse.* "A December baby, a Christmas design," Marit had said when she saw it, beaming.

Sigrid made several stitches before putting the bib back down. She was tired. She seemed to be tired all the time these days. A little nauseated, too. And worried.

Maybe she should try to meet up with Marit and Frank later, and ask Marit if maybe they could steal a little girl-time. Marit was one of her dearest friends. She could talk with Marit about anything.

Then Sigrid shook her head. She could talk with Marit about *almost* anything. Some secrets were just too big to share.

TEN

IN THE TOWER ROOM, Chloe stretched. It had been fun to read about the huge party Decorahans had thrown to celebrate the town's Centennial. Still, something about the yellowed photos and brittle articles made her feel sad. Or maybe, Chloe thought, I just can't shake the shadows of these past couple of days.

Looking over her shoulder, she realized that the lights had gone out in the kitchen—Violet must have gone up to bed. Chloe tried to shed her melancholy. This room should be a haven. Sigrid had done a lovely job arranging what could have been an awkward space. The toys might have been Violet's, like the baby doll with a head of molded vinyl and blue go-to-sleep eyes. Before tucking the doll into the rocker, Sigrid had added a handmade bib with an embroidered *nisse*. Chloe touched it, trying to absorb the joy of whatever happy child had last played with the doll. But she couldn't find joy, and her sadness remained.

Chloe realized that she'd had all she could take for one evening. Ten minutes later she was settled into a four-poster bed in her guest room, listening to the wind and wondering if Roelke was lying awake, too. Think about something else, she instructed herself. Their current state of détente was of her own making. Besides, she wasn't afraid to be alone.

But tonight, with a killer wandering Decorah and a December wind rattling the windows, she really, *really* wished she could fall asleep in his arms.

❦

It was still dark when Roelke's alarm buzzed. The day before he'd asked Chloe to meet him at a café for breakfast before classes started. "How 'bout six-thirty?"

Her expression suggested that he'd asked her to donate a kidney. "Six-thirty? Are you kidding?"

"No. We've hardly had a moment together."

"Well, I can't argue with that." She'd sighed. "OK, but you're buyin'. I'm not really a morning person, especially when it's cold and dark outside." Since Roelke was a morning person, that seemed fair.

Now, once he dressed, Roelke went outside just as Emil was coming in with a bucket of steaming milk. "See you in class," Roelke said cheerfully, and headed up the twisting driveway. He passed an outbuilding perched on foot-tall posts and noticed a cross neatly painted near the peak of the roof. Roelke wasn't much of a churchgoer these days, but he found the Christian symbol reassuring. Maybe Emil is active in his church, Roelke thought, turning onto Skyline Road. Or maybe Emil belonged to one of those Norwegian men's groups, like Chloe's dad. That would be good.

Roelke saw few headlights as he trudged to town in the blue-gray quiet of pre-dawn. At the café he snagged a table by the front window so he could watch for Chloe. Fifteen minutes later he spotted her striding down the sidewalk. Her hands were in her pockets, and she wore a heavy scarf and matching wool hat. Her parka, however, was unzipped—as if her Scandinavian genes scoffed at the cold.

She waved through the glass and something zipped through his insides like electricity. This complicated, difficult, amazing woman is waving at me, he thought. Nobody else. Just *me*.

When she came inside he stood, ready to help her shed the bulky layers. Her cheeks were so red that he found himself cradling them instead, and settling in for a proper good-morning kiss.

When they finally pulled apart she said, "Well, that's the best part of my day so far."

"Too bad I know your day's only what … thirty minutes old? Forty?"

"Forty-five, at least." She shrugged out of her coat and draped it over an empty chair. "OK. I need caffeine and sugar."

A few minutes later she was settled with coffee and a piece of almond pastry, and a bowl of granola that Roelke had ordered for her. "You look tired," he said. "Did you sleep well?"

"Not really," she admitted. She poured a generous dollop of cream from a little silver pitcher into the steaming mug and stirred. "Too much stuff circling around my brain. Did you get any good news when you went to the police station last night? Does that investigator guy—what's his name?"

"Buzzelli."

"Does he have any leads? Knowing that Petra Lekstrom's killer was in jail would help my mood."

Roelke wished he could reassure her. "It's early yet," he hedged. "And the DPD and the DCI can't share any specific information about the investigation with me."

She gave him an *I'm waiting* look.

Roelke sighed. "I didn't get the impression that they've made a lot of headway. Did you ask your mom what Petra did to make Lavinia stop painting?"

"Last night was not a good time to pump my mom for information," Chloe said flatly. "Maybe I can find out from Sigrid. I tried asking Violet, but she didn't know. Oh—Violet wants you and Emil to come to dinner tonight."

"I'll tell him. Speaking of Emil … I heard a story about Petra that said a lot about the type of person she was." He told her the tale.

"Good for Emil and Oscar," Chloe said. "*Chisler*, hunh? Can I call you that?"

"Absolutely not."

She let that one go with obvious reluctance. "The investigator—Buzzelli? He pulled a couple of people out of class yesterday to question them. People who'd already left the reception by the time we found … you know."

"He'll be talking to everyone." Roelke glanced up when the waitress paused at his elbow with a pot of coffee and an inquiring expression. He held up his cup for a refill. Once she was out of earshot, he continued. "You and I have the clear impression that Petra wasn't well-liked, but Buzzelli said he hasn't gotten much corroboration on that."

Chloe shrugged. "He's interviewing a bunch of people who are mostly Norwegian-Americans. Many are related by birth or marriage. They're all way too polite to say anything unkind."

"That's pretty much what I thought." What Moyer thought too, he suspected, which is why the chief had made such a point of asking Roelke to listen and learn.

"I'm not real keen on passing gossip along either," Chloe said, "but I did pick up some intel last night." By the time she got to what she'd learned about Howard Hoff and Petra's romance, she was leaning close and whispering. "Violet said her mother saw them in a passionate embrace," she concluded. "Sigrid wouldn't make up something like that."

"I saw Hoff looking at his wife's photo," Roelke muttered, "and there was something in his face ... something beyond grief." Not a bad observation, he added silently, rather pleased with himself.

"Maybe that's why he didn't want his daughter to visit Decorah."

"Could be," he agreed. "Maybe he was afraid that she'd hear gossip about him and Petra."

Chloe looked pensively at her coffee.

Well, that was enough about that. "How is your mom doing?" he asked. "I know you two got off to a rocky start, but I thought maybe—"

"She's not talking to me."

"She—what? Why isn't she speaking to you?"

Chloe circled her fingers in a dismissive gesture. "She's speaking to me. She just isn't *talking* to me, you know?"

Not really, he thought warily.

She poked a banana slice with her fork and evidently found it unworthy. "There have been times in the past few years when I really could have used some support from her, and she never wanted to listen to what was really going on in my life. That was hard." She pushed an apple slice around the bowl. "But things have been going better for me lately..." She lifted her head and gave him a tremulous smile.

Is it really possible that *I* brought that smile to her face? Roelke thought. The very possibility was intoxicating. "I'm glad."

"Me too. So I thought, OK, I can be the one to make things better with Mom. I came to Decorah for her, and I'm ready to be a good listener. But she just won't *let* me."

Roelke ransacked his brain. There had to be some way he could help *fix* this situation. There had to be something he could say, something he could do. But he came up with exactly... nothing. "I'm sorry," he said finally, which was lame. And inadequate.

"Thanks." She squeezed his hand.

"How did your interview go last night?" he asked.

"I visited a nice lady who is the epitome of everything good. It reminded me of when I was a little kid, helping my grandma make cookies." She shrugged, looking a little self-conscious, then tipped her head. "What are your favorite Christmas memories?"

He had to think about that. "Christmas was pretty normal when I was a kid. Stockings, a few presents under the tree. And my mother always put everyone's shoes out for St. Nicholas Day."

"That was a nice way to honor the German part of your heritage."

"Mostly I just liked getting presents on a day when a lot of my friends didn't," Roelke admitted. "And my grandmother made really good marzipan pigs so we'd have good luck in the new year."

Chloe laughed. "When we get back to Wisconsin, I'll make you a marzipan pig," she promised. "Listen, this will probably sound stupid, but I need to ask you something. How do you want me to introduce you to people? What should I call you?"

"How about your boyfriend? That works for me." It worked quite well, actually.

"That would make me feel like we're in junior high."

He considered. "Is there some historical term you'd like?"

"Beau? Suitor? Gentleman caller?"

OK, that idea wasn't as clever as he'd hoped. "Those would make me feel like we're living in some PBS show." And if one of his friends ever heard Chloe refer to him as her "gentleman caller," he'd never live it down.

"Yeah, you're right." She gave him a smile that was both sheepish and endearing. "We better go."

They walked to Vesterheim, every breath puffing white. The pale sun was up now, glinting on jagged rows of icicles hanging from the eaves. They entered the door closest to the stairwell that led up to the rosemaling classrooms. "Can we meet for lunch again?" he asked.

"I sure hope so—"

"*There* you are!"

Roelke turned and saw Marit emerging from the elevator. "Good morning," he said, in his best *I am suitable for your daughter* voice.

"I'm glad I caught you," Marit said. "Chloe, Howard was hoping you'd have a moment to stop by his office before class begins."

"Sure, I can do that."

"I think he wants an update about the folklore project." Marit beamed. "And he's got an amazing wedding rug up there you'll want to see. It just arrived from someone who is considering donating it to Vesterheim. It was used by the same family for three hundred years! Think how many weddings—"

"Mom," Chloe said in a strangled voice, "for the love of God, would you *please* stop with the wedding chatter?"

The smile slipped from Marit's face. Snippets of conversation came from the supply shop down the hall: "…Any more filbert brushes, size 4?" Two students burst through the door with a blast of cold air and punched the elevator button. They chattered about an *ambar*, whatever that was, seemingly oblivious to the tense scene they'd interrupted. After a short eternity the elevator arrived, they stepped inside, and the doors glided closed.

Only then did Marit speak. "The rug dates to 1675, Chloe. If the donation is finalized, it will become the earliest dated textile in the museum collection. I know you don't particularly care for rose-maled artifacts, but since you *do* like textiles, I thought that might be of interest to you." Two pink circles had appeared on Marit's cheeks. "I apologize for my mistake." With that, she turned and shoved open the door to the stairwell, letting it slam behind her.

Chloe leaned against the wall and closed her eyes. "Well, shit," she muttered. "That was my fault."

"Pretty much," he agreed. She opened her eyes and frowned at him. He decided to keep additional observations to himself. At least for now.

"I think my hopes of having a better day in rosemaling class today are gone with the winter wind." Chloe sighed. Then she touched his cheek. "I'm glad we can meet for lunch. And after dinner with Violet and the moms, maybe we can spend the evening together? I've got to make another visit for the folklore project, but you might enjoy it."

"Sorry." He shook his head. "I don't know yet if I'll be free. Chief Moyer said he'd like to meet again—"

"What for?" She pushed herself erect. "I know you've got stuff to report, but do you really think it will take all evening?"

"I don't know."

She leaned closer and spoke in a low tone. "Look, the chief asked you to keep your eyes and ears open. I get that. But I didn't realize this would turn into actual police work on your part."

"I'm not saying that every evening will be spoken for," he began. "And—"

"Save it," she said. "I've gotta go. I'll see you later." She punched the stairwell door even harder than Marit had, and began stamping up the steps.

Roelke watched the heavy door slam in his face for the second time in three minutes. Great, he thought. Ju-u-ust great. What was he supposed to do? Was he supposed to refuse the police chief's request for assistance? Of course not. Chloe was being unreasonable.

A little bit, anyway.

Roelke raked his fingers through his hair. The truth was, he *could* have said he'd make time for Chloe that evening. He could have said he'd tell Moyer that any meeting had to be short and sweet—which was, after all, the only kind he'd had with the Decorah cops. So why hadn't he?

Because being a cop was the only thing he was really good at. The situation between Chloe and Marit was a mess. He didn't know how to help them. But helping Moyer? That he could do.

Roelke blew out a long, slow breath. Well, for the moment, the heck with it. Class was about to start. And Emil Bergsbakken, chip carver extraordinaire, had said that he, Roelke McKenna, had done good work the day before.

Lovely, Chloe thought. As if bickering with her mom wasn't bad enough, now she was bickering with her—her—her *what?* She shook her head. If she was going to date Roelke McKenna, she really needed to figure out how to refer to the man. Anyway, the salient point was this: The mom-daughter bonding experience in Decorah had turned into a royal flustercluck.

When Chloe reached the second floor landing she paused, trying to compose herself. Staff offices were on this floor, and she didn't want to emerge muttering like a harpie. Breathe in, breathe out. It took a few moments, but she was able to saunter from the stairwell with, she hoped, an attitude of pleasant calm.

That calm took a sucker punch to the solar plexus when she approached Howard's office and saw the wedding rug. It was spread flat on a cushion of acid-free tissue now, but—Holy cow, over three *centuries* of bridal couples had entered matrimony cushioned on its fibers. It was amazing ... but it made her cheeks hot, too. What *was* Roelke thinking about all of Mom's subtle-as-a-sledgehammer comments regarding love, Norwegian-style?

OK, enough of that. Chloe knocked on the door frame.

Howard Hoff, who'd been sitting hunched like Bob Cratchit over several sheets of paper with columns of numbers on them, looked up with an expression that was half pleading, half nervous. She almost expected the man to ask for a half-day off, if you please Mr. Scrooge, just a half-day off in honor of Christmas.

"Pardon me for interrupting," Chloe began, "but—"

"It's no interruption, believe me." Hoff stacked up the budget sheets and set them aside.

"Mom said you wanted a progress report?" Chloe perched in an empty chair facing his desk. "I interviewed Bestemor Sabo last night."

"Good." Howard swiveled in his chair and touched a framed photo. "She and Phyllis were friends."

"I'm very sorry for your loss," Chloe said. Roelke was right, she thought. Howard Hoff's grief was terribly shadowed by guilt. If Howard had been unfaithful, he'd done a stupid and horrible thing. But there was no doubt that he had loved his late wife dearly. And still did.

Howard turned away from the photo. "Anyway, Chloe, I thank you. It's kind of you to lend us your time and talents."

Chloe felt her last bit of resentment slip away. "No problem," she said sincerely. "I'm glad to help out. I won't have time to transcribe the tapes, though."

He waved a dismissive hand. "One of our volunteers is a whiz at transcribing."

"OK, then. I'll keep you posted. Now, I better get to class." Chloe stood.

"Did your mother mention that I have another favor to ask?"

Chloe sat back down. "No-o."

Howard's hands moved nervously over his desk—adjusting a cup full of pens, thumbing the top file on a towering stack, fiddling with a paperclip. "She suggested it, actually. She didn't tell you?"

"No-o-o," Chloe repeated. "She did not." Resentment made a U-turn, took up residence in her chest, and hammered to make itself known in word or deed.

"I was wondering if you would accompany Emil's class into the collections storage area tomorrow during the afternoon break. The chance to study artifacts is a unique privilege for our students, but I have another commitment that day, and I need someone with curatorial experience to be along, and it's not that I don't trust Emil, since he's been teaching here for many years, but—"

"Sure," Chloe said, as much to stem the tide as anything else. "I'll do it." She tried to stifle a resigned sigh, but didn't quite pull it off.

"It's this damn accreditation thing!" Howard exploded. "Not to mention the Luther cabal."

"I beg your pardon?" Maybe "cabal" meant something different in Norwegian.

"*Sorry.*" He rubbed his eyes. "Forgive my outburst."

Chloe hesitated. She was already late for class, no doubt falling even more hopelessly behind. Besides, she thought, I really don't want to sink any deeper in Howard's pond of woe.

Yes you do, said Roelke's voice in her brain. *For God's sake, listen to what the man has to say!*

ELEVEN

Chloe waited until Howard looked up. "What accreditation thing?" she asked. "And ... did you just mention a cabal?"

Howard leaned back in his chair. "Vesterheim was accredited by the American Association of Museums in 1973."

"Really? You must have been one of the very first museums to earn accreditation. That's impressive."

"Yes, yes. But accreditation has to be reconfirmed every decade. We're due."

A dusty, low-watt bulb flickered on in Chloe's brain. "Oh."

"Everyone is thrilled with the museum renovation. But the costs far exceeded initial estimates, financial donations have dropped off because of the recession, we lost revenue when the museum shop was closed during construction, and my last grant request was not funded. We projected that we'd end the year $200,000 in debt. It looks now as if the final tally will be closer to $500,000."

"Yikes." Chloe's eyes went wide. This was why she had no aspirations to climb the museum ladder. She had enough trouble managing her measly curatorial budget.

"My curator resigned." Howard's voice was rising again. "And—lest we forget—one of our folk art instructors was just attacked inside the museum. *And,* not only was she left to die, she was left to die inside an accessioned trunk."

The man made a good case for despair, she had to admit. "So this is not really a good time for an inside-out inspection by a jury of your peers," Chloe said sympathetically. "And … the cabal?"

"Oh." Hoff pushed to his feet and walked to the window, as if he might see clear to the Luther College campus a mile or so away. "As I'm sure you know, our museum was founded in 1877 as part of Luther. It didn't become a separate entity for ninety years, when the Norwegian-American Museum incorporated. All of those original artifacts still belong to Luther. Legally, they're here on long-term loan."

That was not unheard of in the museum world. "And?"

"And I've been hearing rumors that a few professors would like to see the objects that originally came from Luther, and possibly management of Vesterheim itself, returned to the auspices of the college." Howard shoved his hands into his pockets.

"But … why?"

"As of *course* you know, Vesterheim is the oldest, most comprehensive American museum devoted to a single immigrant ethnic group."

"Ah, yes," Chloe murmured sagely, although she actually hadn't known that.

"Our collection numbers over 24,000 artifacts. Some of our buildings are listed on the National Register of Historic Places. We've created something very special."

"Absolutely."

Howard turned from the window and faced her. "And while of course we are indebted to what Luther College started ... it's taken incredible resources to bring the museum closer to its full potential. And now, a few people at Luther evidently think it would help the college to—and I quote—'bring the museum home.'"

"Hmm." Chloe was skeptical. Assuming control of the museum would be the collegiate sugarplum in theory only. It was one thing to grab ownership; quite another to commit funds to ongoing staffing, programming, and upkeep. Any bigwig donors or granting agencies that might initially fling open their pocketbooks would quickly grow leery if collections care or the visitor experience went downhill.

"Well," she said, "the fact that Vesterheim earned accreditation *after* it became a separate entity is in your favor, right?"

"But losing accreditation would be worse than never having it," Howard said glumly. "I've poured my heart and soul into this museum! Lots of good people have done the same. And now I feel as if Vesterheim is teetering on the brink of collapse. One more calamity ..." His voice trailed away.

"I'm truly sorry, Howard."

"Please ... forgive me. I know I shouldn't have burdened you with all of this. It's just that since Phyllis died, I—I don't have anyone to talk to. Anyone who understands. I can't burden the staff and volunteers here. It would be inappropriate, and terrible for morale."

Chloe was briefly distracted as she tried to imagine having a director at Old World Wisconsin who actually worried about staff and volunteer morale. OK, focus. "Things can only get better," she said, hoping that was true. "And—of course, I'm happy to accompany the carving class to the storage area."

That seemed to shake Howard from his mental abyss. "What? Oh—yes."

"I'll work out the details with Emil."

"Thank you. Just make sure that no one moves an artifact, or picks one up improperly. Emil's done this a hundred times, and I trust him implicitly, but with reaccreditation hanging in the balance, it's just that—"

"Of course," Chloe murmured soothingly. She really did need to get back to class at some point today. Her tablemate Gwen had probably painted three bowls, two platters, and a four-post bed while the museum director had been unburdening his soul.

Howard pulled open a desk drawer and spent a good minute scrabbling through its contents. At last he extracted a key and held it out. "Here's a master key. Why don't you just keep it for the rest of the week?" He arranged his mouth in a wan smile. "It's good to have a curator around, even if only for a short while."

Chloe pocketed the key, said "I'm happy to help" one more time, and made her escape.

Once in the hall, she resisted the urge to bang her head against the wall. She truly did know how it felt to fight the good fight against outside critics, a crushing workload, and inadequate resources. Howard had a lot of weight on his shoulders, and no one to share the load.

Which reminded her that at her worst moments in the past six months, she'd *had* someone to help shoulder the load. Someone who gladly would, if she let him, take her burdens on altogether. She'd never let him do it. But it was pretty darn nice that he wanted to.

Chloe headed for the stairwell. She regretted the spitting match she'd shared with her mother that morning, and was even sorrier that she'd snapped at Roelke. I have some humble pie on the menu, she thought, and indulged in a sigh of profound resignation.

In her rosemaling classroom, Chloe's fellow students were silently bent over their work—work that had progressed far, far beyond where they'd been the day before. Mom looked at Chloe with raised eyebrows: *So nice of you to join us.*

And I used a week of vacation for this, Chloe thought. She settled down to paint.

∽

"At the bottom of this long triangle, you want the point of the knife to reach the center," Emil said. "See how I do that?"

When the master carver demonstrated a technique, Roelke never knew if he should watch with complete attention or take notes. Watch, he decided now. If need be he could ask Emil questions later.

"You don't want this cut to get too deep," Emil continued. "Straighten the blade gradually, and bring the tip—"

"*God Jul!*" several adolescent boys hollered from the hall. *Wham!* The heavy classroom door slammed shut.

"Oh!" Lavinia gasped. Roelke jumped.

Emil jumped too. His blade dug a gouge into the wood. He slammed down his practice board with what could only be an impressive Norwegian curse. Then he stamped across the floor, jerked open the door, and shook his fist—actually shook his fist, Roelke observed; you didn't see that too often—after the miscreants. "Stop with your pranks!" Emil shouted. "We're working with sharp knives in here! You try that again and I'll turn every one of you over my knee!"

It was the threat that broke the tension. One of Emil's students sniggered. Roelke coughed to hide a smile. As Emil turned back toward the classroom the anger left his shoulders, and he grinned sheepishly. "I could do it, too," he said. "Now. I'll show you how to fix a mistake."

When the demonstration was complete, the students tried the new pattern. Roelke worked carefully, fascinated by the emerging design. Not bad, he thought. Not bad at all.

Lavinia, his tablemate, nodded with a knowing smile. "It's addictive, isn't it?"

"It is," Roelke admitted.

"Carving has filled a lot of pleasant hours since my husband died. The funny thing is, I didn't like geometry in school." Lavinia reached for her can of ginger ale and raised it in a salute before taking a sip. "Now, I can't get enough of it. The possibilities are endless."

Roelke ran a finger over his work. Geometry ... maybe that was it. His cousin Libby had called him "rigid" more than once. He preferred "meticulous." Either way, the precision of chip carving appealed to him.

Lavinia cocked her head toward two of their fellow students. "And that father-son team—isn't it wonderful that they're taking the class together?"

Roelke followed her gaze. The two men—one in his sixties, the other perhaps twenty-five years younger—worked in companionable silence. Something twitched beneath Roelke's ribcage. Although his own father had introduced him to whittling, Roelke couldn't imagine his dad taking a class. His dad's carving instructions to him and his brother had been pretty basic: *Don't cut your finger off, Patrick. You want to carve a bird, Roelke? Just carve away everything that doesn't look like a bird.* In his memory, Roelke heard his father laughing. But the laughter hadn't been unkind, or the drunken, derisive hoots that came later. Those carving sessions were among the few good memories Roelke had of his father.

"Knives down," Emil called from the front of the room. "We're going to talk about your first rosette." He beamed with anticipation.

Roelke reached for his notebook and pen. He wanted to learn how to design and carve rosettes. He wanted to design and carve rosettes with, as Lavinia had observed earlier, stunning energy and symmetry.

And maybe, if Chloe played her cards right, he'd carve something special just for her.

❦

Chloe watched the clock's minute hand creep toward noon, poised to bolt. *Yes—*

"Remember," Mom called, "I'd like everyone to finish the three largest scrolls before going to lunch. We don't want anyone to get farther behind."

Chloe had not finished painting the three largest scrolls. She didn't care. She was going to go eat lunch with her... with her... Darn it! She was going to eat lunch with Roelke.

Besides, Chloe thought, if I hear Mom use "remember" and the royal "we" one more time, I will shriek. *Remember, please label and date any snacks you leave in the refrigerator. We don't want spoilage! Remember, since linseed oil is flammable, any oily rags must go in the red trash can, not the brown one. We don't want to flirt with fire! Remember, it's important to arrive promptly, and be ready to work at the designated hour. We don't want to cause delays for other students!*

Chloe was pretty sure that last one was aimed at her. Since Mom had volunteered her for extra errands and activities, that really didn't seem fair.

Roelke wasn't in the lounge, so she trotted down the steps and headed toward his classroom. When she got to the doorway, her feet stopped moving. Roelke was intent on his work—board held on his lap with his left hand, and knife held in his right—and there was something about him, something... different.

Finally it came to her. He's totally relaxed, she thought in amazement. Roelke McKenna usually moved through life coiled and ready to spring. He loved his cousin Libby's kids, and she'd seen him playing with them, laughing, tussling—but he was protective of them too, always on alert for any possible hazard or threat.

And he's the same way with me, Chloe realized, with a poignant pang. She didn't *want* Roelke on alert when they were together. She'd have to think about what she might be able to do about that.

"Miss Ellefson." Emil beckoned her into the room.

"Hey!" Roelke looked up, blinked, smiled. "Sorry. I didn't realize it was lunchtime."

"No problem."

Emil stepped closer. "Howard says you'll go with us to collections storage tomorrow afternoon. *Ja?*"

"*Ja.* My pleasure."

"Good, good." He nodded and returned to the chalkboard.

Roelke put his knife in a protective case and his board on the table. So simple, Chloe thought wistfully. Oil paints had to be coddled like cranky infants.

"See you later, Emil," Roelke called. He grabbed his coat.

In the hall Chloe said, "Sorry about this morning. Are we good?"

He smiled. "We're good."

They left the building. "Since we met for breakfast at such an ungodly hour, I didn't get lunches made," Chloe said. "Want to go to the Oneota Co-op? Lots of organic food, locally produced."

Roelke approved that suggestion, and they set out on the short walk down Water Street. Snow had started to fall, and the sound of shovels scraping pavement collided with the Christmas carols piped from one of the shops. "Gotta stay ahead of it," one man said, tossing a bladeful of powder onto a three-foot pile.

Chloe navigated around the drift. "So," she told Roelke, "I got quite the earful from Howard this morning."

"Yeah?"

She told him about the museum director's litany of troubles. "This is a small institution to confront that much of a financial obligation," she concluded.

"The museum will end the year $500,000 in debt?"

"Yeah. Can you imagine how fast interest payments on that rack up?"

Roelke whistled. "Pretty fast. Sounds like a downward spiral."

"I really feel sorry for Howard. Middle management ain't always fun, but he's clearly lonely at the top."

"This accreditation thing—it's a big deal?" Roelke asked. As they reached a corner he stepped from the sidewalk, then back onto the curb as the crossing light changed. Officer Roelke McKenna was not one to walk against a light. "Can't he just put off the inspection?"

"It would look bad," Chloe said. "And a delay could be the same thing as losing accreditation."

"So?"

"So, being recognized by the American Association of Museums is proof that Vesterheim is meeting the highest standards of professional excellence, in every way. It's not just about ... yikes." She was diverted by a window display of Cabbage Patch dolls, cheerfully if incongruously attired in Norwegian folk costume. She struggled to recapture her thought. "It's not just about bragging rights. Being accredited can make a big difference to granting agencies and wealthy donors."

"Which Hoff needs right now."

"Big time."

The light changed again. Roelke grabbed her hand as they walked the last stretch. Chloe liked the way her mittened hand fit into his gloved one, as if the strength in his fingers were enough to ward away all the bad stuff. As they reached the Co-op, she briefly let her head rest against his shoulder. "Let's take a break from talking about Petra's murder and Howard's problems, OK?"

"Sure," he agreed. But his eyes were narrowed, and his voice sounded far away. She could tell his mind was still turning over this new information, examining it from all angles, seeing where it might fit. And she was pretty sure that as soon as they settled down for lunch, he'd whip out a stack of index cards and start making notes.

TWELVE

Food at the Co-op was so tasty that Chloe returned to the Education Center with renewed resolve. "Looks good," she called to the volunteers adorning a Christmas tree with straw ornaments.

One of the women eyed them with a sly smile. "Did you know that straw figures once symbolized fertility?"

It's a freaking conspiracy, Chloe thought. She kissed Roelke quickly and fled without catching his eye.

Back in the classroom, she began work on the motif she'd been instructed to complete before lunch. In an effort to make nice, she carried her tray to the front of the room. "Mom, where should my brush be to start this scroll?"

"One brush edge faces 11:00. Turn it to 1:00 and curve out, down, back in." Mom briskly demonstrated the stroke on a scrap piece of tagboard.

"Thanks," Chloe said, and returned to her seat to try the sequence herself. Moments later she sat back and sighed. "My scroll looks like a pregnant grandfather clock."

Gwen, who had finished *all* her scrolls, big and small, chuckled. "It just takes practice."

Chloe ground her teeth, dipped her brush into the blob of red on her palette, and bent back over her tray. I will persevere, she vowed grimly.

She was so intent on gritting through that she didn't notice a fellow student standing at her shoulder until the young woman cleared her throat. Chloe's paintbrush made an unexpected detour.

"Oh, sorry!" the other student whispered, peering anxiously from beneath a heavy fringe of bangs that needed trimming so badly that Chloe's hand twitched involuntarily toward her scissors. "I didn't mean to spoil—"

"You didn't," Chloe assured her.

"Do you know where your mother is?"

Chloe instinctively scanned the classroom, as if this earnest young woman had somehow missed a five-foot-eight instructor. No Mom.

"She went to get an example of transparent Telemark," Miss Long Bangs said. "But she's been gone for a long time."

Chloe put her brush aside. "I'll find her," she promised, although since she had no idea what transparent Telemark was, she had no idea where to look.

The student lounge was empty. So was the ladies' room. Out of ideas, Chloe tiptoed into the other classroom—and gaped at shelves full of finished bowls, platters, porridge containers, even a baby cradle.

Sigrid joined her. "My students are doing really fine work," she murmured happily.

"They've done all this in a day and a half?" Chloe squawked. Sure, this was an advanced class, but—holy cow. She couldn't even *imagine* doing such work so quickly. She couldn't imagine doing such work ever, period.

"I'm glad you're inspired, my dear," Sigrid said, patting Chloe's hand affectionately.

Back to business. "Aunt Sigrid, have you seen my mom? She went to fetch an example of transparent Telemark...?"

"She's not back yet?" The smile faded from Sigrid's face.

"Back from where?"

Sigrid clutched Chloe's wrist and towed her into the hall. "From the vault."

"There's a vault?"

"There's an old vault in the museum basement, probably left over from when the building was a hotel. It's not climate-controlled, so it's used as overflow storage for the less valuable prints and paintings."

"That's where Mom went?"

"Marit asked me for the combination, but Chloe, she should have been back by now." Sigrid stared at Chloe with growing alarm. "What if she got locked in by mistake? I always worry about that when I—"

"Let's check." Chloe made herself smile reassuringly. "Did Mom write the combination down, or did she take yours?"

Sigrid darted back into the classroom. A moment later she returned, clutching a piece of well-creased paper. "She must have copied it."

"Good. Let's go." Chloe led the way, trying to ignore the frisson of unease skittering over her skin. If this vault was not climate-controlled, what kind of ventilation system did it have? Did it even *have* a ventilation system?

And if Mom had somehow ended up locked inside ... how much time would she have?

❧

"You're running out of time," Emil told his carving students, "if you haven't picked your class project yet. Remember, pieces carved in the Norwegian tradition are beautiful *and* functional."

Roelke bounced one knee as he tried to think. What would Chloe like?

"What are you going to carve?" Lavinia asked him.

"I have absolutely no idea," he confessed. "You?"

"A serving platter." With obvious effort, she opened her huge three-ring notebook and flipped to a section near the front. "I save everything," she confided, looking a big chagrined. "I have a couple of sketches in here somewhere ..." She scanned through dog-eared pieces of lined paper covered with written notes, mimeographed pattern sheets, and a few black and white photographs taped to individual pages.

Suddenly Roelke's gaze caught two unexpected words: *Petra Lekstrom*, written in blue ink—with a violent black marker slash added later. His hand shot out toward the page. "Did Petra Lekstrom take a chip carving class?"

Lavinia firmly removed his hand. "No," she said, also firmly. She flipped a few more pages. "Ah, here we go. What do you think of these two?"

"They're both pretty," he said absently. "I do like that one better." He pointed. Lavinia considered his choice, but did not ask why that particular design appealed to him. That was good, because his brain had stalled on that unexpected reference to the dead woman.

So far, Chloe hadn't delivered on her task of finding out what Petra had done to drive Lavinia from rosemaling. Lavinia did not appear to be a woman easily cowed. Need to follow up on that, he thought, watching Lavinia close the stuffed notebook and slide it back into her canvas totebag.

Chloe and Sigrid hurried down the stairwell and rushed outside. "You should go back and grab your coat," Chloe told Sigrid. Snow still drifted from low gray clouds, and the wind was sharp. The older woman ignored her. She's really frightened, Chloe thought grimly.

When they reached the museum, Chloe and Sigrid cut through the lobby and plunged down a stairwell. "This way," Sigrid said. She hurried through the "Immigrants at Leisure" exhibit—deserted at the moment. Then she stopped.

The door to the vault was smack-dab between a case full of toys and a display of sleds and skis. It looked like something from an old movie—heavy black metal, maybe six feet tall. It was embellished with faded scrolls and flourishes that any rosemaler might envy, and the words "Diebold Safe and Lock Co." in gothic script.

Chloe tugged the handle without success before pounding the closed door. "Mom? Are you in there? Mom!" She paused, pressing her ear against the metal. Nothing. Did that mean Mom wasn't in there at all? Was the door so heavy that no sound could pass from one side to the other? Or ...

Sigrid pointed to a newer tumbler in the door, and held out the combination code. "You try. It's tricky."

Chloe dropped to her knees and began working the tumbler. The combination *was* tricky—long and convoluted. "Turn right to seventeen ... turn three complete revolutions to the left ... turn right to six ..." She completed the sequence once without effect. "Dammit!" she exploded, and handed the paper back to Sigrid. "I screwed it up. Would you read it out loud? Slowly."

It took four tries but finally, *finally*, they managed to release the lock. Chloe heard the grudging click, scrambled to her feet, and heaved the door open. A wave of musty air emerged from the darkness. "Mom?"

The narrow vault was lined on both sides with storage slots for artwork. In the dim light Chloe saw her mother sitting on the floor in the center aisle with her legs extended in front of her. Her breathing came in audible gasps.

"Oh Marit, honey." Sigrid flicked a light switch. Marit raised one arm, shielding her eyes.

Chloe ran inside and crouched beside her mother. "Are you all right?"

Mom made a visible effort to rally. "I ... I ... yes."

"Let's get out of here." Chloe grasped one of her mother's arms and helped haul her upright. They stumbled from the vault together.

Mom gulped several times, as if trying to flush fresh air through her lungs. Her face was white and dotted with perspiration. Finally she gave a forced, shaky little laugh. "Thank you for rescuing me."

"What happened?" Sigrid exclaimed.

"I don't know," Mom said. "I made sure to open the door all the way, resting it back against that wall." She pointed. Except for a small plywood *nisse* propped against it, the wall was blank.

Chloe glared at the offensive folk figure as she experimented with the vault door. "This wouldn't have shut by itself. And I don't think a *nisse* is responsible. Someone must have come along and deliberately closed the door." The thought turned her ribs to ice.

"It didn't just close," Mom said. "It *slammed*. I was looking for the painting I wanted, toward the back." She made a vague gesture with one hand. "There was enough ambient light from the hallway, so I didn't turn on the overhead light. But once the door shut, I—I ..." She shuddered, and a sheen of tears appeared in her eyes. "I couldn't find the light switch, and ..."

"Oh, Mom." Chloe pulled her mother close in a spontaneous hug.

A hug Mom tolerated for about two seconds. "I'm fine, now." She poked at her hair, avoiding eye contact. "Really."

"It's those kids running around," Sigrid said angrily. "A little holiday hijinks is one thing, but this prank went way too far. Let's go talk to Howard. He needs to tell parents and grandparents that—"

"No." Mom shook her head. "There's no need to tell Howard. Or anyone else."

"Mom," Chloe protested, "if some kids thought this was a fun prank, they need to understand that—"

"Neither of you will say one word about this to anyone." Mom looked sternly from her daughter to her friend. "Perhaps a staff member or volunteer saw the door open, didn't see me inside since the light was off, and thought they were doing the responsible thing by closing the door."

"It's hard to believe that anyone would close the vault without checking to be sure no one was inside," Chloe said. "I really think we need to—"

"*No.*" Mom's face was red. "I've been humiliated enough for one day. All I want to do now is get back to class. My poor students must think I abandoned them." She turned and marched away.

Chloe looked at Sigrid: *Can you talk some sense into her?*

Sigrid gave a helpless little hitch of her shoulders: *No.* Then she followed her friend toward the stairwell.

Chloe trailed behind, both sympathetic and frustrated. She understood that there was no room in Marit-world for public embarrassment, vulnerability, loss of poise. But this is serious, Chloe thought. Too serious to let go. That meant *she* would have to talk to Howard, who then would—she hoped—put the mighty fear of God into whatever wise-ass adolescent posse was running wild in the name of Christmas merrymaking.

An image of Petra Lekstrom in the immigrant trunk popped into Chloe's memory like a flash bulb. *Someone* had found Petra alone in a deserted room in the museum—and killed her. And Mom had been alone in just such a deserted spot…

But Mom was *not* attacked. If Petra's killer had been looking for another victim, he—or she—had stumbled on a perfect opportunity for assault, and passed.

Chloe paused as she reached the entrance lobby. Should she ask the ticket seller who had gone to the basement floor lately? That would likely do more harm than good. There was more than one way to get into the exhibit areas on each floor. Whoever had slammed the door, locking Mom into the old vault, had obviously attracted no particular notice. He or she might have been in the museum for hours before slipping down to the basement. He or she might have been a visitor, a volunteer, a member of the staff... or just some punk kid.

When Chloe went back outside, she glimpsed Sigrid and Mom down the block as they disappeared back inside the Education Center. Chloe knew she had to make a detour to Howard's office—missing more class time in the process. Not only would she be dinged for that, Mom would realize that Chloe had ignored her wishes.

Well, joy to the world, Chloe thought. Maybe Mom should just put me up for adoption and be done with it.

She gave herself one moment to feel sorry for herself. Then she hunched her shoulders against the wind and went to find Howard Hoff.

THIRTEEN

THAT EVENING, ROELKE TUCKED happily enough into Violet's boiled cod and root veggies in wine sauce. But friction crackled faintly just beneath the surface of polite conversation. Marit and Chloe never looked each other in the eye. Emil, away from his tools and his wood, didn't look anyone in the eye. Sigrid poked silently at her food. It was all very awkward.

The meal ended with bowls of fruit soup. In Roelke's world "soup" and "dessert" didn't go together, but the dish was delicious—warm and thick and cinnamon-y. "So," Violet said, as everyone scooped up their last bite, "what is on everyone's agenda for the evening?"

Chloe studiously scraped one last raisin from the bottom of her dish. "I've got another interview lined up."

"I'm heading back to the classroom," Mom told the tablecloth.

"Me too," Sigrid echoed.

Emil cleared a throat rusty from recent disuse. "I will escort you ladies back to the classrooms."

"And I'll walk with you to your interview," Roelke told Chloe, choosing his words carefully. He figured she wouldn't want to be "escorted" anywhere. "That is … if it's in walking distance?"

She nodded. "Just a couple of blocks from here."

After thanking Violet, Roelke and Chloe bundled up and headed out into a snowy evening. "Do you know these people you're visiting?" Roelke asked. He didn't like the idea of her visiting strangers, alone. Maybe he should blow off his meeting with the chief after all.

"Stand down, officer," Chloe said. "I'm visiting Adelle and Tom Rimestad. I haven't met them, but they're tight with my mom and Sigrid. Adelle is one of the Sixty-Sevens."

"OK, then." Roelke pulled his trusty yellow flashlight from his pocket and illuminated a bizarre lawn ornament—a three-foot gnome dangling a huge plastic spider. "What's with that? Seems more Halloween than Christmas."

"The *nisse* is a prankster," Chloe said. Snowflakes had caught on her wool hat. A lamp pole by the driveway cast a soft glow on her cheeks.

God, she was lovely.

He belatedly realized she was waiting for some response from him. "Um … yeah?"

"If the milkmaid didn't remember to leave a dish of porridge out for their *nisse*, for example, he might dangle a spider the next morning to startle her into spilling the family's milk."

"Oh."

Chloe started walking again. "Speaking of pranks …" She told him what had happened to Marit that afternoon. "Mom *ordered* me and Sigrid not to say anything to anyone," she concluded. "I know kids have been playing tricks, but ..." She stopped walking abruptly, looking perplexed. "That makes no sense."

"What?" Roelke demanded. Sometimes Chloe's insights helped him sort out complicated problems.

"Why would someone add Greek revival columns to a house with gothic features?" She pointed across the street. "Odd choice, but still, you could teach an entire architectural survey course in this neighborhood."

And sometimes, Chloe's insights did nothing helpful at all. Roelke tugged her hand and they started walking again. "A few boys slammed the door to our classroom today," he told her. "Right when Emil was making a delicate cut."

"I know the kids are excited to be out of school, but these pranks are going too far." She twisted her mouth. "I thought Howard should know, so I told him. Now Mom's more pissed at me than ever."

"You did the right thing."

"And now I'm telling you. Don't mention it to her though, OK?"

"I won't," Roelke said. If I can help it, he added silently.

They reached a brick house a block or so east of the courthouse, with a large plastic manger scene arranged on the front lawn. Chloe checked the name on the mailbox. "This is the place."

"You want to call me when you're done?" Roelke asked. "My meeting with Chief Moyer won't take long, and I'm sure Emil would loan me his truck."

"No thanks," Chloe said. "There's no reason for you to go all Neanderthal on me." He opened his mouth, but she continued before he could object. "I don't want to argue with you on this trip, Roelke. I've got all I can handle with my mom." She leaned closer and kissed him.

"OK," he mumbled when she finally pulled away, because blood was rushing to regions other than his head. "Breakfast tomorrow?"

"Sure." She gave him a breathless smile, blew him a final kiss, and turned away.

Roelke did have the presence of mind to watch as she climbed the front steps. A short, round man opened the door before she could reach the bell. She disappeared inside without a backward glance.

∞

"Miss Ellefson? I'm Tom Rimestad. Please, come in!" Tom had receding gray hair, a broad smile, and friendly brown eyes behind thick glasses in black plastic frames. He wore dark corduroys and a Luther Alumni sweatshirt.

"Is this still a good time?" Chloe asked. She knew that his wife, Adelle, was struggling with lung disease.

"Yes," Tom said firmly. "Adelle's excited. Visitors are a real treat."

After pulling off her boots, Chloe padded after Tom. The family room was a Hallmark card of holiday cheer. On the Christmas tree, traditional red and white decorations were mixed with child-made ornaments. Greeting cards were festooned on a loop of red yarn. Several candles glowed, and the air smelled of pine and cinnamon. Even Chloe's jaded soul felt ready to sing *Silent Night* along with the record on the player: *Glade jul, hellige jul! Engler daler ned i skjul...*

Adelle waited in an easy chair. Plastic tubing, held in place below her nose by an elastic band, ran down to a portable oxygen tank on the floor. Every labored breath was audible. The hand Chloe gently clasped in welcome returned only a mild squeeze. But Adelle's eyes sparkled, and her smile was warm.

"You must be Chloe." Her speech was a little breathy.

"I'm delighted to meet you both," Chloe said. "You have a beautiful home."

Tom squeezed his wife's shoulder. "Christmas is Adelle's favorite time of year."

"Your collection of *nisser* is wonderful," Chloe added. Dozens of hand-carved Christmas elves were displayed around the room. They ranged from several inches to several feet in height. The longer Chloe looked, the more she spotted—peeking from behind a chair, hiding on a top shelf. "Tom, did you carve them?"

He grinned. "No, indeed. I've been known to whittle, but my wife is the true artist."

"Really?" Chloe asked, then felt herself flush. "I just thought…my mom mentioned that you were a member of the Sixty-Seven Club, Adelle. Do you paint *and* carve?"

"I am a Sixty-Seven," she agreed, "but I gave up rosemaling long ago."

Just like Lavinia, Chloe thought. Did they migrate together, or had Petra managed to drive two different women from painting?

"I tried chip carving and acanthus," Adelle was saying, "but figures are my favorite. I go out to my workshop even now, on good days. I'm happy there."

"You are obviously a woman of many talents," Chloe said. She settled into a chair and pulled out a notebook and tape recorder. "Now, as I said on the phone, Vesterheim's goal is to document the persistence of Norwegian Christmas traditions in the community. The notes I received suggested that you both have some experience with *julebukking*?" She gave Adelle a *Please tell me all about it!* smile, hoping it hid her discomfort with the topic.

"Oh, yes," Adelle said. "When I was a child, it was quite common. Do you understand the basic idea?"

Chloe did, but this project was not about her. "Why don't you explain it." She started the tape player.

"Well," the older woman began, "it usually took place between Christmas and New Year's Day. A group of people would dress up in masks and homemade costumes. Often women would wear men's clothes, and vice-versa." She paused for a moment to catch her breath. "I'm sorry. I'm afraid I won't make a very good tape recording."

"It will be just fine," Chloe assured her. "All that matters is your stories. Do you know how the custom got started?"

Adelle considered. "Well, my parents said the tradition went back to pagan times in old Norway. Something about Thor?" She looked at Tom.

"That's how I learned it, too," Tom affirmed. "In Norse mythology, Thor traveled through the sky in a chariot pulled by goats. Once, when Thor needed food, he killed the goats. Then he used his hammer and brought them back to life again. My father told me that when *his* father was a boy, the lead *julebukker* dressed up in a goatskin and carried a real goat's head on a pole."

Chloe struggled to keep her expression neutral. She'd also been introduced to *julebukking* as a young child, when some friends of her parents decided a "traditional" surprise visit from costumed revelers was in order. She'd been terrified when the masked men shoved into her house, the leader carrying an actual goat head on a pole...

"But there's been nothing pagan about it for a long time now," Tom said hastily, as if sensing Chloe's discomfort.

"Heavens, no," Adelle agreed. "Folks just wanted a little fun after harvest time, is all. People might go out fooling on Saturday night, but they go to church on Sunday morning."

"I grew up in Minnesota, and my family always went *julebukking*," Tom said. "My dad carved a goat head from wood and put it on a stick so he could carry it. Those were such fun times!" Tom's face held a faraway look. "We'd spend hours making some crazy costumes, and then after dark we'd just show up at somebody's house. The people had to let us in. We'd disguise our voices, and they'd try to guess who we were."

"That's how we did it, too." Adelle added. "Once people identified everyone in costume, they'd bring out trays of coffee and cookies and we'd take off our masks."

Tom gave his wife's hand an affectionate squeeze. "And then we'd be off again. The custom was that someone from the first house we visited had to dress up and come with us, and so on and so on."

"How large a group might you have by the end of the night?" Chloe asked.

"Oh, maybe twenty or thirty." Tom leaned back in his chair, grinning. "I remember one time we got to a farmhouse and everything was dark, the family already in bed. We started banging tin buckets and hollering. They all got up and let us in, and then a couple of the boys put on costumes and came along with us."

"So," Chloe asked, "is *julebukking* still taking place, or has the custom faded away?"

"Norwegian people in my hometown have always done it," Tom assured her. "I've still got a nephew there, and he goes out every year."

Adelle said, "I grew up in a little town about forty miles from here. People went *julebukking* until I was... oh, I don't know, a young woman. Then a chicken plant opened nearby, and lots of other people moved in for the jobs. Once Norwegian people were the minority, the whole thing sort of died out. I think maybe people were afraid the newcomers would laugh. That was right about the time I married Tom, and we moved to Decorah."

The microcassette clicked off. Chloe turned the tape over and jabbed the appropriate button.

"We've lived here for thirty-four years," Tom said. "I can't say that a whole lot of *julebukking* has gone on. The town's too big, probably. Lots of Norwegians, but we're spread out. And contrary to what we like to believe, not everyone in Decorah is Norwegian."

"Once the Vesterheim people started talking about *julebukking*, though," Adelle interjected, "it got lots of people reminiscing. It's been fun for us old folks." She smiled a little sadly. "Things change."

"Which is why it's so important to preserve your memories," Chloe said. She had jotted down more questions to ask, but it looked as if Adelle was getting tired. "Thank you for sharing your stories."

"When the curator called about this project we said yes right away," Tom assured her. "We've always been big supporters of Vesterheim. Adelle volunteered there for years."

"I gave tours in the Open Air Division," Adelle said. "That was before the Valdres House arrived ... what, maybe five years ago?" She looked at Tom.

He confirmed that with a nod. "Right. That came in seventy-seven, the first year I sat on the museum Board." He looked at Chloe. "Have you seen it?"

"Not yet." She tucked the cassette player into her bag. "Thanks again for talking with me. I'm grateful, and I know Howard is, too. Let him know if you think of more stories, or of someone else who should be interviewed."

"Poor Howard." Adelle sighed. "He's a different person since Phyllis died." She looked at her husband with an expression that hurt Chloe's heart.

Tom's kissed Adelle's hand, and snugged an afghan over her lap. "At least I'm smart enough to know how lucky I am," he murmured. "Not like—"

"Now, Tom," Adelle scolded mildly. "This nice young woman didn't come here to listen to gossip. You go fetch out the cookies."

"Cookies?" Chloe echoed. Dear Lord in Heaven, she hadn't yet recovered from her visit to Bestemor Sabo's industrial-strength cookie factory the night before.

Tom produced a platter of goodies—beautiful enough to grace a magazine cover, large enough to sugar-buzz a small army. Chloe felt her jeans grow tighter just from inhaling. Adelle beamed, waiting for Chloe to help herself. Chloe sampled a gingersnap. "Delicious."

"We've gotten hundreds of cookies from friends and neighbors," Adelle said ruefully. "I had to send some along to Vesterheim with Tom for that reception last Sunday."

So, Chloe thought, Tom was at Vesterheim on Sunday. She filed that tidbit aside and, after two more cookies, said good-bye. "My mom is looking forward to visiting," she added.

Adelle's eyes sparkled again. "I look forward to that. We Sixty-Sevens are a tight-knit group." She pressed Chloe's hand. "And Tom and I are having an open house on Thursday evening. You'll come, won't you?"

Chloe promised that she'd try, then followed Tom back through the house to the entryway. "I hope I didn't stay too long," she said, as she pulled on her boots.

"No." Tom's face a mixture of grief and resignation. "She loves company, and ... and at this point, it doesn't really matter. She has idiopathic pulmonary fibrosis."

"I'm so sorry. Is that uncommon? I don't think I've ever heard of it before."

"'Idiopathic' is just a fancy way of saying 'of no known origin,'" Tom said. "It came on so gradually that the disease was well-established before we knew anything was wrong. Something is damaging her lungs, causing scarring. Scarred tissue can't process oxygen." He spread his hands helplessly. "She smoked for a little while, back during the war, but she quit long ago. The doctors say it sometimes happens that way. She was on the waiting list for a lung transplant for a while, but ..." He shook his head. "It's not going to happen."

"She's lucky to have you," Chloe said gently. "And to be here at home, surrounded by people and things she loves."

"That does give me a bit of comfort." Tom picked up a whimsical wooden elf pulling a sleigh. "And she's leaving a legacy." He studied the *nisse*. "After what happened with the rosemaling, I was against the idea of her taking up carving. But she insisted. We got a little workshop set up out in the garage. And she was happy as a clam. She's taken lots of classes from Emil, and from visiting instructors too—even some from Norway. And you know what? No one's ever been anything but nice to her."

His hand had tightened on the carved figure so hard that his knuckles were white. I'm missing something, Chloe thought. "Something happened when Adelle was rosemaling?"

"She got driven out."

Chloe felt her eyebrows rise. "Driven out?"

"By Petra," he muttered. "That woman had no conscience."

So it *was* Petra, Chloe thought. "Oh?"

"When I realized what she'd done to my sweet Adelle, I…" His voice began to tremble. With visible effort he paused, striving for a calmer tone. "Well, it was a long time ago, and doesn't bear speaking of now."

Yep, Chloe thought, the curse of polite Norwegians is thriving.

"Besides, switching to carving was the best thing that could have happened for my wife," Tom was saying. "Her friend Lavinia Carmichael quit painting too, and the two of them had a fine time taking carving classes together."

Ah, Chloe thought. Maybe a single incident had shoved both women from painting to carving.

"Adelle stayed clear of Petra after that. Not like Howard, who—well." Tom cleared his throat. "I need to get back to Adelle."

"Of course," Chloe murmured, although she really, *really* would have liked to know what Tom had been about to say. Did Tom know more than Violet did about the rumored dalliance between Howard and Petra? Or was there something else altogether?

"Please do come on Thursday night, if you can," Tom said.

Chloe impulsively hugged him good-bye before stepping into the night. The porch lamp went dark as she crossed the lawn.

She paused on the front sidewalk, wondering where Roelke was. Holed up at the PD talking shop? She sighed. This was not how she imagined that the week would unfold.

Which was not good. She and Roelke were in a holding pattern that she didn't know how to break. When she'd met Roelke the previous May, her personal life had pretty much been a sucking quagmire for quite a while. Then she'd almost made a disastrous decision about an old lover. That had gnawed at what little self-confidence she had left, romance-wise.

When she'd finally agreed to go out with Roelke, she'd wanted to take things slowly. Roelke's patience had given her a chance to take a deep breath; to spend time thinking about the future instead of fixating on the past. His patience had given her time to discover that he liked peanut butter and honey sandwiches better than PB & J, and that his favorite color was brown. It had given her time to notice that he looked sexier in jeans than his uniform, and that he liked to cradle her cheeks in his palms when he kissed her, and that they could both nap on his sofa if she lay on her side with her head on his shoulder.

All good. Still, maybe it was time to discover a few *more* things about Roelke McKenna.

But that clearly ain't gonna happen in Decorah, Chloe thought. Not when they were each boarding with chaperones, in separate houses, on opposite sides of the river.

The snow had stopped. The sky was clearing and the temperature was dropping. A sharp wind nipped at her earlobes with icy teeth. Chloe hunched her shoulders, bent her head, and walked away.

FOURTEEN

ROELKE'S MEETING WITH CHIEF Moyer and Buzzelli was short and sweet. Roelke repeated what Hoff had revealed to Chloe. "Yeah, we pretty much knew all that already," Buzzelli said.

"Just sharing what I hear, as promised," Roelke said cheerfully. Seriously, though, meeting with the chief and Buzzelli wasn't proving as satisfying as he'd hoped.

"And we appreciate it," Moyer said. "Check in tomorrow?"

"Will do," Roelke said, and left them to it.

By the time Roelke got back to the farm, his face burned with cold. His toes did too, despite the shearling liners in his Sorels. He'd wear an extra pair of wool socks when he left the house the next morning. He hadn't expected to do so much walking, but he prided himself on being prepared for any contingency.

He found Emil in the living room. "Did Marit and Sigrid get to their classrooms this evening without trouble?" Roelke asked.

"Oh, *ja*," Emil said absently. "There were plenty of students up there, and a policeman was inside when we got there, too."

Roelke dropped into a chair. "Good."

Emil held up a board with an air of supreme satisfaction. "Isn't this a fine piece of wood?"

"It is," Roelke agreed, although one plank looked pretty much like any other to him. "Where do you get your carving wood, Emil?"

Emil looked baffled. "In the forest!"

"No, I meant…" Roelke let his question trail away. Surely this little old man didn't—no. Surely not.

Emil set his wood aside and stood. "Put your boots on."

Sixty seconds later, Roelke followed his host outside. "Where are we going?"

"To the woods."

This did not strike Roelke as logical. It was dark. A wind stung his cheeks and whipped the fresh snow into little cyclones, and he hadn't thawed out from his last walk yet. But Emil was already trekking up the driveway.

The steep forested bluff overlooking the Upper Iowa River was a dark mass against the sky. Emil led him silently across the deserted road. Then he started trudging through the snow that had drifted high on what appeared to be a service lane. "This is my land," he said, gesturing vaguely at both the fence-lined pasture on their right and the woods on their left.

"Um…OK. But—"

"You got the makings of a good carver," Emil said over his shoulder. "But you got a lot to learn."

That was enough to shut Roelke up. He wanted to learn, he really did. Besides, he wasn't as practiced at walking uphill in knee-deep snow as Emil, and needed to concentrate on that. If he fell on his ass and rolled down the hill, Emil might give up on him altogether.

The lane ended when they reached the far edge of the pasture. Without a backward glance, Emil pushed on into the woods. Roelke followed doggedly, dodging low branches, getting snow dumped down his collar. Moonlight filtered through the trees and reflected off snow, filling the forest with faint blue-gray light.

Emil stopped walking abruptly. He wasn't even breathing hard. "You got to understand your wood," he said. "You got to understand the tree it came from. You got to understand the forest where that tree grew. You got to *respect* that forest. You don't just march into the woods and attack any old tree with an ax. You following me?"

Roelke hesitated.

"Look," Emil said. "I don't know how you do your job. But you don't look at just the victim after a crime, right? A victim like that Petra Lekstrom?"

"Well, no," Roelke allowed.

"You got to know the community, right? And the place she had in it? There are lots of people in Decorah, but Petra Lekstrom had her own place in this town. Right?"

"Right."

"Same thing with a forest. With each tree in a forest. This—" he patted a nearby tree—"is not just an oak tree. How much sun it gets, how high it is on the hill, what kind of trees and plants grow nearby, what kind of soil there is—everything affects the wood, the grain, the color, the way it feels in your hand. The good carvers, they understand this. They choose a tree for each project knowing this."

"Well ... hunh." Roelke stood still. He was starting to catch on.

"In the old country, carvers mostly used pine and birch. Here, they had to switch to walnut and maple. I like to carve basswood.

Do you understand the difference between all those trees? Do you have a favorite kind of tree?"

"No," Roelke admitted humbly. He vaguely understood the difference between softwoods and hardwoods, but that was about it.

"Like I said, you got a lot to learn." Emil patted the tree trunk one last time, as if saying farewell to a friend. Then he began marching back out of the woods. Roelke followed, trying to decide if this little foray had been intended to inspire him or put him in his place.

"I can teach you," Emil added over his shoulder.

Good, Roelke wanted to say, but one foot slipped and he got distracted by the effort to stay upright. Once stable, he decided to believe that Emil was trying to inspire him. They waded down the slope together, footsteps crunching, the farmhouse lights glowing softly below.

"So," Emil said as they reached his driveway. "Is Marit's daughter your girlfriend?"

OK, Roelke thought. This man does not believe in verbal turn signals, ever. "Yeah."

"You got trouble there."

Roelke bristled. "What do you mean?"

"She's Norwegian. You're not."

The bristling subsided. Roelke had been afraid that Emil was about to make some unwanted but insightful observation that spelled doom for his relationship with Chloe, but *that* pronouncement was not news. "So?"

"What kind of name is McKenna?"

"Irish."

"You should find a good Irish girl."

They'd reached the front porch. Roelke paused to kick snow from his boots. "I'm part German, too."

"Or a German girl, then."

"Emil, come on," Roelke said mildly. "That may have been true a century ago, but now? Are you really worried about mixing bloodlines or something?"

"I'm not talking about mixing bloodlines. I'm talking about two people who can *understand* each other—where they come from, what they know, who they are. I don't see how two people can make a go of it if they don't know all the answers to those questions." Emil climbed the steps, opened the door, and disappeared inside.

Which was good, because Roelke had no idea what to say.

He stood on the step for a moment, staring back at the dark wooded hill. When it came to carving, Emil was a master. When it came to romance, Roelke didn't know if Emil was a wise soul or a crazy coot. But the old man's pronouncement flicked a sensitive nerve. Chloe had once said much the same thing: *We're very different people, we have nothing in common, blah-blah-blah.*

Suddenly, Roelke felt profoundly sad. He'd wanted a relationship with Chloe since the day he met her. Was that foolishness, obvious to everyone but him?

Teeth clenched, he followed Emil inside. Enough with the dating stuff. It was time for a cup of hot tea and a session with the index cards he'd been using to collect his thoughts about Lekstrom's murder. He wasn't officially on the case, and he knew only a fraction of what the local officers and DCI agents knew. But he was a pretty good cop, with pretty good instincts. Maybe, just maybe, he'd find some new angle, some new detail, that would make a difference.

Chloe stayed vigilant as she walked back to Sigrid's house, but the streets were deserted. Again, the Christmas lights she passed seemed like a frail and futile attempt to ward away the darkness. Too much sadness at the Rimestad house, Chloe thought. And although Adelle and Tom had good memories of *julebukkers*, their tales brought back the terror her dad's friends had bestowed on her six-year-old self, way back when.

Sigrid and Violet had set electric candles on the windowsills. A wreath and *God Jul* sign decorated the front door. Three straw goats in graduated sizes waited on the porch. "Nicer than bloody skulls, anyway," Chloe muttered, and let herself inside.

Light spilled from a door behind the dining room. Chloe followed it to a small studio. Design sketches and practice samples were pinned to one cork-covered wall. Shelves held a variety of rosemaled woodenware—some bare, some backgrounded only, some painted, some varnished. Violet sat at a table littered with tubes of paint, brush holders, and the various other clutter that filled the workshops and drained the wallets of rosemalers everywhere.

Chloe waited until Violet paused before lightly knocking on the door frame. "Hey, Violet. Just wanted to let you know I'm back."

Violet swiveled in her chair. "Oh, hi. Did you have a nice evening?"

Chloe couldn't help noticing that Violet wore the clothes she'd come home from work in—plaid wool skirt, white blouse, pink cardigan—and they showed not the slightest streak of wayward paint. If Chloe hadn't worn one of her mother's aprons in class, she'd have ruined everything she owned.

"Chloe?"

"Sorry. My evening was quite pleasant." She gestured to a row of clear glass balls Violet had rosemaled and left to dry. "Don't let me interrupt you."

"I need to quit for the night anyway."

Chloe took a closer look at the ornaments. "Those are gorgeous, by the way. Are they for one of the folk art trees at Vesterheim?"

"These are just for gifts." Violet contemplated her handiwork. "Only Gold Medalists were invited to contribute to the rosemaling tree."

Ouch, Chloe thought.

Violet began tidying up. "How did your interview go?"

"I enjoyed meeting the Rimestads. I didn't realize that Adelle had stopped painting, though."

"I think Adelle and Lavinia quit rosemaling at the same time," Violet said.

"Tom said his wife was driven out by Petra."

Violet reached for a jar of murky liquid. "Of the Sixty-Sevens who eventually chose to enter the annual Exhibition, Petra was the last to earn her Gold Medal." She began swishing a brush in the turpentine. "My mom, your mom—they got there with mostly blue ribbons, each worth three points. Petra limped along...a white ribbon one year, another three or four years later. And let me tell you,

Petra wanted a Medal *real* bad. It's not hard to imagine that she'd say or do something to cut down on the competition."

"I see." Chloe turned that over in her mind. It had never occurred to her to wonder about the timing of Petra's crowning achievement. And...how long had Violet been entering her work in the Exhibition? Just how badly did *she* want a Medal?

Then Chloe shook her head, disgusted with herself. If she wasn't careful, she'd end up standing in corners with folded arms and narrowed eyes and jiggling knee, suspicious of *everyone*.

"Well," she said, remembering the whimsical *nisser* she'd seen, "it was nice of Emil to help Adelle get started in a new direction."

"Emil's kind of shy unless he's got a carving knife in his hand." Violet reached for another brush. "I guess that's what happens when you grow up with just a dad and older brother." She smiled. "He's a nice guy, though. Did you see that Noah's Ark in the tower room? One Christmas when I was a kid, and my dad was away, Emil carved it for me. He's made gifts for other kids too, and for people in nursing homes."

"I know Roelke's enjoying his class," Chloe said absently. She wasn't quite ready to move on from Petra. "And now that they've opened the Exhibition to carvers, Emil could start competing. If he even wants to. I never realized how frenzied the whole Medal thing can get."

"It's not like that for everyone," Violet said. "Most of the people going for Medals keep their perspective. But for a few..." She shrugged. "It can get intense. Your mom gets the *Rosemaling Newsletter*, right? A while back the editor invited subscribers to submit original designs for the masthead, and a couple of people got completely crazed about it. Did your mom go for it?"

"I don't know," Chloe admitted. "She's a finalist in the Christmas card design contest, though."

"I guarantee that no matter how spectacular all of the final card designs are, someone is bound to get her nose out of joint if she doesn't win."

"So much for peace on earth, good will to all rosemalers." Chloe hesitated, watching Violet return paint tubes to a plastic tub. "Violet? Tell me if I'm out of line here, but I can't help wondering how you feel about competing." Her cheeks grew warm, and she tried to camouflage her discomfort by pulling off her sweater. A pox on whoever killed Petra Lekstrom, she thought, and a pox on chief what's-his-name for dragging Roelke—and therefore me—into the investigation.

Violet snapped off the lamp at her workstation. "Everyone thinks I should be outraged that Petra won a Gold Medal last summer and I didn't. But you know what? I'm fine with it. Petra painted an antique trunk with traditional Telemark designs and a traditional Telemark palette. Judges tend to like that approach. I went with the Trøndelag style. It's not as well known, but sometimes I like to go graphic instead of organic, don't you?"

Chloe had absolutely no idea what Violet was talking about. "I sure do."

"And I pushed the boundaries with my colors. The painters I admire most blend tradition with fresh ideas. That's what I tried to do on my butter churn. I knew it was a gamble."

"Oh," Chloe said. She felt slimy for bringing it up.

"Besides," Violet added, "I did get a red ribbon. That's pretty darn good. I really resent the people who want me to feel bad about that."

"You have no reason to feel bad," Chloe agreed. She felt even slimier.

Violet snapped the lid on her storage tub. "I'm only one point away from a Medal. Maybe I'll get it one day. Maybe I won't. So be it."

O-kay, Chloe thought. Time to change the subject. "May I ask you about something else? I had a long talk with Howard this morning, and he referred to a 'Luther cabal.'" Chloe flicked her fingers to indicate quote marks. "Since you work at the college—"

"Oh, please," Violet scoffed. "Howard's a dear man, and God knows he has plenty to worry about, but he's jumping at shadows on that one. Someone at some meeting lamented the transfer of such an incredible collection, but Howard is the only one who took it seriously. How could Luther possibly take on management of the museum? What good would splitting the collection do? It's ridiculous."

What's ridiculous, Chloe thought, is that I'm trying to squeeze information from this woman. "I thought it sounded absurd too," she confessed. "Did you hear about it from Howard? Or did the rumor reach the music department?"

"I don't work in the music department anymore. Didn't you know? I transferred to Scandinavian studies."

"Oh! No, I didn't know that." Chloe wasn't sure why that felt so surprising, but it did.

"The secretary gig in the music department was supposed to be temporary. I was saving money for grad school, but then Dad died. Mom went through a bad spell, so I moved back into the house. I got more serious about painting, and decided I wasn't ready to go for my masters. Luther's music program is superb, but I decided that if I'm going to spend my days taking notes and typing letters, I'd rather work in a department that interests me."

"I imagine so," Chloe said. "Well, thanks for setting me straight on the rumors. I know Vesterheim is in debt, so it's understandable that Howard's feeling pressured."

"The money will be raised," Violet said firmly. "But I know that a few people have given him a hard time about the big renovation. There have been some grumbles because Decorah residents have been asked to raise ten percent of the deficit."

Chloe chewed that tidbit over. "That's a lot of money."

"Not when you consider that Vesterheim annually contributes almost six times that amount to the local economy! It's only been a decade since Vesterheim renovated the main museum building, and some people think that Howard reached too high with this latest project. But now there's space for artifact conservation, and for the folk art program. Both of those are *essential* to the museum's mission. He couldn't let precious artifacts deteriorate, could he? Or let master artists pass away without sharing their knowledge with students?"

"No," Chloe agreed. She couldn't fault or dispute a single thing Violet had said. And yet... something about Violet's demeanor was making her uneasy.

The sound of a slammed door echoed to the back of the house. "We're ho-ome," Sigrid called in a high sing-song. She and Mom walked into the studio. "One of my students gave us a lift."

"Since it's going on eleven, I'm glad to hear that," Violet exclaimed. She greeted her mother with a kiss on the cheek. Chloe stayed where she was.

"Oh, you know how painters get when they have studio time," Sigrid said.

"I thought you might stop by, Chloe," Mom said. "Since you're so behind."

Chloe felt her blood temperature rise by a whole lot of degrees. "I had to conduct an interview—"

"After the interview, I meant."

"—with Adelle and Tom Rimestad," Chloe finished, and her voice level rose too. "I hardly wanted to rush off."

Mom had the grace to look nonplussed. "Oh," she said, with an honest catch in her voice. "How is Adelle?"

Violet, still standing between the two older women, reached out and squeezed Mom's hand.

Chloe bit her tongue on purpose while she struggled to set aside the stab of—of what, resentment? Envy?—prompted by Violet's gesture. After regaining control she said, "Adelle's spirits seem good. She's looking forward to seeing you."

"I'll visit her tomorrow," Mom said. "Good-night, all." She turned and left the room.

"I'm heading up too," Violet said.

Chloe closed her eyes. Her tongue hurt. Her heart hurt. And this week was only half over. Suggesting this excursion was the dumbest thing she'd ever done—which was, she reflected irritably, actually saying quite a lot. Right now all she wanted to do was go home. Roelke could come along, but Mom could jolly well stay in Decorah and live with Sigrid and Violet.

"Sweetie."

Chloe's eyes flew open. She hadn't realized that Sigrid was still in the room.

"Marit knows you told Howard that she got locked in the vault this morning." Sigrid cocked her head. "You did tell him, right?"

"He needed to know," Chloe said defensively. "Mom could have gotten into serious trouble in there!"

"I know," Sigrid said. The joy she'd carried home from the classroom was gone.

"Aunt Sigrid, I'm sorry this friction between Mom and me is adding extra stress to a difficult week." Chloe was troubled by the strain that was evident on Sigrid's face. "Are you doing OK? You look exhausted."

"Petra's attack was such a shock." Sigrid stared blindly at the carpet. "And this is always a difficult month for me. My husband died in December, very close to Violet's birthday."

"I'm sorry," Chloe said. "It's hard to have sad anniversaries close to holidays."

Sigrid blinked and straightened her shoulders. "It was years ago, now. I'm fine." She stepped close and squeezed Chloe's shoulder. "Listen, sweetie, you did the right thing to talk to Howard. But try to understand, your mother was embarrassed. There's nothing she hates more than that. She's not truly angry at you."

Yeah, she is, Chloe thought. But there was no point in debating. Instead, she took advantage of the rare quiet moment alone with her mother's friend. "Aunt Sigrid? I enjoyed meeting Adelle Rimestad tonight. She's such a talented carver that it's hard to believe she didn't choose to study woodwork first. Do you know why she stopped rosemaling? Her and Lavinia? From the stories I've heard, you Sixty-Sevens were a pretty tight bunch." All except Petra Lekstrom, of course.

"Oh, Chloe. I don't want to think about that nastiness. It was over and done a decade ago, and Adelle found her true calling."

Sigrid looked so troubled, so tired, so—so *fragile*, that Chloe couldn't bring herself to ask anything more.

FIFTEEN

Roelke was waiting on the sidewalk at 6 A.M. Wednesday morning when the café proprietress flipped the *Closed* sign and unlocked the front door. This time he opted for a booth in the back corner. He ordered oatmeal from the same efficient waitress and turned his big mug over: *Fill 'er up, and keep it comin'.* She poured steaming coffee with practiced speed, tipping the pot back at just the right moment, before disappearing again.

The café smelled of spices and floury things. This is good, Roelke thought. He loved early mornings. He especially liked beating the sun up during these longest, darkest days of winter, knowing that he wouldn't miss a moment of light. He wished Chloe could appreciate these pre-dawn moments too.

Then he wished he hadn't wished that. The thought evoked Emil's summation from the night before: *You got trouble there.*

Yeah, well, I'm not taking relationship advice from a lifelong bachelor, Roelke thought, as the waitress returned with his oatmeal.

He added just a bit of brown sugar, pulled a stack of index cards from his pocket, and settled down to think.

His bowl was empty and his cards arranged on the table by the time he became aware of someone standing by the table: Chloe. "Oh—hey!" he exclaimed, chagrined that he hadn't noticed her coming in. He tried to rise, banged both knees on the table, sat back down abruptly. Smooth move, McKenna, he thought. Very smooth.

"For a minute I thought I'd actually gotten here first." She slid into the booth across the table from him. "You're almost invisible."

"I wanted privacy." He gestured to the cards he'd been arranging, considering, rearranging. Some contained people's names. Some contained the few facts he knew about Petra Lekstrom. Some contained possible motives for her attack.

Chloe surveyed the cards with resignation. "You're working on the murder."

"Yeah. I was noodling on this last night, but I'd really like your take on things."

The waitress appeared and filled Chloe's mug. "What'll it be?"

Chloe held up one hand in Roelke's direction, palm out to forestall any nutritional observations. "I'd like a piece of almond pastry. From the middle of the pan, if you don't mind, not one of the corners. And some lingonberry jam. Thanks."

Roelke watched Chloe stir cream into her coffee. She picked up her mug, inhaled deeply, sipped, closed her eyes in obvious homage to the caffeine gods. Something pulsed in his chest as it often did when she was around, something good and achy at the same time.

Oblivious, she remained in her happy place through several more appreciative sips. Finally she put the mug down and looked at him. "OK. Tell me what you've got."

Right. Back to business. "Let's start with the possible suspects I've—"

"I hate this, you know."

"I know." He picked up his People stack and put the top card down by her napkin.

"Howard Hoff." Chloe sighed. "Well, he did have good reason to be angry at Petra. Whether they had a fling or a flirtation, it seems clear that she went after him."

"Right. And after his wife's death Hoff may be particularly unsettled, emotionally speaking." Roelke considered, bouncing his knee beneath the table. Affairs of the heart were often behind volatile crimes. "Maybe he happened to run into Petra in the Norwegian House. If she taunted him, he might have just snapped."

"He was anxious during the reception," Chloe said reluctantly. "Although from what Violet and Sigrid have said, he's generally anxious these days. And with good reason, I might add. His career is in the canner."

"In the … what?"

"You know." She gestured impatiently. "Hot water, simmering, pressure building—oh, never mind. Who else—*oh*, thank you." She gazed reverently at the almond pastry the waitress had just deposited.

"Are you scheduled to see Hoff again?" he asked.

"Nothing formal."

"Well, stop by today, will you? Tell him about your interview last night or something."

"Why?"

"You never know. You might see something, hear something..." He shrugged.

Chloe's eyes narrowed in an expression of reluctance, so he chose to move on before she could argue. "So, who else had reason to hate Petra?" he asked.

"It's a long list," Chloe mumbled around her first bite. "According to Tom, Petra did something cruel that made Adelle give up rosemaling and switch to figure carving. He wouldn't give me details, though. Violet doesn't know, and Sigrid wouldn't tell me. It happened a long time ago."

"Things can fester for years before a killer takes action."

"I assure you, Adelle's health is too frail to even consider her involvement in Petra's death," Chloe said flatly. Then she hesitated. "But her husband, Tom... he's still angry."

"His frustration and helplessness about his wife's failing health might lead to rage," Roelke mused. "Only problem with that theory is that he wasn't at the reception."

"No, but he was in the museum that afternoon. Adelle said he dropped off some cookies."

Roelke started a new card and jotted some notes.

"You're putting Tom on the suspect list, aren't you." Chloe gazed at him. "I gotta tell you, it's hard to imagine him attacking anyone. He's quite pleasant. And a bit on the pudgy side."

"Pudgy people lose control just like anyone else."

"I do know that." She sighed. "He's also a Luther College grad, and sits on Vesterheim's Board of Directors, for whatever those tidbits might be worth."

"Could be important." He noted both facts.

"I also learned that Lavinia quit rosemaling when Adelle did."

"Well, hunh." Roelke thought that through. He fished out his Lavinia card, which had been pretty blank, and filled in what he'd just learned. "Did you ask your mother why?"

"No. I did ask Sigrid, but she wouldn't tell me."

"Is Sigrid deliberately trying to hide something, do you think?"

"I don't think so." Chloe worried her lower lip. "She looked very … strained, but it's probably what I said earlier—we're trying to get sordid info from people who are way too polite and reserved for malicious gossip." She nibbled a bite of pastry and licked her fingers. "This is a totally sucky way to start a day. Are we about done?"

"Not hardly." Roelke played another card.

When Chloe read the name, her eyebrows rose with surprise. "Emil? You consider him a suspect?"

"Not in particular," Roelke admitted. "But I have to consider every possibility, including instructors."

"My mom has a pretty good alibi," Chloe observed. "You and me." When he shot her an exasperated glance she added defensively, "I'm just sayin'."

"Marit is *obviously* not on my list," he said. "But Emil and Sigrid are. Emil admitted to clashing with Petra once—"

"That whole chisler-turpentine sniffer feud thing?" Chloe leaned back in her seat. "That doesn't strike me as motive for murder, especially since Emil got the last laugh. Not quite on the level of the way Howard Hoff and Tom Rimestad might feel, for example."

"I agree," Roelke said. "I'm not aware of any recent conflict between Petra and Emil. He's a bit quirky, but harmless. As for Sigrid—"

"No way."

"Chloe—"

"I'm *telling* you, no way. I've known her all my life. She's one of my mother's best friends." She gave him an indignant look.

Which was completely spoiled by the dab of powdered sugar at the corner of her mouth. Roelke was tempted to lean close and kiss it away, but didn't want to risk another unfortunate defeat-by-immovable furniture moment. His hand twitched with wanting. Something else started to twitch—

Jesus. He cleared his throat, studied his cards, shuffled through them a couple of times to give the impression he was considering complex possibilities.

Chloe cupped her mug in her hands, interlacing her fingers, which were long and lovely...

Get it *together,* he ordered himself. He was a cop. He was in charge of this conversation. He shuffled again, found Sigrid's card, placed it deliberately on the table.

Chloe put down the mug and folded her arms.

"We knew before we even found Petra that people resented her for winning that Medal," Roelke reminded her. "*Especially* because Sigrid's daughter did not win a Medal."

Chloe opened her mouth, closed it again.

"Look, I am not saying that *I* think Sigrid attacked Petra," he muttered. "But you can be sure that Buzzelli and Chief Moyer and the DCI agents are considering that maybe Sigrid was a jealous mama—"

"Seriously?" Chloe looked horrified. "They've labeled Sigrid a suspect?"

Roelke scrubbed his face with his palms. "I have no idea who they've labeled a suspect. That's the point of this little exercise. I have no official role in the investigation, but at the same time I'm right in the middle of it. *We're* right in the middle of it. I can't just report to Moyer once a day and walk away whistling *Dixie* and forget all about it."

"No." She sighed. "I don't suppose you can."

"Do you have any idea what Sigrid was doing in the hour or so before we arrived at the reception Sunday evening?"

"No. And don't ask me to ask her."

"I won't ask you to ask her," Roelke promised, although he'd been planning to.

Chloe looked at his cards. "What about Violet?"

He found his Violet card. It held a single line: *Didn't get her Medal July 1982.*

"She says she's not upset about what happened, and that she's upset by people who think she should be upset."

Roelke decided not to write that down.

"But … on some level she's *got* to be frustrated about it. And sometimes Violet is just a teensy bit too calm and sweet to be true." Chloe fidgeted with her napkin. "Did I say that out loud?"

"What's up between you and Violet?"

"She keeps cozying up to my mother. I know that sounds pathetic, but there it is. Every time I try to make some honest headway with my mom, offering her sympathy or support or something, I get rejected and Violet steps in instead. It's quite annoying."

"Oh." Roelke decided not to write that down, either.

"I did find out one fact about Violet last night. She works for the Scandinavian Studies department at Luther College."

"Does that matter?"

"Only in the context of Howard's cabal theory." She shrugged. "Violet speaks of Howard as a close family friend. Howard thinks there's a secret plot afoot on campus to dismantle the museum and return some of the earliest, most valuable artifacts to the college. Violet denies it, but is she in cahoots with this scurrilous unnamed professor?"

Roelke sensed a whiff of mockery. "Cahoots? Scurrilous? Who are you, Dudley Do-Right?"

"I'm sorry. I know this is serious. But the truth is, Petra might have pissed off any number of people in this town over the years. How could we ever identify them all?"

"We can't." He beat a frustrated rhythm on the tabletop with his pencil. Buzzelli and the DCI agents might have a long list of suspects, but they weren't going to share that list with him. That was both wholly appropriate and completely maddening.

"I keep wondering if the attack occurring *inside* the museum has some significance," Chloe added. "If someone planned to hurt Petra, wouldn't they have chosen a safer location? Safer for making a getaway?"

"I've thought about that too," Roelke said. "Any visitor might have wandered into the Norwegian House just in time to see the attack taking place. And the trunk Petra got dumped in was right below the window that opens to the main corridor, which doubled the risk. That suggests that the attack was spontaneous."

"And no sign of a struggle, right?" Chloe asked.

Roelke increased the tempo of his pencil. "Not that I'm *aware* of. Nothing obvious at the scene, anyway." If forensics had turned up something else, nobody had told him.

"So … it seems likely that Petra was approached by someone she knew, she said or did something to enrage that guy, and that guy snatched up a handy artifact—the *lefse* pin—and struck her with it."

"We don't know for sure the attack came from a man," Roelke reminded her. "Petra was a small woman, and the pin was a very effective weapon. It's heavy, but the handle would make it easy for anyone to swing with a lot of force."

Chloe pushed her plate away. "I don't want to talk about this anymore right now."

"OK." Roelke collected his cards, tapped the edges, and tucked the stack into his shirt pocket. "Thanks, though. This was helpful."

She slid one hand across the table until her fingers rested lightly on his. "This week isn't turning out at all like I expected. I got sucked into museum work, and you got sucked into this crime stuff. Since you dragged me out at this ungodly hour, it would be fun to at least savor a little you-and-me time."

"You'll get no argument from me on *that.*"

Her smile was sly, even seductive. "I was thinking that maybe—"

Roelke desperately wanted to hear what Chloe was thinking. Unfortunately, a sudden clamor drowned her out as half a dozen people shoved in to the café. Several were banging spoons on tin pans. One was blowing a child's toy horn, and another twirling some wooden gizmo that made a ratcheting noise. All were dressed in outrageous costumes, like Halloween trick-or-treaters on steroids. He couldn't even tell if he was looking at men or women.

Chatter in the café died. The intruders paraded among the tables, extracting the highest decibel level possible from their noise-makers.

"What the hell?" Roelke muttered. Some of the other customers looked as baffled as he felt. Others were grinning.

The parade approached the back corner. The lead marcher wore a voluminous red bathrobe over a parka and what appeared to be heavy overalls. A mask concealed whatever facial features weren't hidden by a lampshade hat and a wig made from several string mops. Instead of a noisemaker, this person carried what on first glance Roelke saw as a child's toy—an animal head on a stick that boys a century ago might have galloped about on. But this wasn't some cheerful and fanciful rendition of a stallion. It appeared to be a wooden goat's head, carved with wide glaring eyes and long flaring horns and a mouth that snapped open and closed. The leader shook the goat head at them as the parade circled by.

"What—the—*hell*?" Roelke repeated. He glanced at Chloe, and was alarmed at her expression. "Hey, you OK?"

She licked her lips before giving him a shaky nod. "Damn *julebukkers*," she murmured. "Sorry. They startled me, that's all."

Roelke remembered something Chloe had said when her mother saddled her with the folklore project. *Now I'll be spending my evenings talking about goats. Julebukkers. Don't ask. I hate them.*

The *julebukkers* completed their circuit and lined up near the front door. "Nels Andahl, you old goat, I know that's you!" a patron at the counter shouted. A man wearing a woman's dress removed his lion mask, grinning sheepishly. Within moments the revelers had all been unmasked. The efficient waitress—with an uncharacteristic grin on her face—came from the kitchen with a tray of pastries and cookies for them.

"OK," Roelke said. "I need an explanation."

"It's an old Norwegian tradition." Chloe managed a shaky smile. "In this country, it's only persisted in a few areas of heavy Norwegian settlement. People dress up and visit their neighbors. All in fun."

"You're not laughing."

"I got creeped out when I was a kid. In the way-back days people carried a goat's head around, symbolizing the goats slaughtered at this time of year. When I was little, some friends of my dad's showed up at my house with a real head on a pole. They shoved into our house without knocking. I was terrified."

"Any kid would be."

"When I started screaming they whipped their costumes off so I could see who they were," Chloe added. "But I cried for days. My dad told me that the goat had died of old age on one of their farms, but I didn't believe it."

What a stupid-ass thing to do to a child! Roelke frowned at the *julebukkers*.

"Relax, officer," Chloe said. She patted his hand. "I need to get over that childhood trauma. Tom and Adelle told me last night that Vesterheim's folklore project has revived some of the old traditions. People are just having a good time."

Roelke had more questions, but decided not to press Chloe for details. Maybe I can ask someone else, he thought. He didn't understand this custom. He didn't understand this community.

Emil's voice rang in his memory: *You got trouble there.*

Yeah, well, screw it. Roelke looked at Chloe's face—still tense, still pale—and felt something inside snap like a brittle twig. He was tired of seeing her upset. He was tired of reporting to the cops like some obedient puppy. He needed to stop talking and take action.

SIXTEEN

"Remember," Mom chirped, "anyone using spray varnish needs to step out on the fire escape. We don't want fumes to collect in the classroom! Just prop the door open so you don't get locked out."

Varnish, Chloe thought. Yeah, right. Only people who'd actually finished a project needed varnish. She dipped her brush in the red paint on her palette. It was drying out, so she added a few drops of linseed oil. ... A few too many drops, apparently. Globs of pigment now floated in oil. "Shit," she whispered.

Her tablemate looked up from the recipe box she was sanding. Gwen had finished the assigned tray and was filling time with projects of her own. "Problem?"

"I just ruined my middle red."

Gwen looked at Chloe's palette. "Yes you did. Want some of mine?"

"That—would—be—*great*," Chloe said, trying to inflect each word with profound gratitude. "Thanks."

"No problem." Gwen scooped up her leftovers with a palette knife. "My middle red won't be an exact match for yours, though."

"I do not care," Chloe admitted. "I just want to get this tray done."

"Especially since we'll start on our next project tomorrow," Gwen reminded her cheerfully. "A bowl with a *nisse* in the center. That will be fun."

Since Chloe hadn't mastered the most basic of strokes, much less color theory, it was hard to imagine that the Christmas-themed bowl wouldn't be an even bigger disaster than the tray.

"Remember," Mom called, "don't turn your pieces as you paint. We need to train ourselves to make strokes in any direction."

Chloe's tray was upside-down, and she left it that way. After forcing herself to finish one more motif, she took a break and headed to Howard's office.

He was on the phone, but beckoned her inside. "How long... of course. I see." He sighed. "Well, I appreciate whatever you can do to speed the process along, but care of the artifacts is my primary concern. Will your technicians... OK. I'll meet you there."

Chloe sat down as he replaced the receiver to its cradle. "Were you talking about the Norwegian House?"

"I was." Howard blew out a very long, very slow sigh. "The police have released it, but it's a mess. Did you know that fingerprint powder is black? I always imagined it was white."

Chloe winced as she imagined artifacts covered with powder of any color. "Who's going to clean up?"

"I contacted a professional service out of Dubuque. They have experience with crime scenes—"

"Do they have experience with priceless artifacts?"

Howard turned a gaze on her that was half worried, half weary.

Chloe was already regretting her words. She tensed, expecting Howard to pounce: *You're right, Chloe. Could you clean the Norwegian House? Could you at least supervise the crew?*

But he surprised her. "It's my responsibility. I'll do my best to keep the cleaners in line."

"I—I suppose I could be there when you meet the crew. Just to impress the basics on them."

Howard sat taller and shook his head. "Absolutely not. I've imposed on you too much already." He made an obvious effort to find a more cheerful topic. "Are you enjoying your class? I'm sure that any daughter of Marit's—"

"It's fine. And I interviewed Tom and Adelle Rimestad about *julebukking* last evening. Tonight I'm meeting someone named Edwina Ree."

"Edwina?" His expression changed. "Ah. Of course. Edwina."

Chloe couldn't quite decipher the look in his eyes. "What can you tell me about her?"

"She's an interesting lady." He busied himself arranging a cup of pens. "She worked as an archivist at Luther College for years. She's in her nineties, so she comes at all this with both professional interest and personal experience."

"I'll let you know how it goes." Chloe rubbed her palms on her jeans and stood. "By the way, I encountered a group of *julebukkers* this morning."

"I heard about that." The ghost of a smile quirked one corner of Howard's mouth. "They hit several businesses, delighting the Norwegians and bewildering everyone else."

"Evidently the museum's Christmas folklore project is inspiring people to resurrect some old customs."

"Old customs," Howard repeated. His voice sounded strained.

"Howard?" She sat back down.

"Oh. Sorry. It's probably nothing—"

"*What's* nothing?"

"I shouldn't burden you. It's just that … do you know what a *budstikke* is?"

Chloe hadn't been expecting a quiz on material culture. "Um … a wooden tube, right? Used for delivering messages in days of yore?"

"Right. One end has a metal spike so it can be thrust into a door." He took a shuddery breath. "A few months ago I came to work one morning—quite early, I was the first to arrive—and found a *budstikke* stabbed into my desk." With an effort he shifted one of the towering piles of paper, revealing a gash.

The raw gouge gave Chloe a chill. "My God! Do you lock your office at night?"

"I do now."

"Was there something inside the tube?"

"A note. Unsigned." He got up, paced his office twice, finally stopped by the window. "It was a—a rant. Someone raging because Petra won her Gold Medal at the Exhibition last July. Whoever wrote the note said that the only reason Petra won was …" He turned abruptly. "The person blamed me! As if I could influence the judges. As if anything I did could influence—well. It was ridiculous."

OK, Chloe thought, I'm catching on. Someone had complained that Petra benefitted from her supposed relationship with Vesterheim's director. "Did you give the note to the police?"

"I destroyed it. It was just—just someone venting. Someone who entered the competition and didn't get a ribbon."

"But how did that person get into the building? You said you were the first to arrive the day you found it."

He shrugged. "They probably slipped in the evening before, when someone was working late in the building. It happens. Decorah is a safe town."

Tell that to Petra Lekstrom, Chloe thought. "Did you tell the police about this after Petra was killed?"

"Well, no. I—I couldn't imagine that one thing is related to the other. But … it *has* been preying on my mind this week."

Yep, Chloe thought, Roelke is going to love this. "Did you destroy the message tube, too?"

"Good Lord, of course not!" His look of horror suggested that she'd proposed destroying the Holy Grail while Christ himself looked on. "It's at least a century old." He stepped to a tall filing cabinet, crouched, opened the bottom drawer, and scrabbled past files to the very back. Then he withdrew the antique in question and handed it to her.

The *budstikke* was about four inches in diameter and six or eight inches long. The carver had created a flowing design of acanthus vines that seemed at odds with the wicked-looking spike protruding from one end. A wooden cap fit snugly over the bottom.

"It's a marvelous piece, really," Howard said bleakly.

"It is, but I think you need to show that to the police." Chloe stood and passed it back. "And I need to get to class."

∞

Lavinia Carmichael was conspicuously absent when Roelke arrived in the classroom at 8:45 that morning. Fifteen minutes later Emil shrugged and began class without her. "You've all done good, real good, with practice boards," he announced. "Today, I want you to develop the design for your own project. I'll come around and help."

Roelke was still stewing about Petra Lekstrom's murder, but Emil's instruction knocked that frustration on its ass. He'd stopped by the museum shop earlier and picked out a wooden piece to carve, but had no idea what to do with it.

He hadn't gotten far with any design sketches when Lavinia hurried into the classroom. She dropped her totebag to the ground, hung her parka on the back of her chair, and settled down. The elderly woman's mouth was pressed into a tight line.

"You OK?" Roelke murmured.

"No, I am not." The long pull she took from her soda suggested that the can was filled with brandy, not ginger ale. "So. What are we doing?"

"Emil's coming around to talk with us about our projects."

"Good." Lavinia smoothed her wool skirt over her knees. She picked up a pencil, put it back down. She picked up her knife and put that back down, too. Then she leaned close to Roelke. "I was called back to the police station this morning!" she hissed.

Lavinia? Back for a second round of questioning? Roelke frowned thoughtfully. Had the cops called Lavinia in because of what *he'd* told them? He'd mentioned two days ago that there had been some bad blood between Lavinia and Petra, but he still didn't know the details. Maybe Buzzelli got tired of waiting for him to discover that information. Maybe the cops had uncovered something else about Lavinia in the course of their investigation. "What did they want?" he whispered.

"The investigator and the Criminal Investigation agent questioned me again! They wanted to know how long I'd known Petra, what my relationship with her was like—things like that." She sniffed indignantly. "I told them once again that I didn't *have* a relationship with Petra. That I'd washed my hands of her years ago."

Roelke considered, remembering the marked-out name he'd spotted in Lavinia's notebook.

"It was most upsetting," Lavinia added tartly, "to be interrogated like some criminal."

Roelke's knee began to bounce. Dammit! It was *so* frustrating to hover on the periphery of this investigation. "I imagine it was just routine," he tried. "The cops need to gather information so they can start eliminating people who knew the victim from the suspect list as soon as possible."

"Hmmph," Lavinia snorted. "Well, I resent being made late for class. I'm eager to show Emil my project plan." Her bulging notebook stayed in her totebag today, and instead she pulled out a single page. "I worked on this last night." She held an elaborate penciled design up for review.

He whistled in admiration. "Holy toboggans."

"I need Emil's advice about the border," she said. "How about you?"

He showed her his plate, approximately one-sixth the size of hers. "I picked this out, but I don't have a design yet."

"Then you better get to it."

Roelke nodded. He wanted to lose himself in the pleasure of chip carving again, wanted to enjoy it, wanted to make Emil proud. But his conversation with Lavinia brought all of the questions swirling in his brain back to the frontal lobe. He shot her a sideways glance, assessing this gray-haired lady who wore sensible shoes and butterflies in her hair. *Interrogated like a criminal*, she'd said. Was that Lavinia's take on routine questioning? Or did Buzzelli have good cause to go digging for information from Lavinia Carmichael?

SEVENTEEN:
AUGUST, 1967

"THERE, YOU SEE?" SIGMUND Aarseth held up his canvas so the students could study the flower he'd just painted. "Just like that."

Just like that, Lavinia thought. Although it was a fun challenge to contemplate, she'd need a lot of practice to come anywhere close to "that."

"Remember," Sigmund added, "you should not rely on patterns. Free yourself! Let your design be original, expressing your own artistry within the tradition."

Most of the women clustered around their instructor's chair nodded. Lavinia glanced at Adelle and saw concern on her friend's face.

"We will talk more of this after lunch," Sigmund said, pushing back his chair. "I will see you in an hour."

A few students followed Sigmund out of their makeshift classroom—several tables set up in the museum lounge. Others paused to finish scribbling notes. Lavinia nudged Adelle. "Let's go down to the diner, all right?"

"Perhaps I should stay," Adelle said in a low tone. "I'm feeling overwhelmed. I didn't know he'd expect us to design our own patterns! I've never done anything but copy designs."

Lavinia untied her apron and draped it over her chair. "And I'm a complete beginner," she reminded Adelle, "so you're way ahead of me."

"I just want to make the most of this opportunity. The pace is a bit . . . intense. Sigmund Aarseth is so talented, and such a generous instructor. I don't want to disappoint him."

"You couldn't possibly—"

"Petra!" Marit Kallerud's sharp tone stilled all other conversation. "I wanted to copy that!"

Lavinia turned and saw Petra Lekstrom at the chalkboard with an eraser poised above Sigmund's morning notes and sketches.

"Oh, I'm sorry," Petra said, with honey dripping from every word. "I was just trying to be helpful. I thought Sigmund would appreciate a clean board to start the afternoon."

"Well, please stop," Sigrid Sorensen chimed in. "I haven't copied it yet either."

Lavinia rolled her eyes and grabbed her friend's hand. "Come on." She waited until they'd left the room before picking up their conversation. "It's only the second day of class, Adelle. You'll do fine. *We'll* do fine."

"I wish I had your self-confidence," Adelle said wistfully.

Lavinia was surprised. Self-confidence? Is that what she projected? She'd only signed up for the class because Adelle had asked her to. "I have no idea if I can become a competent rosemaler, but

I'm having fun," she said honestly. "I realized last night that the class was so new and challenging that for the first time since Sid died, I didn't think about him and the farm all day. It was … restful."

"Oh, I'm glad!" Adelle exclaimed. "After everything that's happened in the past few years, you deserve that."

I do, Lavinia thought. Three years ago she had a husband, children to care for, a farm to help manage. Two years ago her husband died of flu, and the social worker had removed the foster kids Lavinia loved as her own—"So they have a stable home." Less than a year ago, Lavinia's house had been struck by lightning and set on fire. She and her dog had escaped to safety, but she'd lost almost everything else. Three months ago she'd sold the farm.

The two women emerged into a muggy heat, and Adelle paused to search through her handbag for sunglasses. "Decorah seems so *quiet*. After Nordic Fest, I mean. I hope they make it an annual event."

"Since thirty-seven thousand people showed up," Lavinia said, "I imagine Nordic Fest will become a tradition." She and Adelle had helped the museum prepare for the community festival, and she'd been lucky enough to score a plum volunteer assignment— serving refreshments out front, which let her enjoy the folk dancing and Luren Singers' concert in Water Street.

"It was marvelous," Adelle agreed. "Since Tom is on the museum's Board of Directors, he had a lot more to worry about. And there's no rest for the Board. They met last night, and Tom reported that they're hoping to revise the museum's contract with Luther College. Having so many artifacts on long-term loan creates some unique challenges. But he also reported that everyone is thrilled with the response to the first National Exhibition. The museum definitely will make that an annual event."

"Do you think you'll enter a piece one day?"

"I'd love to," Adelle admitted, "but I don't think I'd ever find the courage. Not when the entries are put on public display! How about you?"

"Absolutely not," Lavinia said flatly. "I'm just pleased to have a new hobby." She had never shied from helping Sid in the barn or the fields when needed, so for years she hadn't needed extra activities. But after losing her husband, her children, and her home, she had too many quiet hours to fill.

"You know," Adelle began, "Tom's gotten friendly with a new gentleman on the Board. He's a widower, and—"

"No, thank you," Lavinia said firmly, as she'd said more than once since Sid died. She had adored her husband, and that was that. "But as I was saying, I welcome the chance to make new friends in the rosemaling class."

They paused in front of the Ben Franklin store, waiting for a boy on a bicycle to pedal past so they could cross the street to the diner. "It's interesting to meet painters from other states," Adelle said. "Everyone is so nice."

"Well, *almost* everyone." Lavinia held the door open, and was greeted by the smell of frying hamburgers. "Petra Lekstrom is a bit too full of herself." She'd met Petra several times earlier, at various museum events, but this was her first opportunity to spend time with the woman.

"She's all right," Adelle said. They approached the counter and settled onto swivel seats. "I'm sure she didn't mean to inconvenience anyone by erasing the chalkboard."

Lavinia held her tongue. Adelle was the sweetest person in the world, and she'd only be distressed if Lavinia pushed the issue. But *I'm right on this one,* Lavinia thought. She was a very good judge of character, and if she still owned a farm, she'd bet every acre that Petra Lekstrom was trouble.

EIGHTEEN

By MID-MORNING ROELKE HAD made little progress with either his project design or conclusions about Lavinia's role in the official investigation. Then he noticed Chloe at the classroom door. She cocked her head toward the hallway: *Can you come outside?* He got up at once, pleased for all kinds of reasons.

"Sorry to interrupt you," she murmured. "But Howard Hoff told me something just now you need to know." She told her tale quickly.

When she finished, he still felt fuzzy on the details. "Explain again what this thing is?"

"It's a wooden tube. Once upon a time rural people used them to send important messages from house to house, farm to farm."

"Always bad stuff? Or 'Hey, how are you?' things too?"

"I'm not sure." She scratched her nose. "Anyway, I don't trust Howard to tell the cops about it. The note reflects his personal life in a way he'd surely rather not broadcast."

"I'll let Moyer and Buzzelli know."

Chloe leaned against the wall and gave him a bleak look. "I've become Decorah's number one snitch. First I told Howard about Mom getting locked in the vault. Now I'm telling you—and therefore, the cops—about Howard's little ... problem. There may not be a person left speaking to me by the end of the week."

"I will be speaking to you," he promised, and kissed the tip of her right ear. "Listen, I feel like I should stop by the PD over the lunch hour ..." His voice trailed away as her shoulders slumped. "Sorry. Any chance we can have dinner together?"

"That would work. I'm interviewing my last informant tonight, but she asked me not to come before eight o'clock." Chloe shrugged. "Maybe what *I'll* do over the lunch break is see what I can learn about *budstikker*."

"That would be good, but consider dinner together a done deal," he said firmly. "Maybe there will be time to swing by Emil's place. You'd love it. I feel like I'm staying in a museum."

She gifted him with a glowing smile. "Folk art and dinner? Consider it a date."

Score, Roelke thought. And Emil, put that in your pipe and smoke it. Maybe he, German/Irish-American cop, was actually starting to figure out what could make Chloe Ellefson, Norwegian-American curator, happy.

❧

At lunchtime, Chloe grabbed a caprese sandwich at the Co-op—tomatoes, basil, and mozzarella cheese so fresh that she almost swooned. That powered her through twenty minutes in Vesterheim's small and deserted research library. She found an article—"*Budstikker* Use in Northern Europe"—that detailed protocol when a king wanted to spread word about meetings or new regulations. It all sounded very pompous.

Frustrated, she backtracked to a pay phone in the hall. After stacking her change in case quick additions were needed, she called Old World Wisconsin and asked to be connected with her intern.

"Nika Austin," a young woman said briskly after one ring.

"Wow," Chloe said. "I'm amazed I actually caught you." Nika was starting on her Ph.D. and only worked ten hours a week now.

"It's more amazing than you thought," Nika said dryly. "Petty cut my hours in half."

Chloe's free hand clenched into a fist. "Why? He promised us ten hours a week through the off-season!" Nika had worked for free the previous season, and was only making minimum wage now.

"Director Petty giveth and Director Petty taketh away. He did not reveal his thoughts to a lowly intern."

"Another Petty atrocity," Chloe muttered. "I'll talk to him when I get back."

"Don't worry," Nika said. "I'll still finish my projects. So, what can I do for you?"

"A favor, if you will. I'm looking for information about *budstikker*…"

Five minutes later, Chloe hung up. Nika was an intellectual bloodhound. If there were more to learn, Nika would find it.

Chloe returned to the library, sat at the table, and tried to organize her thoughts. She wished that Howard hadn't destroyed the message he'd received. Had the "rant" been a complaint, or an actual threat? She leaned back in her chair, trying to think, trying to connect dots that danced like mischievous *nisser* just out of reach.

Was it possible that Petra hadn't been the killer's only target? Was it possible that whoever was angry at Petra—angry enough to attack her—was equally angry at Howard? Or even Vesterheim itself?

Chloe nibbled her lower lip. Her own foray into rosemaling was a complete debacle. Nonetheless, it was horrid to think that a beloved folk art tradition could be at the root of such evil.

Don't assume you understand anything, she told herself. She grabbed a piece of paper from the copy machine stack and liberated a pencil from a handy supply left for any researcher foolish enough to think it was permissible to examine old books with ink pen in hand. Then she captured some notes, starting with the obvious.

1. Some disgruntled rosemaler hated Petra for winning her Medal; maybe held Howard and the museum responsible

That one would not be easy to pin down. The Sixty-Sevens had a long history of disliking Petra. Violet had, in some observers' views, been cheated last July. But anyone who entered the competition—a ribbon winner or not—might resent Petra's success.

2. Someone angry because Howard took the museum into debt

Before last night, Chloe would have pegged some staff member for that one, or a museum Board of Directors member. But hearing about the impact of the debt on the entire city cast new light on that point. Having a museum of Vesterheim's caliber in Decorah could only be a boon for the local economy, but that didn't mean all locals would appreciate the fundraising campaign.

OK, what else? What was less obvious? What might they all be missing?

3. Someone trying to keep Vesterheim from being reaccredited

That seemed ridiculous. Chloe nibbled her lower lip, trying to imagine who would care. Someone with an ax to grind against Howard Hoff, maybe. But it would have to be someone from the museum world. She was willing to bet that most people in Decorah, both fans of the museum and foes of the fundraising drive, had never heard of museum accreditation.

4. Someone with ties to Luther College wants V to look bad, so collection can be returned

That seemed more ridiculous, and almost impossible to pursue. Violet worked at Luther—but so did a whole lot of people who lived in Decorah. Tom Rimestad was a Luther grad—but again, so were a whole lot of other people, including Mom. And Petra, but if that had relevance, she didn't see it.

5. Someone wants an artifact—maybe the wedding rug?— donated to their institution instead of Vesterheim

That seemed most ridiculous of all. You are more than grasping at straws, Ellefson, Chloe told herself. You are grasping at pieces of straw. You are grasping at specks of chaff blown away by a wailing winter wind.

She massaged her temples, trying to think of another reason why someone might harbor Howard-hatred in their hearts. Nothing came. Finally she folded the paper, stuffed it into a pocket in her jeans, and headed for the door. She was out of ideas, and it was time for class.

❧

The modern collections storage building, where Chloe was to meet Emil's class during afternoon break, was around the corner on North Mechanic street. The one minute walk took her past the eastern edge of Vesterheim's Open Air Division, a dozen buildings ranging from tiny immigrant cabins to a huge flour mill.

According to an informational sign, the Upper Iowa River had once flowed through the site. After World War II, the Army Corps of Engineers had rerouted the river to minimize flooding. That had left a vertical drop of perhaps fifteen feet in the middle of the grounds, but Vesterheim staff had put it to good use. From the low ground below, Chloe could see the back corners of two historic structures propped up on tall stacks of stones—suggesting the construction techniques used in the deep fjord landscape of rural Norway.

Vesterheim's staff and volunteers really have created something very special, Chloe thought. She was starting to feel protective about the museum.

In the storage building, the first thing Chloe saw was a collection of painted immigrant trunks. She flashed on the memory of Petra Lekstrom, dumped inside just such a trunk. Petra might have been a hound dog's mama, but *nobody* deserved that. Evidently, Chloe thought, I am starting to take the murder personally, too.

She took a few deep breaths and purposefully walked down the center aisle. Nothing was more fun than poking around another institution's collections facility. On either side, rows of metal shelving held artifacts neatly arranged on acid-free paper. "Ooh," she breathed, spotting a particularly splendid Hardangar fiddle.

Unfortunately, Emil and his students arrived before she could wander too far. Roelke surprised her with a wolfish eyebrow-wiggle that made the backs of her knees tingle. Other parts of her too, actually. Was Roelke as frustrated by this week's boarding school arrangement as she was? Or were her own frustrations causing her to—

"Miss Ellefson?" Emil asked politely. Chloe realized that it was not the first time the carver had spoken her name. "The artifacts I want to show my students are on shelf 7B." He pointed.

As Howard had promised, her presence was merely a safeguard against any possible criticism of museum policy. Emil donned a pair of white cotton gloves before affectionately stroking a porridge container. "Of all the Norwegian folk arts," he began softly, "wood carving has been the most consistently practiced by immigrants and their descendants."

Chloe noticed that Roelke wasn't tossing furtive glances her way anymore. He looked like he wanted to stroke the porridge container too.

"Norwegian-American carvers have always created beautiful and useful pieces," Emil said with obvious pride. "Rosemaling gets more attention, but people forget that painting almost died out completely before being revived fifty years ago. Woodcarving is the most true expression of Norwegian heritage."

Whack! Chloe thought. She wondered what Mom would think of Emil's claim. The question conjured an interesting mental image of Marit and Emil duking it out—in cotton gloves, of course.

Emil put the porridge container down and gestured toward a rectangular box. "This example dates to 1754. See how the rosettes are combined with bands and fan shapes? Each section is perfectly balanced. The overall design is perfectly balanced."

Some students made hasty sketches in their notebooks. Roelke leaned close to study the artifact with his own brand of intensity. Chloe felt that tingle again.

"How come the wood surface is black?" one of the students asked.

"The surface was stained black before carving, so the design stands out," Emil explained. "In rural Norway, everyone understood that life is a balance of good and evil, darkness and light."

He moved farther down the aisle. "See the similar positive and negative effect in this chip-carved mangle from 1820? Even this symbol of romantic love contains both light and shadows."

Yeah, Chloe thought. All parties understood that in a system that embraced traditional gender roles, romantic love could quickly become a drudgery of household chores.

When Emil picked up a second mangle, she wandered across the aisle to another bank of shelves—which contained a collection of wedding spoons. Geez Louise, had her mother arranged storage so that all matrimonial artifacts were glaringly prominent? Enough with the mangles and love spoons, already!

Behind the spoons were several *primstavs*, similar to the one she and Roelke had seen in the museum. Ironic, Chloe thought, that this particular shelf included love spoons symbolizing joyful beginnings and the calendar sticks that so often included symbols of Christian martyrs' tortured deaths. Each stick had its own style. One had been painted black, so the simple carved marks and pictographs depicting the calendar were barely distinct. Its neighbor had been carved from a pale wood. Darkness and light, Chloe thought. She stepped closer ... and felt a vague wave of discomfort that quickened her breath and tensed her muscles. It was hard to define, but *something* in that aisle was giving off a bad vibe.

Without moving, she studied the shelves. Small pieces were arrayed above and below the calendar sticks—darning eggs, pastry cutters, a child's donut-shaped teething ring. The ring raised all kinds of scarlet flags in her psyche ... an old loss of her own, her mother's not-so-subtle attempts to steer her and Roelke toward marriage and family, her muddled feelings on both issues.

She glanced over her shoulder. Emil had moved on from the mangle and was now analyzing a carved footstool. I am outta here, Chloe thought, retracing her steps. Her perceptive gifts seemed to be evolving, and the notion that individual artifacts in a museum collection might reach out to flick her senses was not welcome. Her job had enough challenges without that sweet little extra.

She met the others in the central aisle. "Thank you, Miss Ellefson," Emil said. "We're finished." As the carvers filed out Roelke gave her a distracted nod. So much for romance.

Alone again, Chloe took one last look behind her. *Something* back there had carried some melancholy through the years. *Was* it the teething ring? Was she starting to project her own dreams and doubts—

"*No,*" she said, and abruptly turned her back. Like she didn't already have enough to worry about? She was not actually responsible for anything in this room. Hallelujah.

Chloe closed the door behind her, turned the key in the lock, and headed back to class.

NINETEEN

CHLOE FINISHED THE AFTERNOON without finishing her tray. So be it, she thought. I've got a date. When she spotted Roelke waiting in the student lounge, her heart did a happy dance that Snoopy would envy.

"Since the lady I'm interviewing tonight lives out of town, Mom loaned me her car," she announced, dangling a key ring enticingly. "We are on the lam."

Roelke looked perplexed. "'On the lam' means 'on the run,'" he said. "So unless you're fleeing the mob, or Investigator Buzzelli has drawn a really bizarre conclusion, we aren't really—"

"Yeah, yeah." She grabbed his hand. "Let's go."

They emerged from the building into a deep blue twilight. "Temp's dropping," Roelke said, tugging the zipper of his parka higher.

"It's going to be clear tonight," Chloe agreed, gazing skyward. No clouds, no snow, no heat bubble.

"Emil's still helping someone in the classroom," Roelke said, "but I'm sure it would be fine if we stopped by his place."

"How far is it? Can we walk? I like the idea of zooming off in Mom's car, but honestly, I've been cooped up inside way too much this week."

"Sure, if you want. It's less than two miles from here."

They set off at a brisk pace, moving from pool to pool of light below the street lamps. "So," he said. "At lunchtime I told Buzzelli about the message-thing Hoff got last summer. Buzzelli will follow up with him."

"Lovely." Chloe pictured Howard's reaction when Investigator Buzzelli came calling to discuss his relationship with Petra. Well, she simply couldn't help that.

They soon reached the river's landscape of drifted snow and frozen water, with steep wooded bluffs beyond, all in shades of black, gray, purple. "Cool bridge," Chloe said, pausing to admire the geometry of the twin sets of trusses.

"Yeah," Roelke said. "All those angles remind me of carving designs. Is it like that for you? Are you starting to think about painting even when you're not in class?"

"Nope," Chloe said, but it didn't matter because her spirits were rising. "I'm glad we decided to walk. I think turpentine fumes were getting to me."

Once across the bridge, they walked along the road in the narrow space cleared by a snowplow. Roelke positioned himself between her and any oncoming traffic. Since seeing her beau/ gentleman caller/young man struck by a car wouldn't be any less traumatic than getting struck herself, Chloe started to protest his gallantry. Instead, she tucked one hand through the crook of his arm. "Hey, Roelke? It was nice of you to come with Mom and me this week. Even if you had no idea what you were getting into."

"I was naïve," he admitted. "But I'm glad I tagged along."

She was too. This challenging week would have been much *more* challenging without him.

"So," she said, "I want to run some ideas past you. Whoever attacked Petra was angry at her. Whoever left that threat for Howard last summer was angry at him. I spent some time over the lunch break trying to figure out how those things might be connected."

"Shoot."

She talked. He listened as she listed her ideas about motivation for Petra's attack: anger about Vesterheim's debt, a furtive drive to prevent Vesterheim from being reaccredited, a desire to re-engage Luther College, etc., etc.

"The rosemaling competition might connect the threat against Howard and Petra's death," he said. "But how likely is it that someone killed her to get back at Howard for taking on a big restoration project, or in hopes of making Vesterheim look bad? Money is always a prime motivator to consider, but if that's it, I don't understand Lekstrom's role."

Chloe exhaled slowly. "Well … I don't either. I'm probably way off base."

"It's good to air out any ideas," he assured her. "You never know where they might lead."

Five minutes later they rounded a bend that revealed a pretty little farm sleeping quietly in the rising moon's pale light. "That's Emil's place," Roelke told her.

"It's lovely. And—Emil has a *stabbur!*" She pointed to the small storage building perched on posts, a rare remnant of vernacular architecture.

"This place has been in his family since they came over from Norway," Roelke said.

She squinted. "He's put out a sheaf of grain for the birds. How charming." That was one of her favorite traditions from the Norske canon.

"Chloe, do you have a favorite tree?"

She blinked—where the heck had *that* come from? "Do I have to pick just one? Walnut, maybe—I love the nuts *and* the wood. Sugar maples for color in the fall and syrup in the spring. And oaks just because they are amazing. I love the way they look in the oak-savannah prairie landscape—"

"Yeah, OK," he said. Evidently she was telling him more than he wanted to know.

She studied him. "So … why did you ask?"

He waved one arm toward the wooded slope across the road. "Emil's land stretches partway up that hill. Last night he walked me up there and gave me what-for about needing to learn more about trees. You two probably could have had quite the conversation."

Roelke didn't sound annoyed by that, just a bit wistful. "Well, let's go up there!" she suggested.

"Now?"

"Why not? I'm tired of crouching on a chair the size of a postage stamp, squinting at chalk lines on a tray that I'm never going to finish painting."

"Are your chairs really too small? Ours are quite comfortable."

"Our chairs are fine, Roelke. That's not the point. I just—I just …" Chloe decided against an explanation. Her buddy Ethan would understand that in the middle of this stressful week, being around trees would do her a whole lot of good. She wasn't sure if Roelke would get that or not.

Evidently he either got it or was at least willing to follow her lead. "Sure, we can do that."

They walked up the hill in silence, aiming for the footprints left from the evening before. Chloe's lungs began to burn pleasantly with the exertion. They paused when the service lane ended. Stars were appearing in the evening sky. Leafless tree limbs whispered in the wind.

"Roelke?" Chloe heard herself say. "Maybe we should just go home to Wisconsin."

"Seriously?"

"Well, yeah. My rosemaling class is a disaster. We could just … you know. Leave."

"I promised the chief I'd keep my eyes and ears open all week. And don't you have more interviews to do for the folklore project?"

"Just the one tonight."

He was silent. A car passed on the road below them, its headlights carving the night like twin spotlights before disappearing around the bend. "I don't want to leave now," he said at last. "I want to finish my class. I might never have another opportunity to study from a master carver."

Chloe remembered how content he'd looked when she'd watched him carving the day before. How absorbed he'd been, how relaxed. Somehow this class was turning into a very good thing for Roelke. "OK," she said. "It was just an idea. I'm glad you're enjoying the class."

She felt his tension ease. "You really need to talk with Emil about trees sometime, Chloe. You two would get on."

"I wish I'd taken his carving class instead of the rosemaling," she said. "I went to forestry school, not art school. The painting workshop has hurt my relationship with Mom instead of helping it."

Roelke folded his arms. "Can't you put the whole mother-thing aside? Maybe get excited by the class itself?"

"That's kinda hard to do when my mother is the teacher," Chloe observed. "I will never, ever live up to the expectations of Marit Kallerud, sainted Sixty-Seven and Gold Medalist."

Roelke was silent again, this time for even longer. Chloe stamped her feet to keep blood flowing. Finally Roelke said, "Hunh."

"What?"

"Nothing."

She frowned. "*What?* There's obviously something on your mind."

"It's just that … I've never heard you whine before. I never thought of you as a quitter."

"I'm not a quitter!"

He shrugged. "You just said you wanted to go home. And you've already decided that your painting class can only end in failure."

Chloe opened her mouth, closed it again. They stood for a long moment. The intimacy she'd been savoring had vanished. So had her pleasure at being in the woods. At last she said, "We better get going."

"You still want to see Emil's carvings?"

A sudden blast of wind brought tears to her eyes. "Let's do that another time."

They trudged back down the hill. Roelke was painfully aware of the silence, the distance, that had come between them.

When they reached the road Chloe said, "I think I better go to Sigrid's house and—and change my clothes before heading out for tonight's interview." She didn't meet his gaze.

"I'll walk you back—"

"No. I'll see you tomorrow." She lifted one hand in vague fare-well and started striding toward town—hands in pockets, head down.

Roelke watched until she disappeared from sight, his jaw tight. Well, hell. He and Chloe had experienced some mighty arguments. She'd stalked away from him in anger more than once. But this quiet chill was a first. And it sucked.

My observation was fair, though, he thought. He couldn't claim to know much about maintaining a serious relationship, but being truthful was important. Right? Honestly, he just didn't understand Chloe's attitude on this whole painting thing. Sure, Marit could be difficult. And he wasn't so stupid as to assume he had an *inkling* of how complicated Marit's relationship with Chloe was. But Marit was basically a nice person. She was passionate about a folk art and wanted to share that with her daughter.

These classes are special, Roelke thought. Why didn't Chloe get that? Expert instructors, rare antiques for inspiration … He wished he could have shared something like this with one of his own parents. And he really did think that Chloe should cut her mom some slack. Just a little.

A truck threw some slush as it passed, startling Roelke from his roadside reverie. Standing here all evening wouldn't accomplish anything. He considered his options. Then he walked back toward town himself.

He went straight to the police station. Moyer was in. Buzzelli was not. "I know I'm early," Roelke told the chief. "I was free, and figured that—"

"No problem," Moyer said. "Anything new to report?"

"Did you hear about that message tube thing?"

Chief Moyer's expression made it clear that he had not. "The... what?"

"I guess Investigator Buzzelli hasn't had a chance to brief you yet," Roelke said blandly. He explained.

The chief held his hands tent-like in front of him, tapping the tips. "I wish Mr. Hoff had been forthcoming about this. I understand that his relationship with Ms. Lekstrom—whatever it was—is a sensitive topic. But for God's sake, we're investigating her murder."

"It makes me wonder," Roelke agreed. "Hoff tried to hide his true relationship with the victim. What else might he be hiding?"

"Exactly," Moyer muttered.

Roelke tried to gauge the chief's mood. A very fine line existed between what Moyer could and could not reveal to an out-of-town cop, and Roelke knew he was walking it. "Has the ME's report come in yet?" he asked, as casually as humanly possible.

"The ME confirms that the head wound was consistent with a blow made by that *lefse* pin."

"Any prints on the pin? Or the trunk?"

"Nope.

"So the killer probably struck Lekstrom in a sudden rage. He or she then panicked and tried to hide the body and weapon in the trunk, but was still composed enough to wipe away prints. How about the angle of the blow? Was it one-handed or two-handed?"

"One. The ME believes the attacker grabbed the pin in his or her right hand and swung it laterally."

"Hunh." Roelke considered. "I've hefted a similar pin. It would take some strength to swing it with one hand."

"I'm not ruling women out, but I suspect we're looking for a man."

"I understand that the investigator and the DCI agent talked with Lavinia Carmichael again early this morning," Roelke said. "Anything new come of that?"

Moyer hesitated, then shook his head. "Investigator Buzzelli briefed me just before lunch, and he didn't mention her."

Roelke could tell he'd heard everything he was going to hear. He left the police station and paused on the front step, replaying what he'd learned. Moyer was being straight with him, but Buzzelli might be holding some cards close to his chest. Besides, this was a DCI case. Roelke had no access to whatever Buzzelli and the agent had learned about Lekstrom's acquaintances—who had alibis, who was still a possible suspect, who had been eliminated.

I'll just keep poking at it from this end, he thought. That's all he could do. Although … Chloe thought he was too involved as it was. Roelke's jaw tightened as he remembered her walking away on this dark, cold night. He'd plowed a snowbank between them. Now Chloe was off on her interview—*somewhere*. He had no idea when she'd get back to Sigrid's house. If he tried calling her later he might wake one of the older women. Not that he was a big fan of trying to work something out on the telephone. And right now, he didn't know what to say anyway.

Dammit all, he thought crossly. Talking to Chloe would have to wait until tomorrow.

That pointed him back to police work. OK. He didn't know who the DPD liked for the murder, but *he* had two top suspects: Tom Rimestad and Howard Hoff. He'd already questioned Emil, the only other man he'd met who'd known the victim. Perhaps he could ask some local if there'd ever been any buzz about the carver and the painter, but right now, he wasn't aware of any smoldering animosity or recent conflict.

As for Hoff, Buzzelli and the DCI guy might be talking to him right this minute—examining the antique message tube, asking him to record what he remembered about the threatening note it had contained, maybe scaring the director into revealing some other juicy tidbit he'd tried to keep hidden.

That left Rimestad. He'd clearly harbored a smoldering resentment toward Lekstrom. He'd also been at Vesterheim the day Lekstrom was attacked. Motive and opportunity, right there.

The night is young, Roelke thought. He decided to grab supper at Mabe's. With any luck, pizza would help him figure out how he might learn more about Tom Rimestad.

TWENTY

Edwina Ree lived on an isolated farm several miles west of Decorah. The concentration needed to find it in the dark while avoiding snowy ditches helped Chloe set aside her hillside conversation with Roelke. It had also helped her set aside the phone conversation she'd just had with Nika, who'd turned up an ominous footnote about the old use of *budstikker*.

"I am having just a splendid day," Chloe said, squinting at a mailbox. OK. Here it was.

She cautiously crept down a long unplowed driveway, aiming for a single set of tire tracks. The drive rounded a bend and ended beside a lovely old frame house. Chloe parked and got out. The farm showed no commercial patina of Christmas cheer—no strings of colored lights on the shrubbery, no plastic snowmen, no wreath on the front door. But a sheaf of grain had been tied with a red ribbon on the porch railing for avian visitors, and a porch light provided a welcome glow.

The front door opened and a tall, white-haired woman stepped outside. She clutched a heavy black shawl over her shoulders, but hadn't troubled to pull on coat or mittens. Chloe headed toward the porch, trying to hurry without losing her footing. She didn't want Ms. Ree to get chilled.

Just as Chloe opened her mouth to call a greeting Ms. Ree tipped her head, as if listening for something. All Chloe could hear was the wind sighing with impatience, but the old woman stood motionless for a long moment. Something about her stillness sent a disquieting quiver along Chloe's spine.

Then Ms. Ree turned her head and smiled, and the spookiness disappeared. "Chloe? I'm Edwina. Please, my dear, come in from the cold."

Two minutes later Chloe was ensconced in a parlor that smelled much like every other timeworn Midwestern parlor—some indefinable blend of furniture polish and old upholstery, spiced with the faint whiff of crumbling leather from a huge Bible. Several stern portraits in gilt frames might have been hanging from their decorative cords since Victorian times. A stereopticon sat on a side table beside a stack of the oblong cards that had brought faraway scenes into this Iowa farmhouse a century ago. Only the presence of electric lights, a plastic radio, and lime-green knitting needles poking from a basket kept the room from museum status.

While Edwina busied herself in the kitchen Chloe closed her eyes for a moment, opening herself to whatever might be lingering in this old home. She perceived only a faint swirl of emotions here, nothing unusual. Just the way she liked it.

Edwina emerged from the kitchen without cookies, which at this point was a relief, and served Chloe hot chocolate in a delicate teacup. "Thank you," Chloe said gratefully, wrapping her fingers around the warm china. She studied her hostess surreptitiously as she sipped. Edwina's blue dress reached mid-shin length, and she wore heavy stockings with black shoes. She was quite thin—bony, really—with snowy braids wrapped coronet-style around her head. Her face was a crinkle of fine lines. Her eyes were as bright as a child's, though—intelligent and assessing.

"As I explained on the phone," Chloe began, "I'm helping with Vesterheim's Christmas folklore project."

"The persistence of tradition is of great interest to me," Edwina said. She sat quite still with back straight, hands folded in her lap, legs crossed at the ankle.

Chloe found herself perching erect too. "I understand your family has deep roots in the area?" She turned on her recorder and smiled encouragingly.

"My mother's parents left Norway in 1867 and settled right here, on this land," Edwina said. "My parents died when I was a baby, so my grandparents raised me. My grandfather kept to the old ways, and told me many tales he'd learned as a child, even though my grandmother scoffed at most of them." Edwina paused to sip her own cocoa. "As I grew older their differences fascinated me, and I developed an academic interest in folklore. I studied history at Luther College, and became an archivist in part because I believed it essential to document the beliefs of first- and second-generation immigrants."

"As I've heard about old Christmas traditions this week," Chloe said, "I've been intrigued by the transition of some aspects of holiday celebrations from pagan to Christian times."

Edwina nodded. "Many a good Norwegian family today considers a thorough housecleaning the first essential step of holiday preparation. Women say they do this to welcome the infant Christ. But as children, my grandparents were taught to clean well at Christmas because this period signaled a return of the dead."

"A return of the dead?" Chloe took that in. "I did not know that."

"You were raised in a Christian church?"

"Lutheran."

"Well, it hasn't been all that many generations ago that church leaders labored to Christianize people's worldview," Edwina said. "Preachers urged Norwegian folk to forget stories that had been passed down for centuries. Have you heard of *mørkemakten?*"

"Um … no."

"It refers to the power of darkness. Our ancestors believed that evil forces were present during these dark days."

Chloe was starting to wish that Edwina *had* wanted to talk about Christmas cookies. Seriously, a rosette or two would be good about now. "Evil forces …?"

"*Oskorei*—a group of malevolent spirits that haunted wintertime skies. Too wicked for heaven, they were doomed to roam for all eternity. They descended on farms and villages, howling like a blizzard wind and playing cruel tricks. *Oskorei* might defile a year's worth of new-brewed beer, or run horses until they dropped from exhaustion, or strike down anyone foolish enough to venture out alone in the dark of a December night."

Chloe became aware of the wind shoving at the parlor windows as if searching for entrance. At least she assumed it was the wind. Something Emil had said earlier that day popped into her mind: *In rural Norway, everyone understood that life is a balance of good and evil, of darkness and light.*

"Farm folk did try to protect themselves," Edwina said. "They painted crosses on their barns to discourage the demons from defiling their harvest. They made sure to stable their animals inside before dusk. They spread straw on the floor of their homes, and everyone slept huddled together for protection. Later, the straw was made into figures intended to ward away evil."

Chloe shifted in her chair. There was something disconcerting about sitting in this spotless parlor with this oh-so-proper old lady, discussing ancient evils.

"Another legend tells of a terrifying goat-like creature descending from the sky," Edwina added, "to punish everyone on the farm if things weren't to his liking."

Oh goodie, Chloe thought. A new twist on the creepy Christmas goat. "Is that story connected to the custom of *julebukking*?"

"Yes indeed. People dressed up and made noise to scare away the evil ones."

Maybe I should give *julebukkers* a break, Chloe thought. "And over the years that became something done just for fun—letting hardworking people blow off steam after getting the autumn harvest in."

"Actually, I don't believe *julebukking* survived strictly as a remnant of the ancient custom," Edwina said. "Or even just as something fun."

Chloe wasn't sure where this was going. "Oh?"

Edwina seemed to consider her words carefully. "In a small community, everyone knows everyone else. There are clear expectations about proper behavior. I believe the costumes give people a chance to ignore those expectations and step out of prescribed roles. Once participants put on masks, they may indulge in forbidden behavior. Women wear trousers, for example. Men might feel free to grab a woman's hand."

Chloe pictured the revelers she'd seen as a child, and the group she'd seen that morning at the café. The participants hadn't simply donned costumes. They'd taken pains to disguise their identity.

"Times are changing, of course." Edwina smiled. "Today, people are most often reviving a custom, not perpetuating one. That changes the participants' motivation entirely. But think of old days in Norway. The rugged landscape isolated rural people. Social mores were strict. An evening of fooling and role-play must have been quite liberating."

The recorder snapped off. Chloe fumbled with the machine. "Do you have more stories you'd like to share?" She hadn't even looked at her own list of questions, but honestly, she'd had her fill for the evening.

Edwina studied her guest, then shook her head. "I think that's enough for now."

Chloe passed the list of informants to Edwina. "If you think of anyone else who should be interviewed, you can let Howard know."

"Many of the old traditionalists have passed on," Edwina said. "Have you talked with Emil Bergsbakken? His family stayed close to their roots."

"I'm not sure why the former curator didn't include him," Chloe admitted.

"Emil's mother and I were close friends. I'm afraid a lot of family lore was lost when she died. She was in the family's farm wagon when the horses bolted—quite tragic. Emil was just a boy, now that I think about it, so I doubt he could tell you much now. None of those Bergsbakken men were big talkers." Edwina smiled. "But oh my, carving is in their genes."

Chloe envisioned Roelke, happy and relaxed in the classroom. "Emil's perpetuating his cultural heritage in his own way."

"Indeed," Edwina agreed. "Perhaps I'll see you this weekend. I'll be participating in Vesterheim's Norwegian Christmas festivities."

"I'll look for you." Chloe packed the recorder away and followed her hostess back to the front hall. She stamped into her boots and pulled on her parka and woolens. "As a gesture of appreciation, may I shovel your front walk?"

"How thoughtful!" Edwina said. "The young man who usually takes care of it sprained his ankle playing basketball. A UPS driver made it up the driveway this afternoon, but I do hate to leave things untended. There's a shovel on the porch."

Chloe found the shovel and soon had the walkway cleared from front porch to driveway. For good measure she shoveled a path to a side door, too—probably the kitchen. The temperature had dropped into the single digits, but by the time those steps were cleared she was warm from the inside out.

She surveyed the farmyard as she caught her breath. Several outbuildings showed dark against the snow. The closest was a small stable, tethered to the house by a rope strung shoulder-height. People who kept livestock sometimes used ropes like that to guide them to their barns during blizzards. Surely Edwina didn't tend animals...? Well, maybe chickens or a barn cat. There was no harm in clearing a path.

Chloe scooped her way along the rope's thread-like shadow. Since Edwina might be watching from a back window, Chloe didn't indulge her curiosity and peek inside the stable. But the log structure itself was a find. Superb corner notching argued against hasty construction. Perhaps Edwina's grandparents had thrown up a smaller building in haste for whatever animals they could afford, and built this stable later. Chloe let her gaze follow the rise of beams appreciatively, picturing a farmwife eager to embrace the new world while her husband longed for the old.

Then Chloe saw something that spoke of modern handiwork—a cross, painted high on the stable's front wall, visible because of moonlight reflecting from snow. She remembered what Edwina had said about terrified rural folk: *They painted crosses on their barns to discourage the demons from defiling their harvest.* Chloe also remembered Edwina's stillness when she'd stepped onto the porch, head tipped as if listening for something...

Edwina reminded me of *me*, Chloe thought suddenly. She always instinctively paused in old buildings, receptive to any lingering resonance. Edwina's countenance that night had suggested something similar.

So. Evidently Edwina's interest in ancient folklore wasn't entirely academic.

Chloe tried to find comfort in the discovery of a kindred soul, but comfort didn't appear. Instead, a frozen tree creaked and groaned as a sharp gust blew through the yard. She suddenly felt quite alone in the world. She imagined a rowdy band of spirits, too wicked for heaven, swooping down as she stood in foolish solitude in this farmyard.

OK, she told herself firmly, that's unlikely.

Then she imagined a killer crouched in nearby shadows, watching her.

And that's ridiculous, she told herself even more firmly. Why on earth would Petra's killer appear here on a frigid night?

Still … *something* sent an icy fingernail over her skin. Maybe finding a woman who'd been left for dead in an immigrant trunk was making her jumpy. That was a reasonable response, right? Or maybe genetic memory was kicking in. Perhaps ancient fears of these shortest, darkest, coldest days had been passed down to quiver in her own DNA.

Whatever it was, Chloe decided it was time to head back to town. She retraced her steps, returned the shovel to the front porch, started the car, and managed to execute a three-point turn without getting stuck in a snowbank.

As she started back down the drive, she glanced in the rearview mirror. Edwina had stepped outside again. Was she watching her guest depart? Or was she listening for evil spirits destined to roam forever on long winter nights?

TWENTY-ONE

Since Roelke had walked Chloe to the Rimestad home the night before, he didn't have any trouble finding it again. However, he did have trouble making a stealthy approach. He could have read a newspaper in the glow cast by moonlight on snow. He paused across the street, considering the house and the separate garage at the end of the driveway. The ranch house and station wagon said middle class, lawn decorations spoke of Christian faith, the neatly shoveled front walk and driveway suggested pride in appearance, attention to safety, or both.

Roelke walked on, not wanting to attract notice. After wandering around the block he approached again. This time he walked on the near side of the street. Lights glowed from the front room, but the curtains were drawn. He glanced quickly over both shoulders. There was no way to know if some neighbor happened to be looking out a window, but he didn't see anyone.

OK, he was going for it. He made a quick turn and walked down the Rimestads' driveway. He had absolutely no idea what he hoped to accomplish by prowling about, but he needed to do *something*.

Chloe tried to banish the willies as she drove back into Decorah. She punched on the car radio and turned the knob until she found Alabama singing "Christmas in Dixie," the antithesis of spooky legends from northern Europe or northern Iowa. She slowed when driving by some Luther College students pelting each other with snowballs, and tried to absorb their high spirits. She meditated on Norman Rockwell as she passed twinkling lights on Christmas trees homeowners had obligingly erected in bay windows. The cultural phantoms that had emerged during her visit with Edwina Ree began to fade.

Unfortunately they were replaced not with Christmas cheer, but a melancholy of modern origin. The last conversation she'd had with Roelke elbowed its way to the front of her mind. Cliff Notes version: he thought she was a quitter.

This is what comes from dating, Chloe thought. You open yourself up to someone, start to get comfortable with someone, and *wham*. She tried to mentally compose the insightful, articulate, and pithy response that had failed to emerge on that wooded hill above Emil's farm.

That response still didn't come. And as Chloe turned onto Water Street, she realized why: Roelke had been right.

"Well, shit," she muttered, forcing herself to consider the situation with an open mind. Honestly, it was not entirely her fault that her rosemaling class had turned into a fiasco. Mom was uptight and demanding and distant.

But, Chloe thought, I *have* already concluded failure. I've been going through the motions and whining *Poor me, poor me,* to Roelke every day. It was not a pretty picture.

When she passed Vesterheim, she impulsively pulled over. Lights shone from the Education Center. Several other cars were parked nearby. It was only 9:30. At least a few industrious students were up in the classrooms.

Chloe lifted her chin. OK. She was going to join them.

On the third floor, all six of Sigrid's students were at work. In her own room, Chloe found five students bent over their projects. Gwen grinned as Chloe sat down. "Hey, Chloe! I didn't expect to see you this evening."

"I wanted to see if I could catch up." Chloe regarded her tray dubiously. No freaking *way* could she catch up—but, no; that was not the right attitude. "At least a little," she amended.

"Let me know if you get stuck," Gwen said. "Your mom usually stays late, but she said she and Sigrid were visiting friends this evening."

Chloe peeled plastic wrap from her palette. "You've been busy," she observed. Gwen had been painting Christmas ornaments cut from thin plywood. A dozen bells, stars, and trees were lined up to dry.

"They're fun to paint." Gwen gestured toward a pile of blank ornaments. "Help yourself if you want to try something different. I know you're not enjoying the class project."

Chloe sighed. Did everyone in Decorah know how much fun she was *not* having in class? Evidently. She dredged up her most chipper smile. "Thanks, Gwen, but I'll stick to the tray."

She approached it with grim resolve. At least Mom's written instructions were clear and thorough. And without Mom on hand to interrupt, criticize, or speed the class along, Chloe found herself— astonishingly—making tentative progress.

An hour or so later a policeman stuck his head in the door. "You two OK? I've been through the building, and the doors are locked."

"Thanks," Gwen called. She began cleaning her supplies. "I'm calling it a night."

Chloe look up, surprised to find that everyone else was gone. She did not want to stay in the building alone. She also was kinda on a roll, and hated to stop now. "Is anyone left next door?"

Gwen checked. "A couple of people are still there," she reported. "And I'll make sure the front door locks behind me. See you in the morning."

Chloe settled back in to work. The solitude and quiet were soothing. She hadn't realized how intimidated she'd been by Gwen's fast and flawless work. Now, with only herself to set the pace, she was able to filter out the negative vibes her subconscious had been whispering all week. Her strokes were still clumsy but maybe, just maybe, she could actually finish the tray.

At eleven o'clock she grabbed a soda from the lounge fridge. Bring on the caffeine, she thought as she returned to her work. She was jazzed now.

Half an hour later she was ready to try a cornucopia painted with three colors applied in a single stroke. Chloe did a couple practice strokes with a triple-loaded brush on a scrap of tagboard, dashed out with annoyance for a restroom break—she was *such* an idiot; she should have skipped the soda—and settled back down. She held her breath and leaned close to the tray. With one stroke the colors blended nicely. She felt quite pleased with herself in particular and life in general—

Until she smelled smoke.

She dropped the brush and jumped to her feet, blood pulsing. Two trash cans sat near the door, a brown one for miscellaneous trash and a red one for oily rags. Someone had left the lid on the red one ajar. Smoke was seeping from the crack.

Chloe ran to the cans. She *meant* to push the lid firmly back in place, but it clattered to the floor. Black smoke billowed high above the can. Flames shot up too, greedy for oxygen, crackling with glee.

"*Shit!*" Chloe ran to the sink. The only containers in sight were a jelly jar and a yogurt container someone had forgotten to wash. By the time she'd filled them, the fire had jumped from the red can to a huge roll of the paper used to cover the tables. Flames wicked up the paper tube to the shelf it leaned against, setting someone's notebook alight. A pile of wadded paper towels on the floor caught at the same moment.

Chloe tossed what water she hadn't spilled at the blaze. After a quick angry hiss, flames jumped from the notebook to a stack of practice tagboard someone had covered with lovely C- and S-strokes. The work was consumed as fire raced along the shelf.

Forget water, she thought. I need a fire extinguisher. Or a phone— a phone would be good too.

But she didn't *see* a fire extinguisher or a phone. She ran around the classroom, frantically shoving and kicking her classmates' stuff aside as she searched for either of those handy little inventions. Nothing.

The room was filling with smoke, stinging her eyes, filling her nose with an acrid oily stench. The crackling noise was rising. Flames had moved to the wooden cabinet beneath the sink. More flames writhed in jagged lines along the floor. It was time to go for help.

Chloe ran to the closed classroom door—why was the door closed?—and grabbed the handle. It turned in her hand, but the door didn't move. She threw her shoulder against it, Hollywood-style. No luck. She banged on the door. "Hey!" she yelled, hoping any student still working next door might hear. *"Hey! Help me!"*

No response, no sign of rescue. The lounge, visible through a window beside the door, remained horribly deserted. The smoke was getting thicker but she could still see writhing flames, hear their crackle as they found stray bits of combustibles. Chloe's heart beat a panicked staccato.

"I am *not* trapped," she muttered. That beautiful, beautiful student lounge was only a pane of glass away. It took two seconds to consider her options. She snatched up the closest chair. Well, she tried to snatch it up. Vesterheim staff had not skimped on student comfort, and the nicely upholstered chair was heavier than she expected. She rolled it toward the front wall instead.

Chloe had imagined hurling it through the window, but that was out. Gasping with effort she wrestled the chair up to shoulder height and banged it against the window. No tinkling glass—not even an encouraging crack. She slammed the chair harder. Still nothing, and her arms were already quivering. God, she was *such* a weenie, and if she escaped this fire she was seriously going to work on upper body strength—

Stop whimpering! she ordered herself. The room had more than one door, right? She stumbled toward the back of the classroom, and . . . *yes*! There was a back door. If she hadn't freaked so quickly, she would have remembered that. Or at least spotted the neon EXIT sign in the far corner. Mom had asked that any students needing to use varnish step outside on the fire escape.

Blessed, *blessed* fire escape, Chloe sang silently as she ran toward the sign glowing red in the smoky haze. When she slammed against the back door's horizontal panic bar it gave so fast that she almost fell.

She found herself in a tiny anteroom, with a second door and EXIT sign on her left. This one must lead directly onto the fire escape. She slammed against its panic bar—and yelped in pain as metal met hip without giving way.

Chloe's stinging eyes blurred with tears. The door was locked.

But . . . how could that be? Mom's instructions had been quite clear: *Remember, anyone using spray varnish needs to step out on the fire escape . . . Just prop the door open so you don't get locked out.* Fire escape doors didn't have exterior handles or fixtures that locked. They should always be easy to open from the inside.

Which could only mean one thing: someone had jammed this door shut from the outside.

TWENTY-TWO

ROELKE REACHED THE GARAGE without arousing any hostile dogs or vigilant neighbors. He paused by a door in the far wall, out of sight of the Rimestads' house. He put a gloved hand on the knob, and it turned easily. He sighed. Too many people thought that a break-in couldn't happen in their community, to them.

Then he reminded himself that right this minute, the Rimestads' false sense of security was not a bad thing.

Two seconds later he was inside, the door shut softly behind him. He pulled his flashlight from his pocket, let his eyes adjust to the gloom, and began a quick look-see.

The garage had been weatherized, and showed no sign that a car had been parked inside for quite some time. One corner had been turned into a shop, with two workbenches, piles of wood on the floor, more wood on shelves, paint cans, a jigsaw, knives and chisels. In another corner a wheelbarrow, grill, and lawnmower waited for spring. Metal shelves along one wall were cluttered with suburban detritus: a red gas can, a collection of birdfeeders, hoes and hedge clippers, miscellaneous bits of hardware. Cardboard cartons with notes marked on the sides lined two shelves: Halloween decorations, dehumidifier, croquet set, Goodwill.

Roelke tapped fingers against his thigh. He'd found no handy weapons collection displayed on the wall, no boxes conveniently labeled "antique message tubes," no fist-sized holes in the drywall suggesting bursts of rage. He was tempted to root around the closed cardboard cartons, but decided against it. This truly was a fool's errand—not to mention that he was trespassing, in a town where he had absolutely no authority. All of which, he reflected sourly, didn't suggest anything good about his own mental state.

He slipped back outside and paused, keeping to the shadows. Away from the street, Rimestad's tidiness was no longer in evidence. Moonglow revealed paint curling from the door frame and cracks in the garage window. A squirrel's nest visible in a high vent pipe had not been removed, and a wooden trellis had fallen sideways. Several flowerpots lined the wall, skeletal dead blooms poking forlornly through the snow.

Roelke felt a flash of irritation, aimed squarely at himself. Tom Rimestad's lack of maintenance didn't reveal one damn thing about the man other than that he was busy. Given his family situation, Rimestad was doing well to have Christmas decorations up in front. Roelke imagined himself married to . . . well, let's say Chloe . . . and how *he* might feel and function if she was terribly ill. It was not pleasant to contemplate.

A light in the next yard flicked on, startling as a search beacon. "There you go, Muffin," a woman crooned. "Do your business quickly tonight, all right? It's too cold for Mommy to wait long for her precious Muffykins."

O-*kay*, that was enough for now. Roelke decided to head for the street before precious Muffykins caught his scent and came to investigate, yapping merrily all the way.

Roelke had reached the front corner of the garage when he slipped on a bit of ice. Windmilling his arms did not keep him from landing on his ass. Windmilling his arms *did* cause him to whack a downspout, hard. The downspout evidently needed a bit of maintenance too, for one segment fell to the pavement with a metallic clatter surely heard all the way to the state line.

By the time Roelke was on his feet Muffin had streaked through the shrubbery, barking maniacally as only small dogs can. A light over the Rimestads' front door flicked on. The door opened. Three people stepped outside. "Who's there?" a man called.

Roelke swore with silent but mighty force. Then he walked slowly toward the light, hands held a bit away from his sides: *I am not a threat.*

"Good heavens!" Chloe's mother exclaimed. "Roelke? Is that you?" Marit hurried down the sidewalk toward him.

"That's Roelke?" the second woman asked. He recognized Sigrid's voice and beehive hairdo.

"Who is Roelke?" Tom Rimestad demanded.

"It's Chloe's young man," Sigrid confided in a loud aside as the trio surrounded him. She and Marit were already bundled in their coats and hats. Evidently they'd been about to leave as he did his swan dive on the driveway.

Marit frowned. "But ... what are you doing here?"

Roelke was quick, if not steady, on his feet. "I knew Chloe had your car," he said, "and I didn't like the idea of you ladies walking home alone."

That was accepted at once. "How *thoughtful!*" Marit said.

"How *sweet!*" Sigrid said, patting his arm.

"How *good* of you," Rimestad chimed in. He extended a hand and introduced himself with a jovial grin. "The ladies and I got to talking and completely lost track of time."

Chloe was right, Roelke thought. If this man is a killer, he does not look the part.

"I'd been trying to convince these two to let me walk them home," Rimestad continued.

Sigrid made a dismissive gesture. "You need to stay with Adelle. Anyway, now that Roelke—"

Roelke sliced the air with one hand to silence her, catching the sound before they did, and whirled toward the street. The others also went still as the distant wail of sirens came closer. More than one siren, punctuated with the unmistakable blare of a fire engine's horn.

"Oh, dear," Sigrid murmured.

Rimestad frowned. "Sounds like they're stopping downtown."

It sounds like they're stopping near Vesterheim, Roelke thought. "Stay here," he barked. Without a backward glance he hurried away, icy pavement be damned.

❧

Chloe hurled herself against the jammed fire escape door a few more times before accepting defeat. Belatedly she shut the classroom door behind her and crouched on the floor in the tiny anteroom, heart thudding, skin prickling, her turtleneck soaked with sweat. During a fire it was best to stay low, where the air was better, right?

Maybe the fire would burn itself out. Maybe she'd be OK here until help arrived.

Nice theory, but it didn't stave off an immense wave of claustrophobia. She was trapped in this little anteroom. The EXIT sign provided the only light, glowing with ghastly red intensity through the smoke that had billowed into the space with her. She crawled along the bottom of the outside door, scrabbling with fingers desperate to find a space big enough to—to shove something through, maybe. But no such space existed and besides, it was dark outside, and she was on the third floor of the old building. Slipping a note through the crack would have accomplished exactly nothing.

She pressed her hand against the classroom door. It didn't feel hot—yet, at least, and that was something. She crawled to the right of the classroom door, trailing one palm along the wall. Nothing. Almost immediately she hit the corner, and turned again—

And felt another door. Another door!

This one had a doorknob. Chloe tried it, turned it, stumbled through. She emerged into a narrow, twisting corridor. A cloud of smoke followed, not wanting to let her go, but it was half-hearted.

Chloe kicked the door closed behind her. She didn't know exactly where she was. But for the first time since she'd seen flames leap from the red can, she felt hopeful.

❧

When Roelke turned onto Water Street he saw a big city fire engine, aerial truck, rescue truck, and a police car parked in front of the Education Center. As he approached he heard a familiar voice, rising with an intensity that could not signify anything good: "I am quite positive about that!" He slid through a small crowd gathered to see the excitement and saw Chloe, Howard Hoff, and a fireman wearing chief's insignia huddled against the building. In the squad car's pulsing light, Chloe looked furious.

"What happened?" he demanded. "Chloe, are you all right?"

"Yes," she snapped. "But I'd be better if these gentlemen believed what I was telling them."

"But what—happened?" Roelke growled.

Before she could answer, several firefighters pushed through the door. "Fire was already out," one reported. "Cole's still up there, but we're clear."

"Good response, men," the chief said. He was a burly man with an air of competent calm. The firefighters began stowing their gear, and the chief moved away to speak to them.

Roelke took advantage of the lull to grab Chloe's shoulders. He could smell smoke on her coat, in her hair. "What *happened*?"

As she explained, something in his chest went very still and hard. "Once I finally got out," she concluded, "I ended up in the textile classroom and found a fire extinguisher. Then I saw Howard—"

"I came by to make sure all of the students had left for the night, and check that the main door was locked." Howard was wringing his hands with anxiety. "After what happened to Petra—"

"Was the door locked?" Roelke asked.

"Yes. I went upstairs, and you can imagine my horror when I saw the classroom filled with smoke, and—"

"Howard called the fire station," Chloe said. "Then we grabbed fire extinguishers and he opened the classroom door. The fire was out by the time the first firemen got here."

Roelke glowered at the building. "But why wouldn't the fire escape door open?"

"It was jammed," Chloe repeated. "And the door to the lounge must have been too. I should have been able to open it from the inside."

The fire chief rejoined them as she spoke. Unlike his men, who were attired in black from head to toe, he wore a white helmet. "The door on the fire escape opened easily when we tried it."

"It—was—*jammed*," Chloe insisted.

"Ms. Ellefson." The fireman shifted his weight from foot to foot. "Is it possible that because you felt panicked—"

"No!"

A lone firefighter emerged from the Education Center. "Chief? Got a minute?" He cocked his head. The two men walked out of ear-shot as the aerial truck pulled away from the curb.

Chloe glared after the chief. "I know what happened."

Roelke put his arm around Chloe's rigid shoulders. He needed to feel her, safe. "What were you doing here at this time of night anyway?"

"Well, I decided you were right about some things." She sounded a bit defensive. "So I came to work on my painting."

Great, Roelke thought. A fine time for Chloe to decide he was right about something.

"This is a nightmare," Hoff moaned. "What will I tell the Board?"

The chief returned and introduced his companion. "Cole here is our fire marshal. He's on the squad, but he also works for the State of Iowa. He'll be investigating the fire."

That means he's already found something to investigate, Roelke thought grimly.

Marshal Cole asked Chloe and Hoff to go back upstairs and walk him and the chief through the evening's events. Roelke went too. Chloe talked. He eyed the smoke patterns on the walls and ceiling, the charring on the wooden cabinet, the scraps of oily rags.

When Chloe and Hoff had shared all they knew, the chief thanked them. "We'll call if we have any more questions, Miss Ellefson. Director Hoff, we'll need a list of everyone who was in the building today—teachers, students..."

Roelke took Chloe's hand. "Come on. I'm going to walk you back to Sigrid's place."

"I've got the car."

"Then I'll *drive* you back." The point was, he wasn't letting her out of his sight until she was safely inside.

At the car, Chloe slid into the passenger's seat and slammed the door. "Someone set that fire and locked me in."

"I believe you." Roelke didn't want to believe it, because the very thought sucked all the air from his lungs. But he did. "Fasten your seat belt."

Chloe did. "I think someone snuck into the classroom and left oily rags in a spot where they might spontaneously combust. Maybe they did that when everyone was taking a supper break."

"But there'd be no way to predict when, or even if, the rags would burst into flames," Roelke mused as he pulled away from the curb. "And if the bastard actually crept upstairs to toss a match into the can, he would have seen you."

"I *did* take a bathroom break," Chloe reminded him. "That might be when Sigrid's last students left, not realizing I was still around. Or maybe they left earlier and I didn't notice. Anyway, in theory, an arsonist did have enough time to toss in a match, leave the can lid ajar so the fire got a bit of oxygen, and disappear before I went back into the room. It's also at least possible that if he waited around, he could have closed and wedged the classroom door without me noticing. I was in the zone."

"If he tossed a match on the rags while you were in the ladies' room, the fire would have started at once." Roelke tried to think of everything he'd heard about arson. "Maybe he used a cigarette as a fuse, or something similar that would burn down more slowly and give you a chance to get back inside before the rags caught."

"I smelled smoke almost right away after I got back to the classroom, so that might be it," Chloe said. "I suppose the arsonist could have been one of Sigrid's students."

Roelke didn't know anything about any of Sigrid's students, so he set that possibility aside. "But assume, for now, that this guy was hanging around. Wouldn't Sigrid's students have run into him when they left?"

Chloe shook her head. "Not necessarily. Most people use the elevator, and he could have been in the stairwell. Also, the layout up on that floor is sort of circular. I got out through a little hallway at the back of the building. It leads past a couple of offices and into the textile classroom, and on to the front hall. A bunch of looms are in that room. If someone had wanted a place to lie low, waiting for opportunity, it wouldn't have been hard to hide in there."

"It was someone who knows the building well, then." They'd reached Sigrid's house. Roelke parked and reached for Chloe's hand.

"I suppose so."

Roelke stared at the porch blindly, visualizing an arsonist's path. "Once you were focused on fighting the fire, he could have waited until you tried the door before removing the wedge. Same thing on the outside. If he'd crept up the fire escape, he could have listened for you to try the emergency exit door and *then* removed a wedge before—"

"You're hurting my fingers." Chloe pulled her fingers from his.

"The investigator must have spotted something suspicious. He may not be able to prove that someone wedged the doors shut, but he'll be able to tell if arson was involved. If someone splashed linseed oil about, traces will be left. It would burn into the floor."

"Let's talk more about this tomorrow, OK? I'm exhausted."

"Sure."

"And Roelke? I am sorry about the way our conversation ended earlier, when we were up on Emil's hill."

"Me too."

She leaned against him. "Breakfast tomorrow?"

"I'm counting on it." He didn't know whether to feel touched or alarmed by her sudden willingness to rise before dawn. "I will meet you here, though." He wasn't going to accept any arguments about that. No way was he going to let her walk even a few blocks alone, in the dark. Not until they knew what the hell was going on.

TWENTY-THREE

REASSURING MOM, SIGRID, AND Violet that she was truly all right kept Chloe up for an hour. Memories of flames and smoke, stinging eyes and locked doors, kept Chloe awake into the wee hours.

Why would someone want to scare her? Or even … well, best not to ride that train any farther. But the key question remained: *Why?*

Maybe I wasn't the target, she thought. Maybe I was collateral damage. But if someone wasn't after me …

That suspicion produced a new wave of anxiety. She thrashed about for a long while before finally sliding into a fitful sleep.

When her alarm buzzed she opened one eye, shut it again. It was cold. It was dark. Finally, moaning under her breath, she forced herself to throw off the down comforter, dress, and face the day.

Roelke had promised to meet her on the front porch, but when she turned on the outside light and peeked through the window, she saw no one. Well, I'm not going to cower inside like a frightened child, she thought. She flicked the light off again, stepped outside, and eased the front door closed behind her.

Then she turned—and kicked something that hadn't been there the night before. Something that rattled across the porch and down the steps. The clatter inspired the German shepherd next door to a frenzied barking that suggested armageddon, right here, right now.

It took a moment for Chloe's spiked heart rate to succumb to cardiac gravity. When it settled back to a sustainable pace, she tried to find in the pre-dawn gloom whatever she'd stumbled over. She finally spotted a wooden canister, four inches in diameter and six or eight inches long. A loop of twine was attached to a cap at one end. A wicked metal spike protruded from its other end, which was charred.

She jerked away as if it might leap to life and attack. This was *not* good.

Still, she couldn't let the thing lie there. She crept down the steps and crouched to get a better look. The tube had been carved with two symbols: a mitten and a bonfire. She sucked in a steadying lungful of cold air, picked up the tube—and instantly felt a wave of hot black anger reverberate from the wood, through the thick wool of her mittens, into her hand. "Oh, *shit*," she whispered, dropping the tube again.

"Chloe?" Sigrid appeared at the front door, wearing fleecy slippers, long wool robe, and an expression of sleepy confusion. "I heard a racket."

"Chloe?" Roelke turned onto the front walk, wearing boots, parka, and an expression of annoyance. "I told you to wait for me inside."

Chloe looked from one to the other. "I—um—I'm sorry I woke you, Aunt Sigrid," she stammered. "And Roelke, I just stepped out on the porch. And I found this." She gave Roelke a meaningful look, pointing. Instant understanding flashed in his eyes.

"Why...it's a *budstikke!*" Sigrid sounded intrigued. "An antique, by the looks of it. I do hope it wasn't jammed into my front door, though."

"It was on the doormat." Chloe bit back a warning as Roelke picked the horrid thing up, using the tips of his gloved fingers.

His face was hard, but he kept his voice level. "Why don't we go inside."

The three of them settled into the parlor. "May I?" Roelke asked. Without waiting for an answer, he eased off the tube's snug cap and upended it over one still-gloved palm. A small carved goat slid free.

Chloe flinched. Sigrid clapped her hands like a delighted child. "It must be for you, Chloe. Last night Adelle mentioned how much she enjoyed your visit. She said she wanted to give you one of her carvings."

Chloe swallowed hard and tried to smile. "Maybe Tom brought it over after we'd all gone to bed."

"That's just the kind of thing that would make Adelle laugh." Sigrid yawned. "I'll see you early birds later." She patted Chloe's cheek before heading back up the stairs.

"Let's get out of here," Chloe muttered to Roelke.

"Wait." He tipped his head, making sure Sigrid was out of earshot, before poking a finger into the tube and fishing out a piece of paper rolled inside. He held it out for inspection. Someone had written two sentences in flowery cursive: *These are the days of Thor. Beware the power of darkness.*

Chloe felt ice crystals form in her bloodstream.

Roelke gave her a level look. "Do you know what *that's* supposed to mean?"

She wished mightily that she'd never heard of Thor and his damn Christmas goat. This carved goat was charming—just as charming as all the *nisser* she'd seen at the Rimestad home. Still, there was something seriously malevolent about the whole thing. Maybe it was faint ripples from her traumatic childhood incident. Maybe it was the surprise of literally stumbling over the *budstikke* in the dark. Or maybe whoever had left this little trinket was so evil that he or she had imbued the thing with bad ju-ju.

Roelke jiggled one knee up and down impatiently. "What?"

"Please, let's go. We can talk over coffee." She stood and zipped up her coat.

Fifteen minutes later they were settled into the corner booth at the café. Roelke returned Chloe's palm-out gesture while he ordered a healthy breakfast for them both.

"And some almond pastry," Chloe called after the waitress.

Roelke frowned. "You really need to eat better."

"I usually eat OK these days," she objected. "I only eat pastry when I'm stressed. You didn't have to order for me. I would have made up for it at lunchtime."

"My grandmother used to say that sometimes, the only thing you can do for someone you care about is make sure they eat a good meal."

Someone you care about. Jeez, that sounded good—especially in the middle of a week that was proving worse than her wildest imaginings. She opened her mouth to say something mushy.

"Tell me what you know about that goat," Roelke said crisply.

The goat. Right. Chloe took a fortifying swig of a dark roast and felt marginally ready to wade back into the mess. "OK, let's back up," she said. "I talked to Nika last night—remember my intern? Anyway, she did some research and came up with a nasty little tidbit about *budstikker.*" Chloe had no trouble reciting from memory. "A cord attached to one end of the *budstikke,* and a scorch mark on the other, reminded people that disobeying a summons would result in men being hanged and women being burned out of their homes." That reference to burning made her skin prickle.

Roelke's grim expression didn't waver. "I do not like what I'm hearing."

"If the message tube came from a collector, maybe the telling details—the scorch mark, and the cord—don't have any significance. Maybe the Rimestads *did* mean it to be a gift honoring old customs. Or maybe one of Sigrid's Norske neighbors is getting into the holiday spirit by sending party invitations in medieval fashion, and doesn't understand the symbolism."

"Or," Roelke countered, "the cord and scorch mark might have been part of the message."

Chloe thought about the other three women asleep inside when the cylinder had been left, and slumped against worn leather.

"What about those carved symbols?"

"They remind me of what we saw on that calendar stick. A mitten to signify winter, and … maybe the bonfire signifies the solstice."

"Or arson," Roelke said. "I'm going to give this thing to Chief Moyer."

"We should at least ask Tom and Adelle Rimestad if—"

"I am giving the damn thing to Chief Moyer," Roelke growled. "It may be a joke or a gift, but it may be a threat. This is police business."

Chloe sighed reluctantly. "You're right."

The waitress arrived with their OJ and oatmeal, plus pastry and lingonberry jam. Chloe dug in. "Listen," she mumbled over a bite of pastry. "I've been thinking about what happened last night. I was driving *Mom's* car. It's possible that someone saw the car and assumed that she was the one staying late."

Roelke's jaw tightened. "I thought of that too. But why would someone want to hurt your mother?"

"I have no idea. Here's the thing, though. Maybe it's not even just my mom. Maybe it's the Sixty-Sevens. You have to admit they've had a pretty bad run of luck lately. Phyllis Hoff died of cancer. Adelle Rimestad is dying of lung disease. Petra was murdered. Someone shut my mother in the storage vault. Her classroom was set on fire. Then that damned carved goat and spooky message was delivered to Sigrid's porch, in a manner that might have been threatening. Is it possible that the killer's rage wasn't aimed at Petra specifically? Could all of the Sixty-Sevens be at risk?"

"Petra was attacked, and I believe the fire was set. But otherwise … one death from cancer, a woman dying of lung disease. You said yourself that it was likely just kids who shut your mother in the vault. And as far as I know, Lavinia's doing fine."

Chloe rubbed her forehead. She just couldn't fit the week's events into any reasonable box.

Roelke patted his coat pocket. "Does this tube look like the one Hoff got last summer?"

"No. But it's unlikely that it would. A collector would do well to find more than one."

Roelke nodded, and was silent for a moment before asking, "Can you get a list of all the Sixty-Sevens?"

Chloe thought of Sigrid's scrapbooks. "That shouldn't be a problem."

"When I give the message-thing to the local cops, I'll ask if Buzzelli can check on all of your mom's friends. Maybe someone else got a threat, or a note like this, that we're not aware of. A pattern might emerge. At this point, every lead is worth pursuing. I'll head to the PD at lunchtime, so ... how 'bout we plan to meet at the afternoon break?"

"Sure."

He drained the last of his juice. "You about ready to go?"

"One more thing." Chloe twiddled her spoon. "I had an interesting visit with Edwina Ree last night." She quickly summarized Edwina's interest in and knowledge of ancient Scandinavian Christmas traditions, including the howling band of demons waiting to descend from the night sky and wreak havoc. "She used a word I wasn't familiar with," Chloe concluded. "*Mørkemakten.* She said it referred to 'the power of darkness.' And yes, that is an exact quote."

Roelke drummed his fingers on the tabletop. "Do you think she might have something to do with that message in the tube?"

"I think it's extremely unlikely. Edwina seems to be in good shape for a woman in her nineties, but her driveway hadn't even been plowed." Chloe pictured Edwina sitting so still in her old parlor, tipping her head slightly from time to time, listening ...

Chloe shivered once, shaking off the notion of phantoms and ghoulies. Forget the mythology, she ordered herself. Concentrate on the here and now. "There was a set of tire tracks in the snow, so I suppose it's possible that she's more mobile than it appeared. But why would Edwina Ree want to leave a threat?"

"We don't know yet why anyone wants to threaten anybody," Roelke observed. "That's what we need to find out."

How did I get in the middle of this? Chloe thought miserably.

Roelke glanced over his shoulder, then leaned on his forearms. "Howard Hoff is still on my short list of suspects in Petra Lekstrom's murder. Chief Moyer thinks a man most likely swung that *lefse* pin. I agree with him."

"Who else is on the list?"

"As far as I know, the other men in my carving class have never been to Vesterheim before. That leaves Emil, Hoff, and Rimestad."

"Maybe you shouldn't be too quick to rule out a woman as attacker."

Roelke's eyebrows rose. "What makes you say that?"

"All the damn *julebukker* talk. Edwina believes that the disguises gave people in insular communities a rare chance to act up. She wasn't talking about whacking somebody in the head, but still … the point is that today, people with dark feelings might not have even one night to blow off steam. It made me think…" She grimaced, then came out with it. "Maybe one of the good women of Decorah isn't quite as genteel as we think."

‌⁂

"It's a what?" Buzzelli asked, staring at the antique Roelke had placed on his desk. It was a little after noon, and a half-eaten ham and cheese sandwich lay on a napkin in front of the investigator. Chief Moyer was out, so Roelke had brought Buzzelli up to speed.

"A *budstikke*." Roelke flipped his notebook open to the page where he'd had Chloe print the word. "I haven't seen the one Hoff got last summer, but from what I've heard, that one was carved with acanthus vines instead of just these little symbols. Plus no scorch mark, no cord."

Buzzelli leaned back in his chair. "Almost six months have passed since Hoff got his threat. And that one was specifically addressed to him, about a conflict that, frankly, disappeared when Miss Lekstrom died. Other than using these wooden things for delivery, I don't see a direct connection."

"I don't either, but maybe Petra Lekstrom's murder was not an isolated incident," Roelke said carefully. "A number of painters have experienced health problems or other bad luck. I can get you a list of the other local women in that group, if you'd like."

Buzzelli picked up his sandwich. "I think this line of thinking is a waste of time."

"I'm a belt-and-suspenders kind of guy," Roelke said. "Can't be too careful."

The investigator gave one firm, negative headshake. "My priority is solving the Lekstrom murder. I have limited resources. Unless you can give me some real evidence that anyone else is being threatened, I can't justify the time it would take to track those other women down."

"Okey-dokey," Roelke said, still aiming for that *I'm an easy-going colleague with no wish to get in your way* tone. He got to his feet. "See you around."

When the afternoon break came, Chloe was so eager to meet up with Roelke that she bypassed the tray of *krumkakke* left in the lounge. In truth, though, it wasn't just the goodies she wanted to avoid. The Beginning Telemark class had moved to the textile room, and she had no wish to glimpse the fire-scarred classroom they'd vacated even through the oh-so-thick glass window. It was bad enough that the whole building stank of oily smoke.

On the first floor, Roelke treated her to a kiss before murmuring, "Want to take a quick walk? I'll fill you in on my noon visit to the PD."

"Can we go to the museum? I want to look at something."

They didn't bother with coats, and Roelke kept an arm over her shoulders as they strode down the block. Chloe wasn't sure if he was trying to keep her warm, feeling overprotective, or indulging in actual couple stuff. Whatever the motivation, she was happy to go with it.

"Investigator Buzzelli doesn't see a connection between the message cylinder left on Sigrid's porch and the Lekstrom investigation," Roelke told her.

"It's not his mother who might be a target," Chloe muttered.

"We can pursue it ourselves."

"Fine," Chloe said. "I'll start checking in with the other Sixty-Sevens." She wasn't exactly sure how she was going to do that, but she'd figure something out.

"I'm planning to visit Hoff at home this evening. I want to see him away from his work environment."

"I hate to think what might have happened if Howard hadn't come by right when he did last night," Chloe said. "He knew where the phone was, and the fire extinguishers." She hesitated. "But on the other hand..."

"On the other hand, he showed up at quite a convenient time," Roelke finished.

And Howard was actually the reason she'd suggested this little excursion. She felt idiotic for trying to channel some inner Nancy Drew. Still, she felt better for doing *something*.

They'd reached the museum building. "What do you want to see?" Roelke asked.

"I want to go back to the Norwegian House."

Roelke frowned. "That is not a good idea."

"Probably not," she admitted. "But I had a strange conversation with Howard yesterday. He'd just hired a professional crew to come in and clean up, and was worried about protecting the artifacts, but when I offered to talk to them, he declined. In fact, he rather forcefully refused."

"So?"

"So, Howard hasn't hesitated to ask me for all kinds of favors this week. Why not accept my help? I was relieved, but now it makes me wonder. What if there's something in the Norwegian House he didn't want me to see?"

"What could that possibly be?" Roelke asked in an undertone. "You can be sure that cops crawled over every inch of the place."

Chloe gave the volunteer greeter a friendly wave before tugging Roelke through the lobby. He was right, of course. There couldn't possibly be anything helpful to see or find in the Norwegian House exhibit. But she felt compelled to try.

As they walked in, it was impossible not to flash back to the moment she'd found Petra in the trunk. Although most signs of the investigation had been removed, the absence of that trunk was itself glaring. Two nearby blue wallboards had been replaced with raw planks. Chloe pointed at the pale scar. "Why would they take …" she began, then let the question fade away. She didn't need Roelke's *I'd rather not spell things out for you* look to figure it out. The cops must have found traces of Petra's blood on the wall.

Chloe turned away. If there was something here Howard hadn't wanted her to see, what could it possibly be? Think, she told herself. Look hard.

She prowled through the rooms with Roelke a silent escort. Nothing suspicious presented itself. Finally he said, "We better head back."

Chloe took one last look around. "I wish it hadn't happened here. Most of these pieces came from Norway. Look at the sun motifs on that tankard! I think that's where Vesterheim's logo comes from."

"Un-hunh."

"And *geez*, that's magnificent." She pointed at a massive cupboard painted with Biblical scenes. Ornate woodwork panels added to the overall artistry. "Look at the carving."

"It's great," Roelke said, "but it's *acanthus* carving."

Chloe interpreted that observation as *What it's **not** is chip carving, which is what **I'm** interested in, and by the way class has no doubt started again and I really want to get back.*

"Just a sec," she promised, skimming the interpretive label. "This says that someone once covered all the religious scenes with black paint. Whoever would have...?"

But even as she speculated, she flashed on an image of Edwina Ree speaking softly of *mørkemakten.* The power of darkness. Which, Chloe thought, is evidently as much a part of my cultural heritage as almond cookies and rose painting. Maybe the long-gone person who'd slapped black paint on the cupboard had valued darkness more than religious motifs—

"You coming?" Roelke stood at the door, all but tapping his toe with impatience.

A shiver iced Chloe's spine. Then she stiffened that spine, physically and metaphorically. Someone had killed Petra Lekstrom. That same someone might be threatening Mom and her friends. That same someone had most likely set the fire that had scared the living bejeebers out of *her.*

The darkness can be banished, she vowed silently, sending the mental message toward whomever needed to hear it. I don't for a minute believe some shrieking Scandinavian banshees are bringing evil to Decorah. You have pissed me off, and you're pissing off my gentleman companion/personal cop, and you *will* be punished.

TWENTY-FOUR

AT THE END OF the day, Roelke looked up Hoff's address in the phone book and walked three blocks. After his near-disaster while skulking around the Rimestad house, he was going for straightforward with the museum director.

Hoff lived in an old two-story home in the historic district. Chloe would have rattled off some fancy architectural term, but the label that came to Roelke's mind was "depressing." The bricks were dark red; the shutters, black. Hoff had done nothing to brighten the winter night with Christmas cheer. The only decoration in sight was a two-foot straw goat plunked in the snow near the front door. Roelke, remembering Chloe's reaction to the goat-people who'd shown up in the café, shook his head. Weird shit. To each his own, but if ethnic traditions were to be part of Christmas, he'd choose the Germans' St. Nicholas customs any day.

Roelke knocked firmly on the front door. A moment later Hoff opened it. "Why … Roelke! What brings you here?"

"Sorry to bother you, but I wanted a chance to speak away from the museum." Roelke gave an exaggerated shiver and rubbed his arms: *It sure is cold out here.*

Hoff led him into the living room. "I just made a pot of coffee," Hoff said. "Want some?"

"Decaf?"

"Nope."

Unless he pulled a late work shift, Roelke avoided caffeine at night. But this was a late work shift, wasn't it? Besides, he wanted a minute or two alone. "Sure," he said. "Thanks."

After Hoff disappeared, Roelke began a quick visual study. The room seemed formal, with a marble fireplace and fancy wallpaper and furniture that looked really old. The Hoffs had clearly invested time and money in their collection of Norwegian folk art, because a lot of antiques were on display. Colorful weavings hung on the walls. Rosemaled bowls and plates sat on end tables and bookshelves—some so old that the painting was almost worn away; some glowing with vibrant reds and yellows and greens.

The room might once have had a museum quality, but it didn't now. Images flickered from a muted television sitting in front of the fireplace on a wheeled cart. Dolly Parton warbled blather about "A Hard Candy Christmas," whatever the hell that was, from a radio nearby. Newspapers, manila file folders, and mail were piled on every flat surface.

Well, hunh, Roelke thought. Evidence of a grief-stricken and overworked widower came as no surprise, but the antiques confirmed something interesting. "You've got some great stuff," he said when Hoff returned.

Hoff put steaming mugs down on a magazine. "Phyllis and I started searching out Norwegian pieces long ago," he said, considering the room with a sad eye. "It's gotten a lot harder, of course. Prices keep going up." He sat, and gestured Roelke into another chair. "Now. What can I do for you?"

Roelke waved a reassuring hand. "Nothing, sir. But I thought you should know that another one of those carved message cylinders turned up this morning."

The older man twitched with dismay. "Another *budstikke*? Dear God. Where?"

"Chloe found it on Sigrid's porch this morning," Roelke said. He felt comfortable saying that much. Buzzelli hadn't asked him to keep the "gift" quiet, and Sigrid had probably told a dozen people about it already. "I don't know if the person who left it there intended it as a threat or merely some kind of holiday greeting."

"The fire last night, and now another *budstikke*." Hoff put his elbows on his knees and sank his head into his palms for a long moment. Finally he said, "I just don't know what to think anymore. It started with Petra. *Everything* goes back to Petra."

Roelke waited, letting the silence invite confidences. He sipped his coffee, which was surprisingly good. Hoff might be falling apart—or guilty of some criminal act—but the man knew how to brew coffee.

Hoff studied a hangnail on his left thumb. "Petra," he repeated dully.

"Do you think her death might be connected with the two *budstikkes*?"

"*Budstikker*," Hoff corrected him absently. "I have no idea."

OK, this was not getting anywhere. "I can't imagine how difficult everything must be for you," Roelke said. He wasn't a warm-and-fuzzy kind of cop, but he tried hard to sound sympathetic. "You're short-staffed, you've got the workshops going on, and the big Christmas weekend coming up ... that would be enough to overwhelm anyone. Even without the murder of a colleague inside the museum."

Hoff winced, opened his mouth, closed it again. "It is overwhelming," he said at last. "I've given my all to Vesterheim, and until recently loved almost every minute of it. But now, I feel as if everything is teetering on the edge of collapse. Sometimes I just feel so desperate..."

Roelke nodded encouragingly.

But Hoff abruptly sat up straight. "Forgive me, please. Every museum director goes through hard times. Vesterheim will come through all right. It always does. Now, how are you enjoying your class?"

Roelke assured Hoff that he was enjoying the class immensely. "Emil's not just a master carver, he's a good teacher."

"It's too bad you didn't have a chance to study with his brother Oscar, too."

A perfect opening. "Emil told me about a joke he and Oscar played on Petra," Roelke said.

Hoff actually smiled. "That war of words between the painters and the carvers? It's become part of Vesterheim lore."

"It sounded as if the Bergsbakken brothers had the last laugh," Roelke said. "Unless you're aware of any animosity between Emil and Petra that emerged later...?"

"No, nothing like that," Hoff said. "I imagine Emil simply steered clear of her."

The two men chatted about Roelke's first foray into chip carving for a few more moments, but part of Roelke's brain was already processing what he'd learned. Hoff and his wife had been collecting Norwegian antiques for years, so it was possible that one or both *budstikkes (budstikker*—whatever) had come from his own collection. The radio and TV, left on even with a guest present, suggested that Hoff was afraid to be alone with himself. The way he said Petra's name, over and over, indicated the depth of Hoff's anger and frustration with the dead woman. And his use of the word "desperate"—well, that was most revealing of all. Desperation could easily fuel a fit of violent rage, and attempts to cover up afterward.

But if Hoff had killed Petra Lekstrom, where did the message tubes come in? How about the fire in Chloe's classroom? What purpose did *that* serve?

Roelke drained his coffee and stared at the mug in his hand. It was red, with the words *What part of uff-da do you not understand?* emblazoned in white. All of it! he suddenly wanted to shout. He was trying to make sense of scattered bits of information in a Norwegian world he simply did not comprehend.

"Want a warm-up?" Hoff asked.

Roelke figured he'd done all he could do for now. "No thanks. I don't want to interrupt your evening any further."

Hoff hesitated, perhaps torn between a visceral wish for company and the need to return to the open file beside his chair. Roelke decided for him by getting to his feet, shrugging into his coat, and leading the way back toward the front door.

On the far side of the entrance hall an open door led to a dining room. When Roelke glanced inside, something unexpected caught him like a fishhook and reeled him into the room. "That's a practice board on the mantel! Are you a chip carver?"

"No, no," Hoff said. "I've taken a class or two, but I don't keep up with it. I like to see how instructors work with their students. And frankly, it's been a struggle at times to keep the carving workshops afloat. They don't attract the numbers that the painting classes do."

Roelke flipped on an overhead light and walked across the room. The plank resembled the practice board he'd been making that week, with row upon row of different designs. But even to his unskilled eye, Hoff's work far outshone his own. Somehow the practice board had become a piece of folk art in its own right.

"You really should look at Phyllis's rosemaling," Howard said. "She was the family artist. Not me. See that sled?" He pointed proudly. "That's the piece that earned her a Gold Medal."

"Her painting is beautiful," Roelke said. "But since I'm taking a carving class this week, I'm sort of focused on that."

"Ah. Of course." Hoff sounded embarrassed. "Phyllis liked that board, and insisted on displaying it. I suppose now I should take it down, but ..." The words trailed away.

"I know how much work goes into even practice pieces," Roelke said, with forced heartiness. "I say, Leave it where it is." With that, he made his exit.

Outside, the wind was rising. Roelke automatically turned up his collar as he started down the sidewalk, but he scarcely noticed the cold. So Howard Hoff is a carver, he thought. Who knew?

"Howard Hoff is a carver?" Chloe repeated. She was in Sigrid's kitchen, but no one else was home.

"He is," Roelke confirmed. "So he might have carved that little goat. He tried to point my interest elsewhere, but I couldn't tell if he didn't want me to know he carved or just wanted me to admire his wife's work. In terms of the *budstikke*... is it possible to carve something today and then make it look like an antique?"

"Sure. Sandpaper, a Brillo pad, some vinegar... there are lots of ways to distress wood." She twiddled the phone cord, considering. "A conservator could tell, of course, but not your average Joe."

"Could you tell?"

"Possibly. I'm no expert in that field."

"Hunh."

She could hear Roelke thinking; picture him sitting by a phone in Emil's house, knee bouncing. "You think Howard's claim of getting that *budstikke* with the threatening note inside was just a ruse?"

"Could be," Roelke allowed. "If he attacked Petra, and panicked, he might have staged a fake threat to throw suspicion in a different direction."

"He did sort of tell me about it out of the blue," Chloe mused. "So. Maybe he made himself a *budstikke*, and—"

"Or maybe he used one he already had. His house is full of old Norwegian stuff. Is it ethical for a museum director to collect antiques?"

"Well, that's sticky," Chloe admitted. "For all we know the pieces you saw were family heirlooms, or collected during a period when he wasn't working for Vesterheim."

"The point is, Hoff might have had a couple of those antique message tubes," Roelke mused. "Or maybe he even made a couple and scuffed them up before planting one in his own office, and another on Sigrid's front porch."

Chloe hunched her shoulders. She hated thinking that Howard might do something so horrible. Hated having to think about a woman's murder. Hated having this conversation over the phone, instead of cuddled up beside Roelke…

"Chloe?"

She sighed. "I'm still here. Listen, I'm going to the Rimestads' party tonight. There's a good chance I can meet a couple more members of the Sixty-Seven Club. Do you want to come?"

He hesitated. "I asked Emil to help me with my carving, so I think I need to hang by his place this evening. You'll be safe in a crowd, though, and—"

"I'll be fine," she said, although she hadn't realized until that moment just how badly she'd wanted him to come.

"Promise me you won't walk home alone."

"I *won't*. I'll talk to you tomorrow, OK? I gotta go." Chloe hung up the phone. Stupid man. She wasn't yearning for Roelke's protection. What she wanted was something altogether different.

Well, romance was obviously not in the cards tonight. And she had work to do.

Chloe returned to the tower room and sat down on the floor by the shelf of scrapbooks. She checked the dates on each volume until she found a fat one labeled **1967**. It had been a momentous year. Yellowed articles clipped from the *Decorah Journal* described the city's first Nordic Fest and the first Exhibition of Folk Art in the Norwegian Tradition.

More pages were devoted to the inaugural rosemaling class. Sigmund Aarseth, the instructor, was a young man from Norway who wore a white shirt while painting. Several color snapshots showed the master demonstrating while students clustered around him to observe. Mom was leaning over his shoulder, wearing a truly ugly dress beneath her apron. Sigrid's cat's-eye glasses were equally ill-advised, but the photographer had captured the intensity of their interest. Chloe wondered if Sigmund had any idea how profoundly he'd inspired his students.

Chloe also found a more formal photograph with "The Sixty-Seven Club" written beneath it. The women were posed with rose-maled pieces arrayed on a table in front of them, grinning joyfully. Bingo! Chloe slipped the picture from the little black corners affixing it to the page. "Good job, Aunt Sigrid," she whispered, for the name of each student was penciled on the back. On the next page Chloe found a class list with addresses. Even better.

Some names and faces were familiar: Mom, Sigrid, Adelle, Phyllis, Petra, Lavinia. The roster also included two Decorah women Chloe hadn't met, Linda Skatrud and Peggy Nelson. The other six students had traveled from all over the country to attend that first class. Chloe copied all the names and addresses.

She still had some time before she needed to leave for the Rimestads' party, so she flipped through a few more scrapbooks. Sigrid had saved every Exhibition program, and Chloe was able to chart her and Mom's progress as they collected ribbons and points on their march toward their Gold Medals. Petra's name appeared as well, although—as Violet had said—her ribbons came with less frequency. Lavinia Carmichael's name didn't appear at all, so she evidently had never entered the Exhibition. Adelle Rimestad entered a platter in 1972. She did not earn a ribbon, and her name didn't appear in Exhibition records again.

A clock chiming in the parlor jolted Chloe from her survey. She was ready to quit. The women in the photographs looked so young, so excited. Quite the contrast from the sad and worried faces on all sides this week.

Well, except Adelle, she thought fairly. The 1967 Adelle had beamed at the photographer, brush in hand: *I am a rosemaler!* Even though life—and Petra Lekstrom—had pushed her onto a different path, Adelle had somehow maintained her sweet smile.

I'm making progress, Chloe thought. Most of the women she hadn't met were out-of-reach, but with luck, Linda and Peggy still lived in the area. If so, she might be able to learn if either of them had experienced any illnesses, accidents, or threats in the past couple of years. And with a little more luck, she might even learn what Petra had done to drive Adelle out of rosemaling altogether.

TWENTY-FIVE:
JULY, 1972

"Oh my." Adelle Rimestad stopped on the sidewalk in front of the museum and looked from her husband to her best friend. "My stomach is filled with butterflies."

"This is an exciting day," Lavinia said.

Tom kissed Adelle's cheek. "I am *so* proud of you. It took courage to enter a piece in the Exhibition. You're already a winner to me."

Adelle's nerves settled—a little. "I certainly don't expect to win a ribbon," she said. "And I *am* proud." She'd worked hard to develop all the skills Sigmund Aarseth had tried to instill during that first class five years earlier. It had been challenging, exhilarating, frustrating, rewarding. Although Lavinia had continued to attend classes, she'd never developed any interest in competing. But for Adelle, what had started as a niggle in the back of her mind became stronger as her skills developed.

I'm challenging myself, she reminded herself now. Every entrant received the judges' comments. Their advice would help her grow as a painter.

"I'm lucky to have an entourage," she said, as Tom held the door for the two women. "I've had support and encouragement from so many friends and teachers. The rosemaling community is generous." She caught Lavinia's eye. "Even Petra can be nice when she wants to be. She shared some great tips after she got back from her last class in Norway." Adelle knew that Lavinia had never warmed to Petra, but it just took a little patience to draw her out.

"You're a good soul," Tom said fondly. He often said that when he didn't agree with her outlook but didn't want to argue.

"No, really," Adelle insisted. "Petra showed me some examples of colorwork that helped me develop a fresh palette. And when I was dithering over what saying I wanted to paint around the edge of my platter, she came up with the perfect phrase."

They'd reached the Exhibition gallery. The curator, hovering near the door, shuffled through a pouch and handed Adelle a sealed envelope. "The judges' comments," he said.

"Thank you." She was already scanning the room for her piece. *Her* piece, on display in Vesterheim, part of the National Exhibition! Her heart skittered with excitement.

The curator had arranged fifty or so entries with care—some pieces were hung on walls, with others arrayed on platforms. Lavinia pointed across the room. "There it is!"

Adelle saw at once that there was indeed no ribbon hanging beside her platter. Well, that truly was all right. She saw Marit Kallerud beaming beside the blue ribbon that had just earned her a Gold Medal. Good for her, Adelle thought.

As she led Tom and Lavinia across the crowded room several conversations seemed to fade away, and that was a bit thrilling in itself. I'm being recognized as an exhibitor, she thought proudly.

Tom took several Polaroids of Adelle standing beside her platter. While waiting for the prints to develop, Adelle held up the envelope. "Let's see what the judges think," she said, feeling a little breathless. She slid one finger beneath the flap and tore it open.

Three people had judged the exhibit, and she was so excited that it took a moment to focus. "'Excellent brushwork and design,'" she read. "And ... Oh. 'Painter's understanding of color needs improvement.'" She glanced up. "Well, that's helpful to know."

"I like your color scheme just fine," Lavinia said loyally.

Adelle continued reading ... and her mouth opened with shock. Heat scalded her face.

Tom frowned. "Oh, sweetie, what?"

Adelle couldn't find words. She glanced up and saw several people watching her. Sigrid and Marit looked sympathetic. They would know, Adelle thought. Many people here—most, probably—didn't speak Norwegian. But some did.

Then Adelle spotted Petra, watching from a far corner. A little smirk turned up the corners of Petra's mouth.

Lavinia snatched the report. "What's the matter? The judges' comments are supposed to be constructive." She read in silence for a moment before her fist clenched, crumpling the page. "Petra Lekstrom," she said with quiet fury. "That *bitch*."

TWENTY-SIX

At the Rimestads' house, electric candles glowed in every window, and real ones flickered from the mantel. The house smelled of mulled wine. In the dining room, a buffet table sparkled with cut crystal and polished silver. Christmas carols played from the stereo, interrupted occasionally by impromptu performances by members of Decorah's Luren Singers. A few *julebukkers* appeared early, were quickly identified, and divested themselves of costumes to enjoy the party. Only the conversation was a bit off—more subdued than at most festive gatherings, as if the guests hoped that keeping their voices down might help Adelle conserve her strength.

Adelle didn't leave her chair, but her face glowed like the candles. "She's still beautiful, isn't she?" Sigrid whispered to Chloe. "She's so happy to be surrounded by friends."

Chloe, who was feeling sad and very un-sleuth-like, was grateful for the opening. "Other than Lavinia and you and Mom, are there other Sixty-Sevens here?"

"Well, let's see ..." Sigrid scanned the room. "Peggy Nelson's here somewhere. And I know I saw Linda Skatrud earlier—oh, there she is, collecting punch cups."

Chloe followed Linda into the kitchen and introduced herself. Linda was a sixty-ish woman wearing a gorgeous sweater. She beamed when she realized who Chloe was. "Oh, sweetie, it's good to see you. We met back when Marit won her Gold Medal, remember?"

"I do," Chloe lied, since she didn't want to hurt Linda's feelings. "How have you been?"

"Oh fine, honey. Just fine."

Chloe mentally placed a pox on Petra's killer for putting her in this position—trying to pump this nice lady for information at a Christmas party. "I'm glad to hear that," she said. "After ... well, you know."

Linda's pretty smile vanished. "Petra," she said in a clipped tone.

OK, no love lost between Linda Skatrud and Petra. "Well, yes," Chloe murmured. "But I've been a little concerned about other Sixty-Sevens too. My mom looks forward to seeing you all when she visits Decorah, and it seems as if a string of bad luck has been plaguing your group. Phyllis Hoff died of cancer, Adelle's so terribly ill, a fire started in my mom's rosemaling classroom ..." Chloe began stacking cups beside the sink with what she hoped was a sheepish shrug. "I'm not usually so superstitious, but I admit, I've started to wonder."

"Well, wonder no more," Linda said firmly. "I'm healthy as a horse, and can't remember the last time I so much as stumbled." She beamed as Lavinia entered the kitchen with an empty platter. "Some of us are doing just fine. Aren't we, Lavinia?"

"We are," Lavinia confirmed. She headed for a towering stack of cookie tins. "Heavens, I think every woman in Decorah pitched in to make this party happen for Adelle and Tom."

"People are good," Linda agreed. "Most of them, anyway. Now, Chloe." She made a shooing motion with both hands. "You go on back to the party, and let Lavinia and me take care of this."

Chloe obediently returned to the party, considering what she'd learned. Her hypothesis that someone was targeting the Sixty-Sevens appeared to be faulty. Actually, Chloe thought, I didn't learn squat from Linda.

Unless, of course, that Linda and Lavinia hadn't been targeted ... *yet*.

That thought put a snowball in the pit of Chloe's stomach. Don't speculate, she told herself. Focus on facts.

Chloe spotted her mother alone by the enormous Christmas tree, admiring the ornaments. Mom could point out Peggy Nelson and make the introductions. Maybe, Chloe thought hopefully, Mom would even be pleased that I *want* to be introduced to one of her long-time friends. She began eeling through the crowd.

Just as Chloe was about to greet Mom, she heard someone standing on the far side of the tree say "Gold Medal" in such a hushed tone that she instinctively swallowed her words. "... but at least Petra didn't have long to enjoy her Gold Medal," a woman was saying. "That doesn't make things right by you, though."

"It was bad enough to miss a Medal by one point," a second female voice said bitterly, "but having to watch Petra Lekstrom prance about with *her* Medal ... that was hard to take."

That second voice was familiar: Violet Sorensen, Sigrid's daughter. Well, well, well, Chloe thought. Violet isn't quite as Zen about the whole Medal thing as she wants people to believe.

"Everyone knows you should have earned yours last summer."

"It would have been nice," Violet said. "I've never seen such quality work at the Exhibition as we saw last summer, and a blue ribbon would have meant a lot. It's gotten a lot harder to earn a Gold Medal, you know. Those early winners don't know how good they had it."

Chloe's jaw dropped. It was one thing to learn that Violet did indeed resent Petra's win, but *that* jab was unexpected.

"Oh, I know," the first woman was saying. "I wish they hadn't changed the rules last year and let Gold Medalists compete for Best of Show, too. They really should just let those old rosemalers fade away so new talent can be recognized."

Chloe wanted to reach through the pine boughs and whack Violet and her friend with a straw goat. "Old rosemalers" indeed! Those early Medal winners had struggled to learn an art when there was little support and little instruction available, and helped fuel a new revival in the process. Women like Sigrid, and Mom—

Shit. *Mom.* Chloe dared a sideways glance. Mom stood rigid, gaze fixed on the carpet, cheeks bright red, mouth a tight hard line. When Chloe reached toward her, Mom walked away.

After days of cold darkness both figurative and real, Chloe felt a welcome flush of hot anger rising inside. "Pardon me," she murmured to an older couple, causing the gentleman such a start that wine sloshed over the lip of the glass he held. Chloe made her way around the tree. Then she was upon them: Violet Sorensen and a younger woman Chloe didn't recognize.

Chloe stabbed a finger toward Violet's nose. "You are entitled to your opinions," she hissed. "But don't you *ever* diss my mother in a public place again."

Violet's eyes went wide. Her cheeks flamed. She held a glass of something alcoholic, and it shook enough to rattle the ice cubes. "Chloe, I—I—"

"And shame on you for insulting your own mother, too. You're at a party, for God's sake!" Chloe glared from Violet to her friend. "Shame on you both."

"No, I—that is—I didn't mean—"

"Save it, Violet," Chloe snapped. "The damage is done."

⚬⚬⚬

When Roelke got back to Emil's farmhouse he found the old carver just where he'd expected: sitting in his favorite chair with a carving knife in his hand. "You're back earlier than I expected," Emil said. "Did you go to the party at Tom and Adelle's place with your girl-friend?"

Roelke hung his coat on the old coat tree, hiding a wince. He knew Chloe didn't like the word "girlfriend" any more than she liked "boyfriend."

He also knew he'd disappointed Chloe by not attending the Christmas party with her, but he hoped to make it up to her with his Christmas gift . . . a gift he needed Emil's help with. "I'm not big on parties. You didn't go?" It had occurred to Roelke only after turning down Chloe's invite that Emil might not even be home.

"I'm not much on parties either. What do you think of this?" Emil showed Roelke his latest project. "Howard's daughter is getting married. I'm making a set of wedding spoons."

"Amazing," Roelke said sincerely as he plunked down into an over-stuffed chair. "Actually, I stopped by Howard Hoff's place earlier and saw a practice board he did in one of your classes. I didn't realize he was a carver."

"Oh, *ja*," Emil said. "He's taken a lot of carving classes. My brother used to teach figure carving, and Howard took that class a couple of times."

A lot of classes? Roelke thought. Figure carving classes? Interesting. Very interesting.

"Did you finish the design for your project?" Emil asked.

His project. Right. Roelke handed Emil his small wooden plate with a socket in the middle. "What do you think of this? I didn't want to start carving until you'd seen it."

Emil studied the design Roelke had carefully penciled onto the wood. "It would have been easier to pick something with straight edges," he observed.

Roelke wasn't sure if that was a condemnation or a passing observation. "I know," he admitted. "But I figured I should challenge myself while I'm here." Once at home in Palmyra, he would not have access to expert advice.

Emil extended his arm, contemplating the plate. "You got a good design here. A good balance of positive and negative space."

Roelke blew out a breath he hadn't known he was holding. "I was inspired by that trunk you showed us in the storage area. But I don't know if the design is too complex for a beginner."

"That doesn't matter if it's what you want to do. Remember, your design is nothing more than lines and triangles. You know how to carve those."

Lines and triangles, Roelke thought. He could manage that.

"You go ahead and start," Emil told him.

Roelke began sharpening his knife. Emil returned to his carving. Only the occasional metallic *ping* of the iron stove heating up broke the silence. Finally Emil said, "Are the cops gonna find that Petra Lekstrom's killer? Everybody is upset."

"The local cops can't tell me much," Roelke allowed, "but I think they're making progress."

"It's terrible," Emil muttered. "Very sad."

Roelke wished he had more tangible proof of progress. "Chloe and I are following a few leads too."

Emil's hands stilled. "Sometimes I think there is a darkness in Decorah."

Roelke shot a sideways glance at Emil. What the hell did that mean? The carver was staring at the front window, head slightly tipped as if listening to something beyond the frosted glass. The veiled threat left on the note inside the message tube popped into Roelke's head: *These are the days of Thor. Beware the power of darkness.*

"Emil, do you know something about the murder?" he asked. "Something you haven't told anyone?"

"I'm not the one to ask."

"Who *should* I ask?"

"Maybe you should talk to Edwina Ree. You know Edwina?"

Roelke switched mental gears, trying to keep up. "Um…no, I haven't met her. Chloe has, though. She interviewed Ms. Ree about Christmas customs."

Emil got back to work. "That old lady, she knows a lot."

"Do you think Edwina had something to do with Petra's murder?"

Emil gave him a *Don't be ridiculous* look.

"Do you think she knows who did?" Roelke persisted, trying to understand. "If so, you need to talk to the police. Or at least tell me."

"All I'm saying is, that old lady, she knows more about what happens in Decorah than anybody. If you're stuck, you should talk to her. Sometimes she knows things."

Roelke tried to remember what Chloe had said about Edwina Ree. She was quite elderly and evidently housebound by the latest snowfall. And…she'd said something ominous about darkness.

Roelke didn't realize he'd spoken the last word aloud until Emil nodded and said, "*Ja*, darkness. Especially at this time of year."

Right. According to Ms. Ree, this season of ice and darkness had long been feared. Although no way did Roelke believe that some band of howling demons had killed Petra Lekstrom.

So…who *did* kill her? His hand clenched on his knife.

"Hey, what you doing?" Emil barked. "You be careful with that. You got to honor the wood, not hack at it."

Roelke forced his fingers to relax. "Sorry. I'm just frustrated."

Emil looked Roelke in the eye. "You'll find your answers. You go at it cut by cut, piece by piece. Right now, though, you got to decide if you want to think about that Petra Lekstrom or carve. You can't do both."

"I want to carve," Roelke said. He needed a break.

The two men worked in a companionable silence broken only by the occasional gust of wind pushing against the house. When the first section of his design emerged from the wood, Roelke felt a flush of pleasure unlike any he could remember.

At 9:30 Emil put his knife away. "I'm turning in. You close the damper and switch the lights off when you come up, OK?"

"Right," Roelke said. "Good-night." He stared at his plate as Emil's footsteps faded up the stairs. *I really should just leave police work to the local guys,* he thought. *Forget about investigating a murder. Concentrate just on carving while here in Decorah.*

Except that the piece he was carving was intended for Chloe, and thinking of her reminded him that someone had set a fire in her classroom and locked her inside, and thinking of *that* made it hard to breath. His knee began to jiggle up and down. He probably should have gone to the party. Chloe wasn't the most practical person in the world. Her safety—and the safety of anyone else in Marit's circle of pals—was more important than anything else.

Roelke's hand clenched on the knife again. He hadn't known Petra Lekstrom, and a whole bunch of experienced Iowa cops were investigating her death. But someone had almost harmed Chloe. Maybe someone was trying to harm Marit and her friends, too.

He set his jaw and sent a silent message through the winter night: *I'm coming after you.*

∞

After telling off Violet for speaking about Gold Medalists with such contempt, Chloe turned her back and marched away. As well as anyone could march through a crowded living room, anyway. Needing a quiet moment or two, she headed toward the bedroom where guests had piled their coats.

"Chloe! Chloe, dear!" Sigrid was beckoning from across the room.

Lovely, Chloe thought. Just who she did *not* want to see while Violet's nastiness echoed in her ears.

Sigrid had been chatting with a petite woman with Asian features. "Chloe, this is Peggy Nelson." Sigrid beamed. "Peggy, this is Marit's daughter."

Chloe liked to think of herself as beyond stereotypical expectations, but she found herself stammering as helplessly as Violet had two minutes earlier. "You—you're—that is, I'm glad to, um, meet you."

"You look surprised." Peggy smiled with the kind delight of a repeated joke. "My full name is Peggy Villanueva Nelson. I met my husband, a good Iowa boy, in the Philippines during World War II."

Chloe scraped up a bit of composure. "It's a pleasure to meet you. I know my mom has really been looking forward to spending time with some of her dear friends. I hope you've been well. Mom would be terribly upset to hear any more bad news."

"Quite well, thank you—oh, please excuse me." Peggy pressed Chloe's hand lightly before joining another group of friends.

Sigrid had cocked her head to study Chloe. "Are you all right? You look ... I don't know ... flustered."

"Just tired," Chloe said. "I'm going to head back." The hell with her promise not to walk home alone.

"It's been a busy week," Sigrid agreed sympathetically. "Just be sure to say good-bye to Adelle before you leave."

Adelle still presided over the evening from her easy chair. Tom perched nearby, dividing his attention between friends and his wife. Adelle's face was drawn but her eyes lit with pleasure when Chloe sat down beside her. "It's been a lovely evening," Chloe said.

"Hasn't it?" Adelle patted Chloe's hand.

One more awkward question to ask. "Adelle, someone left a little carved goat on Sigrid's front porch this morning. I wondered if…?"

"No, honey." Adelle shook her head. "That carved goat didn't… come from me." She paused to catch her breath. "But I *do* have something for you… Tom, do you remember which one I want?"

"Of course." Tom poked through a tin basin brimming with heart-shaped baskets woven from red and white felt. Each was larger than the usual baskets made to hold bits of candy. He pulled one free and handed it to Chloe.

The soft nest held something hard and lumpy. Chloe peeked inside and gasped. "Oh, Adelle!" She lifted free one of Adelle's carved Christmas *nisser*. The elf was sitting cross-legged, holding a bowl of milk for a kitten. Both the *nisse* and the kitten seemed ready to blink their eyes and come alive.

"Do you… like it?" Adelle asked.

"I adore it!" Chloe exclaimed. "This cat looks just like my sweet little Olympia."

Tom gave his wife a *You done good* smile.

"And the wood itself is gorgeous. Is it maple?" Chloe held the carving high, admiring it from all angles. Adelle had chosen a pale wood with red, black, and brown lines wandering through the grain. "I was just telling someone the other day that maples are among my favorite trees."

"Mine too," Adelle said.

Chloe felt tears threaten. She gave Adelle and Tom each a kiss on the cheek, thanked them humbly for their kindness, and slipped away before she lost her composure altogether.

She made her way to the spare room and excavated her parka from the mound of outerwear on the bed. Then she took a moment to admire her gift again. Adelle truly was an amazing carver... beginning with her choice of material. The dark-and-light variations in the wood suggested marble.

But that's more than just the grain, Chloe thought, holding her carving closer to a lamp. That's—

Her shoulders sagged when she realized what she was seeing. Oh, *God*. She sank onto the bed, staring at the *nisse* and kitten, feeling sick. Then she scanned the room. Half a dozen more of Adelle's carvings were on display, each carved from a gorgeous piece of wood.

Why didn't I notice that when I was here before? Chloe berated herself. How could I have missed it?

She darted to the door and peeked into the hallway. No one was in sight. She closed the door, sat back down on the bed, and dialed the phone. Two minutes later she listened to an operator asking her friend Ethan if he would accept a collect call from Chloe Ellefson. "I will," he said promptly.

Chloe wished she could reach through the line and hug him. "Sorry 'bout the collect call," she said. "I'm at a friend's house."

"No problem. What's up?"

"Tell me about spalted wood."

He was silent for a moment. "Well ... it's beautiful."

"It is. But the designs are caused by a fungus, right?" She was trying to remember a long-ago lecture from their forestry school days.

"Right. Spalting in hardwoods shows up as zone lines or white rot, or sometimes as other kinds of pigmentation."

Chloe closed her eyes. "And carvers love spalted wood."

"They do," he said happily. "Coniferous trees usually show signs of brown rot, which degrades the wood too quickly for use. But I've seen some stunning pieces of spalted hardwood. I think I've got some spalted beech in the garage. Should I use it for that cookbook shelf you want me to make?"

Chloe imagined her best friend smiling with pleasure. "That would be great. But you have to be really careful when you work with spalted wood, don't you?"

Ethan's tone sobered. "Absolutely. When you sand or saw diseased wood in a closed area, you run the risk of inhaling tainted wood dust. That could be bad, but don't worry. I always wear a mask when I run the sander."

"Shit," Chloe whispered.

Silence echoed from the line. Then Ethan asked, "What's going on?"

"I'm horribly afraid that a friend of mine—" She broke off as the door opened. A man stopped abruptly, obviously startled to see her. Chloe motioned toward the coats with a *Be my guest* gesture, then turned back to the phone. "I gotta go. I'll fill you in later, OK? And Ethan ..."

"Yeah?"

"Thanks," she said, even though she wasn't feeling thankful at all.

TWENTY-SEVEN

It was still dark when Roelke came down to the kitchen the next morning, but he found a pot of coffee on the stove and a dirty cereal bowl in the sink. Emil was already out doing chores. Roelke, who was facing a long cold walk to meet Chloe, and then another back to the café, decided he had time for a splash of java himself.

Thus fortified, he went back through the main room. He'd left his boots by the front entry. As he stomped into them, he leaned against the door—and jerked away as something poked painfully into his arm.

What the hell? He flicked on a light and examined the door. Something tiny and sharp extended from the wood.

Roelke jerked the front door open and saw the *budstikke* at once. This ornately carved marvel was rectangular, with a dragon head extending from each end. This time the person who'd left it hadn't contented himself with leaving it on the porch. The sharp iron point extending from one dragon's mouth had been driven into Emil's front door with enough force to splinter through the wood.

Chloe waited for Roelke at Sigrid's house until her patience ran out—about ten minutes past their appointed meeting time—and then struck out for the café. She was too antsy to wait politely for her escort. She'd spent half the night fretting about Adelle Rimestad, and the other half wondering just how angry Violet Sorensen had been at Petra.

She spotted Roelke striding toward her as she turned onto Water Street. "Hey," she began, stopping under a lamppost. "I—"

"Why didn't you wait for me at Sigrid's place?" he demanded, breath steaming in annoyed puffs. "I told you to—"

"I didn't feel like waiting. And since you were late, I—"

"I'm late because I found another one of those damned message things this morning."

That stopped her. "You did? Where?"

"Stabbed into Emil's front door. With enough force to drive the point clear through the wood."

Through *Emil's* front door? Chloe turned that over without finding any logic. "Where is it now?"

"The cops have it. I called them and waited until the guy on duty got there. It may be nothing, but I wanted someone official to photograph the damn thing. That's why I'm late. I thought about trying to call you at Sigrid's, but I was afraid I'd wake the whole house, and—*dammit!* I hate this. I feel like we're living in dormitories."

"Yeah." Chloe kicked one boot against the other, trying to bring feeling back to numb toes. "Complete with chaperones."

"Come on." Roelke put an arm over her shoulder. "We can talk inside."

Once they were ensconced in their back corner booth at the café, Chloe regarded him. "So, tell me about the *budstikke*. Was there a message inside? A carved goat?"

"Yes to both." Roelke ran both hands through his hair. "The container was very different. More of a box than a tube, and covered with decorative carvings. Even I could see that this was very old, very valuable. Who would use something like that to send a threat?"

In spite of everything, Chloe was touched by his indignation on behalf of an artifact so ill used.

"Otherwise, it was the same routine as last time," Roelke was saying. "'These are the days of Thor. Beware the power of darkness.'"

"Scorch mark? Twine?"

"Yep."

"Emil didn't have any idea who might have left it?"

"Nope."

"What the hell is going on?" Chloe demanded in a fierce whisper. This didn't make sense. Nothing was making any sense. "Somebody is using priceless antiques to randomly threaten Norwegian-Americans?"

"Stabbing this one right through Emil's door goes beyond friendly," Roelke said. "But we don't know if they have anything to do with Petra Lekstrom's murder."

"There must be some connection," Chloe insisted.

Roelke leaned forward on his elbows. "What? What is the connection? Lekstrom was most likely attacked in a sudden burst of rage. Someone planned ahead to set a fire in your painting class-room. Your mom got shut into the vault, although we don't know if that was malicious or a prank. Howard Hoff and Emil got vague threats in these *budstikke* things. Another one was left at Sigrid's house, which might have been aimed at her, or your mother, or Violet. Or you, for that matter. If you can make any sense of all that please tell me, because I can't."

Chloe couldn't either. "The only link I can see is that everyone involved is somehow connected to Vesterheim."

"But we have no idea if other people have been threatened. Local people we don't know. People with no connection to Vesterheim."

"Wouldn't the cops tell you?"

"Not necessarily." Roelke glared at the wall. Then he pulled a stack of index cards from the pocket of his flannel shirt.

Chloe watched as he shuffled through them, frowning, shaking his head from time to time. She could feel him straining to make sense of things; to make order. She could feel his frustration. She was frustrated too. At least we can share this with each other, she thought.

The waitress delivered their breakfast and retreated. Roelke placed one card on the table. Even upside down, Chloe could read the name printed on top: Howard Hoff—Director at Vesterheim.

"Remember I told you yesterday that Hoff said he'd taken a class or two?" Roelke asked. "Well, Emil told me that Hoff took several figure carving classes from Emil's brother."

"So ... Howard really could have carved the goats himself."

"Right." Roelke put the Hoff card back into his stack.

"You got a card for Violet in there?"

Roelke rifled through like a poker dealer, extracted a card, slapped on the table. Then he looked at her, a question in his eyes.

"Violet Sorensen is not the sweet little 'nothing bothers me' Pollyanna she wants people to think she is." Chloe told him about the comments that she'd overheard at the Rimestads' party the night before. "Violet and her friend were drinking, and they got quite bitchy about the whole thing. Violet puts on a good show most of the time. However, she is *clearly* angry that she missed her Gold Medal by one point while Petra earned hers."

"Interesting." Roelke beat a thoughtful rhythm on the table. "Angry enough to kill?"

"I'm not saying that."

"I'm not either. Just speculating." The drumbeat increased in tempo.

Could Violet be capable of such a spontaneous fit of rage? Who knew? "I suppose it's possible," Chloe whispered. "Damn, I wish Mom and I weren't staying at Sigrid and Violet's house!"

"We'd have to use dynamite to get your mother out, though," Roelke agreed soberly, "especially since there aren't any hotel rooms available."

"Even without getting paranoid about Violet's emotional stability, I wish she hadn't felt compelled to demean my mother, and her own mother too. You should have seen Mom's face." Remembering made Chloe furious all over again. "I'm glad this week is almost over. Last night Violet didn't come in until the rest of us had gone to bed. But the tension in that house is going to be thick as *rømmegrøt*."

"Thick as …?"

"It's this porridge that …" Chloe waved a hand. "Never mind."

Roelke scribbled something on his Violet card. Then he shuffled through his stack and placed another on the table.

"You made a card for Edwina Ree?" Chloe protested. "Roelke, I told you, the lady is in her nineties."

"Bad people can grow old."

"I *know* that. But Edwina? Kill Petra? No." Edwina might know things Chloe didn't know—things I don't even want to know, she thought—but some strong human had driven the latest *budstikke* through Emil's door.

"I don't really see her as a suspect," Roelke admitted. "But Emil suggested that I talk with her."

"Why on earth does Emil think you should talk to Edwina?"

Roelke slipped his cards away, picked up his spoon, and dug into his oatmeal. "He said she knows more about what happens in Decorah than anyone."

"Well, that may be true," Chloe allowed. Then she slumped in her seat. "Listen, may I change the subject?"

"Sure."

Chloe told him about the gift Adelle Rimestad had given her, and her subsequent conversation with Ethan. "I'm terribly afraid that Adelle's health problem—at least some of it—came from working with the diseased wood."

"Jesus." Roelke shook his head.

"It makes my heart ache. Wouldn't it be horrible if the very thing that's brought her so much joy has contributed to her lung problems? I spent half the night trying to decide if I should say something to Tom. What if the Rimestads didn't know about the dangers, and didn't take precautions? Part of me wants to spare them any knowledge of this. But what if knowing might make a difference in her care?"

Roelke rubbed his face. Finally he said, "How about this? Talk to Lavinia. She's a good friend of Adelle's. And she's known the Rimestads a lot longer than we have."

Chloe felt the weight of solitary knowledge ease. "That's a really good idea. I'll try to catch her after classes end this afternoon."

"Maybe at lunchtime I can take you out to see Emil's carvings," Roelke said. "He's working on a set of wedding spoons that … no, wait." He shook his head. "I really should run by the police station again instead. What you overheard from Violet sheds new light on her state of mind regarding Petra Lekstrom."

"All right." Chloe felt a sense of reprieve. Wedding spoons—symbolic of romance, love, procreation? Awkward. "Don't forget, classes end early so students can attend opening festivities for the Norwegian Christmas event. They're in the Open Air Division."

He looked blank. "The Open Air Division …?"

"Remember passing a few old buildings when you came down to the collections storage building?"

"Yes." He nodded emphatically, but Chloe could tell that his mind was still on criminal activities. Life with a cop, she told herself. Bail now, or get used to it.

Well, she didn't want to bail. "I'll look for you there this afternoon," she said. "Come on. Howard's meeting all of the students in the lounge this morning."

A sleety rain pelted them as they walked to the Education Center. They joined their classmates shucking off coats, stamping slush from boots, pulling off mittens. The lounge smelled of wet wool and coffee.

Howard clapped for attention. "We've reached the last day of classes," he said with hearty good cheer that didn't match his haggard expression. "I commend all the good work you've done."

Well, Chloe thought, *most* of us did good work. God knows I haven't.

"It's been a difficult week for the museum." Howard shoved both hands into his pockets and began playing with their contents. The wrestling mice effect was distracting. Chloe tried to focus.

"Classes end at three o'clock this afternoon," Howard continued. "And our Norwegian Christmas Weekend officially begins at four. I'm afraid the weather forecast is not promising..."

Sigrid filled the silence before it became uncomfortable. "It would take more than snow to keep Norwegians indoors," she called. "And since the Christmas concert at Luther is this weekend, there are lots of visitors in town."

"Yes. So... ahem." Howard cleared his throat. "Thank you for supporting Vesterheim. We are indeed a family here."

A pretty troubled family at the moment, Chloe thought. Howard's misery made her realize just how badly she wanted Petra's murderer to be caught before she and Mom and Roelke drove away.

But time's running out for that, she thought. Time is running out fast.

TWENTY-EIGHT

"Hey, that looks real good!" Emil leaned over Roelke's shoulder late that morning, hands in his pockets, beaming his leprechaun smile. "You must have stayed up late."

Roelke considered his project with what he hoped was a critical eye. "I really want to finish the carving today."

"I think you will." Emil moved on to look at Lavinia's work.

Roelke felt a flush of pleasure. He was happy with the way his plate was turning out, and he had a plan for presenting the gift to Chloe. Some of it would depend on good luck, but this part was under his control. He liked that.

After another student called Emil away, Roelke and Lavinia worked in comfortable silence. The knife felt good in his hand. His design was emerging, tiny triangle by tiny triangle. Cut, cut, cut—pop out the chip. Cut, cut, cut—pop out the chip. Right now, there was no need to think about all the world's chaos. Right now, everything focused down to this ordered, controlled precision...

Lavinia put a hand against his arm.

"How's it going?" he asked absently, testing the knife blade against one thumb. He'd need to resharpen soon.

The hand turned into a talon. Roelke glanced up. Lavinia stared at him, eyes wide, face white, mouth opening and closing soundlessly. Her other hand clawed at her throat.

Jesus. "Medical emergency here," Roelke barked. "Emil, go call—"

"I'm a doctor." The older of the father-son team scrambled to join them. "Retired from the Iowa Lutheran ER. Lavinia, are you having trouble breathing?"

Lavinia's breathing was audible and fast, but she gave a tiny head-shake: *No.* She reached for her pen and scrawled in her notebook: *Felt wood chip go down throat with ginger ale—breathing OK—can't talk.*

Roelke glared at the offending can on the table. Emil, hovering anxiously, muttered something inaudible.

"I suspect the chip got lodged in your larynx," the doctor was saying. "You're going to be fine, but you need to go to the hospital. I'll drive you."

"I'll come too," Emil said. "It's almost noon. The rest of you—take your lunch break."

Roelke helped Lavinia into her coat. "See you later," he said firmly. She gave a shaky nod before letting the two men lead her from the room.

The other students stared at each other. Then someone whispered, "Thank God she's going to be OK," which snapped everyone else from their horrified reverie.

Roelke looked at the son. "And thank God your dad was here."

"He's handy to have around," the man agreed soberly. "Listen, everyone, we were going to invite you all to Mabe's for pizza today to celebrate such a wonderful class. I'd still like to take the rest of you out."

The other students nodded, murmured appreciation, put woodenware aside, and began bundling up and filing toward the door. "How scary for Lavinia," one of the other students muttered. "A freak accident like that."

The son turned to Roelke. "You coming?"

"Sorry," Roelke said. "I already had plans to meet someone. Thanks, though."

He waited until the hall was quiet. Then he sat back down, knee pumping like a piston. *Had* Lavinia suffered a freak accident? It would have been easy for someone to drop a wood chip into Lavinia's open can of ginger ale. Her fellow carvers had easy access, of course, but he couldn't discount the possibility of someone else slipping in. They'd all taken a mid-morning break, and staff members and the occasional curious visitor sometimes wandered through.

On the other hand, Lavinia did constantly have an open can of soda on the table. Everyone was working like mad to get as much done as possible before class ended. Chips had literally been flying. Bottom line: he had no idea if he'd just witnessed the results of a devious attack or a bizarre accident.

Roelke stewed for another few moments without getting anywhere. He glanced over his shoulder—nobody around. Then he reached into Lavinia's overflowing totebag.

He was really, really sorry that Lavinia had swallowed a wood chip. But the incident did provide the opportunity he'd been looking for all week—ever since he'd glimpsed the words "Petra Lekstrom" in Lavinia's binder. He pulled out her huge three-ring notebook, opened it to the first page, and began to read.

"Chloe, will you do me a favor?"

"Sure, Mom." It was time for the lunch break, and Chloe hadn't accomplished much that morning anyway. The progress she'd made on Wednesday night had ended when the fire started. She'd marred her tray with a dropped brush loaded with crimson paint. Her attempt to remove the unwanted streak had left a muddy blot.

"There's a small bowl in the storage area I'd like to show this afternoon, but with everyone working so hard to finish their pieces... well, *most* people are trying to finish—"

"What do you need, Mom?"

"Could you fetch the bowl and bring it here? It would take too much time to have the whole class go over to storage. I'd get it myself, but Howard's being *so* careful about having only museum professionals handle artifacts—"

"No problem." Chloe flashed a chipper smile. Mom was pretending that nothing unpleasant had happened at the Rimestads' Christmas party. Chloe had pretty much decided to go with that.

She wiped what paint smears she could from her fingers with a paper towel. The week was almost over, thank God. Mom was volunteering this afternoon at the opening Christmas Weekend festivities. Tomorrow, Mom and Sigrid would demonstrate rosemaling at the Gold Medalists' table—without Violet, who does not *have* a Medal, Chloe thought with a petty stab of satisfaction. And Sunday, she and Mom and Roelke would jump in the car and get the heck out of Dodge. Yahoo.

She ate her cheese sandwich and carrot sticks while walking to the collections storage facility, and unlocked the door with the key

Howard had entrusted to her. Mom had given her both a description of the bowl and its accession number, and it didn't take long to locate. Chloe found acid-free tissue, bubble wrap, and an appropriate box, and soon had the bowl well-packaged for its trip to the classroom.

She hesitated, once again struck with that delicious sense of privileged access. I'm entitled to look around, she thought. Howard gave me the key. Roelke's busy with cop stuff. And I am a credentialed professional.

She wandered the aisles, hands clasped behind her back. She carefully avoided the immigrant trunks, but there were plenty of other folk art treasures to admire.

Then she came to the aisle of wooden artifacts where she'd seen the calendar sticks. As she slowly walked toward the far end, she once again felt *something*, something dark, emanating from one of the shelves. She stopped where the vibe was the strongest. "Dagnabit," she muttered. The not-knowing niggled at her. She pulled on the cotton gloves she'd stuffed in her back pocket and began touching pieces, one at a time. Not this spoon... not this butter mold... definitely not the teething ring, which seemed to give off a faint but identifiable sense of joy.

She moved on to the calendar sticks. No, no,... *bingo*. The black one.

OK, this time she wouldn't just walk away. The file on this particular piece might tell its story, but she wouldn't know until she checked. Chloe gently picked up the stick and carried it—feeling something unpleasant pulsing into her palms—to a worktable with better light.

Examination, however, left her baffled. She was no expert, but she'd never seen a calendar stick completely coated in paint. And the paint had been sloppily applied, in what looked like several different layers.

"Of course it had to be black paint," she muttered. "Winter, darkness, blah, blah, blah." The universe, if trying to impress her, clearly felt she needed a metaphor of utter simplicity.

The carver had created a decorative dragon head at one end, and drilled a hole at the other end so the stick could be hung on a wall. Chloe ran a gloved finger over some of the symbols that represented either milestones in the agricultural year or saints' days. It was impossible to get a good look through the thick paint.

She turned the stick over. Both sides were carved, which was traditional—one side representing fall and winter, the other spring and summer. The allegory ended there, however, for the season of long sunny days was also coated with unrelieved black.

"So, where's your ID?" Chloe asked. Any museum piece got marked, unobtrusively but indelibly, when it was purchased or accepted from a donor. This *primstav*, however, had no accession number. And without the number, there was no way to find the stick's paper trail.

Chloe felt a moment of disappointment, followed by a sense of relief. "I tried," she told the stick, carrying it back to its place with both arms fully extended in front of her. "You'll have to keep your unhappy story to yourself."

After carefully locking the storage facility, Chloe took the bowl back to the classroom. "Here you go," she told Mom, who was writing notes on the board. "Where's everybody else? I figured people would work through lunch, this being the last day and all."

"I chased them out. Most of my students have been putting in really long hours."

Chloe ground her teeth. Was that a simple observation? It didn't feel like a simple observation. It felt like one more little barb, aimed for the heart and packaged with a calm smile.

And it was just one little barb too many. "Most of your students . . . but not me, right? Isn't that what you meant?"

Mom blinked. "I said what I meant, Chloe. But since you bring it up . . . well, let's just say that I'm disappointed that you haven't seemed to appreciate the class this week. I'm sure that if Sigrid had taught this class as was planned, instead of—"

"*Mom!* This has nothing to do with Sigrid. It's just that—well, rosemaling is supposed to be enjoyable, right? I haven't gotten to the enjoyable part. I never seem to do anything right in your eyes. You volunteer me for all kinds of errands, and then you criticize me for being behind." Chloe rubbed her forehead. "This is a beginners' class, Mom, but you act as if we're all planning to enter our first pieces into competition."

Two little spots of color had blossomed on Mom's cheeks, and her voice was clipped. "I'm trying to provide a foundation, Chloe. My students can go in any direction they wish. I imagine that most will paint purely for pleasure, but two people in this class have already told me that they hope to compete one day. They won't get anywhere—and none of you will understand your choices—if you aren't introduced to proper basic techniques from the start."

"Well, maybe you should have given us more time to practice those basics before jumping into a complicated project. I would have appreciated more time to practice the fundamental strokes."

"Perhaps," Mom countered. "But I've seen students grow bored and quit rosemaling altogether if too much time is spent practicing brushwork. I try to empower beginning students by sending them home with a piece they're proud of."

"I'm not proud of mine," Chloe muttered, but she immediately regretted it. Pull it together, she ordered herself. Telling Mom how you feel is acceptable. Whining like a petulant child is not.

Mom walked from the front of the room back to Chloe's seat. Then she pulled out Gwen's empty chair and gave Chloe an *I'm waiting* look. Chloe plodded over and dropped into the chair.

Mom picked up Chloe's tray. "You haven't done your line work yet, Chloe. Perhaps you should finish the piece before declaring it a failure."

That observation reminded Chloe uncomfortably of Roelke's remark about her being a quitter. In fact, he'd said much the same thing about choosing to fail. She opened her mouth, closed it again. Evidently she was a slow learner on this point.

Her mother picked out the finest of her brushes, dipped the tip in one of the blobs on Chloe's palette, wiped off the excess. In about sixteen seconds she'd added delicate outlines and decorative flourishes to one scroll and flower. Chloe watched with amazement as the motif popped to life.

"See?" Mom said.

"That looks good," Chloe admitted. "But I ruined it, here." She pointed. "I dropped my brush the night of the fire."

Mom studied the tray. Then—a few more strokes in different colors, a bit more with the liner—and the area looked ... if not perfect, much improved.

"That's a lot better," Chloe said. "Um … thanks."

"You could have asked for my help, you know."

She just isn't going to make this easy, Chloe thought. "Yes, Mom. You're right. I should have asked for help."

"You were hedging your bets, Chloe. I think it was a lot easier to *not* ask for help. Then you could declare yourself a rosemaling disaster, with complete permission to never try again."

Chloe didn't have it in her to agree again. She tried to make do with a sigh, open for interpretation.

"Do you know what I have loved most about rosemaling?" Mom asked.

"Winning your Gold Medal."

"No." Mom stared at Chloe's tray, but her gaze had turned inward. "Every time I pick up a brush, I feel connected to the old days when skilled painters traveled through Norway's remote valleys. Rosemaling was done in the winter, so the artists probably traveled by sleigh, or perhaps just on skis. I picture isolated families welcoming the rosemaler into their dark little cabins—back in the days when most people lived in windowless houses with just an open hearth to provide warmth and light. Can you imagine what a joy it would be to have the painter at work while snow fell and wind howled? Can you imagine how people felt while watching the painter bring such vivid life and color to their world during winter's bleakest, darkest days?"

"Well … I can now," Chloe allowed.

Mom looked startled, as if she hadn't expected an answer. "No one today can truly realize how precious rosemaling was to people who had so little," she said briskly. "I know my tiny efforts will never have that kind of impact. Still, I like to think I'm honoring an important tradition."

"You are, Mom," Chloe said quietly. "You truly are." And for a moment she thought Mom might accept the compliment; might squeeze her hand and express appreciation; might even invite more confidences.

Mom picked up Chloe's second class project—the bowl that she'd barely begun. "I don't think you're going to finish this today."

So much for confidences. "No. I am definitely not going to finish that today."

Mom swiveled in her chair and pointed at the Christmas ornaments Gwen had painted. "I have a new assignment for you, Chloe. Go down to the shop, buy an ornament, and paint it. Use whatever colors appeal to you. Do anything you want. Just have fun with it."

For two seconds that promise of rosemaling freedom seemed miraculous. Then that promise of freedom turned overwhelming. Do *anything*? Chloe thought. She had no idea how to "do anything." Not even a clue. "But—"

"Is it OK if we come back in now?" one of the students asked as she hurried into the room. It was the serious young woman with long bangs, surely one of the painters who dreamed of competing one day.

"Of course!" Mom smiled serenely. "Chloe has an errand to run, but I'm ready to teach."

TWENTY-NINE

BY FOUR O'CLOCK, WHEN Chloe wandered out to the Open Air Division, the sleet had given way to an honest snowfall. That should please Howard, she thought. If it was hard to attract visitors to a museum where a murder had recently taken place, it was surely even harder to get those visitors outside and feeling festive while ice flew into their faces like birdshot.

Although one of the Decorah PD's finest was patrolling among the old buildings, and the cloudy sky lent a gray chill to the afternoon, Vesterheim's staff and volunteers had done their best. Old-fashioned lanterns hung from posts along the pathways, and more lamps glowed in cabin windows. Docents were ready to greet guests. Children pelted each other with snowballs. A group of carolers strolled among the buildings singing Norwegian favorites.

Chloe was studying a program of events when strong arms reached around her middle from behind. "Hey, you," Roelke whispered. She closed her eyes, nestling her cheek against his chin. He released her all too soon.

She turned to face him. His cheeks were ruddy from cold. Snow-flakes dusted his dark hair. God, he looked good…

"Hey," she said belatedly. The single syllable sounded husky.

The corner of his mouth quirked up, but all he said was, "What's going on?"

She waved the program. "A bunch of stuff. Volunteers in the drying shed are showing how good Norwegians sprouted barley to make Christmas beer. My mother is in the Valdres House—" she pointed to a red structure—"baking waffles. The Luren Singers are giving a concert in the Bethania Lutheran Church across the street at eight, and I thought maybe we could go to that…?" She studied his face for any sign of Norwegian burnout. "You know, something normal? It could even be like a date."

"A date sounds pretty good," he agreed.

Chloe felt a ripple of something good inside. "But first, Edwina Ree is scheduled for a storytelling session in the church in…" She checked her watch. "Well, soon. If you still want to meet her, I'll introduce you before she gets started."

As they walked across the lawn, Roelke told her what had happened with Lavinia that morning. "She swallowed a chip of wood that had landed in the open can of ginger ale. She didn't choke, but it lodged in her larynx and she couldn't speak."

"How horrid! She's OK?"

"Yeah. But you'll have to wait a day to talk with her about Adelle and that wood fungus thing. Emil said they decided to keep her in the hospital overnight to make sure there's no bleeding. Since she lives alone, I'm glad about that."

They'd reached the steps of the church. Roelke put a hand on Chloe's arm to keep her from joining the guests flowing inside.

"But there's something else. Her trip to the ER gave me a chance to look into the notebook she's kept ever since she started taking classes here way back when. One section is sort of like a journal."

"Learn anything helpful?" Chloe asked. She hated all this prying and poking, but not as much as she hated having a killer wandering around Decorah.

"I found out why Lavinia hated Petra. Adelle dreamed of entering the rosemaling competition, but it took her a while to scrape up the courage. Petra gave her a Norwegian saying to use on her piece. Does that make sense?"

Chloe nodded. "Lots of painted bowls and platters include pithy folk sayings."

"Well, evidently the phrase that Petra translated for Adelle was ever-so-slightly off. Enough to change the meaning from something pithy to something lewd. Adelle was mortified and swore she'd never paint again. Lavinia quit in solidarity."

Petra, Chloe thought, you really were quite the bitch.

Inside the church, Chloe was able to catch Edwina's eye and make introductions. "Quick question," Roelke said. "I'm unofficially consulting with the local cops about Petra Lekstrom's murder, and Emil Bergsbakken suggested that I talk with you."

"Me?" Edwina looked taken aback.

"He said you know more about what happens in Decorah than anyone."

"If I had even a *glimmer* of anything helpful, I'd have spoken with the police already." Edwina shook her head. "Poor Emil. I'm sure he was just trying to be helpful when he suggested you speak with me. Since his brother died, I'm probably the closest friend he has left." She sighed. "But while I'm flattered by his respect, I'm afraid I can't help you."

"Miss Ree?" a volunteer called. "It's time to begin."

Roelke and Chloe lingered at the back of the church for a few moments, but Chloe grew antsy as Edwina began sharing tales of ancient Norway. "…so the period we know as the Twelve Days of Christmas was once known as the Wild Hunt. During these long dark nights a band of the undead raced through the skies, looking for opportunities to harm the peasants cowering below. A foolish soul who ventured out alone might be killed outright. Even the most cautious might find the roof torn from their huts, their wells fouled with urine, or their chimneys clogged with straw."

Chloe caught Roelke's eye and jerked her head toward the door. Once outside, she tugged her wool hat over her ears and led the way down the steps. "I don't want to hear one more word about evil spirits. Let's go say hi to Mom."

"I'll catch up with you, OK?"

She eyed him with sudden suspicion. The man who'd greeted her with an embrace now look distinctly distracted. "Where are you going?"

"I just want to check something. I'll meet you back at the church before the concert."

Chloe watched him walk away. What was that all about?

Clank! Clunk! Clang! A discordant clatter made her forget her errant suitor. She winced as three *julebukkers* emerged from behind a nearby cabin wearing ridiculous costumes over their woollies. One banged a tin pan with a spoon. Visitors crowded around the trio, merrily snapping pictures.

Time to am-scray, Chloe thought. The *julebukkers* might be doing the righteous work of driving away evil spirits, but she was in no mood to watch, thanks all the same. She turned her back and headed for the Valdres House. Maybe Mom would give her a waffle or two.

The Valdres House was a slate-shingled building painted a festive red and green. It perched on a stone foundation atop the hill created when the Iowa River was diverted. Chloe found her mother sitting beside a hearth in the main room, carefully pouring batter onto an old hand-held waffle iron. She'd changed into traditional dress—not her formal *bunad*, but the striped skirt, blouse, colorful vest, and jacket that her peasant ancestors might have worn. In the dim light Chloe felt a touch woozy for a moment, as if she'd stumbled back through the centuries.

"Hey Mom," she said a little too loudly, and tried again. "This is a great house."

"That's right, you haven't seen it before." Mom smiled. "It came all the way from Norway. It's a typical Norwegian landowner's house dating back to 1795, although the covered front entry was added decades later." Balancing the iron's long handles on her knee, she extended the baking surface over the fire.

Roelke's abrupt departure and the *julebukkers'* arrival had jangled Chloe's nerves, but now she felt tight muscles slowly ease. She usually felt at home in old buildings. The furnishings here were simple but appealing. A table that folded down from the wall suggested ingenuity. A flax hackle—a bed of sharp nails used to separate plant fibers before spinning—suggested the comfort of domestic routines. Two decorated wall cupboards, one each for husband and wife to tuck treasures out of reach of childish hands, suggested tradition. The home had a good feel. And Mom did indeed offer warm, sweet waffles. Chloe munched two.

"Chloe, do you and your young man have plans for the evening?" Mom asked. "Sigrid, Howard, and I are going to the concert at the church."

"Roelke and I are going too," Chloe said, and was pleased when a real smile brightened Mom's features.

Then Mom said, "Did you remember to return that artifact bowl to storage?"

Chloe had *meant* to return the bowl after the monumental task of packing up her painting supplies and stowing them in Mom's Buick. Her cheeks warmed as she realized that the errand had slipped her mind in anticipation of meeting up with Roelke. "I was just about to," she lied.

"Please do. We're responsible for the piece until it's back where it belongs." Mom turned as two visitors wandered inside. "Welcome to Christmas at the Valdres House! People from the Valdres region knew this season as 'the strong and powerful days...'"

Chloe slipped outside, berating herself for forgetting the bowl. And just, she thought, when things with Mom were getting a teensy bit better —

"*Oh!*" As Chloe stepped from the entryway, a *julebukker* leapt from a shadowed corner and grabbed Chloe's left wrist. "Let go!" Chloe yelped. She tried to slow her suddenly racing heart and pull her hand free at the same time.

The reveler yanked her away from the door. Through a hazy twilight curtain of snowflakes Chloe saw an enormous polka-dotted housedress and—beneath a wig of black yarn and a towering fur hat that looked like something from *Dr. Zhivago*—a rubbery Satan mask, the kind that covered the wearer's whole head.

"I'm not going with you!" Chloe snapped.

The *julebukker* whipped something from behind his back and shoved it toward her. Chloe glimpsed glowing animal eyes, wicked animal teeth, wildly streaming animal hair—all evoking the childhood memory of the threatening strangers brandishing a bloody goat head on a stick. The waffles she'd just gobbled threatened a sour reappearance.

Chloe tried again to wrench away from the devil-creature. Her boots slipped over the drop-off beside the house. The *julebukker* swung her hard, like a mean child playing crack-the-whip, and released her abruptly. Chloe flew head-first toward the home's stacked-stone foundation.

⟳

Roelke walked as quickly as he dared on the slick sidewalks, head down against the wind and snow, arguing with himself. He felt bad about leaving Chloe so abruptly. Maybe he *should* have tried explaining, even brought her along. Problem was, he was planning to trespass on the Rimestads' property again. Best to go solo.

Besides, he was angry at himself for missing something. Although he'd sympathized when Chloe told him that Adelle Rimestad worked with diseased wood, he hadn't given the story his full attention. But something he'd heard Edwina Ree say in the church that evening had snapped in his brain like a rubber band: *Even the most cautious might find the roof torn from their hut, their well fouled with urine, or their chimney clogged with straw.*

The last time Roelke was here, he'd noticed that a vent leading from Adelle's workshop appeared to be blocked by a squirrel's nest. He hadn't given it another thought ... until hearing Edwina's reference to clogged chimneys. Roelke still considered Tom Rimestad a suspect in Petra Lekstrom's murder, but Chloe had described a devoted couple. The last thing Rimestad needed was any hint that his laxness in maintaining the ventilation system had contributed to Adelle's lung disease.

Lights glowed inside the Rimestad house, but the curtains were drawn. He was glad to see that the garage-side neighbors' home was dark. With any luck, their precious Muffykins was dreaming doggie dreams instead of keeping watch.

Roelke slipped down the driveway and along the side of the garage without attracting attention, canine or otherwise. He aimed his flashlight's beam at several small sticks poking from the vent. Shouldn't there have been some screen over the vent? Maybe it had fallen out. Anyway, it would take just a quick moment to clear the vent. His good deed for the day, and no one would be the wiser.

The vent was too high for him to reach, but Tom had stacked some cinder blocks beside the garage to keep his trashcans out of the snow. Quickly, silently, Roelke moved enough of the blocks to provide the boost he needed.

Closer now, he grabbed one of the sticks and poked it tentatively into the open space. The stick did not meet the soft flesh of a slumbering mammal.

It did, however, hit something hard and unyielding with a tinny thump. What the hell? Roelke reached one gloved hand above his head, into the vent. His fingers met the same obstruction—something hard and flat where nothing hard and flat should be.

His good neighbor vibe disappeared and his senses crackled to full alert. He stepped back to the walkway and added the last of the cinderblocks to his makeshift step. Once he'd balanced on top of the pile, he braced his left hand against the garage wall and held his flashlight in his right. He rose slowly on tiptoes and peered into the vent.

There *was* no vent. A metal plate had been pressed into the shaft, completely sealing it about six inches in. The plate had been there long enough to obtain a layer of rust.

Jesus, Roelke thought. Who would have sealed the vent?

Maybe Tom had when Adelle stopped carving. Except … Chloe had said that Adelle still visited her workshop on good days.

All right, maybe the plate had been intended to be adjustable—closed when the workshop was not in use, open when it was needed. Except … he couldn't see any sign that the plate had ever moved. The metal had been cut slightly larger than the vent pipe, and when pressed into place, the edges had folded back in right angles. There was no handle, no visible way to move or remove it.

Roelke stepped back down and restored the cinder blocks and trashcans to their original position. He walked back down the driveway undetected. With a bit more luck the falling snow would erase his tracks.

His thoughts buzzed as he turned toward the downtown. Who had converted the Rimestad garage into Adelle's workshop? Had Tom cut corners and done the work himself instead of hiring a professional? Had he inexplicably done something that allowed for the vent cover to wedge itself closed? *Or,* had someone who wanted to harm Adelle Rimestad done that deliberately?

If that were the case, who was behind it? Men were most likely to strike hard and fast; women most likely to kill with poison. Wood fungus was an unusual poison, but according to Chloe, poison nonetheless. He remembered that after interviewing Edwina Ree, Chloe had advised against ruling women off the list of suspects. Something about *julebukkers* and acting against expected roles.

Had a woman blocked the vent? What woman hated Adelle Rimestad so much that she'd try to poison her this way? Could it have been Petra? By all accounts, Ms. Lekstrom had been meanness incarnate. And what about Violet Sorensen? Based on what Chloe had overheard, Sigrid's daughter wasn't the sweet daughter of Decorah she presented herself to be—

Roelke skidded on an ice glare. After regaining his footing he forced himself to slow down, physically and mentally. If someone did bear a grudge against Adelle—and he had no idea why anyone would—messing with ventilation was a pretty iffy way to do damage. Still …

He turned onto Water Street. He could see the museum buildings through the falling snow. His hands clenched and unclenched. He *should* go find Chloe. She might be pissed at him for running off.

But his head felt ready to explode with what-ifs and wild theories. Maybe he'd gone completely off his rocker. Maybe he'd completely misconstrued what he'd seen. He could try talking it through with Chloe, but she knew less about the situation than he did. And he didn't have enough to go to the police. He had absolutely nothing except worries and hunches and wild-ass guesses.

I need facts, Roelke thought. And short of knocking on the Rimestads' door and asking, he wasn't sure how to get them.

Unless ... maybe Emil would remember who had designed and constructed the workshop. As Roelke approached Vesterheim he looked for Emil's pickup, but his favorite parking spot on the corner was empty. Damn.

Well, Emil had probably headed for home as soon as class ended. It had been a long week. And unless he was talking woodcarving, Emil wasn't comfortable in crowds.

Roelke stepped under a streetlamp and checked his watch. If he booked it, he would have just enough time before the concert to get to Emil's farm and back on foot.

THIRTY

THE *JULEBUKKER* FLUNG CHLOE at the stone wall as if she were a bale of hay. Instinct brought her forearms up to protect her face. Even through her thick sweater and parka, the slam knocked the breath from her lungs and brought tears of pain to her eyes. A rough stone grabbed her hat as her head grazed the foundation. She fell hard, skidding, her cheek smacking snow with a shock of bare skin against gritty ice crystals.

Rage almost propelled her upwards but the terrain was too slick, too steep. She began tumbling down the slope, breaking through the sleet-glazed crust all the way. Her scrabbling hands found only fistfuls of snow. In the jumble she heard the carolers' harmony drifting from somewhere nearby, children laughing, perhaps even the calm hum of her mother's voice chatting with guests inside the Valdres House. And she heard snow crunch as she thudded to a stop.

A final frisson of pain rattled her bones. She struggled to catch her breath, gingerly testing each limb to see if it still worked. My skull could have cracked like an egg, she thought. The image made her woozy, and she decided to lie in the snow a moment longer.

The wet cold soaking through denim became the most urgent discomfort. With effort she managed to roll onto her hands and knees. When she crawled away from the hill, she found herself staring at the knees of two elderly visitors. "Are you all right?" a woman asked.

Chloe staggered to her feet, panting as if she'd just skied the Birkie. "Did you *see* that guy?"

"What guy was that, dear?"

Chloe squinted at the hill, then looked around the lower grounds. There was no sign of the creature who'd flung her down like a sack of flour. Guests still wandered. Carolers still sang. Lamps still glowed. She could see at least a dozen *julebukkers* now. Two carried wooden goat heads mounted on poles. Several had grabbed the hands of laughing visitors to form a torch-lit parade. Chloe did not see a creature in yarn wig and Cossack hat, but the darkness, the closely situated buildings and changing terrain made it impossible to see everywhere.

The older couple still peered at her with concern. "Never mind," she said. "I'm fine. I just ... um ... slipped."

"It's getting treacherous," the gentleman agreed. "The wind's picking up, too. We're heading back to our car."

Chloe slapped snow from her clothes as she tried to figure out what had just happened. Could someone actually have attacked her right in the middle of the festivities?

Damn straight.

She marched indignantly through the grounds, looking for the nice young police officer she'd noticed earlier. She wanted to make him go find the SOB who'd grabbed her.

Although ... what could she say, really? A guy dressed up in crazy costume—like all the others out there entertaining guests—had gotten too rambunctious? Come to think of it, she wasn't positive her *julebukker* was a guy. The grip on her wrist had felt like iron, but she'd been taken by surprise, and everything had happened in a blur.

Her steps slowed, then stopped. Am I losing it? she asked herself. Did the week's events make me see a demon in an overzealous high school kid enjoying the excuse to act out? Are my nerves so frazzled that I can't tell the difference between holiday fun and evil intent?

According to Edwina, however, holiday fun and evil intent arrived hand-in-hand in Scandi-land this time of year.

Lovely. Chloe wished Roelke hadn't disappeared, and then she wished she hadn't wished that, because she really didn't want to be a needy kind of girl. Maybe a middle course was best: tell the officer what had happened, but without hysterics.

OK, she thought. You've got a cop to find and an artifact bowl to return to the storage building. Get moving.

※

Roelke walked north and east to the sound of boots crunching snow and shovels scraping sidewalks. A few cars passed, moving slowly, throwing fans of slush. The wind drove snowflakes almost sideways through the cones of light cast by street lamps. This may not have been my best-ever idea, Roelke thought as he approached the Upper

Iowa River bridge. He was dressed well for wintry weather, but the snow was slowing him down. Best try to pick up the pace.

Good plan, but he'd no more than tromped onto the bridge when both feet flew out from under him. He landed, once again, on his ass. "Danger," he muttered as he clambered to his feet. "Bridge surface may freeze before road."

There were no lampposts on the bridge. He dug his flashlight from his pocket and scanned the single traffic lane, hoping to identify any additional icy spots. There was nothing to see but snow and the twin ruts of tire tracks. He set out again, this time keeping a hand on the railing.

He was halfway across the narrow bridge when headlights appeared ahead. A car was approaching the bridge, too fast. "Slow down," Roelke muttered. "Slow *down*. Slow down, Goddammit!"

The car didn't slow down. As it hit the bridge the yellow beams went crazy, slicing the snow-hazy night. The vehicle was a dark blur, whirling, sliding, coming his way—*Christ Almighty*—coming his way and there was nowhere to *go*, nowhere to go. The bridge railing bore into Roelke's hip until something had to give, bone or iron, and the car kept coming.

Roelke leaned out over the river, away from the speeding mass of steel. He heard the relentless *shussh* of skidding tires. The car was seconds away from crushing him.

Instinct pushed him over the railing in a wild twisting scramble. He managed to catch one vertical iron bar with his right arm. His other arm shot around too, and he clenched his right elbow with his left hand. The car hit the railing inches beyond the spot where he now dangled. The bridge shuddered. Roelke clenched every muscle. The car fish-tailed once or twice before the driver was able to straighten it out.

Then the car accelerated on toward town. Roelke watched the taillights disappear with stunned disbelief and rising fury.

But there was no time for that now. He was dangling in the snowy dark above the Upper Iowa River, hugging an iron post which dug painfully into his arm. His muscles were already starting to twitch. He had to get back on the bridge.

Roelke tried bringing one leg up and over, but he needed more momentum to make contact. OK, Plan B. He allowed himself one deep inhale and exhale before he deliberately began to swing. Back and forth, back and forth, each movement shooting arrows of pain through his arms. Finally he flung himself sideways and up, quivering with effort, right leg straining to reach over solid iron.

He didn't make it. His legs dropped again with a wrench that shot a groan through gritted teeth. He was still dangling.

Damn, he thought. This is bad. He was aware of the trembling pain in his arms; the ache in his left hand straining to stay locked on the elbow through leather glove and slick nylon sleeve.

He looked down but saw only whirling snow. How far was the drop? Twenty, maybe twenty-five feet? How deep was the water? How thick was the ice? He tried to remember what he'd seen in daylight. His brain felt like slush.

Plan C is to hang on, he told himself. Someone will come. Any minute.

God, his arms ached. Shouldn't *somebody* be driving home right about now? Why wasn't anyone coming?

He tried to prepare for Plan D, a drop to the river. It was actually a pretty piss-poor plan. The fall could kill him outright, and if he broke through the ice, the river might instantly sweep him under. He tried to think of some strategy to minimize the impact. Cannonball, he decided. Going in butt-first might keep bones from snapping, might disperse water and ice most efficiently.

Roelke thought about Chloe. Her Christmas gift was in his pocket. If he froze to death or drowned, and the cops went through his things, would she understand that he'd made it for her? *Why* he'd made it for her?

No, no, *no*, he ordered himself. Don't think about that. Just hang on. And he did, for an eternity that might have lasted moments or hours.

Then his right arm spasmed. His left hand slipped, tried to re-grab the right elbow, skidded down the snow-slick sleeve instead. Both arms gave way.

I'm sorry, Chloe, he thought, and felt himself plummet.

⁂

Chloe reported the mean *julebukker* to the nice young officer as calmly as possible. And since the artifact bowl she'd borrowed for Mom was on the third floor of a now-deserted building that had been hit by an arsonist, she succumbed to the willies and asked him to accompany her inside. His earnest assurances that she was not being silly convinced her that he did think just that. She let him walk her inside the Education Center anyway, and then all the way to the collections storage building around the corner, before she thanked him effusively and sent him on his way.

She locked herself inside and turned on every light in the place. Then she carefully returned the bowl to its home, and removed the note she'd left explaining its absence.

Well, she thought, that task took all of six minutes. Maybe she should have asked the officer to wait for her. She still had time to kill before meeting Roelke. She had no wish to go back to Sigrid's house and risk running into Violet. She *really* had no wish to go back to the revelers celebrating the season pagan style in the Open Air Division.

But there was something here that still bugged her. She retrieved the painted calendar stick from its shelf, brought it back to the work-table, and sat staring at it. "There is nothing to see," she mumbled, but the piece exuded *something* unpleasant, bad ju-ju left from either the carver or someone else who'd once owned the stick. Some long-gone farmer?

Well... maybe not so long-gone. Although the black paint was scuffed, it didn't show signs of age. Which made the fact that the stick had no accession number even harder to understand. She'd glimpsed enough of Vesterheim's artifacts to know that the museum kept scrupulous track of its treasures. A new item that hadn't yet been cataloged would have been kept in a separate location.

So... this odd artifact must not be an accessioned piece.

"I don't know why Vesterheim would even want to accession a piece sloppily coated in black paint," she muttered. There might be delicate carving underneath, but it was impossible to tell. The calendar stick reminded her of the stunning cupboard she'd shown Roelke in the Norwegian House—the one with religious paintings once covered with black paint that hid the creator's Christian-themed artistry until some savvy curator-type had discovered the secret.

Chloe had grown very weary of all things evil, spooky, and dark. Without giving herself time to think she got up, found a clean cloth, and filled a plastic basin with warm water. Then she sat back down, wet the cloth, and began to rub the stick.

The paint came off more easily than she'd expected. She worked cautiously at first, on the off-chance some delicate masterwork might be hiding beneath the top coat, but there was no sign of other pigment. Soon most of the paint had been removed from both sides. She put the stick on a towel and studied it again.

"What on earth *is* this?" she demanded. The carved symbols didn't align with her understanding of seasonal events as usually depicted. She assumed the traditional carved mitten indicated the Winter side of the stick. She found a sled and a leafless tree, which seemed appropriate. A small bonfire had been etched beside it, reminding her uncomfortably of her arson misadventure and the scorched *budstikker*, but this fire probably represented the winter solstice ... except she found another one nearby, which blew that theory. One unfamiliar symbol appeared to be a ladder. Fruit picking time? The Winter side also included a few stick figures that represent saints, each noted with a single letter and a cross.

She turned the *primstav* over to the Summer side. No bonfire here. Few symbols at all, actually, and only two stick figures with letter and cross. Shouldn't there be more saints' days than that? Chloe didn't know enough about such holy days to connect martyrs with particular dates and initials, but she'd thought there were more.

She studied the dragon head carved at one end of the stick. Some might consider that an odd choice for a piece adorned with religious symbols, but Chloe wasn't surprised at the juxtaposition of Christianity and paganism. As Edwina had said, their ancestors hadn't been willing to leave centuries of superstition and tradition behind just on a minister's say-so. "Hedging their bets," Chloe murmured.

She sucked in her lower lip. The phrase had popped out unbidden, but it reminded her of something her mother had said earlier that day. *You were hedging your bets, Chloe. I think it was a lot easier to **not** ask for help. Then you could declare yourself a rosemaling disaster, with complete permission to never try again.*

"Yeah, yeah." Chloe rubbed her forehead. Something about that phrase still poked at her. Where else had she heard it recently? She closed her eyes, trying to remember. Hadn't Mom also used the phrase last Sunday? Yes, in that awful conversation about Norwegian romance she'd had in the car with Roelke. *My husband used to tease that he'd hedged his bets by carving several at once, but I know the mangle he made to propose to me was his one and only...*

A new idea flashed into Chloe's brain, so horrific that it took her breath away. She flipped the calendar stick over again and squinted at a couple of the symbols she hadn't been able to identify.

Then she stumbled to her feet so fast that her stool fell over. "*Shit,*" she breathed, backing away from the stick as if some devil's hand might snatch it and beat her senseless.

❧

Roelke knew an instant of freefall, wind racing past his cheeks, arms circling. He remembered his plan just in time to bring up his knees, pull in his arms, form himself into the human cannonball he'd perfected long-ago during lazy summer days on Wisconsin lakes.

His feet and butt hit first. The snow-covered ice gave way with a sharp crack. He plunged on through.

The shock of aching cold almost paralyzed him but the river, thank God, was only waist deep here. He began floundering toward shore, breaking ice as he went. The current pulled at legs gone numb. The ice broke sulkily, demanding that he use his weight to fracture the surface. It was painfully slow going.

Stay on your feet! he ordered himself. He stumbled on toward shore, broke more ice, went down, and gulped frigid water. He came up choking, shivering, and disoriented in the whirling snow. His bone marrow had frozen. His brain had frozen. The wind shrieked with spiteful glee, and the night was dark and formless.

THIRTY-ONE

CHLOE WANTED TO TALK to Roelke about the calendar stick. That was a bit problematic since she had no idea where he'd gone. *I can at least try Emil's number*, she thought. She dug out the appropriate scrap of paper, found a phone on the curator's desk, dialed, listened to it ring and ring and ring. After slamming the receiver back to its cradle she considered her options.

She didn't know if she was onto something important or completely crackers. She *did* know that with this new idea banging about her brain, patiently waiting for Roelke to reappear at eight o'clock was not an option.

Chloe had Mom's car keys. Mom would be at Vesterheim until after the evening concert. "All righty, then," Chloe announced. "We have a plan." Leaving the mess on the worktable—she'd confront whatever trouble she might be in later—she locked up the storage building, bundled up tight, and headed into the night.

Ten minutes later, after turning the defroster to full blast and scraping two inches of snow and a foundation of ice from the windshield, Chloe drove from the parking lot. She stopped first at the police station, hoping Roelke was talking crime with the local cops. But the station was dark, and no one answered her knock. Any officers on duty tonight were—not surprisingly—out and about.

On to Emil's, then. Chloe got back into the car and made a left turn. Visibility wasn't great, and the road conditions weren't either. You're being kinda stupid, she told herself, when the wheels briefly lost traction and spun on wet snow. What do you hope to gain by driving to Emil's place?

Well, the other side of her brain countered, maybe Roelke just got back from his mysterious errand. Or maybe he's been there all along, and just didn't *want* to answer Emil's phone. Besides... where else are you going to look for him?

Chloe had to backtrack when she missed the turn that led to the river, but in short order she approached the bridge. When her head-lights glanced over a snow-filmed caution sign, she was pretty sure of the hidden warning. "Danger," she muttered, "bridge surface may freeze before road." She stopped, straining to see beyond slapping wiper blades and swirling snow. She did not want to get partway across and then have to back off again, so she made sure that no one else had started over the single-lane span before creeping forward.

Still-visible skid marks showed where somebody had spun out. "Geez," she whispered, and gently braked to a halt. Whoever had lost control had *really* lost control. Tires moving sideways had carved large wedges in the snow. It looked as if the vehicle had hit the iron railing, too.

She was so focused on driving that she'd left the bridge before a cold finger flicked uneasily against her backbone and a stray image belatedly blipped in her consciousness. She eased onto the shoulder—hoping like crazy that she'd be able to pull out again without getting stuck—and parked the car.

When she got out the wind hit with such force that she had to squint against the driving snow. She trudged back along the bridge railing. Without the aid of her headlights she couldn't find the thing that had snagged her attention. She began kicking through the snow in the area where the worst skid tracks were.

After a few minutes her boot hit something solid. When she picked it up her blood turned to snowmelt. She'd found a flashlight. A yellow flashlight. Roelke's yellow flashlight, she was sure of it.

Chloe flicked on the light and played it over the bridge. "Roelke?" Nothing. She leaned over the railing and pointed the beam toward the river. The shaft of light showed driving snow but faded into blackness before reaching the water below. "*Roelke!*" Still no answer. He couldn't have gone over the railing... could he?

The road was empty in both directions. With a sinking sense of loneliness, Chloe struggled to decide what to do. The wind whipped past, keening like—like ...

Abruptly, she turned and slogged off the bridge. Skidding, sliding, she started down the wooded hill towards the river, yelling Roelke's name and playing the beam back and forth. Twice she stumbled. Once she fell. Her brain felt numb. All she knew to do was keep going, keep yelling, keep looking.

When the light finally caught him, her knees almost gave way with relief. Thank *God*.

But Roelke did not look good. He stood leaning against a tree, head down. And his clothes were wet. "Roelke!" she cried.

He didn't look up, just dragged one foot forward and planted it.

She floundered ahead to meet him. "What *happened*?"

"Libby?" His voice was slurred. Libby was his cousin.

Confusion—an early warning sign of hypothermia. Chloe had done her share of winter camping, and she tamped down panic and let old training kick in. "Come on, Roelke. I'll get you to the farm." She ducked under his left arm, straightened, and almost stumbled to her knees as his weight hit her shoulder. "I need your help. Come *on*!"

His violent shivers gave her hope. His body was still fighting, still trying to keep warm. But it took an eternity to get Roelke back up the hill.

When they reached the car, he sagged against the trunk while she wrenched the door open. She tugged off his sodden coat and whipped off her own. Once she'd shoved him inside she draped him with her dry down-filled parka and pointed the heater vents his way.

Please don't be stuck, she begged the Buick silently as she slid behind the wheel. She eased her foot onto the gas. The car gave one tentative lurch forward before sinking back again, rear wheels spinning. Dammit! She had to get Roelke to the farm, *now*.

"Sorry," she said, "but I need the coats." She scrambled out of the car and jammed a coat beneath each of the back tires. When she tried driving this time, rubber found nylon instead of snow. The car heaved forward and kept going. Hallelujah.

Chloe jerked the car onto the road with just one tiny skid and headed up Skyline Road. "Almost there," she told Roelke. "We'll be at Emil's farm in five minutes."

"C-cat litter," he mumbled.

"*What?*"

"In the t-trunk. D-didn't need to use our c-coats."

"OK," she said, blinking back tears. Of *course* Roelke McKenna had stowed emergency winter gear in the trunk before they set out. "Next time I'll know."

She drove up the winding hill as fast as she dared. Her headlights caught the mailbox with **Bergsbakken** still partly visible beneath the snow. She turned in and saw faint tire marks angled to the barn, but no tracks between the road and the dark house. Since she wasn't exactly sure where the drive was, she hoped for the best and plowed toward Emil's home.

Once she cut the engine she could feel her heart thudding. "We're here," she announced. "You still with me?"

He stirred. "Yeah."

"I'll come 'round and help you out."

Getting Roelke up the hill had been hard. Getting him up the front porch steps was harder. Fishing the key from his ice-crusted jeans pocket without him falling over was hardest of all. Chloe's teeth were chattering too by the time she got the door open and guided him inside.

"Geez," she exclaimed. She flipped a switch in the front hallway, instinctively seeking light.

"What?" Roelke mumbled.

First things first. "Never mind. We've got to get you warmed up." She pulled him into the living room, shoved him down on the sofa, and turned on another lamp. "Get your wet stuff off. I'll go find dry clothes. Upstairs?"

He nodded "First d-door."

She pounded up the narrow stairs. There was energy in the house, stronger than usual, but she couldn't make sense of it. She gritted her teeth against the quivering sensation in her sternum, grabbed what she needed from Roelke's suitcase, and pounded back downstairs.

Roelke was still fumbling with his flannel shirt.

"Let me." She knocked his hands away, ripped open the buttons, roughly jerked off the shirt, and dried his chest and arms with a towel. "What *happened*?"

"S-some idiot hit the b-bridge too fast," Roelke managed. "Skidded. It was either g-get squashed or g-go over."

"Dear God!"

"The river's only waist-deep, but I probably w-would have frozen or drowned if I hadn't stumbled into a fallen t-tree. I m-managed to crawl onto the t-trunk."

The mental picture made Chloe's heart constrict. He's OK, she reminded herself. He's OK. She buttoned him into a dry wool shirt and pulled a thick sweater on over that. "Better?"

"Much."

Chloe crouched at Roelke's feet and tugged off soaking boots and socks. She didn't see any sign of frostbite on his toes, thank God. Then she reached for the zipper on his jeans.

"Chloe?" he said. "I th-thought you weren't r-ready for this."

A hiccup of hysteria popped out. "Roelke …"

With an obvious effort he pushed up from the sofa. "Go away. I can do it."

Chloe stood and turned her back. Unoccupied, the emotive energy lingering in the house struck her again. It was still difficult to sort through the jumble. Hope … happiness … something dark, too. Normal for any old house, she reminded herself. Maybe her anxiety was increasing her reception.

"You need help?" she called over her shoulder.

"No." Roelke's voice was blessedly stronger already. "Did you bring socks down?"

"I—um—no. I will." She dashed back up the stairs. *Something in Emil Bergsbakken's house was off-kilter.* That sense was stronger on the second floor. But all that really mattered right now was making sure that Roelke was truly all right.

Back downstairs, she threw the socks at him. "Put all the socks on, one over another. We're leaving."

Roelke looked bewildered. "I was hoping you'd make some hot tea."

"I want a doctor to check you out."

"I don't need—"

"I don't care what you think you don't need. We're going back to Decorah."

He tugged on three layers of socks while she pulled the sodden wool liners from his boots and tossed them aside. When he jammed his feet into the boots, she laced them up tightly. "You better stay inside until I'm sure I can get the car turned around," she advised. Maybe careening blindly through the snow hadn't been the best idea after all.

Chloe ran back into the night. The cold air stole her breath. Was she being wise, or reckless? Maybe all Roelke really needed was a warm bath and hot tea …

She hesitated, shivering. Emil's farm felt many miles removed from Decorah—from anyone. Except for the lamps she'd turned on inside, she couldn't see a single light. Driving snow stung her cheeks. Ice-slick tree branches rattled.

And the wind shrieked down the hill with a wild fury that might, just might, hold unearthly laughter. Chloe froze with the same icy terror that must have seized her ancestors on restless winter nights centuries ago.

Then a blazing fury seared up inside. She planted both boots and faced the night sky. "The hell with you!" she howled back. "We are *leaving*!"

Ten minutes later she had the car turned around, the heater blasting, and Roelke wrapped in an old wool granny-square afghan and buckled in. "I was kinda in a hurry when we got here," she reminded him. "Hold on." They had to crest a rise to get back to the road, and she hit the gas.

"Jesus, Chloe!" Roelke braced himself as the car crowned the hill and skidded sideways onto the road.

"We're fine," she said, once she'd gotten the sedan pointed in the right direction. She didn't care if they slid all the way back to Decorah. She craved people. She craved lights.

Roelke took a deep breath. "What are you doing here, anyway? How did you find me?"

"I came looking. I wanted to tell you about this weird calendar stick I found. There's no identification number on it, and I have no idea why it was in the storage building, but it gave me the willies, and..." They'd reached the bridge and she stopped talking until she'd safely crossed.

"And?" he prompted.

"Roelke, under the black paint I found some symbols and these stick figures, each one with an initial and a cross. I assumed they represented saints, so at first I didn't pay much attention to the initials. But—I know this sounds crazy—there's a darkness embedded in that piece."

"What do you mean?"

"What if someone made that calendar stick as a record of people he or she has harmed in some way?"

"Who?"

"It could have been Emil. He's a carver, and he probably could have gotten his hands on a key. The carving is primitive, though."

"Emil's a possibility," Roelke said, "but not likely. None of the carvings I've seen have paint on them, and I don't know if he has it in him to do anything you'd call primitive. Maybe Tom Rimestad made the stick."

"It would have been much harder for him to come by a Vesterheim key." Chloe paused at a corner while a snow plow lumbered past. "Although—he is a Board member."

"So it wouldn't have been impossible."

"No." She eased through the intersection. "Or, maybe Howard carved it. He could get into the storage building any time he wanted to."

Roelke held his hands in front of the air vent. "Why would Hoff make a calendar stick like that and plant it on a shelf among the old stuff?"

"I have no idea," Chloe admitted. "But think about it. Howard's the one person with access to everything. He could have carved the little wooden goats and left the message tubes on Sigrid's porch and in Emil's door. Howard could have set the fire in the classroom that night, and then pretended to arrive and be the hero. And the night we arrived, he was acting very nervous even before we found Petra Lekstrom's body in that trunk, remember?"

"We do know that Hoff had motive to attack Lekstrom," Roelke admitted. "And there's one more thing."

"What?"

300

"I found a plate of solid metal earlier this evening blocking the ventilation pipe leading from Adelle Rimestad's workshop."

Something sick and frightening pooled in Chloe's belly as she took that in. "Phyllis Hoff and Petra Lekstrom are dead," she said. "Adelle is quite ill. We know Lavinia's safe in the hospital tonight, but—oh God, Roelke, what about Sigrid and my mom?"

Roelke was silent.

"Mom got locked in the vault. That threatening *budstikke* could have been intended for her, and the fire in the classroom almost certainly was." Chloe squeezed the steering wheel, fighting panic. "Are you doing OK?"

"I am," he said firmly.

Chloe thought about the maniacal *julebukker* who'd thrown her down the hill and felt the temperature drop a few degrees. "I'm stopping at Vesterheim. I want to find my mother."

They arrived back at the museum block ten minutes before closing time, but the grounds appeared deserted. Chloe parked on Mechanic Street near the collections storage building. "Why down here?" Roelke asked.

"My mom was working in the Valdres House—" Chloe pointed, although the house above was invisible in the snowy darkness— "and I want to make sure she didn't slip and fall down the drop-off. You can stay in here with the heater on."

"No way." Roelke got out of the car.

She didn't argue. He put one arm around her shoulders as they trudged through the snow toward the bottom of the steep hill, and she didn't argue with that either. He'd also taken charge of the flashlight again, playing it over the hill, the ground at the bottom.

There was no sign that Mom or anyone else had tumbled down the rise—or been slammed into the house's stone foundation.

"Let's go 'round and make our way to the top of the hill," Chloe said. "Maybe Mom's still inside the Valdres house, happily making waffles."

It took several minutes to wind through the Open Air area. Across Mill Street, light glowed from the windows of Bethania Lutheran Church as concertgoers straggled up the steps. The main museum grounds were quiet, though, with only a few sputtering torches casting wildly flickering shadows on the snow.

As Chloe and Roelke approached the Valdres House, a caped woman emerged from the small enclosed entryway. For three seconds Chloe felt relieved and foolish. She *had* been letting her imagination run wild. Mom was fine.

Then Chloe recognized Sigrid, and anxiety roared back.

"Chloe!" Sigrid met them on the path. "Do you know where your mother is? We were going to meet Howard here so we could all go over to the concert together, but the house is locked." Sigrid spread her hands, looking bewildered. "There's no sign of either of them."

THIRTY-TWO

No sign of either of them. No sign of either of them. Chloe squeezed Roelke's hand.

"Sigrid, go wait inside the church," he said in his *You will do what I say* cop tone. "We'll find Marit and Howard and join you."

"But…" Sigrid peered at them anxiously. "Where are your coats? Shouldn't *you* go—"

"We're *fine*," Chloe said. All she wanted was to get Sigrid over with the other concert-goers. "We'll be right along." She and Roelke watched until Sigrid had crossed the street and disappeared into the church.

"Where should we look?" Roelke asked grimly. "If the house is locked—"

"I've got a key." Chloe led him into the entryway. Sheltered from the wind, she worked the lock and burst into the Valdres House. "Mom? You still here?"

A gust rattled the windows. Lamps in the main room had been extinguished, but coals still glowed in the open hearth. Chloe felt a hitch in her chest and pointed at the embers. "That's not right."

"Why not?"

"Mom would never leave an historic structure without thoroughly dousing the fire." Chloe felt another hitch beneath her ribs, tighter and colder.

Two doorways led left from the living space to smaller rooms. She darted into the closest. Roelke followed, shining his flashlight beam about. A large loom took up most of the space, but a huge immigrant trunk also stood against one wall.

"Please, no," Chloe whispered, fumbling at the heavy lid with numb fingers. Roelke snatched the lid and let it bang back against the wall as he flashed the beam inside.

Mom lay in the trunk, crumpled and still.

"Go get help," Roelke ordered. "Chloe! Go!"

Chloe swallowed hard, fighting nausea. This wasn't a stranger dumped in a trunk. This was Mom. Dear God, this was *Mom*. She wasn't moving. Was she still breathing? Chloe's knees banged onto the floorboards. Her hand went inside the trunk, trying to find warmth, trying to find a pulse, trying to provide a shred of comfort if these were Mom's final moments.

"OK, *I'll* go." Chloe heard Roelke's footsteps pound from the room, around the corner, out the door.

Then she heard a startled exclamation and a muffled thump.

"Roelke?" she called. No response. She bit her lip, hard. *Roelke?* Her voice quavered this time. He'd taken the flashlight. Darkness shrouded the weaving room. Heart racing, she scrambled silently to her feet and tiptoed to the main room—just as some haunted creature burst through the front door. In the dying fire's faint shadows, she recognized the Satan who'd accosted her earlier—same tall hat, same wig, same hideous mask. He lifted the same stick-mounted wooden goat head high over his head.

Chloe stumbled backwards, skirting the hearth, scrambling past the table, into a corner. The *julebukker* came after her with eerie certainty, as if he were indeed part of the band of undead roaming the skies. Whatever he was, this—this *thing* had almost certainly killed Petra Lekstrom. He may have killed Mom.

Chloe felt the same scorching rage she'd summoned at Emil's farm. No way in hell was she going to let this apparition crack her skull with a goat head.

The flax hackle she'd admired was still on the windowsill, its wicked bed of sharpened nails affixed to a sturdy wooden base. She grabbed that base with one hand and lunged forward, swinging the hackle with all her strength.

Her attacker jumped backwards. The goat head dropped with a wooden clatter. Chloe was thrown off-balance when the hackle sliced air instead of flesh. She fell hard against the table but managed to stay on her feet. As he gathered himself and snatched up his own weapon, she swung the hackle again.

This time she felt it connect. She heard his unearthly howl. She saw him stumble away, clutching his left arm.

"Come on, you bastard!" She clenched the wood, raised the hackle, readied for another swing.

Another shadow roared into the room. Roelke seized the long-handled waffle iron Mom had left propped against one wall. He held it like a baseball bat and swung with a force that ripped the air. The iron connected with the *julebukker's* right arm. The creature cried out in pain as he fell to his knees.

"Lay down on your belly," Roelke growled. He planted himself, iron still held at the ready. "Do it! *Now!*"

The *julebukker* complied.

"Chloe. You OK?" Roelke asked, not looking at her.

"Yeah." Her chest was heaving. "But Mom—"

More heavy footsteps sounded in the entryway. Another strong flashlight beam sliced the darkness. The policeman Chloe had met earlier entered the room cautiously, with Sigrid hovering behind him.

He whipped his gun from its holster when he saw the tableau. "What's going on here?" he demanded. Sigrid gasped and pressed both hands over her mouth.

"Call an ambulance." Roelke waited until the officer pulled his radio free, pressed a button, and made the call. "I'm an off-duty cop," Roelke added. "This man attacked us. He may have killed Petra Lekstrom, and I believe he also attacked Marit Kallerud."

"*What?*" Sigrid wailed.

"She's in the big trunk," Chloe told Sigrid. "Please—go be with her." She couldn't turn away from the thing on the floor. Sigrid darted into the weaving room.

The cop pulled out his handcuffs.

"His left arm is bleeding," Roelke said. "His right arm is probably broken."

"He's not going anywhere." The young man put one foot lightly on the man's back. "We'll wait for the EMTs."

Roelke reached down and roughly pulled off the *julebukker's* fur hat and wig. Then he grabbed the rubber mask and jerked it free. The ancient specter of icy winter nights disappeared.

Roelke staggered backward. "Emil." The word was an exhalation, full of grief. "You? *You* did all this?"

Emil didn't move. One cheek was pressed to the floor. In the deep flickering shadows, Chloe couldn't read his expression.

"Emil!" Roelke implored.

"I ..." The old man sighed. "*Ja*. I killed Petra. I think I killed Marit—"

Chloe launched at the carver. The cop pushed her away. "Let the law handle this," he said.

"You'll be tried for murder." Roelke sounded dazed. "How could ... why did ... how could you look at me all week? Talk with me all week?"

"You just remember what I said. You got the makings of a fine carver."

Roelke shook his head.

"It's all right," Emil said. "I'm tired. I've been fighting for a long time."

Roelke dropped onto a bench.

"It's all right," Emil said again. "Someone needed to stop me." He blew out one long sigh. "Sometimes the darkness is inside."

∞

Chloe pressed herself into one corner of the curtained cubicle. Mom had regained consciousness by the time the ambulance arrived at the hospital, groggily mumbling about a headache, but Chloe couldn't breathe normally until the doctor finished her examination. "I think your mother's going to be fine," the young woman said. "But we don't take chances with head injuries. I'm going to send her up for a CAT scan."

"OK." Chloe struggled to squeeze even two syllables past the salty lump in her throat.

"We'll keep her for observation for a while, but I expect to release her either later this evening or tomorrow morning. Chances are good that the only lingering effects will be headaches for a day or so. If she experiences dizziness, nausea, or loss of memory, contact us at once."

Chloe swiped at her eyes. "OK."

"You can wait out in the reception area."

"OK. Um... see you soon, Mom." Chloe waited until Mom had been wheeled away before retracing her steps to the waiting room.

Roelke and Sigrid jumped to their feet. Howard, who'd arrived at the Valdres House just after the ambulance crew, was waiting too. "She's going to be all right," Chloe told them. "They just want to run another test and watch her for a while."

Sigrid dropped back into her chair, sniffling. Howard closed his eyes.

Roelke pulled Chloe against him and wrapped both arms around her. After a moment he whispered, "Emil was in the shadows beside the house when I dashed out to find a phone. He hit my knees and I went down and slid down that drop. I came back as fast as I could. When I saw him going after you..."

She pressed her face against his shoulder. "I'm all right," she whispered back. "What about you?"

"I talked to a nurse. I'm fine."

Chloe was glad that Roelke had been checked for signs of frost-bite or fever, but that wasn't what worried her. She stepped back so she could look him in the eye. What she saw hurt her heart.

While they all waited in still-stunned silence, Chloe struggled to sort through the evening's events. A young couple rushed past car-rying a child wrapped in a blanket. A woman's voice paged a doctor. A janitor began mopping the floor, leaving a strong disinfectant smell behind. Finally Chloe asked, "Does anyone know why Emil would do what he did?"

"He's obviously mentally ill," Howard muttered.

"But his attacks weren't random," Chloe said. "Why Petra? Why Mom?" Roelke gave her a tiny warning headshake, but she already knew better than to share their speculation about Adelle.

Chief Moyer appeared in the doorway, dapper as ever in another plaid sports jacket. He pointed at Roelke and beckoned. Chloe fol-lowed too. She deserved—needed—to hear whatever was to be said.

They huddled in a quiet corner. "I'm very glad your mother is recovering," Moyer told Chloe.

"What about Emil?" Roelke asked curtly.

"He's getting his broken arm set," Moyer said. "Investigator Buzzelli is with him. Bergsbakken also needed stitches and a teta-nus shot."

I did that, Chloe thought. The memory of swinging that hackle made her sick to her stomach ... until she remembered why she'd done it.

"Now," Moyer was saying, "we'll need a statement from each of you—"

"Can we go to the farm?" Chloe asked.

"No," Moyer and Roelke said in unison. "I've already got people there," the chief added.

Roelke said, "And I don't want you anywhere near anything to do with Emil Bergsbakken."

"I understand all that, but—the thing is, I really, *really* need to go back there."

"Why?" Roelke asked.

This was not the moment to describe what she'd perceived swirling through the layers of time in Emil's farmhouse. "I think I can help figure out what's been happening."

The men exchanged a glance.

"Please do not patronize me," Chloe snapped, before Moyer had a chance to launch into a *Don't worry your pretty little head* speech. "Just give me a chance. The best cops in the world might miss something that I would understand."

"She may be right," Roelke said quietly. "She's helped me with stuff like this before."

Moyer spread his hands in acquiescence. "All right. My car's outside." He started to shrug into the overcoat he'd been holding over his arm, then frowned. "Don't you two have coats?"

"We're *fine!*" Chloe shouted, and headed toward the door.

⁂

Ten minutes later Moyer eased his car into Emil Bergsbakken's drive. Three other vehicles were already parked by the house. Light streamed from every window.

"You sure about this?" Roelke asked Chloe.

"Yeah." She was worried about him, actually, but this had to be done. As they started up the front steps she paused, looking up at the night. The phantoms were gone.

Chloe and Roelke followed Moyer into the front hall. He held a whispered conversation with his officers. When Roelke toed off his boots Chloe did the same, and they both accepted the booties one of the techs offered. "To the best of our knowledge this isn't a crime scene," the chief said. "But I don't want to take chances. Please don't touch anything." He nodded to Chloe. "After you."

Something indefinable, ephemeral, still vibrated in the house. She straightened her shoulders. "Let's start upstairs."

She stopped at the top of the steps, trying to open herself. When Moyer started to speak, she held up one hand to silence him. The vibes were definitely stronger up here, but she sensed that she hadn't gone far enough.

She walked slowly down the hall. The quivering beneath her sternum increased, pulling her past both bedroom doors to the end of the corridor. I don't get it, she thought. Maybe I'm about to make a fool of myself.

Then she looked up and saw a small rope loop dangling from a square wooden hatch in the ceiling. "Up there."

Moyer grabbed the loop and pulled. When the hatch creaked opened, a narrow set of steps eased down to the floor. Chloe felt Roelke's stern gaze upon her: *You will **not** bolt up those stairs.*

The chief called two of his men to join them. "The lady wants to see the attic. Take a look around."

She waited impatiently as footsteps creaked above her head. The officers came down brushing cobwebs from their clothes. "It's clear," one of them said.

Chloe climbed to the cold attic with Chief Moyer and Roelke on her heels. Energy pulsed in the stale air, but she still couldn't define the emotion behind it. That alone was disconcerting. What on earth had happened up here?

They could stand straight only in the center of the room because the eaves sloped down sharply. In the weak light cast by an overhead bulb, Moyer surveyed cardboard cartons, dusty chairs, a couple of suitcases, straw-filled milk crates with bits of china peeking through. "Not much here," he observed.

Chloe turned around, drawn toward the back gable wall. Something here throbbed with a tangible energy. She pulled a dangling string and another bare bulb flickered on.

"Dear God," Chloe whispered. She understood, now. Everything.

Roelke and Moyer were on her heels. She pointed to the wall.

"What?" Roelke demanded. "It's just some of Emil's carved stuff."

"It's not just stuff." Chloe stared at the carved pieces hung in a precise row. "Those are mangles."

Moyer leaned closer. "They're … what?"

Chloe gritted her teeth and stepped closer. Each mangle was unique, each a miracle of craftsmanship. Two initials and a date had been carved at the base of every one. Chloe pointed at the first. "'P. L., 1982.' Petra Lekstrom."

The men exchanged another silent look.

"I don't quite get this one." Chloe pointed to a mangle carved with 'S. J.' and two dates, 1943 and 1977. "Sigrid, maybe?" she mused. "Before she married and again after her husband died?"

Roelke pressed one knuckle against his forehead. "Jesus Holy Christ."

"'L. C., 1966.' Lavinia Carmichael? Maybe after she was widowed?" Chloe looked on down the row. "This one, 'A. G., 1952,' might be Adelle before she married Tom." She didn't recognize the next set of initials but she paused before 'P. E., 1950' and pointed. "Same thing here. This could be Phyllis, Howard's wife. I don't know her birth name."

When Chloe looked at the final mangle it took a moment to find her voice. "'M. K., 1946.' Marit Kallerud. Mom didn't change her name when she married my dad."

Chief Moyer was clearly bewildered. "You're going to have to help me out here, Miss Ellefson."

Roelke touched her arm. "I'm trying to remember exactly what your mother said."

"Men traditionally carved personalized mangles for the women they hoped to marry," Chloe told him wearily. "A suitor would leave the mangle on the woman's doorstep, and if she took it inside, it meant she accepted his proposal. A few men tried to hedge their bets by carving more than one mangle, because once a woman had declined a proposal gift, it couldn't be offered to anyone else."

"I still don't get it." Moyer rubbed his chin, staring at the carvings.

"Old Norwegians have a saying," Chloe told him. "Beware the man with many mangles."

THIRTY-THREE

AT EIGHT A.M. THE next morning Chloe drove Mom home from the hospital. "Thank you Chloe," Mom said, adjusting her wrap-around sunglasses. "For this, and for last night."

Chloe tried to find words to describe the terror she'd felt when she'd found Mom in the trunk at the Valdres House. Since she couldn't, she finally settled for, "You're welcome."

The sky had cleared. Sunlight glittered on every ice crystal. Chloe parked in front of Sigrid's house and insisted that Mom take her arm as they made their way up the steps.

They found Sigrid sitting alone in the tower room, surrounded by scrapbooks, dolls, the charming parade of wooden animals marching toward the Ark. "Oh, Marit," she cried. "Sit down. Are you sure you're all right?"

"*Yes,*" Mom said with a touch of her usual asperity.

Sigrid had been holding the *nisse*-embroidered baby bib, but she set it aside and led the way into the parlor. "I brewed some coffee—"

"None for me," Chloe replied. She hung up Mom's coat before sinking into a chair. "I may take a nap. I'm exhausted."

"I am too," Sigrid admitted. "But I couldn't sleep. Has anyone been able to make sense of what Emil has done?"

"Some of it." Chloe glanced at her mother. "Mom? Are you up for this conversation, or do you want to go to bed?"

Mom crossed her arms. "I want to hear what you have to say."

"OK, then." Chloe tried to assemble and condense everything she'd learned overnight. "Evidently Emil wanted a good Norwegian wife. And evidently her ethnic heritage mattered more than anything else. Mom? Did Emil propose to you in 1946?"

"He ... well, yes, he did." Mom studied her hands. "It was quite awkward. He even made a mangle for me. I declined as gently as I could, and I thought he'd put the episode aside. We got to be friends after that. At least I thought we were friends."

"Emil Bergsbakken made a lot of mangles, and hung on to a lot of grudges," Chloe continued. "I found a calendar stick he'd made to keep track of the women who'd turned him down. The police are sorting everything out, but it seems he updated the stick each time he tried to harm someone. I saw a letter M beside a symbol that resembles a ladder. Does that mean anything to you?"

"A ladder?" Mom looked baffled. "No, I can't imagine what ... oh." Her expression changed. "Might that symbol have been railroad tracks?"

"Well ... maybe. What would that mean?"

"A long time ago," Mom said, "I almost fell from the platform right in front of an oncoming train. It happened here at the Decorah station."

Sigrid moaned softly.

"In fact," Marit continued faintly, "that's how I met your father, Chloe. He caught me."

Chloe clenched her chair's armrests as she thought about how the cosmos would have changed had Mom died before meeting Dad. It took her a moment to find her voice again. "He may have tried to harm you several times before. Maybe little accidents that happened while you visited over the years weren't really accidents. He didn't shut you in the vault—evidently that really was a prank— but Emil set the fire in your classroom."

Mom shook her head, winced, went still.

Chloe was glad that Chief Moyer had asked her and Roelke not to speak of Adelle, Lavinia, or Phyllis. Emil had admitted to blocking the vent from Adelle's workshop and putting the wood chip in Lavinia's soda can. He'd also replaced some of Phyllis's oil paints with older, more toxic formulations, and noted the attempt by carving a sled to represent the piece that earned her a Gold Medal. Lavinia was fine, and it would be hard to prove that Emil's actions had caused the other women's illnesses. "We know that Bergsbakken killed Petra Lekstrom," the chief had said, "and we've got him for assault as well. He'll be in prison for the rest of his life."

"Emil confessed to killing Petra," Chloe told the older women. "He didn't like her more than anyone else did, but after his brother died, he was lonely. He was also running out of single 'Norwegian' women to fantasize about. He decided that he and Petra would make the perfect team—him carving woodenware and her painting it."

"Heavens," Mom murmured.

"When Petra arrived at Vesterheim last Sunday, Emil found her in the Norwegian House and proposed on the spot. Unlike you, Mom, she didn't try to let him down gently. He told the police that she laughed at him. Scorned him. Something inside him just...just snapped, I guess. He grabbed the *lefse* pin and...well, you know the rest."

Sigrid clasped her arms across her chest.

"Roelke and I tried and tried to see a pattern." Chloe rested her head back against the chair. "I was trying to figure out if Sixty-Sevens were being targeted, but Peggy Nelson and Linda Skatrud both said they hadn't experienced any bad luck or illness. In Emil's mind, though, neither of those women would have been a suitable partner. Peggy is Filipina. Linda's not Norwegian either—she started rosemaling to learn more about her husband's heritage. Emil wanted a woman of pure Norwegian descent. That included Lavinia. Her family had Norwegian roots, even though she married a man who wasn't Scandinavian."

"I just can't believe this of Emil," Mom whispered.

Chloe didn't add that Emil had evidently proposed to a couple of other women as well, Norwegian ladies who weren't Sixty-Sevens. The police were tracking them down with mangles in hand.

Mom's voice trembled. "He's been part of the Vesterheim family all his life! How could he *do* something like this? How could he hide this part of himself?"

Sigrid straightened wearily. "I wonder if it doesn't go back to his mother's death, when Emil was just a boy. He told me once how it happened."

"A runaway horse, wasn't it?" Mom asked. "His mother was in the farm wagon?"

"Yes," Sigrid said. "But his father had asked Emil to hold the lines. He got distracted by a dragonfly and wandered away. The horses bolted, and his mother was thrown against a tree. She died instantly."

Sigrid reached for a tissue, which she crumpled in her hands. "It's hard to imagine what something like that would do to a boy. Perhaps he's been looking for a 'good Norwegian woman' ever since."

Chloe said, "And with every rejection, his growing hurt and rage got harder to hide."

"Oscar was a good influence on him," Sigrid said. "He was generally cheerful. Without even knowing it, Oscar may have helped Emil suppress his dark urges."

"And maybe..." Chloe hesitated, then plunged out with it. "There were a lot more carvings on the Winter side of the calendar stick than the Summer side. I think the season contributed to Emil's mental illness. The short days, the darkness...even the *julebukking* tradition. Edwina Ree told me that *julebukking* gave people an opportunity to act in ways that were normally forbidden—"

"Not like this!" Sigrid cried sharply.

Chloe reached out to squeeze the older woman's hand. "Of course not. And for whatever it's worth, I think Emil really struggled against the dark impulses. Part of him was horrified by what he did, and wanted to be stopped. I think he left that calendar stick in the collections storage area in hopes that someone would find it and figure things out. He advised Roelke to talk to Edwina Ree about Petra's murder because he thought that if anyone could see into his soul, it would be Edwina. And believe it or not, he told the investigator that he left that *budstikke* here for you, Mom, not as a threat, but to warn you." Chloe stood abruptly and walked to the window. "On the other hand, after Roelke mentioned that he and I were following some leads, Emil panicked and slammed one into his own door in an attempt to point attention elsewhere." She didn't mention Emil's attacks against her and Roelke. All the details would emerge in time.

318

Mom lifted her hands, then let them drop helplessly back to her lap. "I simply can't grasp what has been going on in that man's head."

"He's been at war with himself for decades," Chloe said quietly. She remembered Emil lying on the floor of the Valdres House looking small and helpless. *I've been fighting for a long time…Someone needed to stop me…Sometimes the darkness is inside.* But that reminded her of the pain in Roelke's eyes. He'd been with her for most of what came after Emil's arrest—the trip to the farm, the trip to the police station—but then he'd withdrawn from her. And she had no idea what to do about that.

Maybe I can think of something after I get some sleep, she thought. Recent events and a night spent dozing in an uncomfortable hospital chair had left her weary to the bone. Howard had taken Roelke back to his place, but they'd agreed to meet up later. Maybe by then she'd know how to help Roelke through this.

She longed to rise and trudge to her guestroom, right now. But there was one thing she didn't understand. "Sigrid," she said, "we found a mangle in Emil's house that was carved with the initials 'S. J.' Was that you?"

Sigrid rubbed one thumb. "Yes. My maiden name was Jensen. And Emil did ask me to marry him. Twice, actually. Before I married Bill, and again after Bill died."

Chloe waited, hoping Sigrid would continue on her own. Seconds ticked past. Mom lifted her head and looked at her friend. Sigrid didn't meet her gaze.

"I don't recall seeing an S figure on Emil's calendar stick," Chloe said finally. "So I have to ask. Why do you think Emil never tried to harm you?"

Sigrid abandoned thumb-rubbing and clutched her hands together. "I can only imagine that it's because ... because Emil is probably Violet's father."

Mom gasped. "What?"

Chloe remembered Sigrid's sadness about Violet's birthday, the exquisite Noah's Ark, the sorrow contained in the hand-stitched baby bib. I thought the gloom came from my own mood, Chloe thought. But Sigrid's regrets lingered in the tower room.

"Emil proposed to me before I married Bill. Later, when things with Bill became ... strained ... Emil and I had a very, very brief relationship, which I have regretted every day since." A tear trickled down Sigrid's cheek. "Except for Violet. I could never regret Violet."

"Aunt Sigrid, does Violet know?"

"No. Violet doesn't know. And my husband never knew. Emil— well, we never discussed it, but he could do the math." She gave Mom and Chloe a beseeching look. "I married in such haste. Lots of us did, during the war. Bill could be difficult. I—"

"But how could you keep such a secret?" Mom looked stunned. "How could you not tell Violet? How could you not tell me? We were pregnant at the same time! I thought we shared *everything*!"

Sigrid didn't answer.

"I need to lie down." Mom rose and walked stiffly from the room. Her footsteps faded as she went upstairs.

Sigrid buried her face in her hands, weeping. Chloe gave her a few moments before touching her shoulder. "Aunt Sigrid? I'm so sorry. Is there anything I can do?"

After a few more sniffles Sigrid sat up and grabbed another tissue. She looked a decade older than she had a week ago. "No, honey. There's nothing anyone can do. I need to gather my strength so I can talk to Violet. I believe I'll go up to my room as well." She pushed to her feet and left Chloe alone.

Chloe sat in the empty room. She felt stunned, too—and not just because of Emil. Mom and Sigrid had been best friends for decades. Now both of them were miserable, in pain, and feeling alone just when they needed each other the most. And there's not a thing I can do, Chloe thought. Not a thing to help Mom, or Sigrid, or Roelke either. She *hated* feeling helpless.

Except ... maybe there was something she could do. Chloe got to her feet, grabbed Sigrid's cloak and Mom's car keys, and headed for the door.

⚮

Sometime later she was back at Sigrid's house, chopping an onion in the kitchen, when she heard the front door open and close. A moment later Violet appeared in the doorway. "Hey," she said cautiously.

"Hey."

"I heard about what's been happening," Violet said. "Some of it, anyway. Did Emil really kill Petra?"

Chloe stepped to the stove. Minced onion sizzled into the hot skillet she'd prepared. "He confessed."

"I can scarcely believe it," Violet said. "I've been out for a walk, just trying to wrap my head around things."

Violet would soon have a whole lot more to wrap her head around. Chloe's residual anger about Violet's snide comments at the Rimestads' party faded away.

"Look, I need to apologize for what I said the other night," Violet said. "I was just sounding off." She leaned against the door frame. "Obviously the results of the Exhibition last summer *did* bug me. A lot more than I've been willing to admit, even to myself. Last summer I was … unkind to Howard about it. I regret being so stupid and impulsive. And I truly didn't mean what I said about the older rosemalers. I know how hard they worked."

"Yeah," Chloe said. "They did." The onions were turning translucent, and she turned down the heat under the pan.

"I feel just horrible that Aunt Marit overheard us. She was already having a tough week." Violet drummed the heel of one shoe against the toe of the other. "I know she felt slighted because my mom was given the advanced class to teach instead of her. And even though she's taught beginners for years, she felt unprepared. You know how methodically she approaches teaching."

"Yeah," Chloe said again, although honestly, she'd never thought about it.

"And Aunt Marit was *so* upset after not winning Best of Show in the Exhibition last summer—"

"She was?" Chloe moved the pan and turned to face Violet.

"Well, sure!" Violet sounded perplexed. "Gold Medalists can't compete for ribbons, of course, but last year their entries were eligible for Best of Show for the first time. That hanging cupboard your mom entered was stunning. But so was the piece that won."

I had no idea, Chloe thought. This was the first she'd known Mom had even entered a piece in the Exhibition.

"I'd do anything to take back what I said," Violet said miserably. "I tried to apologize to Aunt Marit, but she won't listen. Do you think she'll ever forgive me?"

Chloe thought about Mom and opened her mouth to say *Honestly? I doubt it.* Instead, something entirely different came out. "All you can do is keep trying, Violet. You just have to keep trying."

"I will." Violet sighed. Then she gestured at a big bowl of chopped tomatoes on the counter. "What are you doing?"

"I'm making tomato soup with wild rice and kale," Chloe told her. "A very big batch. As Roelke's grandma used to say, sometimes the only thing you can do for people you care about is make sure they eat a good meal."

THIRTY-FOUR

At eleven-thirty Chloe left the fragrant soup simmering in a Crock-Pot and walked to the museum. It was a Christmas card, snow-dazzle kind of day, and she hardly noticed the cold.

Roelke was waiting in the lobby. "Hey," she said, and kissed him. "How are you doing?"

"OK."

He didn't look OK. He looked tired and depressed. The night before, though, they'd promised Howard that they would attend the grand highlight of Vesterheim's Norwegian Christmas weekend, singing and dancing around a huge Christmas tree. Chloe would bet her last candy cane that Roelke wasn't going to dance, but if Howard's greatest fear came true—that visitors, horrified by headlines in the morning paper, completely spurned the museum—at least Chloe and Roelke would add to the head count.

But visitors were, thank Heaven, coming. Families, groups of friends, and couples crowded inside, filling the lobby with smiles and chatter, forming an impromptu receiving line to greet Howard. When the festivities began, Roelke and Chloe watched the children's delight as they circled around the tree. A *julenisse* passed out candy. A beaming volunteer read a story.

And not a *julebukker* in sight, Chloe thought with profound relief. "Howard should be pleased," she murmured to Roelke as the ceremonies came to an end. Then she straightened. "Is that my mother?"

"It looks like your mother," he agreed.

Mom saw them and made her way through the crowd. "Thank you for leaving the soup, Chloe," she said. "It was just what I needed."

"You're welcome," Chloe said, feeling ridiculously pleased. "But didn't the doctor tell you to rest today? I don't think you should be here."

"Oh, stop fussing. I wanted to be here for Howard's sake."

Right on cue, Howard pushed through the crowd to a podium. "Thank you for coming," he began. "As most of you know, we have had a wrenching week. I arrived at the museum before dawn this morning with a heavy heart. But the logo on Vesterheim's sign gave me hope."

Chloe glanced at the closest sign. Sure enough, there was the sunburst design she'd admired on the old tankard.

"To me, the design represents the best of our heritage: our belief that a bright new day will always dawn," Howard continued. "It represents warmth and goodness. It represents the ancient tradition of lighting bonfires on these shortest, darkest days to welcome the return of the sun."

Much to her astonishment, Chloe felt a lump rise in her throat.

"I am reminded of something I told our folk art students a week ago." Howard looked over the gathering. "The Vesterheim community is a family. Together, we can see any dark days through. I thank you all for your love and support."

Applause rippled through the crowd.

Howard blew his nose before continuing. "Now, it is my pleasure to announce the winner of our Christmas Card contest."

Mom stiffened.

Now I get why she's here, Chloe thought.

"All Gold Medalists were invited to submit a design," Howard was saying, "and the top choice was determined by popular vote. Please help me congratulate the winning painter, who's come all the way from Colorado..."

"Never mind, Mom," Chloe said loyally, squeezing her mother's hand. "I liked your design best."

Mom pulled her hand away. "It's just a silly competition. The winning design was well-executed." But her eyes sparkled with unshed tears.

Chloe's shoulders slumped. "Oh, Mom. After everything that's happened, *please* tell me you're not crying because your Christmas card design wasn't chosen."

"If I'm crying, it's because I'm getting a headache." Mom blinked rapidly. "I think I should go take another nap."

"I'll go with you," Chloe began, but Mom was already sailing toward the front door.

Chloe looked at Roelke. "Should I go after her?"

He considered, then shook his head. "I don't think so."

"She's a Gold Medalist. She's a beloved member of the Vesterheim community. Why isn't that enough for her?"

"I do not know."

"This trip was for her."

Roelke regarded Chloe with—finally—some honest sympathy. "What are you going to do?"

"I'm going to keep trying," she said. "Just keep trying."

"Good."

Chloe turned to face him. "Listen, do you want to get out of here? You've probably had your fill of all things Norske."

He shook his head. "Let's at least walk through."

So they chatted with the craftspeople who'd come to demonstrate straw weaving and Norwegian embroidery. They lingered in one of the galleries as the Luren Singing Society performed a few favorites. They admired the decorations volunteers had worked so hard on. They paused by tables where excited children were making woven hearts. They accepted warm *krumkakke* offered by elderly women in traditional clothing.

And to Chloe's amazement, she found her sadness easing. Vesterheim's Norwegian Christmas celebration provided the balance she'd so desperately needed. Yes, her heritage included a dark chapter or two. Her ancestors had feared the long nights of this icy season. Edwina Ree's folklore studies were an important part of understanding the historical Norwegian psyche. And dark things *had* happened this week—horrible things and revelations that would reverberate through Decorah for years to come.

But today, light was shining into every corner. Today Christmas was all it should be—joyful, sparkling, and filled with grace.

"Where to?" Chloe asked as she and Roelke stepped outside. "I can offer you a nutritious and delicious meal at Sigrid's house, prepared by yours truly, but the atmosphere there may be a bit … tense."

"No." Roelke shook his head. "We have dinner reservations at the Winneshiek Hotel."

Chloe felt a smile spread over her face. "We do?"

"We do. All I could get was an early seating, though, so let's go."

As they made their way down the sidewalk Chloe pointed skyward. "See those fluffy clouds? I could paint those. It's all C-strokes and S-strokes."

Roelke didn't answer, but he took her hand.

The historic hotel was as lovely inside as its exterior had suggested. In the restaurant, they even scored a window table. "Would you like to start with a drink?" the pleasant waitress asked.

"Oh, yeah," Chloe said. They each ordered wine.

When the goblets arrived Chloe sipped gratefully. "Do you want to talk about the nasty stuff?" she asked. "I've got a few updates."

Roelke nodded. "Let's just get through that and be done with it."

"I stopped at Lavinia's house this morning—"

"She could have choked to death right beside me." Roelke's face hardened.

"But she didn't. She's completely recovered. She's also wondering if a fire that destroyed her home years ago was a lightning strike after all. There were two bonfires carved on that calendar stick."

A muscle worked in Roelke's jaw.

"I told Lavinia about the spalted wood and the blocked ventilation system." Chloe rolled her glass, watching the wine swirl. "She thinks we should try to keep that from the Rimestads, if possible.

It's too late to undo the damage, and wondering would only torment Tom."

"It certainly would."

"Emil's been doing bad stuff for decades, but it seems as if he was more sporadic in the old days," Chloe mused. "Then this week, all kinds of things happened. Why do you think that is?"

Roelke exhaled slowly. "My best guess is that actually attacking Petra face-to-face changed him. Excited his dark side, maybe. Or maybe that same dark part of him knew the cops would close in on him sooner or later, and he felt compelled to do as much harm as possible first."

The waitress arrived with their dinners, broiled trout for Roelke and broccoli soup and a salad for Chloe. "So," Roelke said, "how did it go at Sigrid's place this morning? All this has got to be hard on her and your mom. How much did you tell them?"

Chloe watched a woman walk past with a black lab on a leash. The dog had a big bow tied on his collar, and looked quite pleased with himself. "Just the basics. But I did ask Sigrid if she had any idea why Emil never seemed to target her." She shared Sigrid's explanation. "My mom was shocked. She was pregnant with my sister Kari about the same time Sigrid was pregnant with Violet."

Roelke leaned back in his chair. "Holy toboggans."

"Remember how awkward dinner was that evening when you and Emil came over?" Chloe asked. "Neither Sigrid nor Emil said a word. I just figured Sigrid was upset about the vault episode, and Petra. Violet had no idea she had invited her biological father over for fruit soup."

"I had no clue."

"How could you have?" Chloe asked. She chose not to mention *her* clue—the baby bib embroidered with such sorrow.

"I should have known!" The words burst out in a low growl. "I should have picked up on *something*. I stayed in Emil Bergsbakken's house, for God's sake! I even asked him about his mother's *lefse* pin. How could I not have seen?"

"Emil fooled a lot of people, for a very long time," Chloe reminded him. "People who knew him a lot better than you did—"

"But I'm a cop. And there were signs. He's shy and pleasant … but when some kids were playing tricks and snapped off our classroom lights, he flew into a rage. When he tried to give me relationship advice—"

"Emil gave you *relationship* advice?"

"He told me to find a good Irish or German girl."

That bothered Chloe more than she would have guessed. "The word 'hubris' comes to mind," she said tartly.

"He said I needed a woman who could understand where I came from. What I know. Stuff like that."

Chloe struggled to purge her brain of the image of Emil Bergsbakken, mass murderer, giving Roelke advice about *her*.

"Everybody's heard stories about the nice man next door who turns out to be a serial killer," Roelke was saying bitterly. "But there were indications that Emil's mental state was … crumbling. He said something about his dead brother coming back this Christmas."

"Old-time Norwegians believed that about family members," Chloe said. "Maybe Emil was frightened Oscar would come back and punish him for killing Petra. I saw the cross painted on the stabbur to ward away spirits."

"I thought it just meant Emil was a Christian." Roelke scrubbed his face with his palms. "It's like there were two Emils."

"I know," Chloe agreed soberly. "Part of him had horrible urges; the other part of him longed to be stopped."

"I was too open with him. If I hadn't told him that you and I were pursuing a couple of ideas, you never would have become a target."

"Not just me. When I think about what happened on the bridge…" Chloe felt pain in her hand and realized she was squeezing her fork. They'd learned the night before that Emil had used Oscar's old car to try to ram Roelke on the bridge. He'd told the cops that he drove up and down Skyline Road a dozen times, waiting to see Roelke walking back to his place. "I didn't ever hear about the *budstikker*, though. I assume those came from Emil too?"

"He left the one at Sigrid's house," Roelke confirmed. "And he jammed that carved *budstikke* into his own front door, too. Evidently his grandfather made that one. Emil did not leave the one Howard got—that one must have actually come from some disgruntled painter."

"I think it was Violet," Chloe said. He gave her a questioning look. "It's just a hunch."

Roelke picked up his goblet, put it down. "I still can't take it in. *Emil.* I should have seen it."

"You're not a mind reader."

"I should have picked up on something. I should have, and I didn't. I was so focused on carving that—"

"That's what you were supposed to be focused on!"

"—Lavinia was hurt. Your mom was hurt. You were almost…"

Chloe reached across the table. "Give me your hand." She waited until he reluctantly complied. "Listen to me. This was *not* your fault. None of this was your fault. And please don't forget that you got him in the end—despite teetering on the edge of hypothermia."

"You were holding your own."

"I'm not sure I could have taken him down with a hackle," she said honestly. "But I didn't have to, because you came. You got him."

Roelke shrugged. Chloe reluctantly released his hand, knowing she hadn't convinced him of a darn thing.

They ate in silence for a few moments. Then Roelke looked up. "Chloe? You were the one who wanted to go back to Emil's house with Moyer. And you led us straight up to those damn mangles. How did you know?"

Chloe sipped her wine. She watched a little boy skip past their table. She pleated her napkin. "We-ell," she said at last, "there's something I've kinda wanted to talk to you about for a long time. Roelke, sometimes I can perceive strong emotions that linger in old places. Most of the time when I go in an old building—like this one—if I think about it, I get sort of a faint jumble. No big deal. But sometimes, a really strong emotion comes through. I can sense it."

"Like instinct? Cops need good instincts. I can't explain exactly what that means, but I know it's real."

Chloe was tempted to go with that; to let him think he understood. But Roelke deserved the truth. "No, this is different from instinct, or intuition." She rubbed her forehead, groping for words. "It's so hard to explain. I have instincts sometimes, when I think I know something. What I'm talking about is literally *feeling* something. When it happens, it's like some resonance is sort of … vibrating through time. In a physical way. It's visceral."

After a long, considering pause Roelke said, "Well, hunh. And you felt something like that at Emil's place?"

"Yes."

"What was the emotion?"

"It was confusing. I got flickers of something dark, but happiness and hope too." She picked up her fork and played with a candied walnut. "All I can figure is that I picked up on how terribly conflicted Emil felt over the years. Just like I picked up on that calendar stick he left in the storage building. I would never have noticed it on my own if I hadn't *felt* something."

"Does this kind of thing happen a lot?"

"Not a lot. Just sometimes, and there's no predicting it. But it's been happening ever since I was a little girl. I've never told anyone about it before." She looked at him anxiously. "It's true, Roelke. I wanted to tell you back when we were on Rock Island, but I just couldn't find the words. I didn't want you to think I was a fruitcake."

"I don't think that."

"These flashes I get ... they can be quite inconvenient. I can go for months without perceiving anything unusual, and then— bam."

He looked out the window. Finally he said, "Thank you for telling me."

Chloe felt compelled to make sure she was understanding what this often-rigid, oh-so-German man was saying. "So ... what I've just told you, this perception thing, it's not a deal breaker?"

His mouth hinted at an actual smile. "Definitely not."

Chloe felt happier than she'd felt all week. I think I feel happier than I've felt all year, she thought, a bit dazed.

She polished off her wine. "This is a treat. I haven't liked us being apart so much. With the separate classes, the folklore project, trying to figure out what was going on, staying in separate places—it's been frustrating."

"For me too."

On impulse, Chloe grabbed her totebag. "Close your eyes for a minute. I was going to give you this later, but..." She extracted a Tupperware sandwich container, pulled off the top, and pushed it across the table. "Here. Merry Christmas."

Roelke opened his eyes and stared at the rosemaled star inside. "Did you paint this?"

"I did. It's an ornament," she added, in case it wasn't obvious. "It's taped to the bottom of the tub because the paint isn't dry, so don't touch it."

"I thought you were rosemaling a tray and a bowl."

"My classmates painted trays and bowls. This is what I painted. It's my sole accomplishment for the week, and I want you to have it."

"It's really good. I like it a lot." He met her gaze. "And I have a surprise for you."

Chloe felt a tingle of anticipation. "What is it?"

"When I made our dinner reservation yesterday morning, I spoke with the desk clerk and asked if anyone had cancelled for tonight. And guess what? Someone had. We've got a room waiting upstairs."

Chloe wasn't sure what she'd expected, but this wasn't it. "We do?"

"We do. Is that OK?"

Chloe had no idea if that was OK. What she did know is that Roelke needed her. "Yes. It is."

"Do you need to let your mother know you're not staying at Sigrid's place tonight?"

"Absolutely not!" The very thought made Chloe's cheeks flame. "I'm a big girl."

The waitress appeared. "Anyone save room for dessert?"

"I don't think so," Roelke said. "Just the check."

Chloe tried to collect her wits while he took care of the bill. She tried to collect her wits as they left the restaurant. She tried to collect her wits as Roelke led her up an elegant flight of stairs. Oh my, she thought. What if we're not ready for this? What if this ruins everything? What if my bra doesn't match my panties?

When they reached their room Roelke unlocked the door and stepped back, letting her enter first. Inside, Chloe found that a street lamp outside provided just enough illumination to make more light unnecessary. "This is very nice," she said. Her voice sounded higher than usual.

"I have one more gift for you." Roelke sat down on the bed.

Chloe sat down beside him. It's going to be OK, she thought, and felt her spasm of worries fade. This is the man I want to be with.

Roelke reached into the pocket of the coat Howard had loaned him and pulled out a package wrapped in plain white paper. "Merry Christmas, Chloe."

She accepted the gift and pulled away the paper. Inside was a small candleholder.

"It's a candleplate," he said, as if unsure she could tell.

Chloe ran her finger along the lovely design circling the socket. "It's *beautiful*! You carved this for me?"

"I did," he said. "I've got a candle to fit it, too." But there was no joy in his voice.

Chloe felt her heart break. "Oh, Roelke." She lay her head on his shoulder.

They sat in silence for a long time. Finally Roelke spoke in a voice so low she strained to hear. "I always believed I was a good cop."

"You *are* a good cop. A very good one."

He didn't answer.

"And you're a very good boyfriend, too," Chloe added. "Roelke? Light the candle."

⚮

Hours later Roelke lay awake, staring into the dark. Chloe was sleeping peacefully with her head on his shoulder. He could feel the satin of her skin, the softness of her long hair, the curve of her hip bone, the beat of her heart. Down in the restaurant earlier he had almost stopped short of admitting he'd scored a room. God knew the timing was bad. But as the candle burned low Chloe had, for a while, made him forget.

Now, though, all he could think about was Emil. He is a killer, Roelke thought. I was with him more than anyone this week, and I didn't see it.

Roelke knew that he'd done a few things right. Once he'd gotten Emil on the floor of the Valdres House he hadn't kicked the old man, or pounded his head against the floor. But did that even reflect control on his part? Or did it reflect the fact that despite everything Roelke had seen and heard, he'd still felt as if he'd just broken the arm of a kindly old uncle?

An uncle who would live in prison for the rest of his life. An uncle who would never again hold a carving knife in his knowing hand.

Chloe stirred in her sleep and Roelke pulled up the sheet, tucking it gently over her shoulder so she wouldn't get chilled. He thought again of the miracle in his arms, this beautiful, smart, brave, passionate woman. He knew that telling him about sensing stuff had made her feel anxious, but honestly, it was no big deal. He didn't understand it, but there were lots of things about Chloe he didn't understand. Like why she had finally decided that she really did want to be with him.

Unwanted, Emil's gruff advice came back: *I'm talking about two people who can understand each other—where they come from, what they know, who they are. I don't see how two people can make a go of it if they don't know all the answers to those questions.*

Roelke wasn't Norwegian. He didn't have a college degree. He didn't know anything about old stuff. Hell, he didn't even have a favorite tree.

He'd *thought* he could protect her. Evidently he couldn't even do that. She'd saved him from freezing to death. Had he even thanked her for that? He couldn't remember.

I took Emil down in the end, Roelke thought. But Chloe had already done some serious damage.

His closed his eyes, but the question remained: How could he be a good partner for Chloe when he had nothing to give?

When dawn came Roelke had yet to figure that out. Chloe stirred, touched his cheek. "Have you slept at all?" she whispered.

"I can't."

"Roelke." She raised herself on one elbow. "You'll have lots of time to figure out how to carry all this. But now, it's time for you to rest. I'll keep watch for a while."

"It's not your job to—"

"Sometimes, it is." Her voice was low but firm. She kissed him gently before easing back down.

Soft morning light spilled through the curtains. Roelke tightened one arm around his girlfriend, and let himself drift off to sleep.

Rosemaled Bowl, Telemark Style
(Vesterheim Norwegian-American Museum, Decorah, Iowa)

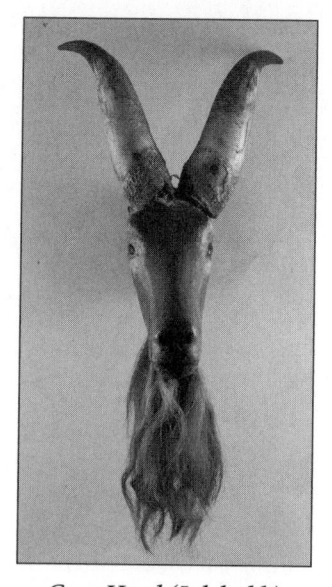

Goat Head (Julebukk)
(Vesterheim Norwegian-American Museum, Decorah, Iowa)

Chip Carved Mangle (Mangletre)
(Vesterheim Norwegian-American Museum, Decorah, Iowa)

Mangle Carving Detail
(Vesterheim Norwegian-American Museum, Decorah, Iowa)

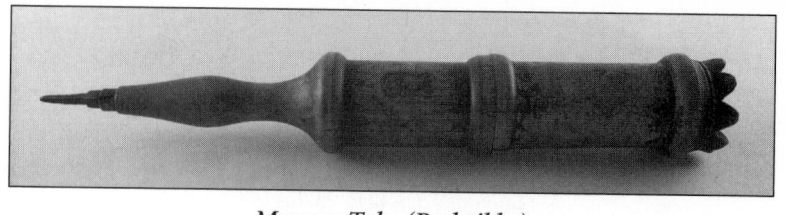

Message Tube (Budstikke)
(Vesterheim Norwegian-American Museum, Decorah, Iowa)

Message Tube Open
(Vesterheim Norwegian-American Museum, Decorah, Iowa)

Calendar Stick (Primstav)
(Vesterheim Norwegian-American Museum, Decorah, Iowa)

Calendar Stick Detail
(Vesterheim Norwegian-American Museum, Decorah, Iowa)

Julebukker, 1908 (Minnesota Historical Society)

ACKNOWLEDGMENTS

Heartfelt thanks to Alison Dwyer, Collections Manager at Vesterheim Norwegian-American Museum, for assistance with artifacts, photographs, and a myriad of other details. Thanks also to Ken Koop and Martha Griesheimer for welcoming me at special events. I am enormously indebted to *all* Vesterheim staff and volunteers for their assistance and support as this book developed.

I'm grateful to my patient and inspiring rosemaling instructors, Gold Medalists Joanne MacVey and Patti Goke, and Turid Helle Fatland of Norway; and Education Specialists Diane Weston and Darlene Fossum-Martin, whose work has done so much to preserve traditions and enrich the lives of students. Huge thanks also to Ellen Macdonald, chip carver extraordinaire, for sharing her love of the art.

Chief Bill Nixon of the Decorah Police Department and Jerry Thompson, formerly of the Decorah Fire Department, were kind enough to answer questions. I appreciate their help.

Huge thanks to Andrea Cascardi, and to everyone at Transatlantic Literary; and to Terri Bischoff and the Midnight Ink team.

I'm lucky to have many friends involved with Project Chloe, and I thank you all: Laurie Rosengren, editorial assistance; Kay Klubertanz, photography; the team at Cedar Creek, website programming; Tom Micksch, video editing; Alisha Rapp and the Prairie Café crew, cakes and mochas; and Katie Mead and Robert Alexander, who provided the perfect retreat. Special thanks to my extended family, and to Scott Meeker—partner in all things.

If any readers are interested in learning more about the historic roots of Norwegian Christmas customs, I highly recommend *Keeping Christmas: Yuletide Traditions in Norway and the New Land*, by Kathleen Stokker (Minnesota Historical Society Press, 2001).

Geri Gerold © Kathleen Ernst

ABOUT THE AUTHOR

Kathleen Ernst is a novelist, social historian, and educator. She moved to Wisconsin in 1982 to take an interpreter job at Old World Wisconsin, and later served as a Curator of Interpretation and Collections at the historic site.

Heritage of Darkness is Kathleen's fourth Chloe Ellefson mystery. Her historical fiction for children and young adults includes eight historical mysteries. Honors for her fiction include Edgar and Agatha nominations.

Kathleen lives and writes in Middleton, Wisconsin, and still visits historic sites every chance she gets! She also blogs about the relationship between fiction and museums at www.sitesandstories.wordpress.com. Learn more about Kathleen and her work at www.kathleenernst.com.